Jack Cavanaugh

whom
sha
i
fear?

whom shall i fear?

athol dickson

ZondervanPublishingHouse
Grand Rapids, Michigan

A Division of HarperCollins*Publishers*

Whom Shall I Fear?

Requests for information should be addressed to:

ZondervanPublishingHouse
Grand Rapids, Michigan 49530

Library of Congress Cataloging-in-Publication Data

Dickson, Athol, 1955–
Whom shall I fear? / Athol Dickson.
p. cm.
ISBN: 0-310-20760-6 (softcover)
I. Title.
PS3554.I3264W48 1996
813'.54—dc20 96-30314
CIP

Published in association with the literary agency of Alive Communications, Inc., 1465 Kelly Johnson Boulevard, #320, Colorado Springs, CO 80920

Interior design by Sherri Hoffman

Printed in the United States of America

97 98 99 00 01 02 03 /❖ DH/ 10 9 8 7 6 5 4

This novel is dedicated to my very best friend. . . .
He knows who He is.

Acknowledgments

THIS NOVEL WAS PUBLISHED BECAUSE of an extraordinary chain of events that began with my new friend, Allen Pusey. His encouragement and selfless gifts of time and professional guidance gave me confidence in my writing and my witness. His daily practice of the Golden Rule is an ongoing inspiration to me. Thank you, Allen.

There are so many others in the chain of friends (and sometimes strangers) who helped the book along in so many ways. Thanks to my "editors": Mark and Vicki Blaskovich, Cathy Edson, Ned and Dee Lidval, Gene and Audrey Chilcott, and Tim Purselley. Thanks to Janet Manus, the second professional to offer encouragement. Thank you, Dorrie Fern and Loy Newton. Your attention to detail made my job much easier. And without the help of Stan Potocki and Gene Getz, I would not have met Greg Johnson, the man who made this dream a reality—thanks to all of you.

Then there's Mary Dickson—my personal editor and friend. Thanks, Mom.

Finally, I want to remember that morning on the "deck/dock" five years ago, before it all began, when Sue dangled her toes in the water of our little cove, turned her big green eyes toward me, and said, "You can do it."

Poopsie, with you beside me, I can do anything.

The LORD is my light and my salvation—
whom shall I fear?
The LORD is the stronghold of my life—
of whom shall I be afraid?
When evil men advance against me
to devour my flesh,
when my enemies and my foes attack me,
they will stumble and fall.
Though an army besiege me,
my heart will not fear;
though war break out against me,
even then will I be confident.

—PSALM 27:1–3

CHAPTER 1

IT SHOULD HAVE BEEN A GOOD DAY. Gathering an old pair of blue jeans, a favorite faded polo shirt, and my good-luck sneakers, I slipped out of the bedroom without waking Mary Jo. I dressed in the kitchen while the coffee brewed, poured some of it into a thermos, and left the rest on the hot plate along with a note saying I'd be back about eight. I didn't brush my teeth or comb my hair. Where I was going, nobody would notice.

Outside, the whippoorwills were winding down for the night. I descended through the woods, following my flashlight's beam along the path. It was copperhead season, or I wouldn't have bothered with the light. At the bottom of the hill, I stepped from the tree line onto an old crooked pier that meandered over the water to a cedar boathouse with a rusty metal roof. I wandered to the end of the pier and stood alongside the boat for a moment, looking out across the lake. The faint glow of sunrise licked the treetops on the far shore like a forest fire raging in from the next county. Cattails waved in lazy unison along the shore as the first light calls of goldfinches and cardinals trickled through the woods, and the final good-nights of bullfrogs and katydids faded into rhythmic obscurity.

The feeling rose within me again, swelling my chest and whispering that I ought to kneel and say a thankful prayer for all this beauty. I didn't do it, of course. Didn't know how. The moment passed, as such moments always did, leaving nothing behind but a vague dissatisfaction, easily ignored.

It took three minutes to drop the boat into the water with the electric winch. I stepped aboard, squeezed the fuel pump, and started the outboard in three tries, filling the air with oily blue smoke. Soon the motor warmed up and the exhaust cleared. I backed out of the boathouse and nosed around to follow the shoreline at idle speed, pouring a cup of coffee into a thermos lid as I inched along.

Half a mile to the west was a small cove where I usually got started. I'd caught a twelve-pound bass there when I was fifteen years old, and a thirty-six-pound channel catfish twenty years later. Just before I turned into the cove, a great blue heron rose with an awful honk from the high branches beside me and flopped across the pale gray sky like a gawky airborne dinosaur. I remember thinking herons bring good luck. I remember being happy. I was in my favorite place, a lucky place for me. Lucky, anyway, until that morning, when I found the old man.

His filthy little boat lay mired in the shallows, with lily pads scattered around it like emerald stepping stones. It was a peaceful scene, disturbed only by the old man's odd snorting and giggling.

Cruising slowly, sipping coffee, and enjoying the spreading sunrise, I approached the little boat. The old man was making a lot of noise. He didn't seem to see me. I called from about fifty feet away and called again as I drew closer. Finally, I came alongside.

"Mr. Martin? Mr. Martin? What's so funny?"

Nothing but silly laughter.

I looked at him carefully, filled with a growing sense of uneasiness. Drool coated his chin like foam on a rabid dog and dripped elastically from the gray stubble of his beard to his shirt front. He was up to his shoelaces in motor oil and lake water. He reeked of bug spray and stink bait. His shirt was dotted with tobacco juice stains, as were the sparse gray whiskers beneath the spit on his chin. Above his head, flood lamps dangled from a makeshift scaffold built of old cane poles, the intensity of their glare just beginning to fade in competition with the rising sun. Thousands of bugs fluttered in the cone of light, drawn to the glow like drunks to a downtown bar. They filled the air so thickly that collisions were unavoidable, causing them to crash and spin and flop to the water, where their predicament attracted bass and crappie—which, of course, was the point of the lights.

The old man held a twenty-pound test line in his calloused and cracked hands with the gentleness of a mother holding a child. I got the sense that he would not react when a strike came, that he wouldn't understand what was happening. He didn't seem to realize that I was there, even when I tied our boats together.

Thinking he might respond to an offer of coffee, I stepped onto his boat with a freshly poured cupful. The steaming container in my outstretched hand bore a strip of tape inscribed with my name. He ignored it.

"Come on, Mr. Martin, a little coffee will do you good."

His eyes never focused on me. The manic giggling continued. Careful not to turn my back to him, I set the coffee on the seat and looked around for a rope, intending to tow him to shore. I saw that he had hooked the end of a chain fish stringer around a cleat, the other end dangling in the water, probably with a few fish attached. I grabbed it to bring it aboard. The old man stopped giggling. I pulled at the stringer.

From the murky water of the lake rose a mud-gray corpse. It rolled on the surface with its face framed by limp fish and moss, its cheek stretched like putty by a steel stringer hook.

I dropped the stringer and sprang from the side. The little boat tossed and rolled with the sudden movement, lightbulbs violently slapping the cane-pole scaffold, lake water splashing aboard. I gripped the scaffolding to regain my balance. Long minutes passed while the rocking boat and swaying lights overhead slowed and stopped. When all was steady, the old man began to giggle again. Then, for the first time, he moved. Slowly, carefully, he leaned over the side of the boat. The giggling grew louder. He leaned farther. With his wrinkled face almost touching the water above the sunken corpse, the old man stopped snickering and said one word in a chilling, little-boy's voice.

The word was, "Daddy?"

CHAPTER 2

I DON'T REMEMBER DECIDING NOT TO tell them my name. A woman answered the telephone and put me on hold. As I waited, that smirking gray-green face in the water bobbed through my memory, complete with a sound track of crazy giggles. It was a face I knew, a face I'd never wanted to see again. The warm lake water had bloated his melting features, pumping his cheeks full of gas like a party balloon, but enough remained to create an aching fear that the corpse was Ernest B. Martin, the old man's son. When a deputy came on the line, I told him what I'd seen and hung up before he could ask any questions. My hand left a sheen of sweat on the telephone. Ernest B. was dead, and Old Man Martin had lost his mind. Would they blame me?

I spent the next two days slugging it out with fear and guilt—fear that I'd be blamed for Ernest B.'s death, and guilt for leaving the old man alone with the body.

It was hard to feel much sympathy for Old Man Martin, though. He was stingy rich, and he smelled like a skid row mattress. Maybe he was too lazy to bathe, or maybe it was the reek of his sour disposition. Either way, I'd learned long ago to deal with him from an upwind position with a hand on my wallet.

Greed and poor hygiene notwithstanding, our southern traditions are dearly held by Mary Jo. The death of a neighbor calls for a covered dish, so she had a casserole fixed by lunch time, which I was to carry over to the Martin home place with our condolences. Old Man Martin lived about a mile west of our place, down a two-lane, blacktop road. The old folks say that Ernest B.'s great-grandfather surveyed and built the original road a hundred and twenty years ago, during the horse-and-buggy days. It is very narrow. In most places the roadbed sinks between mossy, fern-covered banks. Huge pines and live oak trees lean together overhead, forming a serpentine canopy of deep, speckled shade. Spanish moss trails from the branches, giving the road an elegantly timeworn, Southern character.

I turned in at the open Martin gate, my tires rumbling over a rusty iron cattle guard, and followed the twisting drive through the woods for several hundred yards until the old house came into view. A squad car was parked in front. That was to be expected, given Ernest B's. condition.

I parked behind the black-and-white. As I stepped out of my pickup, a uniformed deputy watched me from the shade of the front porch. I didn't recognize him.

"Help you, mister?"

"I'm a neighbor, and I wanted to drop by to pay my condolences. Got a casserole here for Mr. Martin." I lifted the covered dish a little in case he hadn't noticed.

He said, "Mr. Martin's not really up to visitin' right now, sir. There's a couple of folks from the Silver Leaf Home here to move him out. Maybe it'd be best if you left the dish with me. I'll see that one of the ladies takes good care of it."

"All right."

The deputy stepped down the wide steps to meet me. "Who shall I say called?"

"I'm Garrison Reed."

The man's hand settled unconsciously onto the grip of his holstered pistol. "I've heard your name, Mr. Reed. Hang on a minute. I believe the sheriff would like to have a word." He turned his head and gave a loud yell for the sheriff. The noise spooked a flock of crows in the nearby woods. They rose from the treetops, filling the air with beating wings and cranky squawks.

I said, "What does he want to talk about, Deputy?"

"Well, sir, we'd better wait and let the sheriff have his say."

We stood together in uneasy silence, sweating in the midday sun. I watched the deputy from the corner of my eye. He was a big man, about my size, with a crisply starched uniform and a bright polish on his Sam Browne. With his square jaw, close-cropped blond hair, athletic build, ice-blue eyes, freckles, and pug nose, he looked like Clark Kent in a cop uniform. Or Dennis the Menace with muscles.

The Martin house was centered in a clearing below a low hill, completely surrounded by virgin timber. Lean-to roofs covered rooms that angled off in several directions from the center part of the building, the product of a hundred years of additions. Somehow, this haphazard expansion had not diluted the simple dignity of the original farmhouse. But in places, the peeling white paint curled up to expose gray wood siding underneath, like the skin of a partially scaled fish. The sight made me melancholy. This had been my best friend's home, where we'd spent many happy hours playing children's games together. It was hard to see the damage done by the passing of time.

The house stood on a hundred acres or so of heavily wooded land, all that remained of the old Martin home place. The rest had been sold or now lay under water. Behind the house, an ancient stone barn seemed to grow from the red limestone hillside. The wooded slope rose above the barn for a hundred feet, dropping on the other side to the shore of Martin Pool—the lake where Ernest B. died.

Sheriff Clyde Barker stepped out of the house, taking care that the screen door didn't slam behind him. He was a small man, about sixty-five, with the pale copper-colored hair of a blond going gray. His movements suggested grace and athletic ability. He wore no gun or uniform, just a gray felt Stetson cowboy hat, a plaid shirt, chino slacks, and dusty Nocona walking boots. He looked middle-class country, like a rancher or the owner of a hardware store in town. But he was the son of an old family in the area, with enough connections and political savvy to hold his elected office for thirty-eight years.

"Jimmy, what in the world's gotten into you, boy? Your hollerin's got Mr. Martin acting goofy again just when it looked like he might start talkin' sense."

The deputy said, "This here's Mr. Reed, Sheriff. Thought you'd want to talk to him now instead of sending somebody later."

The sheriff shifted his pale gray eyes from the deputy to me.

"I know who this is, Jimmy. Garr and I know each other real good. Whatcha got there, Garr? Somethin' for the old man? That's real nice."

I climbed the porch steps with the casserole, glad to step into the shade. I noticed some dog food in a bowl beside the door, and wondered who was going to take care of Old Man Martin's coon hounds.

Sheriff Barker took the dish from my hands with a smile and set it on a table next to the rocker. "Garr, come to think of it, maybe we should have a little talk." Grasping my elbow, he led me back down the steps. We passed the deputy, and Barker said, "Jimmy, you step on inside there and stay real close to Mr. Martin. Make sure you're standin' nearby if he starts talkin' now, hear?"

With an odd smile, Dennis the Menace went inside.

Watching him go, the sheriff said, "He's a new one, Garr. Just hired him away from the Shreveport Police Department. What do you think?"

I said, "He's a big fellow,"

Sheriff Barker looked up at me and smiled, "Almost big as you, ain't he? Let's take a little stroll."

As we moved away from the house, I lifted my arm to make the sheriff release his grip.

"What is it, Clyde? I don't have long. I just drove over to see how the old man was doing."

"I know, Garr. Say, how long's it been, anyway? I declare, we ought to get together more often. Spend some time talkin' about the old days. Yessir, I just don't see enough of you since your daddy died." The ice in his eyes belied the warmth in his voice.

"I wish you'd tell me what this is all about."

"We'll get to that soon enough, Garr. Let's just walk a bit here in the shade, all right?"

We moved far enough along the drive for the trees to block our view of the house. The air was still and full of the fertile, musty smell of the woods. It was fifteen degrees cooler in the dappled shade. Barker pulled a blue bandanna from his hip pocket, removed his Stetson, and wiped his forehead. "Hot as the dickens, ain't it? I sure like it over on this side of the lake, though. Don't believe it gets as hot, 'cause the water cools the south winds as they blow over."

I had decided not to say a word until he got to the point. We strolled farther along the gravel road in silence, passing a sweetly scented jumble of honeysuckle.

"You know, Old Man Martin and my daddy used to hunt coons together down in the hollows around this end of the lake when they was boys. 'Course, that was before there *was* a lake." He replaced the Stetson on his head and folded the bandanna. "I remember Daddy tellin' me about one time when they'd got this big ol' coon treed up around here somewhere. Maybe right near here. Anyway, they had this coon up top of this tree, you know, and they each took a shot at him and missed."

With his hands the sheriff mimed taking aim at a branch overhead. He looked up at me sideways, still holding the imaginary rifle aimed at the treetops, and said, "They would've kept at it, too, but they'd already used all their rounds."

After a moment he dropped his arms and continued, "So Old Man Martin, he tells Daddy it weren't no use, they'd just as well get on home since the coon sure weren't about to climb down to 'em.

"Well, they did go on home, and the next mornin', Old Man Martin was walkin' through there to get to school. He passed under that tree without givin' it much thought, and just as he passed, that ol' coon dropped down out of the tree, dead. Seems one of 'em had shot him after all. The doggone thing was just too stubborn to let loose for a while."

I checked my watch elaborately, and said, "Clyde, I told Mary Jo I'd be right back. Maybe I'd better start heading that way."

"Sure, sure, Garr. I do go on sometimes. It's just, havin' Ernest B. pop up dead this way, after bein' gone for a while, and walking these woods like we are, I guess the two things sort of reminded me of that story."

"Uh-huh. Well, I'd like to stay and talk some more, but I've still got a few chores to take care of, so if you don't mind, I'll just head back now." I turned toward the house.

Barker didn't follow. After I'd taken several steps, he spoke. "You and Ernest B. had a little problem a while back, didn't you?"

Finally, he was getting down to it.

I stopped and said, "You might say he *was* the problem. He was stealin' me blind until I split up with him. But you know all about that."

He looked over my shoulder, his eyes focused on something deep in the woods. "Oh yes, I do, Garr. Indeed I do."

I didn't want to think about the last time I had seen Ernest B. Martin alive. He had been my best friend since we were kids and a minority partner in my family's construction business. Then our bookkeeper caught him with his hand in the till. I wanted to sue him, to swear out criminal charges, to go after him with my fists. No punishment was too severe for such a betrayal. But Mary Jo wouldn't have it. She calmly spoke of turning the other cheek, quoting from her beloved Bible, searching my eyes for a sign of the Christian charity I had long pretended to share. It was swallow my anger or expose my lie, so rather than getting the law involved, I met with him the next morning at our bank and handed him what was left of his share in cash along with a letter of resignation that he signed on the spot.

But Ernest B. didn't have sense enough to know when he'd been let off easy. A few weeks later, he came to our house, wanting more money. I told him to get off my land. He left for a while, but returned about midnight, sloppy drunk. He fired a shotgun in the air and called me out of the house. Mary Jo telephoned the sheriff's department while I stood on the front porch trying to reason with him. When he heard the sirens screaming down our road, he took a shot at me and ran for it. I hadn't seen him since. Not alive, anyway.

Eventually the anger faded, leaving me with a deep sadness. My oldest and best friend had betrayed me. How could a man change so much? It was as if Ernest B. had been replaced by a stranger.

And now I had to deal with the pain of his death—a hard thing to face, made worse by the cruel and demeaning way I'd found him, floating like a bloated carp on his daddy's fish stringer.

Of course, if anyone had a good reason to kill him, I did. The man had stolen from me, threatened me. That was why I hadn't told them who I was when I called. I didn't even want them to know I'd seen his body. Perhaps that was a mistake.

As if he was reading my mind, Barker asked, "You seen him since then?"

"Why do you ask?"

The easygoing good-ol'-boy demeanor was gone in an instant, replaced by an ice-cold stare. "Indulge me, Garrison. Have you seen or heard from Ernest B. since that night out at your place?"

"No, Sheriff. He sent me a postcard a few weeks later, that's all."

"Where from?"

"Mexico."

"What did it say?"

I looked at him for a moment, then said, "'Thanks for nothing.'"

His pale gray eyes rested on my face, unamused. Finally he said, "That's all?"

"Yes."

He put back on his country grin. "Well, that's just fine. Y'all run on home now. We'll talk again."

I gave him a slow nod and turned back toward the house. After a moment he called out once more, "Garr, you goin' to be staying 'round here for the next few weeks? Might be best if y'all don't take a vacation just now. It's getting too hot for that anyway. Hot as the dickens, ain't it?"

I walked away, feeling his frigid stare on my back, fighting the thought that he knew I was lying.

Chapter 3

Mt. Sinai, home of the annual Tri-County Cotton Fair, is the Jackson County seat. Within its boundaries are the last working mule-powered cotton gin in the United States, a Caddo Indian archeological dig, a sugar-cane syrup factory, the remains of a red brick Confederate armory, and what has been officially documented as the third-largest paper-shell pecan tree in Texas. Framing the town square are four state highways and farm-to-market roads leading out of town. Mistaking one of these roads for another is about the only way to get lost in Mt. Sinai. The streets form a grid system, which peters out altogether about fifteen blocks from the square. Centered in the town square is a four-story red granite courthouse, composed of massive Romanesque arches and delicate Gothic turrets. It was built at the turn of the century by a Yankee architect from Pennsylvania and a team of itinerant Italian stonemasons who were responsible for similar county courthouses all over east Texas and Louisiana. In front of the building is a landscaped fieldstone plaza where festivals and civic ceremonies are often held.

The plaza is shaded by a dozen ancient live oak trees that were planted by a farming family—the first Anglos to settle in the area—around 1820. A hard freeze killed one of the trees when I was twelve. It was a sad day when the old bare trunk was cut down. The city council decided that the job would be done by hand because the tooth-rattling whine of a chainsaw would be an affront to the oak's advanced age and majestic dignity. There was a solemn ceremony. Speeches were made. The gathered crowd was reminded that the oak had been hauled in a wagon from Georgia to be planted near the solitary log house of the founding family of our town. The great oak had prospered through the Indian wars and stood in mute witness to Texas's role in the War Between the States. It had provided shade for the Sunday afternoon courtships of our great-great-grandparents.

When the teeth of the antique two-man bow saw began to slice through the gnarled gray bark of the dead oak, women and children were crying and grown men dabbed their eyes.

History is important in Mt. Sinai, Texas.

• • •

DRIVING AROUND THE SQUARE ON ONE-WAY blacktop streets, I stopped at traffic lights at each intersection. Straightforward country folk in mud-splattered pickup trucks with shotguns mounted against their rear windows cruised slowly beside me. Texans are well armed, a tradition that dates to the days of the Republic when we lived with the constant threat of a Mexican invasion. These days, the threat is more likely to come from a cocaine addict trying to finance his habit.

I nosed into a parking place in front of our building. The Reed Construction office is in one of the old red brick two-story buildings that surround the courthouse. Out front, cantilevered canopies provide welcome shade for the window shoppers strolling along the sidewalks. A few of the buildings are vacant. The others offer everything from farm insurance to videotape rentals. There are a couple of antique shops, a Radio Shack, Pedro's Cafe, an old movie theater, and the First National Bank. Sales are advertised with hand-lettered signs, taped to the storefront glass. Many of the second-floor windows are filthy and fly specked, signifying empty rooms, long unused.

Inside, I found Mrs. P. at her desk in the reception area, as usual. She is devoted to the company and has been our office manager since my father hired her twenty years ago. She was a family friend for years before that. She looks like a black Buddha in drag, piled onto her chair like a generous helping of soft chocolate ice cream, her heavy arms and jowls vibrating with every move. I have never seen her hair, since she sports a different wig every day. They come in a wide variety of colors and styles and migrate across her huge head seldom encumbered by bobby pins, striking jaunty angles that reveal glimpses of a Spandex turban underneath.

When she is aggravated, which is most of the time, she buries the unfortunate source of her annoyance beneath a landslide of creative insults and withering sarcasm. Only two or three people in town are willing to risk her wrath, and they're either crazy or deaf.

Mrs. P.'s husband made his escape soon after they were married, which is why she won't use his name. The P. stands for Polanski, but only a fool would remind her of it. A less imposing woman might have been subjected to an endless stream of wisecracks about being the only black Polanski in our neck of the woods, but with her impressive bulk and repertoire of rapid-fire insults, somehow the subject never comes up.

As usual, she skipped the pleasantries and said, "Already heard from your wife three times this morning, Garr."

Mary Jo was still on probation with Mrs. P. even though we'd been married for fourteen years. Perhaps in another fourteen years Mrs. P. will actually speak her name.

"Why she can't have her say before you leave home is beyond me." She adjusted her bra beneath her ample floral muumuu, snapping the elastic in place. "Must think we got nothing better to do than sit around here waiting on her to call."

I'd long ago decided to put up with Mrs. P.'s attitude. She was an excellent office manager, but more than that, she was a living link to the past, to my father. Still, sometimes I spent too much energy avoiding harsh words with her. To change the subject, I asked, "Have you had a chance to go over that culvert bid this morning?"

"In between answering fool questions about your whereabouts I have." She handed me the documents. "It's a wonder to me how I get anything done at all around here. It really is. Garr, you got to get me a girl to help out. I ain't getting any younger. I got to start taperin' off."

Nodding my head with a concerned look, I left her grumbling and shuffling papers and went into my office. I had hired four women in the past two years to help Mrs. P. She'd fired each of them in less than a month, claiming they were either "foolin' with my filin' system" or "spending all their time making moon eyes at the hands." The fact was, Mrs. P. enjoyed complaining about being overworked and couldn't stand to share her duties with anyone. Even I wasn't welcome in her files.

As I looked over the bid, I sat at my desk and dialed my home number absentmindedly.

Mary Jo answered on the first ring. "Garr, I need you to come home."

"What's going on?"

"There's some men here from the sheriff's office. They're searching the house."

"Did they say what for?"

Her voice sounded frantic, on the verge of screaming. "They have a warrant to look for evidence about Ernest B. I'm scared, Garr. They're looking everywhere, making a mess out of everything."

"Are they still there?"

Mary Jo's attempt at calm broke down. She screamed, "Yes they're here! I've got some idiot going through my panty drawer. I want you home. Right now!"

"All right, baby. I'm coming, but try to calm down, okay? I'm sure this is just some sort of mistake."

I hung up, but stayed seated at my desk for a moment. How could they know? I didn't recognize the voice on the phone when I called about the body, so they couldn't have known it was me. Unless—maybe they could trace the call. Could they? What if they actually considered me a suspect in Ernest B.'s death? Or else this could be a mistake. Yes, I thought, it is probably a mistake.

Walking past Mrs. P.'s desk, I paused to tell her I had to go back home. Then I asked if she'd heard about Ernest B.'s death.

"'Course I heard about it. You think I sit around doin' nothin' all weekend? I got friends. I hear about everything that goes on."

"I didn't mean—" I took a deep breath and tried again. "I was just wondering, who do you think would want to kill Ernest B.?"

"Some hopped-up-no-'count-city-boy, probably. Else maybe his old man. I wouldn't put it past that old coot to do anything."

"But why would he? He and Ernest B. got along all right."

"You don't hear things like I do. I got my contacts 'round here. I get the straight poop."

"Poop?"

"Don't get sassy."

"All right. What exactly have you heard? I need to know right now."

Her nostrils flared, and she raised her triple chins with an air of outraged dignity. "You best take another tone with me, Garrison Reed. I was there the day you was born. I seen you in the altogether more times than I can count when you was just a scrawny little brat. So don't you take that high tone with me. Nosir!"

"Mrs. P., there are sheriff's deputies out at my place right now. I think they might be looking for evidence that I had something to do with Ernest B.'s death. Please, if you've heard something, I really need to know."

"Well, why didn't you ask nice, then? You know I'm easy to get along with if people give me the respect I'm due."

"Mrs. P.!"

"All right, all right. I just heard from Mabel Simmons over at Karol's Kuntry Kuts this Saturday while I was having my nails done—say, did you know that a lot of men are having manicures these days? I think it's just about the most sickenin' thing a man could do. Except maybe get his ear pierced."

I balled my fists and put them on her desk, leaning over until I could look her in the eye. "Mrs. P., I don't have time for this. I really do not. I need you to tell me what you heard about Old Man Martin and Ernest B. Do you understand?"

Mrs. P. stared at me like I'd gone mad, her eyes wide and mouth open. After a long pause she took a deep breath and said, "Mabel told me some woman named Suzy who works over at the Wash 'n' Save said she heard Ernest B. and the old man arguin' in the parkin' lot at the Nowhere Club. She said Old Man Martin was yellin' 'bout how Ernest B. wasn't goin' to run the Martin name through the mud and how he wasn't 'bout to just sit by and let him."

"That's all you heard?"

She stared at me with her wig low over her left ear. "Yes, Garrison. That's all."

"Thank you, then." I straightened up and stepped toward the door. "I'm going home now. You'll handle things for me here, won't you?"

"Don't I always?" she said, lifting her chins high again.

"Yes, you do, Mrs. P."

"Well, all right then."

I couldn't help but slam the door on my way out.

• • •

MARY JO STOOD ON THE GRAVEL DRIVE OUTside our house, with her hands on her slender hips, yelling at a sheriff's deputy. As I stepped from the pickup truck, ducking my head to avoid bumping the door frame, I heard her say he was nothing but a mindless robot.

She shook a finger under the man's nose. "Why don't you people just bring a bulldozer in here and level our place while you're at it? You've got absolutely no reason to be doing this. You should be ashamed. Ashamed!"

She turned my way when I called, her face set in a grim look of fear and anger. The deputy quickly went inside the house, glancing back over his shoulder as he went. I could almost see his ears smoking.

I held my arms out toward Mary Jo, and she ran to me. She runs well, with long-legged, even strides. The sunlight struck her wavy auburn hair from behind, framing her face with a burnt-sienna halo. As we held each other, she pressed her cheek against my chest, making little choking noises.

Finally her anger dissolved into tears and she sobbed, "I couldn't stand to stay in there any longer, Garr. I was going to make sure they didn't break anything, but I couldn't watch them tearing up our house!"

"It's all right, baby. It's all right."

She said, "We've got to tell them the truth."

Hugging her tighter, I said, "No. Too late for that."

"But they already know something, Garr. They must have found out it was you that called about the body, or else why would they be here? Maybe they found your fingerprints on Mr. Martin's boat."

"I've never been fingerprinted."

"Well, they must have found something."

"Maybe. Let's wait and see."

We stood together for several more minutes, until our breathing was synchronized and she had calmed herself. She stepped back and wiped her eyes with the back of her hand. Her eyes are the color of pine needles. Irish eyes.

I said, "Wait out here. Let me go in and see what they're doing."

The first deputy I saw inside was Jimmy, from the Martin place. He met me in our narrow entry hall, holding my .22

squirrel rifle and my twelve-gauge shotgun with a friendly smile on his freckled face.

"Howdy, Mr. Reed. Are these the only weapons on the property?"

"I keep a short-barreled shotgun down at the boathouse. For snakes. What do you think you're doing here?"

His cheerful smile vanished at the aggravated tone in my voice. He said, "I'm sorry, Mr. Reed. I thought I overheard Mrs. Reed explaining the situation to you on the phone earlier. We have a warrant from the District Court to search this property for evidence in connection with the death and possible murder of Ernest Martin."

"Was he shot?"

"Why would you think that, Mr. Reed?"

"Because you're taking my guns, of course!"

"I'm not at liberty to tell you anything about our investigation, Mr. Reed."

He might look like Dennis the Menace on steroids, but he was sounding more like Barney Fife all the time. I said, "Listen, you idiot! I've had enough of your—"

"Settle down, Garr!" the sheriff snapped as he walked up behind the deputy. Reaching up, he put his hand on the man's shoulder and said, "That's all right, Jimmy, we won't be needing Mr. Reed's guns just yet. You set 'em back where you found 'em."

As Jimmy squeezed past me belly to belly in the narrow hall, I turned my head sideways and said, "Clyde, what is going on here? Am I seriously supposed to be involved in this business with Ernest B.?"

"Now, Garr settle down. Why don't you and I step on out to the back here and give my boys room to work while we go over a few things in private?"

I followed him through the house to the back deck, trying to calm myself. This was no time to let emotions take control. I tried to ignore the uniformed men in the living room who were rolling up the rug and tipping over our furniture.

Barker opened a French door and held it for me with elaborate courtesy as I passed through to the back porch. He sat in the porch swing—my favorite chair—and waved his hand at a rocker. "Have a seat, Garr," he said. "This may take a little while."

"Why, thank you, Sheriff. It's so nice to feel at home."

Ignoring my sarcasm, he said, "Y'all got a beautiful place here. Trees between the house and the lake and all. I suppose most folks thin 'em out so as to have a clear view, but I like the way y'all left everything natural. I surely do. The way the hill slopes down to the water, and this porch up here high like this. Like being in a tree house. Real nice."

I could just make out some men down at our boathouse. They had taken my scuba gear outside and were examining it closely. Sunlight sparkled from the chrome around my face mask as one of the men turned it in his hands. There was a distant hiss as another man opened the valve on my air tank. They had emptied my boat. Life jackets, fishing gear, and a coffee thermos littered the pier. I saw that the thermos top was missing and wondered where it was. Funny how you focus on the little things.

I said, "Clyde, just tell me what you're doing here, will you?"

"Good to make a little small talk first, Garr. Eases you into these things."

I was silent as the woods around us hummed and chirped with wildlife. The brief morning coolness had passed, and it was getting hot. The sheriff shifted his weight and pulled a small knife from his pocket. He leaned forward with his elbows on his knees and began to clean his fingernails with the blade.

Finally he got down to it. "You got yourself a little problem here, Garr." He finished scraping his left thumbnail and moved to his index finger. "We done some checkin' around, and it seems you and Ernest B. had some pretty bad things to say about each other before that little sheebang on your front porch a while back. Now he's shown up floatin' in the lake over yonder, right near your place." He waved his pocketknife vaguely toward the lake. "You understand, we got to look into things like that."

I took a deep breath. "It's true, Ernest B. and I had some words a few months ago. But I haven't seen him since your deputies ran him off."

Barker looked directly at my eyes. "You sure about that?"

I thought about the way the stringer hook had pulled at the flesh on his cheek. If only I had told them who I was over the telephone. Lies beget lies.

"Answer the question, Garr. Are you sure you haven't seen Ernest B. since that night?"

"Yes! Of course I'm sure! Now listen: You obviously think I had something to do with his death. And you know he was stealing from my company. I showed you the books myself. But you also know I bought him out and sent him on his way scot-free instead of prosecuting. Why would I do that if I planned to kill him?"

"These things get out of hand sometimes, Garr. Maybe he came back for more. Maybe he tried to pressure you somehow."

"You're the one pressuring me! You weren't this interested in catching Ernest B. when he took a shot at me!"

"That was a case of assault. We're talkin' murder here."

At that moment I began to understand that I should be afraid. Everything seemed to slip a notch. Sounds were amplified, motions slowed, and tiny details assumed extreme importance. The wind in the treetops sounded like a moan. I was outside myself, listening in on our conversation. When the sheriff spoke again, it was as if he were far away.

"How did you spend last Friday, Garr?"

"I'm not sure . . . no, wait." I held up my hand, palm out. It was hard to think. Barker moved to the next fingernail, apparently willing to sit there forever.

After a moment I said, "I woke up around five-thirty. Went fishing for an hour or two."

"Which way?"

"West."

"Toward the Martin place." It wasn't a question.

"I went way past their place, almost to the dam and back."

"See anyone?"

"I almost never do. A couple of boats went by, I don't know who they were. Had breakfast right here on the porch with Mary Jo. Drove over to a little culvert project we've got going on the Henderson Highway."

The sheriff looked up and said, "So you saw some of your boys out there, right?"

"Sure. Allan Mason and Mark Tasco were there. Maybe some others. I can't remember."

"And you didn't see anyone other than Mary Jo before that?"

"No."

"Where'd you go after you left that job?"

"Over to the office. Mrs. P. was there. She could tell you when that was. I know I was there 'til lunchtime, then I went over to Pedro's for something to eat."

"Who'd you eat with?"

"I ate alone. I don't know if anyone who was there would remember me. Pedro might."

The sheriff gave no indication that he was listening. He was working on a black spot under the corner of his left little finger. The birds around us seemed to chirp louder and louder. I wiped a drop of sweat from my forehead and fought the feeling that this wasn't really happening.

"Clyde, I heard a rumor that Ernest B. was in bad shape when they found him. Like he'd been in the water for a while. If that's true, he wasn't killed on Friday, so why is it so important for you to know where I was on that day?"

He looked at me with a little smile, "You heard how we found him?"

"Stuck on his fish stringer . . . oh, I see." It was pretty unlikely that the body had floated onto the stringer all by itself. Someone had to put the body on the hook, and they'd probably done it on Friday. Which brought a question to mind.

"Why aren't you talking to Old Man Martin? Maybe he did it, or knows who did. It's pretty hard to imagine someone stringing up Ernest B. like that without him noticing."

Barker nodded. "Yessir. Hard to imagine all right. Almost as hard to imagine as the sight of that frail old man hauling his own boy up from the lake and sticking a hook through his cheek and draggin' him around all night like a string of bass."

"You're saying Martin's too nice a guy to kill Ernest B.? He's meaner than a junkyard dog. Everyone knows they never got along."

"That so? Didn't get along? Say, that could be a motive for murder all right. Father waits forty-three years to kill his son because they didn't get along."

I felt anger rising again and made an effort to hide it. "All right, then, explain how someone could string up Ernest B. right under the old man's nose without him noticing. And while you're at it, how about telling me how he was killed?"

"First off, I don't have to explain nothin' to you, Garr, but seein' as how you're askin' so nice, I will tell you this: The old man hasn't been able to tell us a single thing about that night. Maybe he did watch them do it. Maybe that's why he's gone nuts. And I don't know how Ernest B. was killed yet. Haven't seen the coroner's report." He returned his attention to his fingernails. "Now, then. I need to know what you were doin' the whole day last Friday, and I'm all done explainin'. You'd about got done eatin' dinner at Pedro's, right?"

I sighed. "That's right. And then I went back to the office. I think I stayed there all afternoon, it's hard to remember. I must have gone home about seven or seven-thirty, because I remember thinking it was going to be a pretty sunset."

Jimmy walked out of the house and stood between the sheriff and me, waiting for permission to speak. A small spot of sunlight shone through the canopy of leaves overhead and glittered on his polished Sam Browne. His dull gray .45 automatic hung on the belt at my eye level. The crazy thought flashed through my mind that I could grab it and make them both go away.

The sheriff didn't look up from his pocketknife. He said, "What is it, Jimmy?"

"Well, Sheriff, we're about done inside, and the boys're finished down to the boathouse."

"All right. Wait for me around front."

After Jimmy left the deck, I said, "Clyde, am I under arrest?"

Before answering, he clicked the knife shut and put it back in his pocket. "Not right this minute you're not. We'll just wait and see what my boys have come up with, then we'll take it from there." He stood and reached behind to pull his sweaty shirt away from his back. It made a sucking sound as it peeled away from his skin. "You be sure you stay right here in Jackson County 'til you hear from me. I'd hate like the devil to have to go run you down somewhere."

"Where would I go?"

He turned toward the door with a shrug. As he stepped into the house, I said, "Sheriff, what if Old Man Martin's just acting crazy?"

"You seriously sayin' he killed his own boy, then stuck him on his fish stringer next to a bunch of crappie, then sat out there all night waitin' for someone to notice?"

"Maybe. He's not exactly known for his gentle qualities."

The sheriff shook his head.

"Garr, he ain't been able to put two words together since findin' his boy like that. He just sits around the old folks' home drooling and slurping his dinner through a straw when he ain't throwing fits and askin' for his dear ol' daddy. Why would he kill Ernest B. if the boy meant that much to him?"

"Maybe he killed him because he's gone nuts. Maybe he went nuts after he killed him. I don't know. I just know I didn't do it."

"Well, you go on over there and see can you get a confession out of him." Barker chuckled as he stepped through the door. "Yeah, you just go on over and do that."

The door slammed, shutting off his laughter.

CHAPTER 4

THE BACK PORCH SEEMED TO SHRINK around me. The voices of insects and birds surged from the surrounding woods in hypnotic waves of pulsing sound that washed over my consciousness, driving logic and premonition along on its crest, tempting me to surrender all reason to the somnolent rhythm.

I shook my head. I sighed and turned my face to the sky, eyes wide. I had to focus somehow, to find a way out of this inconceivable situation. Yesterday I was a leading citizen in the community. Now my home had been searched, and they thought I had murdered my oldest friend.

They thought I was a *murderer*.

Mary Jo settled onto the porch swing, her eyes swollen and red. She sniffled and wiped her eyes occasionally with a soggy tissue, but I was barely aware of her. My thoughts were running to the past, to Ernest B.

She said, "They carried away our bank and tax records." It was as if she was whispering in a well. "They also took your softball bat and your tackle box from the boathouse. Why would they take your tackle box?"

"Well, I found Ernest B. hooked to a fish stringer."

"Oh, my dear Lord. You didn't tell me that."

"It didn't seem like the kind of thing we should talk about."

"What did Clyde say when you told him you were the one who called it in?"

"I didn't."

"You *still* haven't told him?"

"No."

"You've got to *tell* him, Garr. He'll find out somehow and then how will it look?"

"No worse than it does now."

"I wish you had told him."

"How was I supposed to explain not telling him before? 'Gee, Clyde, I didn't think it mattered,' or maybe 'I was afraid you'd think I killed him.' No way, Mary Jo. Not with that embezzlement thing hanging over my head."

We sat together in silence, each of us caught up in our thoughts. After a while she said, "I've never liked that man." In the psychic way that lovers have, I knew she was talking about Sheriff Barker.

"No? Why not?"

"Because he doesn't like you."

"That's ridiculous."

"No, it's not, Garr. You don't see how he looks at you. I noticed it a long time ago, at church one Sunday. We were singing a hymn, and he was sitting across the aisle. I had this strange feeling, like we were being watched. I looked over and caught him giving you the meanest look. It was scary."

"Another good reason not to go to church."

"Be serious. I'm telling you, it was an evil look. He must have a reason not to like you."

We were quiet again. My thoughts returned to the past. I thought about Ernest B., Old Man Martin, my dad, Clyde Barker. I remembered something.

"There was one time . . ."

"What?"

"It's too crazy."

"Tell me, Garr."

"Well, I caught Clyde cheating at poker. I was about seventeen. My daddy was past sixty by then. He used to hold a poker game every week. There'd be Old Man Martin, Clyde Barker, Aaron Stephens, Bud Carlson, and one or two others. It was a pretty big game stakes-wise.

"Daddy wouldn't let me play, of course, but he thought it was all right for me to sit around and listen in. He always said I could get a good education at those games. I mean, the old boys sitting around the table owned Jackson County's banks, grocery stores, the radio station—just about everything. Aaron Stephens alone owned the grain co-op, dairy plant, and farmer's market. And I guess most of the small farmers and ranchers in the county paid their rent to Old Man Martin.

"Anyway, I used to sit near the wall to watch the game, and I'd get 'em their drinks or something to eat. I'd be real quiet—Daddy didn't like me to interrupt their talk—and maybe Barker forgot I was sitting behind him. He was winning pretty big all night. All of a sudden, I saw a card fall to the floor next to his chair. I was about to go pick it up for him, when he pushed it under the table with his boot. Then I noticed he was still holding a full hand."

"What did you do?"

"Nothing. I didn't really know what to do, so I just sat there for another hour or so, then I went upstairs to bed. I didn't get much sleep though, I'll tell you that for sure."

"I'll bet you didn't." She giggled a little. "No pun intended."

"Spare me."

"Well, you told your father, didn't you?"

"Yep. Next morning at breakfast."

"What happened?"

"I don't know. I guess he must've gone to Barker about it, 'cause Clyde never came to another game."

"So Barker might hold you responsible for embarrassing him in front of the good ol' boys."

"He might. It happened so long ago, and I was just a kid, you know? Nobody's ever said anything to me about it, and Daddy told me to never tell anyone else."

"Well, I'll bet the sheriff hasn't forgotten."

"Maybe not."

I hadn't thought of that night in years. But it was easy to understand why Barker might consider it important. Much was decided about the future of Jackson County at those games.

The sheriff was young then, but the others were all old friends of my father. Their families developed the lake together. Called Martin Pool, it was named after the Martin family because they owned most of the land beneath it. The Martins, Carlsons, Stephens, Barkers, and Reeds formed the first board of directors of the Lake Association back in the early 1930s. They were also charter members of the Jackson County Development Corporation, which owned ninety percent of the shoreline of Martin Pool.

Some said the money for these investments came from large-scale moonshine operations. Moonshine was big business in Jackson County back then. My father always said the families invested their life's savings, honestly earned, in a desperate attempt to turn the cheap land prices of the Great Depression to their advantage. Either way, they timed their enterprise perfectly. The Depression drove the value of land to an all-time low. What little property they didn't already own, they bought for a dime on the dollar. Labor for the construction of the half-mile-long earthen dam was also available at a fraction of the normal rate.

My grandfather built the dam in return for a small share of the Development Corporation and for the rights to log the timber in the valleys that were to be flooded. Taking advantage of his position with the Development Corporation, my grandfather was also able to build hundreds of homes around the lake over the next twenty years, using the lumber from the valleys to increase his profits. My father cut his teeth in the construction business by working as a laborer on the dam and then as a supervisor on many of the houses.

If the sheriff's cheating was revealed to men like my father and his friends, it could have meant his isolation from the power base in the area, and the end of any plans that Barker might have had for the political advancement of his career. Small wonder he seemed so eager to consider me a suspect in Ernest B's. death.

Mary Jo interrupted my thoughts. "I should be ashamed."

"Why, baby?"

"I'm sitting here feeling sorry for us, thinking terrible thoughts about Clyde Barker, and I haven't even bothered to say a prayer for Ernest B. or his daddy. Imagine finding your boy like that . . ." She shivered, then squeezed her swollen eyes shut and bowed her head.

I watched her pray for a moment. Mary Jo never cared for Ernest B. or his father, but she was a good Christian woman and it was like her to be concerned for them both, even at a time like this. Sometimes I envied her faith. Mostly I resented it.

She met Ernest B. and me while I was studying architecture at Tulane. Mary Jo was a preacher's daughter and Louisiana native, majoring in fine art. We took the same sophomore life-drawing class and began dating whenever my busy design-lab schedule permitted.

Ernest B. thought I was wasting my time on a "prissy little altar maid" like Mary Jo. For him, the primary attraction in New Orleans—and one of the reasons he spent so much time visiting me there—was the ladies of the French Quarter. He was convinced that they had a unique appeal.

"It's the voodoo thing, buddy," he said. "Your French Quarter women put their makeup on with snake tails. Makes 'em look like Bridget Bardot even if they got a face like a plate full o' worms. Between the voodoo and the rhythm 'n' booze they got in these clubs down here, makes you wonder, don't it?"

I said, "Rhythm and what?"

"Booze, man. Rhythm 'n' booze."

"Rhythm and booze is a malapropism, Ernest B."

Ernest B. gave me a withering look and said, "See there, buddy, that just proves you ought to spend less time in class and more time down at the Quarter with us common folks. You don't understand what somebody has to say, you right off go to using them fancy words, 'stead of keepin' an open mind on the subject." He shook his head and went on under his breath, "You must think I'm an idiom or something," grinning to show that I wasn't the only one paying attention in English class.

His dumb-good-'ol-boy routine often came in handy, especially later on in our construction business. Many an owner or client underestimated him to their sorrow at the negotiation table. And while Ernest B. never enrolled, he did a lot of unofficial auditing of my courses and spent so much time with me at my apartment on St. Charles that Mary Jo thought we lived together until she and I had been dating for almost a year.

Those were wild times, full of the excitement of new opportunities and the promise of more to come. I often drank through the night with Ernest B., hanging out at the strip joints down on Bourbon and sleeping until Sunday afternoon in the tiny shuttered apartment. Hangovers were a nuisance, but freedom from the bonds of my parents' old-time religion was worth the pain. Until I met Mary Jo, life in New Orleans was a delicate balance of parties and studies. But she soon made it clear that she wasn't interested in my hedonistic lifestyle, so I returned with her to church on Sunday mornings and tapered off on the Saturday night drinking. I walked the aisle one day, to stand with the preacher in front of the podium and "declare my faith" in public. Three weeks later, clothed in a white cotton robe, I was briefly immersed in the tepid waters of a tank behind the choir, baptized into the church as a true believer.

It was the beginning of two decades of lies.

At first, my true goal was to entice her into my bed. I knew her beliefs forbade that, but I thought if I pretended to share the faith I would somehow nullify those antiquated rules. She was a beautiful girl. Seductively beautiful. A few Sundays in the pews would be a small price to pay for the earthly delights her body promised.

But as I watched her face in prayer, while all the other heads were bowed with eyes closed, as I stared at her profile in those publicly private moments when she was unaware of my scrutiny, I began to realize two truths: First, this woman would never sacrifice her faith for me—and second, I was hopelessly in love.

So the lies continued. We married. Twenty years of Sundays passed, and still she did not know that what was so important to her meant nothing to me. It was easy to abandon the superficial signs of paganism for her, the drinking and swearing, the blustery displays of anger. I tempered my outward life to match the lie, and soon enough, those outward ways became habit.

Ernest B. was jealous at first, and that made my choice to indulge Mary Jo's beliefs more difficult. Before I met her, Ernest B. was the best friend I ever had. Most of my memories of early childhood include him. We learned the tough lessons of adolescence together, secure in the knowledge that whether we dropped a touchdown pass or had our heart broken by our latest sweetheart, Ernest B. and I would always be there for each other. He was the best man at my wedding, the only person outside my family who always remembered my birthday, the person I turned to when my mother died.

We remained friends despite the changes my marriage brought to my lifestyle. Hard drinking and womanizing gave way to fishing, hunting, rooting for the Dallas Cowboys, and the occasional boys' night out. But in the years leading up to our split, we'd grown apart. Maybe it was because of the business. Maybe we started to see each other as business partners rather than friends; maybe the hard work together all week made for boring conversation on the weekends. It got to where we never really talked, just dealt with the details. The change in our relationship happened so gradually and was so far along before I noticed that I was unable to talk about it honestly. Then, in the months just before I found out he'd been stealing from the business, Ernest B. had gone through some sort of crisis. He grew moody and distant. Hard to get along with, as if he was being eaten from within by something. Almost as if . . .

"You're off somewhere else, aren't you, baby?" Mary Jo asked.

"I was just thinking back to when we met."

She leaned closer and put her arm around me. "Doesn't seem so long ago, does it?"

We listened to the sounds of the woods for a while. Then she asked, "What are we going to do?"

I looked away from her. Through the trees, the lake shimmered in the glare of the hot morning sun. I said, "First we're going to call our lawyer. Then I'm going to find out who killed Ernest B."

CHAPTER 5

BEFORE LEAVING THE HOUSE, I called Winston Graves, Reed Construction's attorney. He was a friend of my father's and had handled his legal work for fifty years. He was a very old man now, but still sharp and mean as a junkyard dog. Although we used a younger attorney out of Dallas for our day-to-day needs, Winston was always willing to help with what he called "the curiosities"—the unusual or interesting legal wrinkles that pop up from time to time in the construction business.

Once one of our men was digging a trench for a water main and the bucket scooped up a casket. He hopped down into the ditch to look around. Skulls and bones everywhere. Nobody knew the graves were there. Nobody knew who the bodies were. So when a malcontent state bureaucrat down in Austin stopped the project cold, Winston Graves was just the man to make a convincing case for our right to relocate the abandoned cemetery in the name of progress. He had the judge crying in his coffee about the unfair demands society places on construction companies.

Winston's voice was raspy from too many cigars. "I was wondering when you might call, Garrison. I heard our idiotic sheriff has been causing you some anxiety."

I wasn't surprised to learn that Winston had already heard of my troubles. It amused him to stay informed, so nothing of any importance in our community escaped his attention. I could imagine him on the other end of the line: wrinkled white cotton shirt stretched tight over his ample belly, bow tie and black suspenders, soggy cigar stub rolling from one side of his mouth to the other. Like a character from a Faulkner novel, he would be sitting in a cane rocking chair behind the white verandah columns of his plantation-style house, drinking tea (with a touch of Southern Comfort), and looking out across the lawn as he talked to me and fanned himself with the financial section of the *Dallas Morning News*.

He was a widower without children and lived alone except for an elderly black woman who cooked for him and kept his huge house clean. I suppose he was a lonely man, but it didn't show unless you knew him well. And although almost everyone of any financial or political importance in Austin and east Texas knew him, nobody knew him well. My father once told me that Winston had too much money and knew too much about too many people to have real friends. He had clients instead.

While it's true that he was stinking rich, and probably true that he knew the dirty truth about most of the Texas upper crust, I figured the real reason Winston had no friends was simpler than that: He was just too smart. The vast gap between his intelligence and everyone else's was too obvious.

Nobody likes to be reminded that there are people a whole lot smarter than they are—unless they need a lawyer.

"You hear about Barker coming over here and searching my place?" I asked.

"I did."

"That was only an hour ago, Winston. How did you hear so fast?"

There was silence on the line. Stupid question.

I said, "What should I do?"

"Nothing. Say nothing. Do nothing. I will instruct our esteemed sheriff that he is not to contact you in the future unless I am present for the interview. And you stay away from him."

"Can he get away with searching my house like that?"

"Of course he can, if he had a warrant. He did have a search warrant, didn't he?"

I realized that I hadn't asked to see it. But I didn't want to admit a thing like that to the great Winston Graves, so I lied and said yes.

"Humph. Probably obtained the warrant from that senile old fool Warren Stevens. I'll call the learned judge and determine what Barker used as an excuse for the search."

"Can you find out things like that?"

"Judge Stevens knows better than to withhold information from me. Wait a moment."

There was a pause while I heard some muffled conversation in the background, then he came back on the line. "Agatha says lunch is served, Garrison. I'll have to let you go. Don't worry about this thing. I'll work it out. When we are finished, Mr. Barker will wish he had entered another line of work."

"Winston?"

"Yes."

"You didn't ask if I killed Ernest B."

Another long silence, then, "You were his friend, were you not?"

"Absolutely."

"Then why should I entertain the notion that you might have killed him?"

"Other people seem to think I may have."

"Humph. I am not a fool, Garrison, and I am an excellent judge of character. I have often thought that you inherited a bit of your father's ruthless nature. You would most certainly be capable of killing an enemy. But you would never betray a friend. Now, I really must go eat lunch, or Agatha will make the balance of my day most uncomfortable. Good-bye, Garrison."

He hung up before I could ask what he meant about my father's ruthless nature.

• • •

THE HUMIDITY WAS HIGH IN THE LAUNDROMAT. Steam condensed on the storefront glass and rolled down to the low sills, where it fed the dry rot. The only air conditioning was a muggy breeze coming through the screen door. I poked at the decomposing window frame with the toe of my boot while Miss Suzy, the proprietor, transferred a load of laundry to a dryer.

"We do a lot of folks' wash for 'em here, you know," she said. "It's not all self-service. There's folks have the money to buy their own machines that still bring their wash to me. I do a real good job for 'em. They get it back ironed and folded, or hung up." She closed the door on the dryer and set the timer. "I even got a dry cleanin' machine here. We can do folks' church clothes in that."

I'd hardly gotten a word in edgewise since walking through the door. As soon as Miss Suzy learned who I was, she began a rosy description of her business prospects, the abundance of customers, and the ease of operating the Laundromat. I figured she wanted to sell the place.

"Now, Mrs. Powell—lives on Tyler Avenue? She's been bringin' me her wash for twenty years, even after her husband died in that hotel fire down in Houston and she got all that money. She says she just loves the smell I get into her private things." She snickered, "Maybe I shouldn't tell you about that, huh? Professional ethics, don't you know."

I smiled and nodded, wiping my face with my shirtsleeve. It was like a Turkish bath in the Laundromat, but I was sweating mostly from nerves. I wasn't sure how to begin questioning a person about a murder. Perhaps it was best to jump right in.

"Miss Suzy? You remember telling your friend Mabel about a fight that Ernest B. and his daddy had out here?" I pointed over my shoulder at the Nowhere Club across the street.

"Sure do." She was pulling someone's clothes out of another dryer farther down the row. "That was quite a while back."

I raised my voice over the rumbling of the machines. "Could you tell me about it?"

"I suppose," she said, huffing over the wad of clothes that seemed to be caught in the dryer's door. I walked over to help.

"Why, thank you, sir." She stood back as I removed the clothes and dropped them into a rolling wire basket. "It's not often a girl meets a gentleman."

Suzy was no girl. She was about fifty, and life in the Laundromat had been hard. Her hair was piled high on her head like a starched, gray ball of lint. She wore a plain white sleeveless blouse with the shirttail out, dark polyester stretch slacks with a permanent crease, and sensible shoes. Around her neck hung a pair of rhinestone-studded reading glasses on a black cord. Up close, I could see that her hands had suffered from her profession. I knew carpenters with smoother skin.

"When was the fight, exactly?" I asked.

"Oh, I couldn't say. A while back, maybe two, three months."

"Were you over at the Club?"

"Gracious sakes no! I wouldn't set foot in a place like that. I'm a good Baptist woman, Mr. Reed." She rolled the wire basket down the aisle, shaking her head as I followed. "No sir, I surely wouldn't."

A large old black woman walked in with a green garbage sack in each hand. She wore a faded cotton sundress and a filthy pair of pink terry cloth house slippers. Sweat stains spread under her arms and across the back of her dress. She went to the far side of the room and began to remove clothes from the sacks and put them in a washer. I returned my attention to Suzy.

"How did you come to hear them fighting?"

"Oh, you couldn't miss that. I even heard them from in here. That old Mr. Martin sure can holler."

"So he was pretty mad, huh?"

"I imagine." She began to fold the clothes on a water-stained wooden tabletop.

The door swung open with a crash and two small children ran in, screaming and laughing. "Ya'll settle down!" the black woman yelled. Suzy gave all three of them a look of disgust.

"Could you tell what he was saying?"

"No, I had to go outside to hear him better." She glanced at me quickly, as if she'd let something slip. "I'm not a busybody,

Mr. Reed. I just happened to need to go out to my car for something right then. That's how I came to overhear them."

"I understand. Could you tell why Mr. Martin was so upset?"

"Oh, it was that Ernest B., of course. He's never been any good." She clapped her hand over her mouth. "Oh my goodness, listen to me speaking ill of the dead. I forgot that poor boy isn't with us anymore."

The black woman was watching us. The nearest dryer buzzed loudly, and Suzy stepped over to it. "I'm not exactly on my best behavior today, am I?"

"Well, it takes a while for something like this to sink in." Someone had left some coins in the pocket of a pair of pants that were drying. The coins had shaken loose and rattled with every revolution of the dryer's drum. Suzy opened the machine, retrieved the coins, and put them in her pocket.

I said, "You were saying about the fight?"

"Mr. Martin was madder than a wet hen. Something to do with Ernest B's. drinking, I think. He said he wasn't going to allow Ernest B. to drag their name through the mud. Imagine that! Mr. Martin thinking folks around here have any respect for his family name, with the way he treats people."

"What makes you think he was mad about Ernest B.'s drinking?"

"Well, they were standing in front of that bar, Mr. Reed."

"Yes, ma'am, but was there anything said that made you think Ernest B's. drinking was the problem?"

Suzy paused for a moment, staring past the condensation on the window to collect her thoughts. "He used the Lord's name in vain. I remember that. He used a lot of words I won't repeat. He said something like 'I'll be blankety-blanked if I'm going to sit by and do nothing while you blankety-blank on my name.' And he said, 'Don't matter what I did, you're blankety sure not going to spend my money on no bender.'"

She looked at me. "That was a funny thing to say, wasn't it?"

I was about to answer when the old black woman approached us. She looked from Suzy to me uncertainly, then turned to me. "You Mr. Reed's boy, ain'tcha?"

"Yes, ma'am, I'm Garrison Jr."

"I knew yo' daddy real well. He never was one to turn a body down when they asked for help." She appeared to be nervous about Suzy overhearing our conversation and placed herself between us. Lowering her voice, she said, "Could you loan me a little wash money, Mr. Reed? I done got off without it this mornin', and it's an awful long walk back home."

I was reaching for my wallet when Miss Suzy was suddenly at my side.

"Claralee, you get on out of here and take these little pickaninnies with you! I mean now!" She said, "How many times I got to tell you not to be comin' round here beggin'? Now leave Mr. Reed be, and get on outside."

Claralee's eyes dropped, and she slowly shuffled back toward her plastic bags.

Suzy followed the woman and the children closely until they were out the door. Then she turned to me and said, "Mr. Reed, I am so sorry. That old nigger woman's been comin' round here for years with that same story. I just detest a beggar, don't you? 'Specially a nigger beggar."

I said, "Maybe it'd be a more Christian thing—you being a good Baptist and all—to give her a little money."

Her face registered surprise, then hardened as she turned her hate on me. "I heard about you, Mr. High and

Mighty," she spat out. "I heard you was a nigger lover. Well, you can just follow her on out that door, 'cause I sure don't need no preachin' 'bout race relations from a poor little rich boy. No sir, I do not."

Her cold stare chased me out into the bright sunlight. Standing on the sidewalk for a moment to let my eyes adjust to the glare, I considered her parting words and my sanctimonious response. Who was I to talk about Christian things? I wouldn't have set foot inside a church these past fifteen years if not for Mary Jo. An unfocused shame rose inside me as I walked across the road to the Nowhere Club. Before I reached the door, one of the children I had seen in the Laundromat appeared at my side, looking up with his hand out. I gave him five dollars, and he ran away without a word.

It didn't make me feel any better.

CHAPTER 6

LESTER FREDRICKS SAT ON A STOOL behind the bar, chewing tobacco and reading a comic book. He was a mechanic where they service my company's trucks until the Nowhere Club opened. I suppose he decided that lubricating drunks was more rewarding.

As my eyes adjusted to the darkness, I walked to the far end of the bar and sat across from him. He wore a camouflage gimme cap pushed so far back that the bill pointed at the water-stained ceiling. A lightweight cotton shirt hung on his bony frame like an empty sack. The stench of stale beer filled the air. Miniature fake Clydesdales pulled a tiny wagon past a revolving snow scene on the wall. A few feet away, a festive neon sign that read *Una Pearla Por Favor* cast a red glow onto a row of large jars containing huge, fuzzy green pickles and pigs' feet. The pigs' feet reminded me of Ernest B.'s face rising from the lake.

When I ordered a beer, Lester selected a water-spotted glass and drew the beverage from the tap one-handed without moving from his stool or raising his eyes from the comic book. I was impressed.

"You're Lester Fredricks, right?"

"Uh-huh." He turned a page.

"Could I ask you a couple of questions?"

"Uh-huh."

"Do you remember a fight outside here between Ernest B. Martin and his daddy a few months back?"

At last he looked up. His eyes narrowed as they reached my face. He stared at me for a moment while he chewed slowly. Then he leaned to the side and spat a brown stream to the floor.

"Your name Reed?"

"That's right."

Giving me what was supposed to be his tough-guy look, he said, "I don't know nothin' 'bout no Martins," and returned his attention to his comic book with exaggerated concentration. I took a sip from my glass and looked around the dark lounge. Two men were playing pool with their heads and shoulders in the shadows on the other side of the room, talking softly and smoking cigarettes. An old man was asleep at a table. All in all, it looked as if my chances were best with Lester.

I had never bribed anyone before. Feeling awkward, I pulled a twenty from my wallet and laid it next to my glass. Lester's eyes shifted just enough to show that he had noticed.

I said, "Anything you wanted to tell me about that fight, I'd keep it between us."

Pool balls clicked behind me like breaking bones. Lester moved his full attention from the comic book to the twenty. He slid the wad of tobacco into his cheek and said quietly,

"Martin found out I been blabbermouthin' about him, it'd mean my job."

"You work for him?"

"Sure. He owns this joint."

I didn't know that, but it wasn't surprising. Several years before, a bitter political battle had taken place between the conservative Baptists in Jackson County and those who wanted "liquor by the drink." With the Arabs driving down the price of oil and the family farm disappearing fast, the tax revenues inherent in being the only wet county for fifty miles had been too tempting to resist. I had heard rumors that Old Man Martin was the financial force behind the pro-liquor lobby in the referendum. This bar explained why.

"Look. All I want to know is, did Mr. Martin and Ernest B. have a fight here a while back? I'm not going to tell him what you say. If I wanted him to know I was interested, I'd ask him myself."

Lester considered my point. "Why you want to know?"

"Let's just say I'm trying to clear up something you wouldn't want to know about, okay? Now, is this going to be a one-dollar beer or a twenty-dollar beer?"

He leaned over and spat again. Then he picked up the twenty and used it to mark his place in the comic book. He carefully spit the tobacco wad into a trash can and said, "They had some words, all right."

"What about?"

"Same thing they're always goin' on about: Ernest B.'s nose candy."

"His what?"

He looked at me with disdain and said, "Cocaine to you."

"You mean Ernest B. took drugs?"

He let out a short laugh. "Man, he never stopped."

I felt something slip a little inside. There was nothing to say. I reached for my glass and took a long, slow sip, letting this revelation sink in. I was saddened and I was completely surprised, but it didn't occur to me to doubt that Ernest B. had been doing dope. It explained too many of his actions over the past few months.

I asked, "So Old Man Martin was upset about the drugs, eh?"

"Oh, you betcha. Now, I don't personally see a whole lot of difference 'tween pushin' dope and sellin' liquor, but I guess the old man splits a finer hair than me and Ernest B."

"I heard he was yelling something about the family name."

"Yeah, I think that was his main complaint. Didn't really give a rip about Ernest B., you know. Just didn't want folks goin' around sayin' he had a doper for a son."

"Did you hear him threaten Ernest B.?"

I'd pushed too hard. Lester didn't answer; he just returned to his comic book as if I'd disappeared. I put another twenty on the bar. As he reached, I set my glass down on it. "I asked if you heard any threats."

He raised himself a little on the stool and looked over my shoulder toward the pool table. Satisfied that the players weren't paying attention to us, he leaned toward me and said, "Old Man Martin told Ernest B., if he didn't leave the nose candy alone, he'd see to it that Ernest B. didn't have no nose to medicate. Then he slapped Ernest B. like he was a little boy—openhanded, right across the face." Lester snorted. "I swear I thought I'd bust a gut tryin' not to laugh. I mean, here's this codger 'bout a hundred years old, tellin' Ernest B.

he's gonna knock his block off? Shoot, you know Ernest B.—he could probably kick both our keisters simon-taneous, you know? But he let that old coot slap him like that, right in front of everybody." He pulled the twenty from under my glass and shook his head. "Man, that was funny!"

I looked at the bar top, feeling ashamed. How could I have worked with Ernest B. every day without realizing he was using cocaine? Some friend I was! The guy had a serious problem—bad enough to cause him to steal from me—but all I did was push him away. The least I could do was make sure whoever killed him paid for it.

Behind me, one of the pool players said, "Three in the far corner."

The other one said, "Wilson, you been takin' lessons?"

New possibilities flashed through my mind. What if Ernest B. was not killed by his father? What if his death was drug related? After all, Sheriff Barker would not tell me how he died. Maybe he overdosed and whoever was with him dumped his body into the lake to avoid explanations. Or maybe he was killed in a drug deal that went bad.

I said, "Lester, who around here would know about the local cocaine business?"

He scratched his chin and thought. "Well, there's the dealers, I guess."

As I opened my mouth to speak, he shook his head quickly and said, "No way am I gonna name those names, man. Don't even ask."

"Okay, but is there anyone else who'd have a handle on that stuff?"

"I reckon." He gave me a brown-stained smile. "Ask the cops."

One of the pool players walked to the jukebox. Lester's eyes followed him closely. I turned a little, enough to see the man's broad back as he dropped a quarter into the machine and pushed some buttons. He was built like a walking triangle—wide shoulders tapering to a slender waist, tapering to tiny feet. He wore a little pair of black cowboy boots with silver toe and heel protectors. I turned back to Lester.

Patsy Cline began to sing about falling to pieces. The music was loud. I leaned forward a little and spoke up, "Come on, man. I need someone to talk to."

With his eyes on the man at the jukebox, he said, "I got nothin' else to say to you, mister. I don't know nothin' 'bout that."

He stood, ambled down the bar, picked up a soiled dish towel, and began rubbing the grease around on a mug. I sat with my glass for a while, trying to decide what to do. Without more information, my little investigation was going nowhere for sure, but Lester was done with me. I got up to leave.

I walked to the door and pushed. The big guy with the little feet was still at the jukebox. When I opened the door, sunlight slapped his face with a stripe of white. His head was bowed over the gaudy machine as if he were making a selection, but his eyes were rolled up, watching me. They were extraordinary eyes—perfectly clear ovals of white surrounding irises so dark they blended with the pupils. Empty holes. Shark's eyes.

I turned away, instinctively avoiding his gaze. When I pushed the door open wider, he turned and called, "Rack 'em up, Jimmy. I'm gonna get that five-spot back this time."

I stepped out into the parking lot, glad to be leaving, thinking about Lester Fredricks' words: "He slapped Ernest B. like he was a little boy." It reminded me of something that had happened years ago.

• • •

I REMEMBERED THE WAVES AT GALVESTON.

My parents and I went there one August to escape the motionless, stifling heat of the east Texas woods. I cried and cried before we left, not wanting to leave my playmates or miss one day of our summer vacation. Finally they agreed to let me invite one friend. Of course, I asked Ernest B.

The second morning on the beach, my father pointed to a piece of tattered facric tied to the skeletal frame of a pastel-blue lifeguard tower and said, "See the red flag, boys? That means we can't get in the water today. There's an undertow, and it wouldn't be safe."

We walked along the sand, hunting for shells, disappointed that we couldn't swim. Ernest B. found the first man-o'-war, beached at the high-tide line. Its purple sail fluttered listlessly in the offshore breeze. Its tentacles lay tangled in a clump of kelp, like a salad of finely sliced cabbage on a bed of deep-green spinach. I had heard of these animals and warned Ernest B. not to touch it. He took me at my word, content to squat beside the creature and examine it closely while clutching his little tin shovel.

"Do you think it's alive?" he asked.

"Probably," I said. "At least until the sun gets higher and dries it up."

He used his little shovel to poke at the sail, flipping it from side to side, no expression at all on his face. Suddenly he jabbed the shovel into the pale purple bubble. It popped softly.

My father walked up behind us. "Don't torture it, boys. It's got enough pain just lying there, dying slow."

I went back with my father to the part of the beach that my mother had claimed for us with umbrellas and towels. Ernest B. stayed where he was, fascinated by the man-o'-war. I began work on a sand castle, building moats and walls to withstand the rising tide. Time went by. The sun grew stronger, but a steady breeze from the gulf cooled me. The wind roared in my ears when I turned my head just right.

From behind me, higher up on the beach, my mother called, "Garrison, honey, run on down there and get Ernest B., will you? He's going too far away."

I abandoned my castle and strolled along the waterline, dragging my feet and kicking the waves when they flowed in. I passed the place where we had left Ernest B. studying the man-o'-war. A few yards farther along, I saw another one, strung out on the sand. Its sail had been popped as well. I put my hand to my forehead to shield my eyes from the sunlight and looked down the beach. Ernest B. was far away, a tiny black figure dancing in the wavy whiffs of heat that rose from the dull, beige sand. Man-o'-wars lay scattered along the beach between us, one every twenty or thirty feet—hundreds of them, a whole community blown ashore. Ernest B. had killed them all. His footprints stretched from creature to creature, a graphic but temporary record of his path between executions.

I ran to catch up with him, passing the dead animals one by one. He was squatting next to a purple sail, jabbing it again and again with his toy shovel. My shadow fell across him and he turned, squinting up at me.

"Why did you do that?" I asked.

He turned back to the dead man-o'-war and said, "Makes you wonder, don't it?"

"What?"

"They was sure dumb to get stuck up here, wasn't they, Garr? I hate stupid things."

"But Daddy told us not to hurt them, Ernest B. He'll be mad!"

Ernest B. stabbed the man-o'-war faster, harder, again and again. Finally, without emotion, he said, "Will he beat me? You won't let him beat me, will you?"

"Beat you? Why would he do that?"

He rose without answering and set off along the beach, trudging toward my parents with his shoulders stooped by a weight I didn't understand. I followed, resolving to keep his secret. By late afternoon the offshore breeze had filled his footprints with sand.

Chapter 7

THE AFTERNOON SUNSHINE WAS fierce, sapping the earth and everything on it of energy. Folks took shelter in air-conditioned buildings or sat still in the shade, drinking ice water or sweet tea and fanning themselves with whatever was handy. I drove along bubbling blacktop streets from the Nowhere Club to the town square, where I found a parking spot in the shadow of an old live oak.

I had decided it was time to talk to Barker again.

As I walked across the plaza, I passed the monument to Mt. Sinai's Civil War veterans. From its red granite pedestal, the bronze statue of a Confederate soldier stared into the distance, calm and unafraid. The figure wore a floppy, wide-brimmed hat, a bedroll on his back, and a cartridge belt across his chest. He held his carbine with bayonet fixed, as if an order to charge the Yankees was imminent. The pedestal was engraved with the names of those who had served and died in the War Between the States. It has always seemed strange to me that an additional list of names, the veterans of the Spanish-American War, was added below the original engraved area. Apparently their war was not worth the price of its own monument, since it was so brief and the list of names so short. But my grandfather's name is there, and so is Ernest B.'s.

I climbed the steps to the county courthouse entrance. Just as I reached the front doors, they were thrown open and Dr. Alvin Krueger charged out, almost knocking me down. The county coroner was slender and tall, with a beaklike, red-veined nose and tight, angry lips.

"Watch where you're goin', Reed!" he barked as he passed me and marched down the steps. I felt my temper rise, but kept quiet. The last thing I needed was an altercation at the door of the courthouse. There was probably nothing Sheriff Barker would like better.

I yanked the front door open and went inside. My boots slapped the polished marble vestibule floor with a hollow, echoing sound as I crossed to another door with "Sheriff's Department" painted in peeling gold leaf on its frosted glass. A frowning young woman in uniform sat at the front desk, viciously pounding a stack of documents with a rubber stamp. One page at a time, one stamp per page. She had been at it long enough to develop a rhythm that I was hesitant to break, so I stood silently in front of her desk until she looked up.

"What do you want?" she snapped.

"I'm Garrison Reed, here to see Sheriff Barker."

"About what?" Her tone of voice made it clear that she considered me to be just the latest in a long series of unwelcome intrusions into her day.

Enough was enough. I said, "Look, I almost got knocked down a minute ago by a guy who wasn't watching where he was going. Then he blamed me. I'm not having a very good day, so would you try to be civil?"

She set her stamp down on the desk with a sigh. "You're right. Sorry about my tone of voice. It's just that Dr. Krueger . . ." There was an awkward pause, then she said, "Well, anyway, you wanted the sheriff? I'll just see if he's busy."

As she picked up the receiver, I asked, "So this is where the doctor was just now?"

"Yes, sir. And he was very rude. Even for him."

"I know. He's the one who almost knocked me down outside. What was his problem?"

She answered with the telephone to her ear, "He's always like that, only today he was worse than usual. . . . Oh, Sheriff? There's a Mr. Reed here for you. . . . All right." She hung up and said, "He'll be out in just a moment. Would you like to take a seat?"

I thanked her and settled into an old club chair against the wall. A ceiling fan hummed overhead. She resumed her pounding with the stamp. The nameplate on her desk said Sgt. Julie Masters. After a while I asked her, "Do you have any idea why the doctor was so angry today?"

Without breaking her rhythm she said, "Maybe you should ask the sheriff. They were in a meeting and I heard some yelling and then out came Dr. Krueger. He just about flew through here. Knocked some stuff off my desk and didn't even apologize, much less stop to pick it up."

I waited. A wasp flew across the ceiling, buzzing up into the age-yellowed plaster, falling a little, moving on to do it again. The woman pounded. The fan hummed. Time passed.

Just as I was about to ask her to call Sheriff Barker again, he opened his office door.

"Well now, Garr. We're sure seein' a lot of each other today, ain't we?" His smile was as false as his perfect white teeth. "You here to confess? Save us all a lot of trouble if you did."

I smiled, too, pretending to enjoy his little joke. "Not hardly, Clyde. But I do have some information you'll be interested in."

He looked at his watch with the air of an overworked man and said, "You sure you want to talk without Winston here?"

So Winston Graves had already begun to pressure Barker. And I had forgotten his advice about talking to Barker alone. But it was too late to leave gracefully, so I said, "This won't take a minute, and I think I might not need Winston's help after we talk."

Barker sighed and said, "Come on in here then, Garr."

His office was surprisingly small. An ancient air conditioner rattled and wheezed in the window next to his desk, dripping water into a plastic trash can on the floor. The walls were covered with photographs of Barker in poses with various civic leaders. There was a shot of him and my father standing in front of some building. The Texas and United States flags drooped from eagle-topped poles to the left and right of Barker's desk. The Texas flagpole was a little taller.

As I took a seat across from the desk, I asked, "What was the fuss with Dr. Krueger just now?"

He walked around me to sit in his large, brown leather chair and said, "Don't exactly know what you mean, Garr."

"He almost knocked me down running out of here."

Barker chuckled. "Krueger sure does get in a hurry now an' then. He sure does." He leaned back in his chair and put his hands behind his head. The springs in his chair seat creaked with his every move. His shirt was wet at the armpits. "I don't think you could say there was a fuss, though. He was just in a hurry is all." I waited for him to elaborate. The pause got awkward. Finally he said, "What was it you wanted to tell me?"

I told him about my conversation with Suzy, about the fight in the parking lot between Ernest B. and his father, and the threats that Lester Fredricks overheard. I kept Lester's name out of it, but I told Barker that I thought Ernest B. had been doing drugs.

Barker picked up a pencil and bounced the eraser on his desk blotter like a drumstick. "So you're still tryin' to say that the old man killed Ernest B.? Come on now, Garr. I told you he was too far gone to figure out how to go to the bathroom by hisself, much less kill a big ol' boy like Ernest B. 'Sides, I got a real problem believin' the old man would do in his own son just to keep the family name respectable."

"What if Ernest B. got involved in a drug deal that went bad? Isn't that possible?"

"No, Garr. That's not possible." His chair creaked again as he leaned forward, put his forearms on his desk, and watched me with cold policeman's eyes. "Ernest B. wasn't doin' any drug deals. Not in my county. I'd have known about it if he was."

The stare left no room for debate, but I pushed on. "Okay, what if he was just a user? What if he overdosed and someone dumped him in the lake?"

"Nope. Didn't happen. Dr. Krueger has figured out that Ernest B. was killed by a blow from a blunt instrument; meanin' someone beat him to death. 'Sides, if Ernest B. was usin' drugs, I'd have known about that too."

"Clyde, I'm sure you have a real firm grasp on what happens in this county, but couldn't Ernest B. have been involved in something that escaped your attention?"

"If he was to be so mixed up in doin' dope that it killed him, me and my men would've known about it. We would've been keepin' an eye on him, and that's for sure. But we ain't been watchin' Ernest B., Garr. Just like we ain't been watchin' you." He paused, then said, "Though I'm beginning to think we should've been payin' closer attention to both you boys."

"Would you at least look over your arrest records for the last year to see if you can find someone to confirm that Ernest B. was into dope?"

"No, I won't. I appreciate that you're takin' what seems like a natural interest in this murder investigation, but the last thing I need is advice from a suspect." He stood and began to move toward the door. "I told you Ernest B. was not involved in drugs. If he was, I'd have a record of it, and I don't. I didn't even have a file on him until that night he shot up your place, and until last Friday it was a real skinny file at that." He opened the door. "Now unless you got another theory to try out, I've got a mess of work to do this afternoon."

I stood reluctantly. "Could I see the coroner's report?"

I'd gone too far. His face turned red as he said, "Doggone it, Garr! Who do you think you are? You can't come in here, tellin' me how to run my investigation, tellin' me to check records, and askin' to see reports. You're a *suspect,* Garr! Now you get on out of here!"

As I walked past Sergeant Masters' desk, I noticed that she was finished stamping the papers and had stacked them neatly in her out basket. Next to the basket was a manila folder with Ernest B.'s name on it. The label on the folder was dog-eared and faded.

Chapter 8

For reasons long forgotten, the Mt. Sinai cemetery lies in a low, boggy field next to the Big Muddy Bayou. It hasn't flooded since the 1920s, but it's damp bottomland just the same. We bury our dead in small stone and concrete crypts above the ground. It wouldn't do to have caskets popping up like weeds after a heavy rain.

In fact, it had rained all night—a slow, steady summer rain born of faraway waves of thunder that rolled around the horizon like rumbling locomotives. I'd spent most of the night lying in bed, watching flashes of lightning through the bedroom curtains, and thinking about Ernest B.

The storm clouds burned off in the morning, leaving the air thick with humidity and my mind foggy with grief. Steam rose like an army of ghosts from the ground as we laid my old friend's body to rest. Mary Jo and I stood quietly with a small group of mourners while a Baptist minister said the ancient words of solace and resignation. Old Man Martin rocked back and forth in a wheelchair, grinning. A pretty young woman dressed in somber black sat next to him, holding his hand and murmuring soothing sounds now and then when he seemed to become agitated. I guessed she was a nurse, there to look after him and to prevent one of the "attacks" he seemed to be subject to since Ernest B. had shown up at the end of his fish stringer.

Barker, Winston Graves, and the mayor were there, as was at least one member of most of the leading families in the area. I saw Dr. Krueger a few yards from the grave site, leaning against the gnarled trunk of a huge old cypress tree. Spanish moss trailed from the branches above like a widow's veil. Lester Fredricks stood nearby, a solid-black tie looped inexpertly around his neck, his camouflage gimme cap in hand. Behind him, the large man with the little feet I'd seen at the Nowhere Club stood silently observing the ceremony. His empty eyes were hidden behind curved plastic sunglasses, and his shiny black hair was slicked back in a ducktail—a fifties throwback. He wore tight blue jeans and a casual western-cut shirt. A cigarette drooped from his full lips, adding its acrid gray-blue smoke to the drifting steam around us. He took a last deep drag and dropped the butt to the ground, grinding it into the soil beside Ernest B.'s crypt with a tiny silver-covered boot heel.

As the preacher neared the end of his eulogy, I returned my attention to the ceremony. Despite the way Ernest B. had treated me during the last few months of his life, my eyes grew wet as the last prayers were spoken.

We'd "played hooky" from school many times to fish and skinny-dip together in the bayou that now flowed past his grave. We learned to play baseball together when we were six. He saved my life years later when we were scuba diving thirty feet down in Martin Pool. We went on double dates with our high-school sweethearts, defended each other in fistfights, and painted our high-school graduation year on the water tower in broad daylight without getting caught. Those numbers were still up there for all to see—faded and peeling, but still there.

And as the preacher's voice droned on, my mind closed in on one part of our childhood that was tied to this very place.

• • •

ONE SATURDAY WHEN I WAS ABOUT EIGHT, my father took me and Ernest B. to work with him. He said he had a big surprise, something new to show us. My mother wasn't to know. I remember the tingling feel of excitement as I sat next to Dad in the pickup truck. The drive to Mt. Sinai seemed to take hours. Ernest B. wanted to fool around, play scissors-paper-and-rock, but I was too wound up for that.

We both ran from the truck to the office door, panting and giggling as my father walked toward us. "Now, you boys stand out here till I get the lights on," he said. "I'll tell you when to come in."

After a minute or two, he called to us and we charged through the door together. He stood in the center of the waiting room, leaning against a large brown cardboard box, arms crossed, smiling just a little. Ernest B. and I stopped in our tracks a few feet from the box. "What is it?" I asked.

"A console television," said my father. "Brand new and ready to play."

"Play?"

"Yes. See, it's like a radio, only bigger. You plug it in and turn it on and it plays programs just like the radio does, except it shows you pictures at the same time."

"Wow!" said Ernest B. "Makes you wonder, don't it?"

"Yeah, wow!" I said. "Makes you wonder."

"I'm going to unpack it while you boys play outside. Go across to the plaza, and remember to watch out for traffic, all right?"

We spent half an hour pretending to be Confederate soldiers, charging the Yankees alongside the towering statue in front of the courthouse. Eventually my father called us.

The television still stood in the center of the reception room, free now of its packaging. It was plugged in, and the screen glowed white and gray, with rolling bars of light rising from the bottom and disappearing at the top. There was no recognizable image and no sound other than static.

"Should work fine over at the house, fellas," my father said. "Guess we'll have to get a bigger antenna if it doesn't."

I was very disappointed, but Ernest B. seemed more interested in the pile of packing material that my father had removed from the big brown cardboard box. As Dad tinkered with the knobs on the front of the television, I joined Ernest B. in his inspection of the trash.

Most of it was clear plastic and kraft paper, but at the bottom we found a treasure: a three-foot-by-four-foot piece of stiff foam at least six inches thick.

Ernest B. said, "Makes you wonder, don't it?"

I said, "What? Makes you wonder what?"

"Makes you wonder if maybe we can make a boat," whispered Ernest B., always the first to recognize the play potential in simple things.

My father was distracted by the television, trying to make it function so he could present it as a surprise to my mother that evening. He barely heard me when I asked for permission to take the foam board out to play.

Carrying the slab of foam over his head, Ernest B. led me around the block, away from the square. We followed an ancient red-bricked alley for a couple of hundred yards to a low spot, marked by a moss-green concrete culvert and a couple of deformed *bois d'arc* trees, heavy with knobby horse apples. A small, clear stream trickled out of the culvert. The stream was probably the reason the town's founders had picked that spot for their center of commerce. A ready source of water was important in the days of travel by horseback. But eventually, the land over the stream had become more valuable, and the flow had been contained in concrete and buried.

We scurried down the low embankment. Ernest B. looked around us for a moment, then walked over to a tangle of dead wood. He selected two short branches and handed one to me.

"You be the first mate. I'll be the captain, all right?"

"Sure."

"Okay, then, you go ahead onto the boat, and I'll shove off."

He slid the foam onto the slowly flowing water. Gingerly, I crab-walked across it and sat cross-legged on the far end. Ernest B. gave a gentle push and scrambled onto his end, moving too fast and almost swamping us.

"Sit down!" I yelled, and he dropped to all fours, clutching the edges of the foam until the rocking subsided. By the time he found a comfortable position next to me, we were well away from the bank and floating downstream.

It was a joyful thing: two young boys floating toward the unknown on a mild summer day. We were admirals, setting forth to conquer the high seas; Indians, slipping silently along in our birch-bark canoe. We controlled our progress with the little wooden branches, poking the water to check its shallow depth and prodding the shore to negotiate the turns.

I was a good boy—or as good as a boy can be—most of the time. But adventure such as that doesn't come often in life, and when it does, responsibilities can surrender to the passion of the moment. I lost track of time. Hours passed in the instant it took us to travel from the Mississippi River to the Caribbean Sea. We didn't notice that the garbage-strewn banks of the stream in town had given way to taller, wider, cleaner slopes. Before we could escape the pirates that pursued us and return to our tropical island port, our little stream had widened and deepened and taken control. Our meager wooden poles no longer reached the bottom. We were whisked around the curves, caught in the current, given no chance to disembark.

The sun was setting when the stream ejected us into the Big Muddy Bayou, several miles from town. By that time, we were no longer great adventurers, just two very small, very frightened boys in trouble. We sat close together, our poles abandoned, our throats sore from calling for help. We were alone.

The Big Muddy flowed more slowly than the stream, and we were able to make progress toward shore by dog-paddling over the side. After perhaps another mile, we passed beneath an overhanging willow and I got a grip on a branch. Working together, we moved hand over hand to shore.

By then it was dark. Clouds obscured the moon and stars. A low rumbling in the distance threatened rain to come. We scraped and clawed our way up the steep embankment of the bayou, grabbing at roots and bushes, ignoring cutting shale and thorns. Halfway up, I lost my grip and slid back down onto Ernest B. He managed to stop me without losing his hold on a root, and we climbed again. Large raindrops gently tapped our shoulders as we reached the top and found ourselves at the edge of a large open field.

Our clothes were torn and filthy. Our knees and hands were cut and bleeding. We lay side-by-side on our backs, laughing up into the rain.

A crack! Lightning slashed across the sky immediately above us, silencing our laughter. We scrambled to our feet and ran for our lives, blinded by the sudden light. The rain began to fall in earnest, driven by a strong wind in our faces. We stumbled across the field, searching for shelter. I tripped over something, and Ernest B. knelt to help me up. At that moment, another flash of lightning illuminated the field around us.

It was the cemetery, and I had tripped over a baby's crypt.

Ernest B. screamed and ran as if Satan himself were chasing us. I wasn't far behind. But it was too dark and too wet for us to maintain our pace for long. We collapsed against the cold stone wall of a private mausoleum. Ernest B.'s small body shook violently. I put my arm around him, but it didn't help. After a while, I stood to look for a way to get out of the rain.

"Don't leave, Garr!"

"I'm just going to see if we can get inside this place," I said.

Sure enough, the wrought iron gate was unlocked. We took shelter just inside, unwilling to venture any farther into that place of the dead. Ernest B. couldn't stop shaking. I was very scared myself. Then, for some reason, I began to sing:

Jesus loves me, this I know,
For the Bible tells me so;

Little ones to Him belong,
They are weak but He is strong.

I sang for a long time. Ernest B. didn't join in—he'd never been in a church—but when I stopped he said, "Keep singing, Garr. Please."

A childish faith in the religion of my parents comforted us both that night.

Yes, Jesus loves me,
Yes, Jesus loves me,
Yes, Jesus loves me,
The Bible tells me so.

Two old ladies who had come to place flowers at a grave found us asleep in the mausoleum the following morning. My folks were so relieved they didn't punish me; they just gave me a long, long talk about how miserable they would be without me and how I had to be careful for their sakes. But Ernest B.'s father beat him so badly he had to stay home from school for a couple of days.

CHAPTER 9

MARY JO SQUEEZED MY HAND AS Ernest B.'s urn was carried into the crypt. She looked into my eyes, her forehead wrinkled with concern. I smiled wanly and squeezed her hand in return. The preacher continued to pray.

I wallowed in grief, ignoring the preacher's hopeful words. He seemed to think that Ernest B. was a Christian. If so, it had been a well-kept secret. The preacher said that my friend was still alive somewhere out there, enjoying himself in a way we poor mortals could not imagine. As he spoke of eternal rewards, I looked around and saw joy in the faces of a few in the crowd. Joy! From my vantage point of sorrow, I resented their pompous certainty of God and the hereafter. How dare they bring these pie-in-the-sky fantasies to Ernest B.'s funeral! Despite the preacher's words, Ernest B. had wanted no part of them when he was alive—why should he be subjected to them in death? Anger began to crowd the mourning from my mind—until I looked again at Mary Jo.

Joy shone in her face as well. Could I begrudge her that?

Remembering the way my parents' old-time religion had sustained me at this same cemetery so long ago, I felt my anger slowly dissolve into envy. If I had their simple faith, maybe I wouldn't feel so alone, so devastated by Ernest B.'s murder, so afraid. If only I could ignore this whisper that said it was superstition, a trick they played on themselves to hide from the cold realities of life. How could they be so sure of this "God" of theirs? How could they abandon common sense and ignore what my eyes—and presumably theirs as well—saw so clearly? The God they served was useless in the real world. What of war? What of disease? Of starvation, crime, and hatred? Did their faith blind them completely?

The preacher droned on. Ernest B. had a mansion in heaven. He was beyond the pain and sorrows of life. Maybe Christians believed so strongly in the rewards of the next life that they were prepared to ignore the failures of their God in this one.

There were people in the crowd who cared as much as I did for Ernest B., yet somehow they seemed at peace about his death. Their faith did seem to shield them somehow. If I could abandon my pragmatism and accept their superstitions, would I, too, be at peace?

No.

Ernest B. was in the grave. Logic told me he was dead forever in spite of what the preacher said. Everything my old friend was, all that he had done, all that he stood for, was now just so much food for the worms. The same thing would someday be true for me. Someday, even my beloved Mary Jo would vanish from the universe, with nothing left of her extraordinary presence but moldering flesh in a satin-lined box.

It was wrong!

It was wrong that we should be cursed with a consciousness to understand such things, yet blessed with no relief from that same understanding. What good was my logical view of reality if it left no room for escape? Why could I not abandon reason like these religious fanatics? Why could I not share their peaceful ignorance?

I caught a movement out of the corner of my eye and looked to see Dr. Krueger walking away toward the row of parked cars, shaking his head and mumbling to himself.

Something told me to follow. I whispered an explanation to Mary Jo and slowly moved through the mourners. When I was far enough away, I broke into a trot toward the road. The doctor was already in his car when I ran up beside him. I tapped on his window and he rolled it down. The sour smell of whiskey drifted out of the car.

"I'm in a hurry. What do you want?" he said.

"Dr. Krueger, Sheriff Barker told me you've finished your autopsy, and I was wondering if you would take the time to tell me about it. I mean, what you found out."

"Why should I?"

I couldn't think of an alternative explanation, so I told him the truth. "The sheriff thinks I killed Ernest B. I need to find out everything I can about his death to clear myself."

He gave me an odd look and slurred, "The sheriff said you were a suspect?"

"Yes, sir, he did."

His bloodshot eyes turned toward the burial party. "I can't talk to you, Reed. Get away from my car." Without waiting for me to step back, he began to pull away from the shoulder.

I walked alongside his car and said, "Please, Doctor. Your report's going to become a part of the public record anyway. Please just tell me what you found."

He stared straight ahead and rolled up the window as his car accelerated, weaving a little. I turned to go back to Mary Jo and saw Barker staring at me from beside Ernest B.'s grave. Next to him stood Lester Fredricks and the big man with little feet.

• • •

AFTER DROPPING MARY JO OFF AT HOME and changing from my coat and tie into work clothes, I drove out to one of our job sites. The county had hired Reed Construction to replace an old wooden one-lane bridge with a concrete culvert wide enough to allow two lanes. A simple job, but the unusually wet weather we were having made the excavation a tedious process, throwing us weeks behind schedule.

I parked the company pickup about a hundred yards up the road to avoid getting stuck. Our backhoes and bulldozers had torn up the ground in the construction area, and the rain had turned the site into a sea of orange mud.

Leon Martinez saw me picking my way across the mess and came toward me with a broad grin. I felt my spirits lift a little at the sight of his lopsided smile.

"Whatcha say, boss?" he asked. "Gotta be careful 'round here, get that pretty outfit all dirty."

I gave him my best city-boy imitation, "Oh, my goodness, I hadn't anticipated such untidy conditions. Do you think you could carry me?"

He laughed. "Absolutely. And don't you worry one bit about that big puddle yonder. No way I'd drop you in it, I promise."

Leon was one hundred percent Mexican-American and proud of it. His pickup license plates read MEXTEX, and he had a Mexican flag sewn into his seat cover. It didn't matter to him that all four of his great-grandparents had been born in Texas and that he had never set eyes on Mexico. He spoke fluent Spanish and used it daily in his job as a construction supervisor.

Leon was about fifty. He was built like a pit bull: short and broad and pure muscle, with hands like vise grips, raw and rough from years of hard work. His face was creased with wrinkles, although whether they were caused by a hard life outdoors or by his ever-present smile was hard to say. Everyone liked him. He was a really nice guy.

My father had hired him as an unskilled laborer when Leon was a teenager. His intelligence, willingness to work, and natural interest in anything and everything related to construction soon earned him promotions to crew chief, superintendent, and finally construction manager. This last position entailed many hours behind a desk, preparing bids, processing pay requests, and writing reports. After a few months of that, he approached my father with an unusual proposal—he wanted a demotion. He hated office work and wanted to return to the field. They struck a compromise: Leon agreed to continue to handle some of the management responsibilities if he could do it at job trailers at the construction sites and remain involved in the day-to-day work on the jobs.

Leon led me across the muddy storage yard to the job shack, a small trailer set up high on concrete blocks. The sun was drowning the earth with molten yellow heat. Our sweat dripped onto the bleached wood of the job shack stairs as we scraped our boots on the bottom step and entered the blissfully cool, air-conditioned trailer. While Leon poured us both a cup of coffee, I sat at the drawing table, idly leafing through the project's engineering drawings. My fingers left damp spots on every sheet I touched.

"Garr, I might as well tell you now we ain't gonna hit our deadline on the twenty-third," Leon said as he put my cup on the table. I started to respond, but he stopped me with an upraised hand. "You know I'm usually optimistic about our schedules, but last night we had almost an inch of rain. Again. We've had rain eight out of the last thirty days. My guys are spending about as much time keepin' the treads serviced on our bulldozers as they are workin' with them."

"Well, all right," I said. "How late do you think we'll be?"

"Hard to say. Depends on how much more weather we get. And how many more tools get stolen."

"What?"

"Yeah, that's the other part. The storage shed got hit again."

I pounded the table with my fist. "That's the third time this year!"

"Third time this *summer,* Garr. We got to get some dogs or a night watchman or somethin'."

I sighed and said, "What'd they get this time?"

"I got a fellow in there takin' inventory right now, but I already know they got a power auger, an air compressor, a manual winch, and a bunch of chain. And the worst of it is the dynamite we had left over from that bridge job last spring."

"They stole our dynamite? Better report that to Barker right away."

"Already did."

"Man, oh man! How'd they get in, can you tell?"

"Nope. Same as the other times. No sign of them forcin' the door or anything."

I thought about that. Our storage shed had heavily padlocked double doors, yet there was never a sign of forced entry. The first two times, I'd halfway thought it was Ernest B. stealing from me just to rub a little salt in the wound. But he had spent the night at the funeral parlor this time.

"Let me have the list of stolen stuff when you get it put together, and let's see about getting new locks on the doors, okay?"

"Sure thing, boss. I was thinkin' about that earlier. And how about getting a dog or a guard?"

"Yeah, I guess we'd better. Only thing is, we can't afford a guard, and I'm afraid someone will get hurt if we go with a dog."

"Nah. You leave that to me. My nephew Gilbert's got some of the meanest rottweilers you ever saw, but he trains 'em good. They'll do just what you tell 'em to after they get used to you."

"All right. Have him send the bill to the company. Don't charge it to this job—we'll capitalize it against the home office." I smiled. "I wonder what the depreciation schedule is for a dog?"

"Well now, let's see. The schedule on portable equipment is seven years. And a dog year is about seven people years. So I guess you'd either take seven times seven and spread it over forty-nine years, or else you divide and take it all in the first year."

"Or else we could put him on the payroll at our skilled labor hourly rate and deduct the salary as operating expense."

"Yeah, that's probably the way to go. I'll ask Gilbert if he charges more for dogs with a social security number."

We were both grinning, but neither of us was going to acknowledge it, so I asked, "How's everything else going?"

"Well, other than missin' our deadlines and gettin' robbed blind, we're about done with the rough grading for the first culvert. Let's go outside and have a look."

For the next hour we walked the job together, dripping sweat. As usual, Leon had everything moving by the book. His equipment was serviced and his men were organized and as busy as they could be in the mud and the heat. After I'd seen everything, Leon walked me back to my truck. As I was scraping my boots, he looked at the ground between us and put his hands in his jeans pockets.

"Uh, Garr?"

"Yeah?"

"Well, I was wonderin'." He pushed some mud around with the toe of his boot. "Do you think Ethyl would like a little puppy?"

Ethyl was Mrs. P. No one else used her first name as far as I knew. But Leon was sweet on her for some reason. Although she rarely acknowledged his attentions, I suspected that she was flattered by them.

"I don't know, Leon. Owning a puppy's a pretty big responsibility. You might ought to ask her first."

"Nah. I want to surprise her."

"Well, I'd give it some more thought if I was you."

"Okay."

I got into the truck. Leon turned to walk away, then turned back as if he'd just thought of something.

"Garr, you know, there's something funny about that stuff gettin' stolen."

"Yeah?"

"Yeah. Like, they took the compressor last night, but left all the air guns and other hydraulic tools that were stacked up right next to it. And they took the hoses."

"Hmm. Why not take the tools if you're going to take the compressor and hoses?"

"Exactly. And the second time we got hit, they did the same thing. Took a generator and our low-voltage lights, but left a couple hundred feet of power cord and a bunch of power saws and drills and stuff. Why would anyone do that?"

I thought about it all the way to the office.

• • •

MRS. P. WAS UNUSUALLY CALM.

"How was the funeral?" she asked as I picked up the day's mail from her desk.

"Well, 'most everyone was there. Old Man Martin wasn't looking too good."

"Does he ever?" she sniffed. "Bet he was wearing that same ol' sorry pair of overalls."

"Well, he never has been a flashy dresser."

"Man's got no fashion sense at all."

I looked up from the mail. As usual, Mrs. P.'s wig was migrating across her head, barely restrained by several bobby pins clipped to her turban. She was wearing a bright pink muumuu. A green plastic corsage was pinned directly over her left breast like moss on a nose cone. The color of her lipstick matched her muumuu exactly and was applied well above her upper lip in sweeping twin arches.

I turned toward my office, then remembered something I'd wanted to say. "Mrs. P., would you like a dog?"

"You kiddin'? I got a busy enough personal life without runnin' around my backyard with a pooper scooper. Why?"

"Oh, no reason," I said, making a mental note to warn Leon.

There was a message on my desk that Dr. Krueger had called and wanted me to call back. The time on the note was about fifteen minutes after he'd left the funeral. I dialed his number before sitting down.

The phone rang eight times, and I was about to hang up when a woman answered. I told her who I was and who I wanted. She said, "Oh, him," and set her handset down hard. My ear was still ringing when Dr. Krueger said, "Who is this?" His words were slurred.

"It's Garrison Reed, Dr. Krueger. I'm returning your call."

"Can't talk now. You come to my office. At the morgue, County General. Ten-thirty tonight. Don't be late."

He hung up without waiting for my answer.

CHAPTER 10

I TRIED TO GET SOME PAPERWORK DONE, but speculations about Dr. Krueger's summons pushed other thoughts from my mind. Why ask for a meeting tonight if he wouldn't talk to me at the funeral? Did he have information that would help to clear me? He sounded smashed on the telephone. Was his call part of an alcoholic delusion of some sort? I hoped not.

The more I contemplated discussing Ernest B.'s murder with a drunk who might hold the key to my future, the more depressed I became. I should have been mourning my old friend, not trying to dig up dirt on him.

Memories assaulted my mind at the strangest times. A glance at a stand of pines as I drove to the office reminded me of a tree house Ernest B. and I had built together. The way a fellow laughed in Pedro's Cafe made me think of Ernest B.'s stupid practical jokes. But just when I'd begin to succumb to the melancholy, I'd remember the trouble I was in because of his death. I had no time to grieve. I had to find out who killed him.

I sighed and put away the papers. Work was out of the question. I decided to go see Mary Jo.

In the reception area, Mrs. P. was talking on the telephone. As I reached the door, she put her hand over the mouthpiece and whispered, "Garr, hold on a minute."

I stood near the door while she returned to her telephone conversation. She hung up after a few parting words and began moving papers around on her desk. With her eyes lowered, she said, "That was the bank. They wanted us to know that the sheriff's deputies came by with a warrant to pick up copies of all the records on our accounts over there."

Dread tightened its grip on my chest. First my home, now the company's banking records. I felt like a ten-point buck in season.

Mrs. P. continued to shuffle papers as she asked, "I guess this thing with Ernest B. is—well, they're serious about it, ain't they?"

"Yes."

She looked up and met my eye. Her big-bad-mamma act wasn't showing. "You know I'll help you any way I can."

"Sure, Mrs. P., I know that."

Embarrassed, she returned her attention to the things on her desk. I said, "There is one thing you could do."

"Name it."

"Would you call Winston Graves and tell him about your conversation with the bank? I just don't feel like talking to anyone right now."

"All right. You go on and I'll tend to business here."

As I opened the front door, I turned and said, "Mrs. P.? Thanks."

She waved me away with the back of her chubby hand and said, "Get on out of here, boy. I got no time to sit around talkin'."

• • •

MARY JO IS A LANDSCAPE PAINTER. HER work is represented by galleries in New York and Santa Fe. Her canvases sell for five figures. She works in a photo-realist style requiring such time-consuming precision that she produces only two or three paintings a year.

We built a studio for her in a small clearing in the woods several hundred yards from our house. The entire north side of the little building is glass, open to a wall of forest green. On the inside, the wood rafters are exposed. The concrete floor and bare sheetrock walls are covered with multicolored streaks and spots of paint, tangible reminders of every painting she has done. Some of her canvases are very large, so we installed a garage door on one end of the studio to get them in and out.

Mary Jo was so absorbed in her painting that she didn't notice when I stepped into the studio. I love to watch her work. She stood in front of an easel, spraying paint on a large canvas with an airbrush. She had begun the painting just a few days before and was still applying the underlying colors. This is a critical stage in the life of a painting—when the composition is determined and the sense of balance and harmony established. Her paintings are lovely and peaceful, like an early morning walk in the woods.

I stood silently behind her. She moved the air nozzle in fluid, sweeping passes across the canvas, her entire body swaying gracefully from side to side like a ballet dancer in top form. There was a sense of supreme confidence in her movements, as if painting was as natural an act to her as eating. The high-pressure combination of air and paint hissed out of the airbrush, the air compressor rattling and groaning at her side. The noise reverberated in the hard, industrial room, but Mary Jo didn't seem to notice. She had filled the center and top of the canvas with a light blue color. Around it, she was spraying a dark green. Now and then she would make a flicking motion with the airbrush, and a thin veneer of the darker green would cover the blue, allowing the blue to show through. I tried to guess what she was painting, but it was too early to tell.

Finally, she set the airbrush on a small table next to the compressor and stepped back to look at the canvas.

I said, "It needs a circle of Day-Glo orange up in the corner with a happy face, don't you think?"

At the sound of my voice, Mary Jo turned and crossed her arms. "Oh yeah? Well, maybe you ought to hire me to paint happy faces on your trucks. How about that, Mr. Art Critic?"

There was a spot of blue paint beside her nose. Her copper-colored hair was tied back in a loose ponytail. She was dressed in her usual painting outfit: Keds sneakers, loose blue jeans, and one of my old dress shirts, hanging to her knees and covered with paint. She looked fantastic.

"How you doin', sweetie?" she asked.

"Not bad." I pretended to be interested in the air compressor. "The bank called as I was leaving the office. They said sheriff's deputies came by and picked up copies of the company's account records."

"Why on earth would they do that?"

"I guess they're trying to establish that Ernest B. stole from us. That would give me a motive, you know?"

"Oh."

She moved to the sink against the wall and began to clean her airbrush. The water rattled in the pipes when she opened the faucet. Got to fix that, I thought. Funny how you think about the little things while your world is falling apart.

Mary Jo said, "I guess I don't really understand what's going on."

"Well, I suppose Barker thinks Ernest B. might have come back to try to get more money and I killed him."

"But that's ridiculous."

"*Somebody* killed him, Mary Jo."

She was silent as she rinsed her tools under the running water. Then, "But won't they see that he didn't get any more money when they look over the bank records?"

"Yeah, I guess so. But that won't convince them that he didn't try."

The depression I was feeling must have come through in my voice. She set her airbrush down and walked to me with her arms wide. "There, there, baby," she said, running her arms between my elbows and my ribs to hug me tightly. "We'll pray together about this. It'll turn out all right; you'll see."

There it was again: that simple faith. She had always leaned on her image of God. In normal times, I thought of it as leaning on a crutch. Now I wondered: Could it be more like leaning on the shoulder of a friend? If only I could believe, would I share that strength? I stood with my hands in my pockets, letting her hug me, wishing I knew how to experience such confidence. Then I hugged her back, and we stood like that for a while.

"I'm okay, Mary Jo. I am. It just seems so unreal. Sometimes I forget about it when I'm working, and then something like this bank thing happens and it all comes back."

"I know, I know," she said, patting my back.

"I really miss Ernest B. I'm surprised how much I miss him." I took a deep breath and said, "This is hard to talk about."

"Need to, though."

"I guess so."

We continued to hold each other for a little while. Thoughts and feelings swirled through my mind without connection: a chaotic mess. Finally I said, "I see things and they remind me of something he said or something we did. I feel like I need to mourn him, but I'm afraid people will think it's just an act, so I can't seem to talk about it to anyone."

"You can talk to me."

It was like pouring stinging alcohol on an open wound to speak my feelings aloud. "He was always there for me when I needed him. Always! He could be hard to be around, but when it was important, he was there. He cared about me. We didn't talk about it, but I—we—loved each other like brothers, you know?" My eyes grew wet. I thought, This is stupid. You don't do this.

"I know, baby."

"When he went crazy that time, it was like someone beat me senseless. I went around for days feeling sort of cold and distant inside. But it was nothing like this. I guess I always had the knowledge that he was alive and we might patch things up someday. And now—and now everyone's thinking I killed him, and I can't even stand to think of him lying in the lake like that. And I'm just so sorry about everything. So sorry." I took a deep quivering breath. I was glad Mary Jo couldn't see my tears. I was glad she was holding me so tightly.

We stood close together for a long time without speaking. Her hair smelled like a field of bluebonnets. I wanted to bury my face in her hair, to bury myself in her love. But the pain and anger inside me left no room for quiet emotions. I felt the dull driving force of revenge rise to seize my thoughts and bathe my wounds in drifting images of violence. It would be sweet to hurt the man who killed Ernest B.—perhaps to kill him. I visualized his fear, and my own fear slipped away. With eyes tightly closed, I saw the murderer's unknown features twist in pain. I embraced Mary Jo but saw my hands at his throat. With my face buried in Mary Jo's scented hair, I longed for a more fulfilling remedy for the emptiness I felt. I wanted to tell her of my dreadful fantasy of revenge, to ask for her help in resisting that shameful instinct. I needed help, maybe the help of her God.

But I said nothing.

How would she ever understand how satisfying revenge would be to me? Her Bible speaks of "turning the other cheek"—and she believes it, she really does. There had been so many times over the years when I wanted to speak my true thoughts to her but held back, for fear that she would guess that I had lied about everything: the days at church, the Bible on the nightstand, the short prayers before every meal together. All lies. A life of lies, lived to keep her love. Would I lose her if she knew? It was a chance I would not take.

So I hid my lust for vengeance, feeling both the sour relief it brought and the strange dissatisfaction of an unfulfilled desire for something more. I was trapped by my lies, longing for Mary Jo's help to escape the awful lust for revenge, yet restrained by the guilt of twenty years of faithlessness.

Finally Mary Jo pulled away. As she stood back, she began to giggle. "We're a pair for sure, Garr," she said, pointing at my chest. I looked down to see blue and green paint spots on my shirt, a mirror image of the spots on hers. I smiled and wiped my eyes, hiding all of my secrets.

• • •

I CALLED WINSTON GRAVES TO ASK HIM what he thought about the seizure of my bank records.

He said, "That move was to be expected in view of your business relationship with Ernest B., Garrison. I would be surprised if Mr. Barker did any less."

"What did he say when you went to see him about searching our house?"

"I have not yet had an opportunity to meet with him."

I didn't know what to say. The telephone line hummed vaguely while I searched for a tactful way to phrase the obvious question. Finally, I decided to take the direct approach.

"Winston, I'm disappointed. Why haven't you spoken to him?"

"I did not say I have not spoken with him. I said I have not seen him."

"Then you did talk to him about searching our house?"

"No, I did not. I simply called to put him on notice that I would be acting as your attorney in this matter, and I directed him not to attempt to question you further without my presence."

"I wish you had asked him why he searched my house, Winston."

I heard a sigh on his end. "I have a great many other concerns at the moment, Garrison. I will speak to Mr. Barker the next time my business needs take me into town."

"Couldn't you at least call him?"

"I could, but this type of interview is best conducted in person. Now then, I am not accustomed to explaining myself, especially with regard to professional matters. If you wish to engage another attorney to assist you, please do so. However, if you desire my counsel, you will kindly do me the very great favor of allowing me to approach the resolution of this issue in my own way. What is your decision?"

"I want you, Winston, of course. But—"

"There can be no discussion of my methods, Garrison. No conditions. Will you agree to this?"

I felt like a chastened schoolboy. My reply was automatic. "Yes."

"Very well. I will contact you directly with any new information. I expect you to notify me of any changes or new developments as well. Until then, good-bye."

The dial tone buzzed in my ear.

• • •

MARY JO AND I SPENT A QUIET EVENING together. She insisted on doing all of the cooking while I sat and watched. She steamed asparagus and warmed some sourdough bread. She covered two large tuna steaks with Cajun seasoning, then blackened them in a red-hot, cast-iron skillet. The smoke from the seasonings rose like a mushroom cloud, filling the kitchen and making our eyes water, so we opened the windows, turned the air conditioning off, and ate outdoors on the back porch while the house aired out.

It was a still evening. I lit a couple of candles. The flames burned brightly and didn't flicker much. After dinner, we sat in the candlelight, passing the time until my ten-thirty meeting with Dr. Krueger by listening to the crickets chirp and watching the night.

"Look at those fireflies," she said.

"Yes."

"Did you ever catch them when you were little?"

"Sure."

"And put a whole bunch of them in a jar, pretend it was a lantern?"

"I guess so."

"No, you didn't. You would have cut off their tails to watch them keep glowing."

"Well, yes, I guess I did."

We sat in silence some more. Then she said, "Why are little boys like that?"

"Cruel?"

"Yes."

"Well . . . because."

"Oh, I see. Just because. Well, I think maybe cruel little boys are practicing for when they have to grow up and be big and strong." She poked me in the ribs. "Businessmen." Another poke. "Tough guys."

"Hey!" I said, sitting up straighter to escape her jabs.

She said, "Maybe there's something in them that makes little boys know it'll be expected someday, so they might as well get some early practice."

"That's way too deep for me."

"You mean you don't believe it?" She made her voice like Mae West's and said, "So maybe you got a better explanation, tough guy?"

"For why little boys are meaner than little girls?"

"Sure."

"I think it's because they know it's their last chance to be the boss before they grow up and get married and their wives start treating them like bugs, poking them and all. That's what I think."

She giggled and tried another poke at my ribs. Then, suddenly serious, she sat up and said, "Hmm. You could be onto something there. Have you seen the bug spray?"

"Very funny."

We were quiet for a while, listening to the bullfrogs and the crickets compete for air time. Then Mary Jo said, "It's about ten."

"Yep. Gotta go."

"Garr . . ."

"Yes?"

"Want me to go with you?"

I thought about it for a moment, then said, "No, baby, I don't think you should."

"Are you taking Winston?"

"Nope."

"Why not?"

"To tell you the truth, I'm a little ticked off at him right now. He hasn't been to see Clyde about this thing, and when I asked about it he acted like I was questioning his ethics or something."

Mary Jo remained silent. I said, "Well? Don't you think he should have gone to see Clyde by now?"

"I don't know, honey. Maybe he's got a good reason not to go."

"I can't imagine what it would be."

"It could be lots of things. Maybe he thinks Clyde will catch the right person soon, so if he holds off he won't have to charge you for an office call or whatever lawyers call it when they go see someone."

"Charge me? I'd give him this year's profits if he'd get Barker off my back."

"I wish you'd take him with you anyway."

"It's too late for that, Mary Jo. I've got to get right over there."

She nodded. "All right, then. Pretend you're a firefly and don't let 'em stick you in a jar."

I smiled. "Or cut off my tail."

"Especially that."

• • •

ON MY WAY OUT, I STOPPED AT THE KITCHEN phone and dialed a number. The handset buzzed in my ear about twenty times before a sleepy voice answered.

He cleared his throat and said, "Hello?"

"Winston?"

"Yes. This is Winston Graves speaking. Who is this?"

"It's Garr, Winston. Would you meet me over at the hospital? I've got a meeting set up with the coroner over there."

The line was silent for a moment. Then, "Garrison, you must be insane. You've got no business attempting an investigation on your own. You'll play right into their hands."

"No one else is doing anything for me."

"All in good time, Garrison. These things move at their own pace."

"Why is that, Winston? Why do I have to sit around doing nothing, worried half to death, while you sit around doing the same? Shouldn't someone be doing something?"

"Are you questioning my ability again?"

I thought about that for two or three seconds. Then I said, "Winston, you're fired," and hung up softly and went out to the truck.

CHAPTER 11

JACKSON COUNTY GENERAL HOSPITAL is the only medical facility for several counties in any direction. Like every hospital everywhere, it is a maze of identical corridors, designed to disorient visitors and confound the staff. I wasted several minutes trying to find the morgue on my own before a passing nurse directed me to the basement level. Once there, I followed a faded yellow line on the concrete floor to a pair of steel doors. They swung open easily.

In the room beyond was a stainless-steel operating table, glaringly lit from above by a high-intensity light. Crisp, starkly defined shadows struck wild angles across the walls.

The operating table was empty. I was relieved, having half expected to find Dr. Krueger hacking away at a cadaver. There were corpses nearby. The sickly sweet odor of corruption, decay, and chemicals assaulted my nostrils. I breathed through my mouth. Overhead, a tangle of exposed pipes and electrical conduit emphasized the utilitarian function of the room. The walls were lined with display cases full of identical glass jars. I avoided looking at their contents.

"Dr. Krueger?"

My voice sounded too loud—somehow vulgar in those somber surroundings. Its echo faded away, absorbed by the subdued noises of the building systems: a low rumble from the air conditioning, a high-pitched hum from the light.

There was another pair of metal doors on the opposite wall, the kind that swing both ways. I crossed the room and opened one of them. A curtain of clear plastic strips hung just inside the doors to keep in the cold. I parted them and stepped into a totally dark, frigid room. Passing my hand along the clammy wall next to the doors, my palm felt the light switch.

Fluorescent lights bathed a row of corpses covered in pale blue. They were covered by sheets and parked along the walls on gurneys. A foot extended beyond the sheet on the gurney nearest me. The gnarled yellow toenails were caked with mud. To my left was a wall lined with small dull-steel doors. I knew if I opened one, a body would be lying inside on a stainless-steel tray, ready to slide out and be identified. Perhaps Ernest B. had lain behind one of the doors, face up, naked, cold. I shivered.

To my right was an old gray steel desk. Like a boy sleeping in study hall, a man slumped at the desk, his head resting on his arms. Beside his head was an empty bottle of scotch. There was no glass.

"Dr. Krueger?" I said again, more quietly this time.

The man didn't stir. The odor of alcohol drifted through the room like a wraith. Drunk. The man was passed-out drunk.

I stepped around the desk and gently tapped his shoulder. Still no response. I gripped his shoulder more firmly and shook him. He began to slide down in his chair. When I wrapped both arms around him to pull him back up, I realized that his skin was cold—deadly cold, as cold as all of the other corpses in the morgue.

CHAPTER 12

FOR SOME REASON, I DIDN'T PANIC. Maybe it was because the room was already full of cadavers. This was just one more.

I turned the dead man's head to the side. It was Krueger. His face was covered with an oval, masklike purple bruise. The tip of his nose was flat from being pressed against the desktop. He stank of whiskey.

Returning his head to its original position, I stood back, thinking hard. This man had wanted to see me for some reason. It must have been to discuss Ernest B.'s murder. Did he have some evidence that would clear me?

I should search him.

But anyone could come in and catch me. I stood frozen in place, leaning over the man, torn between the desperate need to clear myself and the overwhelming sense that this simply wasn't done. I was a respected businessman, a member of the church, a solid citizen. I was a Republican, for crying out loud. How could I search a dead man?

And yet, what if Krueger had taken some notes during Ernest B.'s autopsy—notes that would clear me? They could be in his pocket right now, inches away.

I had to do it.

Krueger was sitting on the coattails of a white lab smock, making it difficult to search his pants pockets. From behind his chair, I reached around and grasped him in a bear hug, pulled him upright, and slid him and the chair back from the desk. There was a horrible squawk as the chair legs dragged across the concrete floor. I stood absolutely motionless, my arms around the dead man, listening for footsteps. With my face so close to his, the whiskey's stench was overpowering, but I was afraid to move. I breathed through my mouth as I waited. No one came.

I unbuttoned his coat. Searching his front pants pockets, I found the usual: keys, pocketknife, a piece of candy, some change. The contents of his wallet weren't very interesting, either. I dumped all the stuff on the desktop. In his shirt pocket I found a snapshot. It was a Polaroid, showing a close-up of someone's forearm. On the arm was a tattoo: the initials "S.A.W." over a pair of crossed swords. On the back of the snapshot was a name, written in ballpoint blue: "Martin."

I was standing by the body trying to decide what to make of the snapshot when a woman's voice called from the next room: "Dr. Krueger?"

Panic almost overwhelmed me. If I was found there with the man's clothes opened and his pockets turned out, I would be finished. Barker would say I murdered him to cover up the results of Ernest B.'s autopsy.

I raked the contents of Krueger's pockets into a desk drawer and desperately pushed his pocket linings back inside his pants. I couldn't find a better place to hide, so I raised the sheet on the nearest corpse-laden gurney and squatted below it. It was a tight fit. The sheet fell back into place. It was still swaying when the woman entered the room.

There was a soaking wet towel draped across the gurney's frame beneath me. The moisture began to seep through my jeans. There was no way to know if the fluid was water, urine, bile, or blood. I shivered. By balancing precariously on the lower frame of the gurney, I managed to keep my boots from showing below the sheet. I tried to sit perfectly still. My heart was racing, and I couldn't seem to catch my breath. The effort required to remain motionless caused me to shake slightly and reminded me of childhood games of hide-and-seek. I felt very foolish.

I could see the woman through a small gap where the sheet folded. She was the nurse who had directed me to the morgue. Because Dr. Krueger was slumped over in his chair, she made the same assumption I had—that he had passed out drunk. She knew better than to try to speak to him, sighing loudly instead as she walked around the desk, probably intending to check his breathing. Gently placing her hands on each side of his head, she raised it enough to see the lividity and the flattened nose.

"Oh, no!" she said, as her hands moved to his throat, needlessly checking his pulse. After a moment, she allowed his chin to drop back to his chest and stepped away from him, wiping her palms on her uniform. "Well, you old fool, you finally drank too much, didn't you?" she said.

Shaking her head, she left the room.

I stayed where I was until I heard her footsteps fade away. Then, as quickly as I could, I unbent my large frame from the cramped position below the gurney and moved to the doctor's side.

I opened the desk drawer, losing precious time as I tried to remember which item came from which pocket. Finally, I stuffed the things back into his pockets as best I could, hoping no one knew him well enough to notice if his wallet or keys weren't in their usual places. After taking a moment to see that everything else was just as the nurse had left it, I hurried to the door—and suddenly remembered fingerprints. Mine were everywhere.

I ran back to the desk. There was nothing nearby that I could use to wipe away my prints. In desperation, I pulled my polo shirt over my head and began to wipe everything in reach. I thought about the things I had touched that were back in the doctor's pockets, but there was no time. The nurse could return at any moment.

I left the room and passed through the operatory to the hall. Just as I reached the elevator doors, the car arrival bell rang. I squatted behind a laundry cart.

The elevator doors opened and the nurse charged out, followed by two men wearing white lab coats. They passed the laundry cart without a word. As the swinging doors to the operating room at the far end of the hall closed behind them, I rushed to the elevator.

"Come on, come on," I said, bouncing from foot to foot as I stood in front of the doors pushing the "up" button over and over. Finally, the doors opened and I stepped in, jabbing the "close door" button as I entered.

On the ride up, I was sure I'd forgotten something. The car was slowing to a stop at the ground floor when I realized that my shirt was still in my hand. The doors opened, and I stood bare chested, facing a group of old women.

I held my shirt between the thumb and first finger of each hand, my arms extended straight in front of me, and said, "Ladies, please step aside. I've been contaminated." They looked at each other in confusion. I took a firm step forward. They took a hesitant step back. I said, "Ladies, I must ask you to clear away. This is a highly contaminated shirt."

They parted to form a purse-clutching, blue-haired gauntlet. Holding the shirt well away from my body, I walked between them with exaggerated care. Their eyes were glued to the shirt. Good, I thought, maybe they won't remember my face.

As I edged my way across the hospital lobby toward the exit, a young man wearing a white coat with a stethoscope in his pocket stepped in front of me.

"What's going on here?" he asked.

"Miller up in 237 has had another attack. He threw up on me. The nurse said you should get right up there."

Involuntarily, he turned and hurried toward the elevators, obeying his emergency training. I was almost to the exit before he realized that he didn't know of any Miller in room 237. He yelled, "Hey you!" at my back, but I was already running out the door.

I didn't get around to putting on my shirt until I was out of town.

CHAPTER 13

MARY JO WAS ASLEEP WHEN I GOT home. She looked so peaceful that I couldn't bring myself to wake her. I knew I would be up and down all night, worrying about getting arrested for searching Dr. Krueger's body, so I decided to sleep on the sofa.

I got a blanket and a pillow and went downstairs to the living room, replaying the events at the hospital in my mind. Barker was sure to learn that I'd been there. At least ten people had witnessed my ridiculous display in the lobby. And sooner or later, the nurse would remember the man who asked for directions to the morgue. The sheriff would surely come looking for me soon.

Then again, what difference would it make? It was bound to be declared an accidental death. When she found him, the nurse had immediately assumed alcohol poisoning, almost as if she'd been expecting it. His body had reeked of whiskey. And he was already drunk when we spoke in the early afternoon.

My spirits began to lift a little.

But I couldn't quite convince myself. It was just too coincidental. After drinking all of his life, why would Krueger pick the night he was to meet me to overdose on booze? And would he have allowed himself to get that drunk on the job? Hard to believe.

I walked across the living room in the dark, avoiding our furniture by memory, and turned on the reading light next to the sofa. Tiny particles of dust floated through the air below the lamp, caught in the solitary circle of light. I undressed absentmindedly, folded my clothes, and set them on a chair. As I lay on the sofa staring at my shirt and pants, I was reminded of another time when I had taken off my clothing and stacked it neatly without thinking.

• • •

ERNEST B. AND I WERE SIXTEEN OR SEVENTEEN. It was late spring, the season of beginnings, when the air in the east Texas woods is so full of pollen you can smell the musky life of it with every breath.

To stay in school on such a day would have been unthinkable. At our lunch period, we slipped out a side door and drove Ernest B.'s old pickup to my place. We "borrowed" a six-pack from the kitchen and snuck down to the boat house.

My father's bass boat was suspended four feet or so above the water, securely cradled between two wide cloth straps. These were fastened to cables that passed through pulleys hung from above. Ernest B. flipped a switch, an electric motor hummed, and the cables played out slowly. The pulleys screeched and the boat swayed gently as it was lowered into the lake. Mud daubers buzzed the rafters overhead, disturbed by the vibration.

I let Ernest B. drive because he loved it so. We paddled the first hundred feet to avoid making too much noise in case one of my folks was around, then he turned the key, and the motor rumbled to life. Ernest B. knew only two speeds in a boat or a car: stop and hurry. He pushed the throttle lever forward, and the boat plowed through the water with the bow high in the air until the hull rose at last to a level hydroplane.

We roared across Martin Pool in the early afternoon, racing low-flying ducks to the top of the lake where the Big Muddy Bayou fed in. For an hour or two, we sat in a secluded cove drinking beer and talking about sports and girls. Skiers never came this high in the lake because it was too shallow. In the middle of the week, there were very few fishermen. We had the cove to ourselves.

After a while, we ran out of things to talk about. The sunlight shone on our faces and shimmered in the nearby woods. All around the cove, newly sprouted leaves stretched toward the sky. In another week or two, their luminous pale green would begin to weather, turning darker as the leaves matured and baked in the sun. Yellow and brown patches would appear as they suffered the hungry onslaught of a million ravenous insects. But it was still early: the damage of living was yet to come.

Ernest B., staring at the woods, said, "Makes you wonder, don't it?"

I said, "What's that?"

"Oh, all this pretty growing stuff. Sprouting out so fresh and clean every spring. Makes you wonder is all."

I grunted my reply, unsure of what he meant.

Ernest B. stood and removed his boots.

"What are you up to?" I asked.

"We're goin' swimmin'."

"Oh no. You're not gettin' me in there. That water's probably fifty degrees."

"Sissy," Ernest B. said, stripping off his shirt and jeans.

I sat there sullenly, looking away as he dropped his white briefs and prepared to dive.

"Garr honey, looky here," he said in a falsetto voice. I turned and was greeted by the sight of his pale white bottom.

"Give me a break," I grumbled.

Laughing, he held his nose and jumped in. The sound of his laughter was silenced as his head passed beneath the waves. I sat in the boat, waiting. Just as I began to be concerned, his head broke the surface.

"Wooeee! It's sure enough nippy!" he yelled, treading water. "Garr, get in here, or I'm comin' up to *throw* you in." His loud voice echoed from the tree tops.

I sighed and set my beer on the deck. Knowing that Ernest B. meant what he said, I stood and began to strip.

Ernest B. was doing a modified dog paddle around the boat. He said, "Hey, buddy, toss me one of them life jackets, will ya? I'm gettin' tired."

I neatly folded my clothes on the seat. Then I reached into a storage chest and pulled out two life jackets. I threw one to him and strapped on the other.

Ernest B. pulled his jacket below the surface and sat on it, allowing him to float with no hands. He looked up at me and burst out laughing.

And for the rest of his life, whenever we were in a crowd, Ernest B. took great delight in describing the sight of me standing on the boat seat, buck naked and pale white except for my bright orange life jacket.

I lay on the sofa smiling at the memory—until I remembered that he was dead. My smile faded away and I clicked off the light. Quiet, brutal anger surged within me. I wallowed in fantasies of violent revenge, visualizing them, savoring them, longing for the satisfaction of them. The man who killed Ernest B. deserved killing himself. All I had to do was find him—and think of a way to do it without getting caught. I pulled the covers close to my chin and smelled that scent that Mary Jo gets into our laundry. I thought of her, knowing she would be ashamed of my lust for revenge. She would remind me of the words of Jesus Christ: "Turn the other cheek," and "Judge not, lest ye be judged." She would quote her Old Testament God, shouting, "Vengeance is mine!"

And maybe she would be right. Maybe the best thing would be to walk away from these feelings.

But then I thought of Ernest B., and again I longed for revenge. "An eye for an eye." I cursed as confusing emotions whirled through my mind. Love. Hate. Anger. Forgiveness. Dear God, what was happening to me? If only I could talk to Mary Jo. Somehow I knew she would have the answers.

But then her face drifted into view, awash with grief at my decades of lies.

Sleep came hard.

• • •

MARY JO WOKE ME THE NEXT MORNING with a gentle kiss and a cup of coffee.

"What you doin' down here, sweetness?" she asked.

"Didn't want to keep you up."

"You have a bad night?"

"Yeah."

"Well, come on in the kitchen and help me get some breakfast goin', okay?"

"Give me a minute to wake up; I'll be right in."

I lay in a semiconscious fog, listening to the comfortable rattles and clinks in the kitchen as Mary Jo began cooking. My neck hurt from sleeping in the same position all night. Gradually, I remembered the discovery of Dr. Krueger's body. After a while I stretched, stood to put on my robe, and went into the kitchen to help.

I told Mary Jo about Krueger as we worked side-by-side preparing biscuits and gravy, sausage, scrambled eggs, grits, and orange juice. I didn't mention searching his body.

"What a terrible thing, finding that poor man like that," she said.

"Yeah. For some reason, it didn't sink in at the time, but looking back on it, I feel sort of queasy about the whole thing."

"I imagine so." She crossed behind me and opened the oven to check on the biscuits. "What did Sheriff Barker have to say?"

"I don't know."

She stopped what she was doing and turned to me. "You don't know?"

"I didn't stick around to find out."

"You mean you didn't report it?"

"No."

"Shouldn't you have given a statement or something?"

"They'd probably lock me up, Mary Jo."

I lifted the sausage out of the skillet and added some flour and a little pepper to the grease. Soon, the gravy thickened and I scooped it into a bowl. The biscuits were ready. She protected her hands with a dish towel and removed the tray from the oven.

"Why would they do that? All you did was find the body. And the sheriff's likely to figure out you were there anyway, right? I mean, someone must have seen you."

She echoed my thoughts from the night before. I'd been a fool to hide from the nurse and run away. I should have waited for the police and explained that Dr. Krueger was dead when I got there. Instead, I'd searched the body. Very, very stupid. My fingerprints might be found on his wallet or on the desk. How would I explain that?

Then I remembered the snapshot I had found, and my worries were forgotten. I hurried into the living room and rummaged through my clothes, finding it in the back pocket of my jeans.

Back in the kitchen, I handed the photograph to Mary Jo.

"Look at this. I found it on Dr. Krueger."

She looked from the photo to my face with a frown. "You found it on the doctor? What do you mean?"

I told her how I had searched the body and hidden from the nurse and the orderlies. Saying it out loud made it seem worse than stupid. Maybe *idiotic* was a better word.

"Garr, I don't know what to say. If it was anybody else, I'd be sure they'd lost their mind." She put two plates on the counter between us and served the eggs, slapping the plates with the spatula a bit too forcefully.

"Hey, come on. Winston told me I must be insane last night. I don't need that from you too."

"How would you describe an honest man who searches corpses and hides from the police?"

"I *know* it sounds crazy. But all I could think about at the time was that he might have some evidence on him that would clear me. I was searching him before I knew it. Then I heard the nurse coming, and I had to hide. I couldn't let her find me like that, could I?"

"Well, no. I guess not." We picked up our plates and moved across the room to our little antique dining table near the window. Mary Jo and I bowed our heads to bless the meal, as we always did. Mostly, I do that for her sake. This time, I put a little more feeling into it than usual on the off-chance that God was really listening.

Picking up my fork, I said, "Here's the deal: Either the doctor had something to tell me about Ernest B.'s body, or he didn't. If he did, why not tell me at the funeral? I almost begged him to talk to me there, but he refused."

"Maybe he wanted to see you about something else entirely, Garr. You know how drunks are. There's no telling what was going through his mind."

"Well, there's this picture." I picked it up from the table and studied it closely. "It's a Polaroid, so it's probably not a copy. Why isn't this with his autopsy report at the courthouse? Either it's the original, or he shot the tattoo twice. Either way, it's strange that he'd have it in his pocket. Why did he hang onto it?"

"Are you sure it's got anything to do with Ernest B.? I don't remember him having any tattoos."

She had a point. I'd seen Ernest B. with his shirt off many times. If he'd gotten tattooed, it had to have been in the last few months.

"It says 'Martin' here on the back, Mary Jo. That's just too much of a coincidence, don't you think?"

"There are a lot of Martins in Jackson County."

I looked her in the eyes.

She said, "All right. Let's say it *is* a picture of Ernest B.'s arm. What does it prove?"

"I don't have any idea. I just know I found it on a dead man who wanted to talk to me—probably about Ernest B. It must prove *something*."

Mary Jo chewed in silence for a while. Then she said, "Garr, you are a good man. People look up to you." She took another bite and chewed some more, then said, "You had absolutely no business breaking the law like you did. It's not Christian. But what's done is done, so maybe you'd better not tell the sheriff about this after all."

CHAPTER 14

I MOVED SLOWLY AFTER BREAKFAST, favoring the crick in my neck, taking longer than usual to get dressed for work. My mind was preoccupied with questions about the death of Dr. Krueger and the photograph of the tattoo. I was about to leave the house when the telephone rang. It was Mrs. P.

"Garrison, I was beginnin' to wonder if you were all right."

"I'm just fine. Runnin' a little late is all. I was about to call you to see if I had time to go out to Leon's job, or if I should come straight in to the office."

"Garr honey, you had a call from Sheriff Barker first thing this mornin'."

"Oh?" I felt a sudden tightening in my chest. It was becoming a familiar sensation. "What did Clyde want?"

"He said he needed to talk to you right away. Said you'd know why."

I knew why all right. He'd probably already put me at the scene of Dr. Krueger's death.

"Tell you what, Mrs. P. I'll call him from here. Also, I think I'll spend the rest of the morning out at the culvert job with Leon. Don't look for me until later today, okay? In fact, I might take the afternoon off."

"Sure, Garr, you do that. I'll hold the fort here."

I hung up the telephone and hurried outside to my pickup, eager to get away from the house before Barker could corner me about Dr. Krueger. It never crossed my mind to actually return his call.

I drove aimlessly across the county, following tree-lined red dirt roads deep into the bottomland. Everywhere I looked, heat oozed up from the ground, making the distant perspective dance and wiggle. In the fields I passed, the steel rocker arms of oil well pumps slowly rose and fell like giant iron chickens pecking for their dinner. The land around them was lined with white-specked rows of cotton, taller than usual because of the rains. I pulled up behind an old black man on a smoking, mud-splattered Ford tractor. He was towing an empty cotton trailer with tall chicken-wire sides, moving just fast enough to blow the leftover cotton bolls out of the top. The white puffs lined the shoulders of the road like midsummer snow drifts, a familiar sight on the fertile bottomland of the Big Muddy Bayou at cotton harvest time.

Cotton farming was imported to east Texas in the 1840s. Small-time Georgia and Tennessee growers came west when their ancestral fields grew barren from a hundred years of over-cultivation. They brought their slaves and their Southern traditions with them. The old man on the tractor up ahead was probably descended from those slaves. And he was probably farming the same land his great-great-grandfather had, still fertile after five generations because we'd learned long ago to rotate crops.

I thought about my own problems. If Ernest B. was into drugs, it stood to reason that drugs had something to do with his murder. He must have had friends, business associates, or fellow dopers familiar enough with that side of his life to suggest some likely explanations for his death.

Unfortunately, Clyde Barker was so intent on proving that I killed Ernest B. he wouldn't consider alternatives, much less help me find them. And Lester Fredricks wasn't about to get involved. It was going to be up to me to find Ernest B.'s drug connections and then find out what they knew.

A black convertible pulled up behind me, crowding my rear bumper. Two young women sat in it, facing ahead with deadpan looks, eyes obscured by dark sunglasses, hair secured with pastel scarves. They followed me for a half mile or so, waiting for a safe place to pass, then roared on up the road, swirling cotton bolls in their wake. The old man on the tractor waved me around too, but I waved back and stayed where I was, enjoying the slow drive in the dappled shade of the overhanging trees and the Spanish moss.

Since Barker wouldn't give me a look at his arrest records for the last year or so, I'd have to get my leads the hard way—by asking total strangers. But I needed a place to start.

The *Mt. Sinai Daily Herald* had a policy of printing the names of people who'd been arrested on drug charges or for drunk driving, presumably to shame them out of the county. It might be a good idea to look up some back issues and see whether they mentioned names I could use. Besides, Barker wasn't likely to look for me at the library.

I took the next left onto a dirt road marked only by a rusting dead-end sign. It led to a special place, discovered when Ernest B. and I were teenagers, cruising the backwoods roads in our restless search for entertainment. The old road wasn't used by anyone much, just two or three farmers who owned land along its short length. The dead-end sign turned casual Sunday drivers away, and the deep ruts, usually filled with a sienna stew of mud and water, made it passable only by trucks. Even if a car could make it, no one who valued his paint job would drive through the encroaching undergrowth of bottomland brambles and thorn bushes.

I bounced along to the end of the road and parked. It widened into a turnaround at the bank of the Big Muddy. Sixty feet above, the ancient cypress trees along the bayou mingled their moss-strewn branches with the gnarled limbs of red oaks that had probably been alive during the days of Travis and Bowie, Austin and Crockett. An outcropping of rusty limestone ran alongside the road for the last couple hundred feet. At the turnaround, the rocks continued across the bayou, worn by the current in the middle of the stream to a fraction of their original height. The Big Muddy lumbered along like cold molasses until it reached this place. Then it rose behind the limestone and poured over the top with an uncharacteristic low roar. On the downstream side, the short-lived rush of water had carved a deep hole in the bayou bottom before settling back into its normal mile-an-hour pace. Ernest B. and I were convinced that this was the perfect spot to find "ol' granddaddy," the biggest catfish of all. We took to calling the place Granddaddy's Spot.

Throughout our teenage years, we came often with cane poles and our current bait of choice: chicken livers, bacon rinds, or soft white bread rolled up into tight balls. There was a sloped red rock that stood just above the swirling waters of the falls and about six feet from shore, the perfect place to sit and cast a line into the back eddy above the falls. But reaching the rock required great coordination and a bit of courage. The sides of the Big Muddy rise steeply like a manmade trench along most of its length. From the road above, we cleared a rugged path to the water's edge. With pole in hand, we would hurl ourselves down the path, leaping at the last possible moment to take full advantage of our momentum and, hopefully, landing on the big red rock. When we missed, we went tumbling over the falls and into the swirling foam below to be flushed along the bottom for twenty feet or so until we popped up laughing and began the swim to shore. We missed a lot more often in warm weather.

I rolled down the truck's window to let in some breeze and heard the falls, invisible through the brush ahead. It was getting hotter as the sun rose higher, hotter and humid and muggy down near the bayou, just like the day my mother died. I turned toward the open window and breathed deeply, thinking of her death. It had not been unexpected—she had been ill for months—but when you're only fifteen it's easy to deny the future. I hadn't been prepared.

The last time I saw her alive, there was no indication that she knew I was there, just a clicking sound from her throat with every breath. She had been unable to speak for days, lying semicomatose in her hospital bed. I felt oddly unattached as I sat with her, watching the slight rise and fall of the sheets above her breast, holding her hand in both of mine, staring at her face. She was already gone—there was no important part of my mother left there, nothing of love or gentle kindness, no sense of the depth of her spirit that I had taken for granted all of my life. It came to me suddenly that she was dying—was really dead already. The stopping of her heart was just a formality.

When my father came into the room, I put her hand back down on the sheet and left without speaking. Ernest B. wasn't in the waiting room, although he had been there with me most of the past few days, living on Fritos and Dr. Pepper from the vending machines and playing card games to pass the time. I couldn't wait in that uncomfortable room alone. I felt a strong need to be in familiar surroundings. Telling no one where I was going, I walked outside and drove away.

The sun was setting when Ernest B. found me sitting on the big red rock at Granddaddy's Spot. I was watching the water swirl around my bare feet, so lost in thought that I hadn't heard him park the truck or scramble down the bank.

"I figured you'd be down here."

I looked up, too deep in my inner world to be surprised that he was suddenly standing beside me. Without answering, I returned my gaze to the water, which was getting black now as the sunlight faded. He removed his boots and socks and put them beside mine and sat on the damp limestone to my right. His dangling feet formed swirling patterns of their own in the water. We stayed like that while the last of the daylight disappeared and the night creatures began their evening songs. My thoughts drifted away along familiar paths to memories of my mother and father, our home and life together, the many times I had let them down, the many times I had wanted to tell them how I loved them but could not find the words.

Mother's death brought guilt into my life. Guilty knowledge of slights and petty behavior, of unacknowledged sacrifices and long-forgotten favors unappreciated. Death ended all hope of evening the score—not that such hope was real anyway, for who could fully return the unconditional love of a mother or a father? Mother's death brought guilt, and the only thing to do about it was to face myself for what I was: an insufficiently grateful child who could never, never deserve the good in this life, much less life itself.

Your mother and father forgive you, of course, but it isn't enough. They have no right to forgive, because they themselves bear the guilt of betraying their own parents' love. God alone has the right to forgive and give comfort, but God help me, I was too proud to ask. And so it went, in circular fashion until the grief overcame and absorbed the guilt, and everything became a great, swelling mass of indescribable pain that threatened to crack open my chest and suck out my soul.

I scrambled to my feet in the darkness, shaking my head like a dog with a rag in its teeth, trying to stop all the thoughts deep inside. Ernest B., lulled by the dull roar of the falls and our silence for so long, was startled and almost slid into the water.

"She's dying, Ernest B.! She's dying!" I said, the words rising thick and hot from my throat. I tried to go on, to express the thing within that was growing and filling me with so many vile emotions, but words seemed too frail for such a task. How could God allow her to die when I needed her so? I would be alone, completely alone without her. Perhaps that was when I began to abandon the faith of my parents. Standing with my fists clenching and unclenching, staring downstream while Ernest B. crawled back up from the water's edge, I silently cursed God. When he reached the top of the rock, Ernest B. rose to face me. Inches separated us, and I saw real pain in his eyes. We stood like that for a moment, face-to-face, with the bayou flowing around us and the falls' quiet roar below. Slowly, awkwardly, Ernest B.'s hands reached out and he pulled me to him. He held me for a long, long time while I cried. He didn't bother to speak at first, but then, as we awkwardly disengaged from our embrace and stared again at the rushing waters, he said, "Makes you wonder, don't it?"

And in all the years that followed, never once did he mention that night. Even that last time when he came sloppy, tearful drunk and begging for money or his old job back, he knew enough to leave it alone. His unwavering support that long-ago night was a gift he gave me, and by his silence he proved it was given for free.

Now he was dead, and I'd come again to this place. As I sat in the truck listening to the softly rumbling falls below, I searched my mind for some sign from the past, something that would make sense of Ernest B.'s death and of my role in his life. But this time, nobody was there to share my grief, much less my guilt.

I turned the key in the ignition and drove up out of the Big Muddy bottomland toward Mt. Sinai, leaving the promising cotton harvest behind.

• • •

MRS. SEYMOUR WAS SEATED BEHIND HER desk just inside the front doors when I stepped into the cool air of the Mt. Sinai Carnegie Library. On the wall behind her was a poster: "Read As If Your Mind Depends On It."

She had been the head librarian since I was a child. One of my earliest memories was of my mother taking me to Mrs. Seymour's Saturday morning storybook time. Fifteen or twenty of us kids would sit in a semicircle on the carpet, giving Mrs. Seymour our total attention as she read from *Grimm's Fairy Tales* or *Jungle Book*. She had a natural gift for narration. She would peer through her half-framed reading glasses, now at the book, now at us, as her soft Southern voice changed to rise high and squeaky when she spoke the part of the little pigs, or fall low and threatening (but never too scary) when she read the part of the big bad wolf. She never seemed to age. Then, as now, her hair was gray and piled high on her head like fluffy cotton candy. It shook when she became excited about a particular storybook passage, reinforcing the energy of her words.

Although I hadn't been in the library for years, she greeted me as if I'd been to her storybook time just last Saturday.

"Good morning, Garrison. How are you today?"

"I'm fine, thank you, Mrs. Seymour. And you?"

"Oh, lovely. Everything is lovely. We've been so busy with our preparations for the school year. All the new arrivals must be organized, and the card files have to be updated. They've got this new cataloging system now . . . What was the name of it?" She sifted absently through the pile of books and papers on her desk. "Oh well, doesn't matter. I'll not make a change in our Mr. Dewey's lovely system after all these years, not when he's served us so well. Wouldn't be right. No, not right at all."

I stood looking around as she rambled on and on, her hairdo vibrating from side to side. She'd always been an incessant talker. This might well be the only library in Texas where the patrons sometimes asked the librarian to be quiet.

The building was classically magnificent in a compact way. It was wainscoted in solid red-oak paneling, with coved plaster ceilings and a hardwood floor inlaid with complex geometric patterns in contrasting stains. The books were stacked on two long rows of shelves, separated by an open area furnished with six or seven antique reading tables, complete with green glass reading lights and inset felt blotters. There was a comfortably musky smell that reminded me of my grandparents' house.

Eventually, Mrs. Seymour paused for breath, and I quickly asked for the location of the recent back issues of the *Daily Herald.* Her face lit up with pride as she said, "Garrison, I'm so pleased you've asked. We have the most wonderful machines now. They're a gift from the Stephens family. They're called microfiche readers. You'll be interested in this. Come along."

She stepped out from behind her desk and led me to a tall oak door behind the nearest row of shelves, talking all the way. On a table in the small room beyond the door were two machines with screens like television sets, designed for viewing miniature negatives. Each negative could contain four full pages of the *Daily Herald.* As she proudly explained the use of the readers in minute detail, I waited patiently, unwilling to tell her I'd used machines like these in college years ago.

Finally, she left me alone. I sat at a reader and began the laborious process of reviewing the copy. Since I wouldn't have time to read every word of every issue from the last few years, I started with the assumption that Ernest B.'s cocaine habit was a recent one, say two years old at most. Second, I decided that anyone who might know anything about Ernest B.'s enemies would be enough of a heavyweight in local drug circles that his or her arrest would be front-page news. So, no need to waste time on stories after page one.

I opened the first square box of film and placed the first negative in the reader.

Two-and-a-half hours later, I broke for lunch. On the way out, I asked Mrs. Seymour if I could pick up anything for her. It took her a while to get around to it, but she said no.

At 1:00 I was back at the microfiche reader. By 3:00 I had finished the first year. By 4:30 I was losing hope. There didn't seem to *be* a drug community in Jackson County. The paper mentioned very few arrests, and those that did make the news seemed to be kids caught smoking a joint or two. No heavy hitters in narcotics had been arrested in Mt. Sinai in the last twenty-four months.

Maybe Sheriff Barker was right. Maybe he really did have a good handle on the drug situation in Jackson County. Good enough to know about Ernest B.'s drug problem if he'd had one. Good enough to keep the county nearly drug free. Those now-familiar feelings of depression began creeping back in—until I realized how selfish I was to lament the fact that Jackson County was so free of drugs.

An article rolled onto the screen that mirrored that very thought. It was headed "Drug War Victory" and cited statistics on felony arrests for drug offenses. It seemed that the rate of arrests over the past year was down almost ninety percent from the previous five years. The sheriff's office was praised for the apparent success of its techniques in dealing with offenders. Sheriff Barker was quoted as saying "They [the drug pushers] all know they'll do time if they come around Jackson County with that stuff. We've got a good network of folks out here that call us with tips on unusual behavior, and we follow up. No drug dealer is going to get by for long with that kind of public pressure on him."

I flipped to the next edition. At 5:05, Mrs. Seymour put her head in the door and said, "Garrison, we close at five, but I'll be here for a while taking care of a few things. You're welcome to stay if you like."

"Thank you, Mrs. Seymour, but I don't think I'm going to find what I'm looking for anyway." I continued to scroll through the reader.

"Oh, my goodness, that is a shame," she said as she stepped into the room. She glanced at the screen in front of me, saying, "I understand poor Ernest B. Martin was drowned the other day."

I looked up at her. "Yes?"

Her eyes flicked from my face to her hands. She laced her fingers together, palms touching. She said, "I seem to recall that you boys were friends. Is that right?"

"For all of our lives."

"Then it must be very painful for you, Garrison. I am so sorry."

"Thank you. I appreciate that."

"Yes, well . . ." Her last word trailed away to an awkward silence. I returned my attention to the flickering screen, sensing that she had more to say but was uncomfortable for some reason. Finally, she said, "It's not me, you understand. If it were up to me I wouldn't ask, but our resources are so limited. I really must do something."

"Yes?"

"Yes. Truth be told, if it was up to me, I wouldn't dream of asking. I mean, at a time like this, these things can seem so—trivial."

"Why don't you just tell me what's on your mind, Mrs. Seymour?"

She sighed. "It's Ernest B., actually. I believe you were his neighbor as well as his friend?"

"Yes. He lived with his father on the land next to ours."

"In that case, I wonder if you could do us a favor?"

"I'll try."

"Well, I'm afraid your friend has—that is, he had—well, several overdue books. Quite a few, actually. And I was wondering, since you are a friend of the family, and since you live nearby . . . could you possibly drop by their house and collect them for me? I wouldn't ask, except we're so low on funds, and many of them are quite old. Irreplaceable, really. And—that is—"

I interrupted her. "That's no problem, Mrs. Seymour. I'll be glad to do it."

"Oh, bless your heart, Garrison! I feel so awkward asking at a time like this."

"Not at all," I said. "But you know, I'm surprised to hear that Ernest B. checked out books."

She cocked her head, her tall gray hair leaning at a precarious angle. "Really? Why is that?"

"I just didn't know he was much of a reader."

"Oh, gracious me, yes! He was here all the time. That is, for a few weeks. Before that, I don't believe we had seen him since his school days. But recently he has—had—a strong interest. In fact, he spent many a day right there at that machine, going over the same material."

"The same material? Ernest B. was here, looking at the *Herald*?"

"Heavens, yes. In fact, I believe he was interested in that very page. He was here for days and days, while he was working on that story for the New York magazine . . . what was it called?" She raised her head toward the ceiling in thought, and began a verbal listing of every New York-based periodical that she could remember.

I interrupted her again. "Ernest B. was writing an article for a magazine?"

"Why, yes. That's what he said. I knew you were close, so I thought possibly you were here to carry on his work. A sort of ongoing memorial to a fine young man, as it were."

"And he was interested in this page, here on the screen?"

"Yes. I believe he asked for a photocopy of that one. Say, did you know we can do that now? I can make you a copy of anything you find on these machines. Isn't that marvelous?"

"It sure is, Mrs. Seymour. It's just wonderful," I said absentmindedly, looking at the screen. It was displaying a Sunday supplement piece on the recreational wonders of Martin Pool. The headline on the article was "Martin Pool, a County Treasure." I read a few lines while the librarian rambled on about the marvels of modern technology. When she paused for breath, I said, "Mrs. Seymour, do you mind making me a copy of this article?"

"Why, of course not, Garrison. Let me see now, I believe I just need to write down this number on the lower left . . ." As she busied herself with the machine, I sat back in thought.

Ernest B. had never been a writer. I was sure the story he'd told Mrs. Seymour was a lie to conceal his real interest in the article. But it looked like a standard piece on the lake, designed more for weekend residents and tourists than for local consumption. So why would he bother to lie?

I said, "Mrs. Seymour, you've given me an idea. I believe I would like to finish Ernest B.'s story, and you could help."

She stopped fiddling with the machine and turned to me. "What can I do for you, Garrison?"

"Well, is there a way to see everything Ernest B. checked out and got copies of while he was working on the story?"

"I should say so. We keep excellent records of book withdrawals, of course, and I have a pad in my office where I record photocopy requests so I can charge them to the right people."

"That's great. I wonder if we could have a look at those records? It would save time if I didn't have to retrace all of his research."

Within the hour, I was walking to the truck with a pile of photocopies and several books on the seat beside me. Ernest B. had been busy. During the period between eight and two months before his death, he had checked out more books than in the twenty years before that period, including those he never returned. Other than one article in the *Dallas Morning News* about a new restaurant and bar in Deep Ellum, all of his reading selections seemed to be concerned with the local history of Jackson County, and Martin Pool in particular.

I wondered why he was so interested in old stories about the lake? Was there a connection between his newfound curiosity and the fact that Martin Pool was where he'd died?

CHAPTER 15

I FELT GUILTY SPENDING ALL DAY AWAY from the office. We weren't particularly busy, but Mrs. P. was handling more than her share of the workload while I searched for Ernest B.'s murderer. So, since the library was near the office, I decided to stroll over to check on things.

Outside, the heat was intense, something you pushed through, like wading upstream against a current. I only got as far as Pedro's before the need for cool air and a glass of sweet tea drove me inside.

Pedro's Cafe is a Mt. Sinai landmark. For over forty years, Pedro Comacho has served three meals a day in his long, narrow dining room across the square from the courthouse. He worked first as a busboy, then as the cook, waiter, and cashier, saving every penny and learning the business from the elderly gentleman who had operated the restaurant as Harper's Cafe since the turn of the century. After ten years of living on beans and rice in a boardinghouse room, Pedro surprised the old man with a $12,000 cash offer—a lot of money in those days.

Mr. Harper was glad to sell the place and move to be with his daughter in Tyler, Texas.

Nothing but the name changed for the next few years. Then Pedro made history in Jackson County on a stifling hot day in 1961.

He was in the kitchen preparing for lunch and listening to Martin Luther King make a speech on KLIF, one of the old Dallas radio stations. For some reason the great man's words struck home with more force than usual that morning. Pedro stood at a steel table cutting potatoes, dripping with sweat as Dr. King's deep voice boomed over the AM waves. Now and then, when the reverend's speech touched something deep within him, Pedro muttered "*¡Sí!*" under his breath and chopped a little harder. The speech ended with a stirring appeal for peaceful action by every decent man, woman, and child, regardless of race, to achieve freedom for all. It was enough for Pedro.

His white apron billowed behind him as he strode through the restaurant to the front doors. For fifty years, the cafe dining room had been divided into white and "colored" sections. The social mores of the South wouldn't allow Pedro to eat in the Anglo section of his own restaurant. In fact, owning a prosperous business in downtown Mt. Sinai was a step over the line for a Mexican-American in those days. But Pedro wasn't the kind of man to be satisfied with walking a single step when he could run a mile. He wiped potato juice from the butcher knife and used the blade to carefully pry the "Colored Section" sign away from a low wall near the entrance. Then he stood and waited.

As people began to arrive for lunch, Pedro met them at the entry with his arms folded, legs apart, and feet firmly planted. He pointed to the dining section he wanted each group to use. His directions were based on their order of entry, not on their race. First group to the left, second to the right, and so forth.

There was some resistance, of course. Blacks feared for their safety. Whites were outraged at the impudence of the "uppity Mex." But for the most part, Pedro's customers sat where they were told—possibly because, when Pedro pointed to their seat, he did so with the butcher knife.

In the following weeks, Pedro's business declined. Meals were often solitary affairs for the few out-of-town diners who didn't know better. His front windows were broken twice. He considered closing.

Then one Sunday afternoon, as Pedro paced back and forth on the raised sidewalk outside the little restaurant, worrying about laying off his help, he saw a strange thing. A group of black folks dressed in their church-going finest turned the corner of State Highway 121 and Main, diagonally across the square. Immediately behind them another little group of people appeared. Soon a hundred determined Negro men and women were marching across the plaza in front of the courthouse and up the middle of the street toward Pedro, led by the Reverend Clarence T. Brown, pastor of Calvary Baptist Church.

The crowd gathered in front of Pedro's Cafe, silent, serious, and still, waiting for their leader to speak. From the raised sidewalk Pedro could see every face. He knew many of them, and he'd seen the others around town. He searched their eyes for a clue as to why they were there.

Standing in the road blocking traffic, with his congregation at his back, the Reverend Brown looked up at Pedro and said in a loud voice, "We understand your business been a little down these last few weeks, Mr. Comacho. We also understand that where you once had 'bout twenty seats available for our use, you now goin' to let us sit where we please."

"That's right."

"Well, Mr. Camacho, we just finished our Sunday prayer service, and we worked up a powerful hunger for our daily bread!"

A Baptist behind him shouted, "Amen!"

"We hunger and thirst after righteousness!"

Another man shouted, "Tell it, brother!"

"We want to taste the fruits of freedom!"

"Say it again!"

"We're here to consume some manna from heaven!"

The whole crowd began to shout to the sky and wave their hands above their heads. The Reverend Brown turned to them with arms raised, asking for silence. When he again had the undivided attention of everyone in the street, he faced Pedro with a broad smile and said, "In short, Mr. Comacho, we'd like some lunch."

Pedro said, "Well, sir, I don't got no fruits or manna, but I got a chicken-fried blue-plate special that y'all might like."

After that Sunday, Pedro's business never lagged again. To this day, a large part of the congregation of the Calvary Baptist Church makes Pedro's a regular stop on their way home from church. And after a few months, white folks began to return to Pedro's Cafe. His food was just too good to boycott. Occasionally, fights broke out over the seating arrangements, but these were dealt with so decisively (the jail being just across the street) that soon even the hotheads settled down and concentrated on Pedro's cooking.

I tried to make it to Pedro's a couple of times a week for lunch. When I returned from Tulane full of big ideas and liberal politics, he was one of the only members of the older generation in Jackson County who understood the changes I'd been through. He encouraged my new ideas and often came to my defense when one of my father's buddies would chide me for my "darn fool hippie notions."

"You leave Mr. Reed be," he'd say as he set our plates before us, and coming from Pedro, that was a mouthful. It was usually enough to get the good ol' boys to change the subject. And it was more than enough to make me a customer for life.

• • •

I WAS REACHING FOR THE CAFE DOOR WHEN Pedro opened it from the side and said, "You look terrible."

"I haven't been getting much sleep lately," I said.

Pedro gave me a toothless grin and invited me inside. The painted wood floor creaked as we walked to a table near the door. Pedro's knees popped when he bent to sit across from me. He was getting old. His hair was snow white, as was his trademark Pancho Villa mustache, grown long enough to cover his upper lip, which was a good thing considering that he'd taken to leaving his dentures at home lately. As always, he wore a white apron. Some folks joked that he slept in that apron.

He called a waitress over to pour us some coffee. When she walked away, he said, "Garr, I been hearin' 'bout your troubles."

That didn't surprise me. Pedro's Cafe was a favorite place for early-morning coffee and conversation, and Pedro heard it all.

He said, "I understand you been askin' 'round 'bout Ernest B."

"Yeah. Been finding out some stuff I'm not too happy about."

He sipped his coffee and nodded.

"Did you know Ernest B. was using drugs?"

Pedro nodded again. "I wondered if you knew about it, Garr. Thought about askin' you a couple of times, but figured if you wanted a partner who was doin' dope, that was your business."

"I didn't know."

He traced patterns in a ring of water on the old oak tabletop. "I got a nephew, name of Geraldo, a good for nothin'. Went to runnin' with a bunch from Dallas a couple years ago, now we don't see too much of him. But he comes home now an' then, holidays an' special occasions, like when he needs a couple hundred bucks." Pedro sighed. "Anyway, he's been doin' a lot of dope. I can tell 'cause of how he's lost weight an' gotten pale an' his eyes an' hair don't look so good. I guess he's sellin' the stuff too.

"A few months ago, I was sittin' right here at this table, an' Ernest B. walked by the window with Geraldo. Surprised the you-know-what out of me. I hopped up an' went outside to say hello. Before I could say anything, I saw Ernest B. pull out some money an' count it off into Geraldo's hand. You know how you can tell when someone's up to somethin' they shouldn't be? Well, I knew those two didn't want me to see what I just seen, so I went back inside.

"A little later, Geraldo shows up an' pays me back some money I loaned him. New bills, hundreds and fifties. I figure that was Ernest B.'s money. I figure Geraldo sold him somethin' for it."

We sat in silence for a minute, pondering the disappointing frailties of friends and family. I looked away, staring up at the antique tin ceiling without really seeing it, trying to put my feelings into words. Finally I said, "It's like he led a double life."

Pedro sipped his coffee.

"I haven't been able to get around the idea that he spent so much time with me and I didn't know. I just can't get over it."

Pedro cleared his throat and said, "I seen you come in here for what? Fifteen, sixteen years. Learnin' that business of your daddy's an' growin' into it. You been real busy all that time. Get your lunch to go so you can eat it back at your office. Look at you. You an' Mary Jo got no time for kids. Don't get out much. Just work, work, work. Right?"

I had to nod.

"Well then, Garr, how come you're so surprised Ernest B. had a life of his own? When did you have time to keep up with his comin's and goin's? You two ain't kids no more, spendin' all day playing down at the lake. You got your life; he had his."

"My life's getting pretty shaky here lately, Pedro. You know Barker thinks I killed Ernest B.?"

Pedro made a spitting sound. "That old *perro* don't have a clue what goes on 'round here."

"Yeah, I guess. But he's got it in for me anyway. Thinks I killed Ernest B. because he was trying to milk the company."

"Was he?"

"Yes."

"I thought it was something like that."

"What do you mean?"

"Well, that was a big wad of bills he pulled out to buy the drugs from Geraldo. He had to peel a lot of hundreds away to get at the twenties. Must've had four, five thousand dollars in his pocket."

"But Ernest B. was always broke! It got to be a joke between us how he couldn't hang onto his cash."

"Yeah. He used to come in here an' eat an' then tell me he'd have to come back later to pay me 'cause he forgot he just spent his last buck. Never could hang onto a line of credit, you know? American Express even took away his green card. I know, 'cause he made a stupid joke about how the Immigration was gonna come get him since he didn't have no green card." Pedro's toothless grin flashed for a second, then his bushy white eyebrows knitted together and he became serious again. "But this last year or so he's always had plenty of cash. I mean, he did before he . . ."

We sat silently for a few minutes. Maybe the old man was pondering the strange twists of fate that would let him grow so old and take Ernest B. so young. I was thinking about that big wad of money.

I said, "Pedro, do you know any dopers?"

"I met some of Geraldo's friends, yeah."

"I need to meet them too."

He glanced around the room before saying, "Those guys are no good, boy. You stay away from them."

"I figure whoever killed Ernest B. probably did it over drugs or money. The only way I'm going to clear myself is to find another suspect for Barker to go after. And the only way to do that is to talk to some of Ernest B.'s doper buddies."

An old green pickup truck pulled up to the curb outside and Pedro raised a hand to wave at the driver. Without looking at me he said, "You sure you only interested in clearin' yourself?"

"What does that mean?"

"Lotta guys would want a piece of someone that killed their best friend. You doin' any thinkin' along those lines?"

I looked away from him, afraid he would see the truth in my eyes. "I never thought about it that way."

He sat silently for a moment, then said, "Was me, I'd be dreamin' 'bout killin' 'em with my bare hands."

I couldn't answer, afraid that he would hear the truth in spite of any lie I might tell. A mental image rose within me of my hands closing around a throat, of a man choking and begging for mercy. A thrill of pleasure flickered at the thought. There was no hint in my mind that revenge was evil. The desire had become too strong. I smiled.

Pedro had a strange look on his face. He said, "Garr, that ain't gonna solve nothin'. You know better."

"I need to meet Geraldo's friends, Pedro."

He shook his head slowly. "You're fixin' to step knee-deep in pig slop here. Leave this to Barker, *hijo*. Listen to me! Do what you're thinkin' and it will change you, make you one of them."

I just looked at him. After a moment he said, "All right. If you're bound and determined to get yourself hurt, I can't stop you. Let me think."

He stroked his drooping white mustache for a moment, then leaned forward and quietly said, "I know Geraldo likes to whoop it up pretty hard down around that Deep Ellum place in Dallas. I've heard him talkin' 'bout some place down there, some nightclub. Has 'Money' in the name. Wasted Money, Easy Money, somethin' like that."

I remembered the article about a bar in the *Dallas Morning News* that Ernest B. had photocopied. I said, "I've heard of it. But how about closer to home? Know any place around here where I should look?"

"Naw, those fellas don't hang out around here too much. Not exciting enough."

"How about the Nowhere Club?"

"Well, you might go see ol' Lester Fredricks out there. He's dumb, but he keeps up with things."

I told Pedro about my conversation with Lester earlier in the week.

"Didja talk to Victor Sickle?"

"Who's that?"

"Fella's always over there. I think he owns part of the joint."

"What does he look like?"

"Big fella. Real wide in the shoulders. Little bitty feet. Wears his hair kinda long an' slicked back."

I thought of the man at the jukebox. The one who stood near Lester at Ernest B.'s burial and ground cigarette butts into the grass with his little silver-tipped boot. I remembered his black, empty eyes. Shark's eyes.

Pedro said, "On second thought, Garr, you stay away from Victor. He's a bad one." He leaned closer. "I shouldn't tell you this. You keep it to yourself, all right?"

I nodded.

His voice was very low as he said, "I hear Sickle's place is a drop for *las mulas*—the ones who bring the stuff up from Mexico."

"Where is his place?"

His knowing eyes rested on mine for a moment before he answered. "Up near yours, 'bout a mile past the dam on the other side of the lake. But I'm tellin' you, Garr, stay away from there. Those guys'll kill you."

"I thought Barker had all those people run out of the county."

Pedro looked at me with amusement and said, "You *jefes* all think you got this county figured out, but don't none of you know squat 'bout what really goes on 'round here."

"You know, I'm just beginning to understand that."

He glanced around the dining room nervously. "Garr, I always liked you for some reason. I'll be hanged if I know why. You're gettin' into somethin' here that's gonna get you buried. You shouldn't oughta try to play detective. Just hire you the best lawyer you can, and fight it out in court. Shoot, Barker ain't even arrested you yet."

I shook my head no and was about to speak when he continued, almost whispering, "I know you ain't gonna do that. So if you're bound and determined to keep messin' with this thing, look for the money. If you figure out where the money is, you'll know who's pullin' the strings."

"What money are you talking about, Pedro?"

"Garr, don't be stupid. I'm talkin' 'bout the money Ernest B. had. Where he got it. Who knew he had it. They didn't find none on him, did they? So where is it? Find that money and you'll find your answer. And Garr, listen. I'm gonna light a candle for you over at St. Andrew's tonight, just in case."

"Light a candle?"

"Yeah. An' maybe say a little prayer." He leaned closer. "I'm worried about you. You got a look, a bad look, like somethin' ain't right inside. You better think about what I said before. You start fightin' this thing their way and it'll change you. It'll eat you up inside."

With those words he rose slowly, supporting himself with difficulty by leaning on the tabletop. There was more I wanted to ask him, but with the place filling up for dinner, Pedro had become very uneasy, nervously looking around as if we were being watched. Since the moment our conversation had turned to drugs and dealers, he had seemed ill at ease.

As he turned to go, he repeated, "I'll be prayin' for you, Garr. That always helps."

I watched him hobble across the diner and pondered what I'd learned that day. Clyde Barker had said drug dealers didn't exist in Jackson County. And the newspaper backed him up. But why was Pedro Comacho so afraid to speak out loud about drug dealers? What could so frighten a man who had braved lynching by the Ku Klux Klan? It was a train of thought that led to some scary possibilities . . . very scary.

CHAPTER 16

I DECIDED NOT TO VISIT THE OFFICE after all and walked back to my truck deep in thought. I had a couple of new ways to look into the drug angle, thanks to Pedro, and the discovery that Ernest B. had been reading up on Martin Pool and local history gave me another lead to pursue. In my excitement at finding some clues to Ernest B.'s behavior, I forgot to take the roundabout route home and drove through town. A deputy's cruiser appeared in my rearview mirror when I passed the courthouse. It stayed right behind me as I left the city limits.

I drove carefully, following all the traffic laws, one eye on the road ahead and the other on the mirror. The cruiser didn't close the gap between us, maintaining a hundred-yard distance all the way to my house. As I pulled into our drive, the cruiser passed slowly by. When I peeked through the blinds ten minutes later, it was parked by the road outside.

I barely slept that night. Every hour or so, I was drawn to the window to see if the deputy was still parked out front. He never moved.

The next day was our fifteenth wedding anniversary. For months, Mary Jo and I had planned to go someplace wonderfully exotic, but I was uneasy about being gone too long. Barker might overreact and arrest me when we came home. Or they might find more evidence or locate a witness and I would miss out on it. I needed to stay near Mt. Sinai.

There didn't seem to be any point in worrying Mary Jo with all of this, so I cooked up a scheme for a romantic evening in Dallas, claiming a heavy workload and selling her on the idea by promising carte blanche at Neiman Marcus. She agreed enthusiastically.

We left for Dallas early in the morning, waving at the deputy out front as we drove past in Mary Jo's Volvo 940. It was a three-hour trip, nothing at all in a state the size of Texas. The first two hours were a pleasantly scenic tour of rolling pastures and piney woods. Men in the oncoming lane drove with their wrist draped across the top of the steering wheel, raising a finger or two in the usual wave as we passed. Mist stood in the hollows, steam sucked from the ground by the morning heat. The top half of rusty corrugated-steel barns and silos seemed to float in the bottomless vapor. Mary Jo and I had a long-standing tradition about the mist in the mornings; we called it "ghosties." Stands of pines divided the ghosties into manageable groups. Mary Jo insisted that we turn the fog lights on, even though the roadbed was above the specters. We pretended we were involved in a narrow escape from the mystical forces of evil. She sank down on her seat, gathering the collar of her blouse close around her neck and staring at the passing mist with her forehead wrinkled in concern.

She said, "Do you think they'll catch us?"

"Not if we're fast."

"And not if our hearts are pure."

"Yes. We have to be good, too."

"Oh, that's good."

"Yes. Good is good."

"And we are, too."

"Good," we both said at once, smiling just a little. Our tradition was upheld.

The two-lane blacktop sprouted shoulders. Its curves straightened out. Yellow stripes appeared down the center. Too soon, the mist burned off and we reached the interstate. We slowed, turned onto the access road, entered the ramp, and rushed onto the four-lane highway, accelerating to seventy.

An hour away from the city limits, the Dallas/Fort Worth metropolis meets the countryside like a crusty birthmark on a beautiful woman. Green gives way to gray. Trees to Day-Glo billboards. Solitude to manic traffic. The Big D and Cow Town squat on the countryside like a pair of giant toads, a hundred miles of ugly along Interstate 30.

At ten o'clock we pulled into the parking lot of Northpark Mall, Mary Jo's favorite. It is one of the oldest shopping malls in the country, with a Neiman Marcus, a Lord and Taylor, and a Barney's of New York. It is fertile ground for what Mary Jo calls "a good shop."

We share almost everything in life except the love of shopping. I hate it. She lives for it. On some level of consciousness that I can't seem to achieve, it must be fun. When Mary Jo shops, her face assumes a look of obsessive concentration, like a gambler shooting craps. The clothes are not the thing—it is the bargain, the hunt. I know this is true because she usually returns two thirds of what she buys, after basking in the afterglow for a day or two. According to Mary Jo, that is the best thing about clothes shopping: Once you have had your fun, you can change your mind and get your money back. Try that in Las Vegas and see where it gets you.

I spent a lot of time nodding encouragement, while Mary Jo rushed around indulging her addiction, surrounded by admiring salespeople. I think she understood that my real anniversary gift to her was not the roses or the fancy French dinner I had planned but this attempt to share one of her favorite things in life.

It was a long day. At six in the evening we drove downtown to the Adolphus, the backseat and trunk of Mary Jo's Volvo crammed full of boxes. I tipped three bellboys to help carry it all to our room. Mary Jo took a shower while I lay on the bed, trying to recover. Shopping exhausts me. I stretched and enjoyed the comfortable, long bed. Usually my feet hang over the edge of hotel mattresses. I was about to fall asleep when Mary Jo reappeared in the bathroom door, wearing nothing but a saucy smile, her complexion rosy red from the shower. We spent the next half-hour enjoying each other enthusiastically. Hotel rooms have that effect on us.

Afterward, we read and catnapped and grinned at each other for a while, then we dressed and went downstairs to a three-hour dinner at the French Room—the best Dallas has to offer in the way of fine dining. Thirty-foot gilded columns supported barrel-vaulted ceilings frescoed with clouds and angels. The wait staff wore tuxedos (of course). There were more waiters than diners. Even the waiters had waiters. The food was marvelous. Every dish was a new experience in excess, a work of visual art, a culinary masterpiece. Mary Jo and I gave our waiter a hand when he brought our desserts. He played along with a broad smile and deep bow from the waist. Our fellow diners, sophisticates all, looked on with subdued amusement.

When we finished our dessert and coffee, I suggested we take a cab over to Deep Ellum for some local color. It was a good opportunity to check out the bar in the *Morning News* article—which I still hadn't mentioned to Mary Jo.

Downtown Dallas is a ghost town after six. At the end of the workday, the streets are choked with people going home, and home is someplace else. There are no high-rise condominiums, no blocks of brownstones like the cities back east, and no open restaurants or bars, except in the hotels. People work downtown; they don't live or play there.

But across Central Expressway on the eastern edge of the inner city is Deep Ellum, and Deep Ellum is different. It's named for the way black people pronounced the "Elm" in Elm Street back in the twenties, when it was their neighborhood, swaying to the sounds of Leadbelly's rhythm and blues. It's ten or twelve blocks of simple brick storefronts, juke jumpin' joints, pocket cafes, and shoeshine stands. It's punkers and hippies, New Age airheads and winos, cops and neo-nazis, upper class, middle class, lower class, and no class—all dressed up and ready to go. It's a throwback to the days before mirrored high rises and six-lane expressways, to the days when Dallas was just another midsized city patiently minding its own business, to the days before the Fall of Detroit and the Great Exodus South, before Hollywood came up with that television show about J. R. Ewing and the rest of those darn fools.

Deep Ellum is Dallas's last chance at a soul. She'll probably tear it down in the name of progress, but it will party hard between now and then.

The taxi dropped us off, and we enjoyed an evening stroll, Mary Jo in a brand-new Liz Claiborne pleated tartan skirt and white silk blouse and me in my chinos, pastel plaid button-down shirt, and navy blazer. We felt like city folks, smug and swanky, looking for a bar that was worthy of us. I was looking for a sign. After a while, I found it.

On the other side of the street, mounted to the front of a simple red brick storefront, a neon sign said "Easy Money" in bright turquoise and pink. I took Mary Jo's hand and we dashed through the traffic and up to the entrance.

The doorman was a giant. A literal giant. He was over seven feet tall and dressed to the nines. Size-twenty Italian loafers, triple-pleated silk slacks, a jet-black polo shirt under a black-and-brown houndstooth jacket. Padded shoulders would have been redundant.

And he was a doorman, not a bouncer. No bouncer ever had such a gracious manner. He leaned down to speak to Mary Jo, making an unaffected bow. The spray of freckles across his pale white cheeks, and the childish cowlick in his bright red hair seemed at odds with his size, like a boy's head on the shoulders of a titan.

He said, "Good evening, ma'am. Please, do come in."

His voice was soft, melodic. He remained half bent, his head down at our level. I couldn't recall another time when a man had to stoop to my height. Usually, it was the other way around. His size made me nervous, and I didn't meet his eye. A hand like an outfielder's mitt gently grasped the brass door handle and pulled it open. The very effort of holding his upper body so low was a gesture of courtesy, as if he knew how his size affected people, how we needed some assurance of his good intentions.

As we stepped past, he spoke again, very quietly, "Enjoy yourself, sir."

Something in his tone penetrated my uneasiness. I looked directly at his face. His pale blue eyes were amused, aware of my intimidation, expecting it. I smiled. He returned the smile with a tilt of his head and held the door open a bit wider.

Mary Jo led me into a sea of screaming, chaotic, beautiful people. An exotically striking black woman in a tight floral dress greeted us just inside the door. She stuck out her lower lip in a knowing way and nodded her approval when I said that we would stand at the bar, as if my decision was a stroke of genius. A quintet was playing jazz in the corner. They were very good, but no one was paying attention. Taking advantage of my size, I cleared a path through the crowd of bimbos, pretty boys, and sugar daddies, found us a spot to lean against at the bar, and settled into some serious people watching. A short Latino dressed in black with a silver bolo tie took our drink order.

It was very noisy. The crowd and the musicians competed for dominance, each increasing their volume every few minutes to be heard over the other. I leaned across the bar top so I wouldn't have to yell and asked the bartender if he'd seen Ernest B. lately. He gave me a blank look, so I yelled the question. He shook his head and shrugged in that infinitely expressive way some Latinos have.

I sipped my drink and began watching the crowd, hoping to spot a familiar face. Black was in. Everywhere I looked I saw men and women in black and white, milling and bumping together like Holsteins at the trough. A young fellow with a very long, very black ponytail came in from the street. He and the beautiful hostess at the door kissed the air at each other's cheeks, left and right. He looked like he thought he was important. She looked bored.

I turned my attention to the band. They were really very good. It annoyed me that the crowd was so loud. Ponytail appeared at my side, rising onto his toes to look around, his chin up. His face was starkly pale against his black silk shirt and hair. It was too crowded for him to reach the bar, so I asked if I could place his drink order for him. Without lowering his chin, he looked down his nose at me for a moment. Since I was clearly nobody, he decided to play it straight.

"All right. Why not?" he said, returning his attention to the crowd.

I waited for him to tell me what he was drinking, but he ignored me. His eyes were constantly moving, looking at everyone and at no one. Beginning to get irritated, I said, "What do you want to drink?" He pretended not to hear me, even though we were only a foot apart. Suddenly, his tip-toed search was rewarded. He saw someone he knew—someone who was *someone*. He pushed on through the crowd without looking at me again.

I sighed and sipped my drink. The woman next to me lit a cigarette, the smoke rising to my face. She slid an ashtray close to my elbow and put her cigarette in it. I turned toward Mary Jo to avoid the smoke. Every time the woman picked up her cigarette, her elbow rubbed my back. I don't like cigarette smoke, and I don't like strangers touching me. I shifted away from her as much as possible.

Mary Jo stood quietly smiling, surrounded by her peaceful aura, enjoying the show. She's like that: oblivious to little provocations, serenely focused on the positive, cruising blindly past life's potholes like a latter-day Mr. Magoo. Ask her, and she'll say her secret is not that she is unaware but that she ignores what she doesn't like. Simple.

On another night I might have followed her lead and enjoyed the band. But my hunch that this place was connected to Ernest B.'s dope problem was very strong. If I was going to learn anything helpful, now was the time. But what could I do? My plan wasn't exactly well thought out. I had entertained the notion that I would come here and meet some of Ernest B.'s drug buddies, maybe even his dope connection. It was a dumb idea. I wouldn't know a drug dealer if he was sitting on a bale of marijuana.

In the movies, a man in my position would coolly survey the room, ignore the innocent bystanders, and instinctively select a suspect from the crowd. I looked around, but all I saw was a room full of accountants and dental hygienists, spending their big night out pretending to be rich and famous: pseudo-hip bar flies who might have been interesting people if they hadn't been so busy working on their image. They looked more like victims than murderers. Everybody seemed to be drunk or stoned or well on the way, living pointless lives centered on sex and drugs. Finding pleasure at any cost. Avoiding eye contact. Frantically casting about for something or someone to make their night complete. The younger ones and the stupid ones hadn't reached the obvious conclusion yet, but once or twice I saw a crack in the veneer of gaiety. A glance at someone caught off guard revealed the vacuous expression of an aging hedonist straining to ignore the painful truth: sensuous pleasures lose their flavor unless they're tied to something more. Lust without love leaves you empty and lost.

In the end, you have to stand for something. You have to believe in abstract concepts like loyalty and honor and unconditional love. You have to pursue goals that endure, even though you'll never completely attain them. Sex, money, drugs—you can buy or steal them all. Only a fool would base life on something so superficial, something that can be bought or stolen.

I thought about Ernest B., coming to this place to be among these people. I thought about me, working so hard I didn't notice him changing.

Only a fool.

"I've got to get out of here," I whispered in Mary Jo's ear. She nodded and reached for her purse.

The giant held the door as we stepped outside. I tried to tip him a buck, but he wouldn't take it.

"Oh, no sir, that isn't necessary," he said in his strangely mellow voice. "You spend that on a flower for your lady, sir. Enjoy your evening."

I looked up at him. "How do you put up with all those spoiled brats?" I asked.

His eyes glazed over a little, and he lifted them to look beyond my head. I was putting down his bread and butter. "They're not all bad, sir. You just got to bear with 'em now and then."

Mary Jo said, "I'll bet they don't give you too much trouble."

He smiled a little and said, "Oh, some guys, they see me as a challenge, ma'am. The foolish ones give me a try." Another couple walked up, and he turned his attention to them. After they entered the bar, he turned back toward the sidewalk, a little surprised to find us still waiting there.

"You don't happen to know a guy named Ernest B. Martin do you?" I asked.

He frowned in concentration, then shook his head. "No, sir. Don't believe I've had the pleasure."

I watched his face closely. If he was lying, he was very good at it. I said, "Doesn't matter. He's just a friend. I've heard he comes here now and then."

"Lots of folks come here, sir."

"Well, enjoy your evening."

"Yes, sir. You folks do the same."

We strolled arm in arm along the sidewalk. The glass towers of downtown Dallas loomed over Deep Ellum; a couple thousand florescent tubes still twinkled in the offices up there. Five or six wild-looking teenagers wearing scuffed black military boots, black T-shirts, and black caps ran past us, shouting something about burning a car. I pulled Mary Jo closer. The street was jammed with joy riders, cruising with their windows down and their stereos up. Rap, rock, and country music fought for control of the road, a noisy, mixed-up jumble of notes that ebbed and surged with every change of the traffic lights.

I looked back at the Easy Money from half a block down the street. The giant was in close conversation with the attractive black woman in the floral dress. They looked our way. A man stepped out of the door and stood beside them for a moment, then he looked our way too. It was the pool player from the Nowhere Club, the big guy with the little feet who had ground cigarettes into the soil beside Ernest B.'s crypt, the man Pedro Camacho had warned me to avoid. Victor Sickle.

Our eyes locked at thirty yards. Even at that distance, I saw a fierce malevolence in his face. Details around us blurred for an instant, and it seemed there was no one on the street but

Sickle and me. Evil surged my way with an almost physical force. Suddenly, my notion of finding Ernest B.'s drug connections seemed foolhardy at best, especially with Mary Jo along.

I put my arm around her shoulder and led her away from Victor Sickle, picking up our pace a little and wishing I owned a handgun.

CHAPTER 17

SICKLE MIGHT TRY TO FOLLOW US, but I felt fairly safe out on the street. That was probably foolish, but then I'm from a small town where folks are fairly safe almost anywhere. I tried to hurry Mary Jo along just in case, putting some distance between us and the Easy Money. There were hundreds of people strolling the sidewalks around us. We soon got lost in the crowd.

If she noticed our increased pace, she didn't mention it. After a while she said, "You asked for Ernest B. back there. Did that place have something to do with what's going on?"

"Yes."

Her shoulders stiffened. She said, "Oh."

"I'm sorry I didn't tell you about it. I didn't want you to worry on our anniversary."

She didn't answer right away, and I thought she was angry. Then she said, "Please let me worry with you, Garr. You're my husband. I need to be a part of this."

"I'm sorry. I just didn't want to ruin things."

She put her arm around my waist and said, "I know."

We window shopped as we walked. New Age crystals, a gay/lesbian bookstore, Ethiopian imports, a gallery showcasing the work of someone who dipped found objects in plaster of Paris, then spray painted them black.

Mary Jo said, "Black black black. What's the matter with these people, Garr?"

"Beats me."

"It's so boring, all this New Age stuff. And naive."

"Really? Even the crystals? I was sort of hoping all it took was clear rock to put you in touch with a higher power."

She laughed. "Imagine that. And this channeling thing. I mean, didn't they used to call that demonic possession?"

"Oh, times have changed. Now it's good to be possessed."

We passed a couple of kids standing in a recessed doorway. They were dressed in black leather jackets, jeans with holes at the knees, and huge shiny black boots. Both were as pale as corpses, with bruised brown bags under their eyes and impossibly black hair, worn long on one side and shaved close to the skull on the other. They watched us pass without a word, their dull eyes locked blatantly onto Mary Jo's breasts.

"Let's turn back," I said. "I want to go to our hotel."

"All right."

We walked around the block, heading for the hotel. I was keeping an eye out for Sickle. Suddenly, I realized we were passing a tattoo parlor.

"Wait a minute, sweetheart. I've got an idea." I led Mary Jo inside.

"Garrison, I don't love you enough to get tattooed for you."

"I can dream, can't I?"

"Not about that, baby. Not about that."

The place was very clean. It looked a lot like a hair-styling salon. We stood in a waiting area next to a large round chrome-and-glass coffee table piled high with magazines catering to the Harley Davidson leather-and-chains crowd. There were two matching sofas, full of surly looking customers.

I told Mary Jo what I had in mind, and asked her to wait for me there. With her usual self-possession, she sat on the sofa between a skinny teenager with tall purple hair and a very large guy who wore filthy denim blue jeans, a black Harley T-shirt, and fingerless leather gloves with metal studs on the knuckles.

"How do you do?" she asked, smiling sweetly at each of them. They shifted uncomfortably and muttered greetings under their breath.

To the left and right along the central aisle were semiprivate booths. Several of the cubicles contained barber-shop-type chairs, others had the kind of padded adjustable tables they use in examination rooms at a doctor's office. Customers sat or lay on them, sleeves rolled up or shirts off, eyes closed tightly as they concentrated on ignoring the pain of the artist's needle.

About halfway down the aisle, I found a man sitting in one of the adjustable chairs reading a newspaper. He looked out of place: clean shaven, short hair, pressed cotton oxford shirt and slacks. A model citizen.

"Help you, sir?" he asked, peering at me over the top of the paper.

"I was wondering if you could answer some questions for me."

"Well, that depends." He folded the newspaper. "Are you a policeman?

"No, I'm from out of town, and I was wondering about a tattoo a friend of mine has."

"You're not a policeman?"

"No."

"You sort of look like a policeman."

"No, really, I was just passing out front and thought I'd satisfy my curiosity about this tattoo. If you're too busy, perhaps I could pay for some of your time."

"You want a tattoo?"

"No. Just some of your time."

"All right, give me twenty dollars."

I must have shown surprise at the price. He said, "The fees we charge here net us about a hundred dollars an hour, sir. Allowing for a break now and then, twenty dollars would be about right for five to ten minutes per customer. You've already had one."

I gave him the money and said, "Do you have a pen and some paper?" I sketched the tattoo I had seen in the Polaroid snapshot from the morgue. "Ever seen this before?"

He glanced at it for less than two seconds. "No, sir. That's not one of ours."

"How can you be sure?"

"I own this shop, sir."

"Ever had a customer with a tattoo like it?"

He thought for a minute. "Yes, sir, I believe it's similar to the First Cavalry's logo. You know—in the army. Something we see on our customers now and then." He looked at the sketch again. "But it's a little different. This 'S.A.W.' part—I haven't seen that before."

I gave him my business card and another twenty dollars. "Would you ask around, see if you can find out what it means?"

"All right. It's really none of my business, but do you mind telling me why you're so interested?"

"You call me with some information, and I'll satisfy your curiosity, okay?"

"Fair enough."

When I got back to the waiting area, I found Mary Jo in earnest conversation with the huge biker on the sofa. She had spread out a piece of paper on the coffee table, and they were both leaning over it while she sketched. I stood near the door until they finished and she stood up. Both the biker and the kid with the purple hair rose with her, and they shook hands all around.

The biker said, "Thanks, Mary Jo. That'll look real good. I'll see what I can do on that other deal."

When we were back out on the busy sidewalk, I said, "What was that all about?"

"Oh, we were having a lovely talk, and Henry—that's the older one—he said he wasn't sure what kind of tattoo to get. So I told him I was an artist, and offered to sketch him a design."

"What was the 'other deal' he was talking about?"

"You don't think you're the only one who can do detective work, do you? Henry said he'd be very pleased to help us find out about Ernest B.'s tattoo, so we traded phone numbers. He's in some club called the Scorpions, and he said the other members have lots and lots of experience with tattoos."

"You gave that biker our telephone number?"

"Sure. Why not?"

I thought about it, then said, "Well, I guess we need all the help we can get."

"Right. Now get me back to the hotel so I can try on one of my new teddies."

"What color?"

"Black lace, of course."

I said, "Want to race to the cab stand?"

She giggled and wrapped her arm around my waist. "It's only a few blocks." Doing her best Mae West imitation, she said, "Savor the anticipation, big boy."

• • •

THE NEXT MORNING, I LEFT MARY Jo asleep and slipped downstairs for some coffee. I was on page three of the *Dallas Morning News* when Victor Sickle slid into the booth across from me, grinning. He wore a black shirt with a western-style yoke and silver collar tips. A silver and turquoise band around his wrist drew attention to the size of his hands.

How could a man with such tiny feet have such huge hands?

"Hey there, don't I know you from somewhere?" he asked.

I was speechless.

"Sure I do—you're from around Mt. Sinai, ain'tcha? Wait a minute, I'll think of it." He took a slice of toast from the plate in front of me. "Oh sure, you're the guy I saw at ol' Ernest B.'s funeral. Hey. Wasn't that a shame?"

"Did you know Ernest B.?"

He turned his empty eyes on me like a weapon, stabbing me with them while he chewed the toast. He said, "Me an' Ernest B., we was good buddies. Yessir, you could even say best friends."

"He never spoke about you."

"Well maybe he did. I ain't introduced myself yet. I'm Victor. Victor Sickle. Didn't he ever mention me?"

"No."

"Well now. That's sure strange. He told me all about you. 'Bout all that money you boys was makin' buildin' roads and all. He even said we might be partners someday. Say—you *are* Mister Reed, ain'tcha?"

I tried to return his stare, but those eyes were too much. I looked away.

"Hey. How long you think it'd take me to figure out this construction racket, anyway? Think maybe we could be partners after all?"

"Why on earth would I do that?"

"Well, it was one of Ernest B.'s last wishes. And I hear you ain't spending much time around the ol' *oficina* lately."

"I don't know what you're talking about. Do you mind getting out of my booth?"

"Hey, that ain't nice now. Let's be nice here, all right? Ernest B. always said you was a nice fella." Sickle leaned across the table, dominating it. "You *are* Mister Reed, right?"

I shrank away from him in spite of myself. He made no threat, yet there was a looming evil about him. A sense that he had none of the boundaries of normal men. That he would do anything, absolutely anything.

He sat back, satisfied, and said, "You must be Mister Reed. 'Cause here you sit, right where Mary Jo said you'd be. Hey. She's really somethin', ain't she? A real looker. Like one of them New York models."

"You talked to my wife?"

"Sure. Up in room 568. Just a little while ago. Man, she's really put together—"

I was out of the booth and running toward the elevators. Behind me, Victor Sickle laughed and called, "Hey! Tell her I loved that teddy."

When the doors finally opened on the fifth floor, I burst from the elevator and ran down the hall. I fumbled with the key, put it in upside down and, cursing, pulled it out and tried again. Finally, I turned the doorknob and rushed into the room.

On the bed, the sheets stirred and Mary Jo peeked from beneath them, a sleepy smile on her face.

She said, "Hi, baby. What's the matter?"

Sickle had lied, but his point was made.

CHAPTER 18

WHEN WE GOT HOME SUNDAY AFTERNOON, the police cruiser was gone. But thirty minutes after we walked through the door, it showed up in the same place out front. Mary Jo and I didn't mention it, as if by avoiding the subject we could somehow remove the threat it represented.

She walked over to the studio to work on her new painting, and I decided to spend the evening going over the material I'd found at the library. I was just about to get started when the doorbell rang.

It was Clyde Barker. His normally calm features were tight with anger.

"What's the idea, goin' off to Dallas like that?" he said.

"Yesterday was our anniversary, Clyde. We went into town to celebrate."

"You should have told me."

"Would you have tried to stop us?"

"Probably."

"Well, there you go."

His face turned red. "I ought to take you in. You knew better than to run off in the middle of this thing. I told you to stay put."

I took a step closer so he'd have to look up at me and said, "Clyde, either arrest me or get off my land."

He swelled his chest like a rooster. We stood for a moment, staring at each other. Finally, he looked away.

"Not today, Garrison. Not till I'm good and ready. When I run you in, you're goin' in to stay. And I'm gettin' close, boy, I'm gettin' close."

"How's that, Clyde?"

He looked at me slyly. "Well now, you're lookin' a little puny to me, boy. You been to see the doctor lately?"

Barker gave a short bark of a laugh and turned without another word, strutting to his car. Standing in the door, I watched him roll slowly down the driveway and pause by the deputy's cruiser for a moment to exchange a few words before moving on down the road.

I closed the door and sat in the nearest chair, telling myself to relax, to not overreact. If he could prove anything about Krueger, he would have arrested me. He was just playing games, trying to keep the pressure on so he could shake me up.

It was working.

But there was no sense in sitting around waiting to be arrested. I went into the study to collect the books and magazine articles I had found at the library, carried them to our kitchen table, got a cold drink from the refrigerator, and began reading. It felt good to be doing something constructive.

Most of the material concerned the history of Jackson County. There were three books from the University of Texas

Press on the subject. They seemed to be history students' doctoral dissertations. There was a piece from *Texas Monthly* and a couple from the larger Dallas papers. And every year around founder's day, the *Mt. Sinai Daily Herald* comes out with a series of articles on unusual facts and legends about the area. Ernest B. had taken copies of several of these. There were articles about a mysterious man who lived alone for fifty years in the deep woods of the Big Muddy bottomland without the benefit of electricity or running water. He wore clothes made from animal skins and trapped game with ingenious contraptions made of sticks and vines. There was a piece about two boys who found a cave containing the mummies of a family of Caddo Indians, apparently trapped by a landslide and remarkably well preserved by the dry conditions and lack of oxygen their final campfires had created.

I found the material fascinating. The next three articles I read concerned facts I already knew about the construction of Martin Pool, the formation of the Jackson County Development Corporation, and the path to power of the county's leading families—including mine and Ernest B.'s.

The fourth piece was different: an article entitled "Moonshine—Cash Crop of the Thirties." The timing of the article coincided with the debate over liquor-by-the-drink in the county. I read it with interest.

> Jackson County is known for its schools, its cotton farms, its dairy ranches, its churches, and its recreational opportunities, but in the 1930s it was best known for another resource: moonshine. The pristine streams and the densely wooded hills and valleys in the Jackson County area provided moon-

shiners with fresh running water and seclusion. All they had to add was sugar and corn. Federal records from 1935 alone show over fifty arrests of local men involved in the illegal production and distribution of alcoholic beverages. More than thirty moonshine stills were destroyed.

Mr. Jake McKinsey, seventy-five and a resident of the Silver Leaf Home in Mt. Sinai, was a sheriff's deputy at that time. In a recent interview, he described his experiences as a law man dealing with the glut of illegal brew.

"We called Wednesdays choppin' day," he said. "We usually went out on Wednesdays looking for them ol' boys cookin' corn. If we found us one, why we'd get our axes and go to choppin' up their still. I can remember this one fellow, he sat on a log and busted out cryin' right in front of everyone. Said we was ruining months of good, hard, honest work."

Mr. McKinsey told this reporter that there was one alleged moonshiner the sheriff's office and the federal "revenuers" never caught: Mr. E. B. Martin Sr., the patriarch of the Martin family for whom Martin Pool, the area's largest lake, is named.

"Ol' E. B. was a slick one, and that's for sure," Mr. McKinsey said. "We knew he was cookin' up a storm somewhere down in Martin Holler [the popular name for the valley that was flooded to form Martin Pool]. We kept findin' jars with E. B. M. printed on the lids just as neat and pretty as you please. Everyone preferred his liquor—said it was smoother than most 'cause he aged it three months

> or more. Them revenuers would pick up fellows as far away as Shreveport or Tyler with a trunk full of E.B.'s goods. But whenever we'd go out there lookin' for his still, he'd be sittin' on his back porch drinkin' a cold glass of milk."
>
> In addition to the quality of his product and his ability to elude capture, Mr. Martin had another characteristic that distinguished him from his competition. As Mr. McKinsey said, "Remember, this was the middle of the so-called Great Depression. Folks didn't trust paper money too much, not when coins was still solid silver. And E. B. never would take a dollar bill [the price for three jars of moonshine]. He always took his pay in coin. If you didn't have no coin, you didn't get no shine."

There was a grainy photograph of E. B. Martin Sr. standing on the front steps of the Martin home place with his wife, who held a newborn baby. The family resemblance between the moonshiner and Ernest B. was startling. Under the photograph, a caption said, "E. B. Martin Sr., Helen Martin, and their new son Ernest." It was hard to believe Old Man Martin was ever as cute as the pudgy baby in the picture. Hard to imagine anyone calling him Ernest for that matter.

Next to the old photograph was a map of Martin Pool. Someone had drawn a small circle over the water near the Martins' land, and written "need air" in the margin.

I puzzled over the notation for a while, then gave up and skimmed the rest of the article. It went on to describe the usual method of distilling moonshine, as well as the cottage industry's effect on the local economy. A subtle common thread between the books and articles began to occur to me. Each of them contained a reference to Ernest B.'s grandfather. I reached for the article that Mrs. Seymour had noticed on the microfiche reader screen, "Martin Pool, a County Treasure."

Halfway through it, the name E. B. Martin again caught my eye:

> Local legends persist that E. B. Martin, a member of the family for whom the lake was named, collected a substantial number of solid silver coins, which were hidden somewhere on his land. That land was later flooded.
>
> It is believed by some that E. B. Martin mysteriously disappeared just prior to the construction of the Martin Pool, leaving his fortune of silver to be covered by the water. While there is no known evidence that such a treasure ever existed, it is a fact that Mr. Martin did disappear under unusual circumstances. A review of the county records has uncovered a sheriff's department report of a search for Mr. Martin that was undertaken at the request of his wife in the winter of 1939. The search was not successful.
>
> When asked to comment on the rumors of his father's hidden wealth and disappearance, Mr. E. B. Martin Jr. said, "Daddy always was a pack rat. It's possible he stored up some money in those days I guess, but I imagine he took it all with him wherever he went." Mr. Martin Jr. was the youngest member of the Jackson County Development Corporation at the time of its founding in 1940.

I placed the article on the table and sat back in my chair, massaging my stiff neck with one hand. The stories about Ernest B.'s grandfather were interesting, even intriguing in a way. But they were just stories, and old ones at that. Moonshine, mysterious disappearances, and silver treasure sunken below Martin Pool—I'd heard various versions of them all since childhood. They were pages from the same book as the Lady of the Lake and the Swamp Monster.

But why was Ernest B. so interested? Most of this stuff he'd surely heard at his daddy's knee. It wasn't like him to read about history or spend time at a library. Whatever his motivation, I knew two things: It must have been important, and I was missing something.

Time had passed quickly as I sat at the kitchen table reading. Outside, the setting sun streaked dashes of rusty orange across the sky. Eerie silhouettes of treetops stood against the fading glow like old witches holding hands in a pagan rite. I shivered and thought of Mary Jo.

The phone rang. It was her, speaking very quietly. "Garr, thank God you're there. I'm at the studio, and there's someone trying to break in."

Chapter 19

Mary Jo's whispered words dipped my mind into an acid bath of raw panic, burning away every thought except one: Get to her side and protect her. I slipped into remote control, isolated from my actions by fear and anger.

I said, "Stay inside and be as quiet as you can. Keep away from the doors and windows. I'm on my way." I hung up without waiting for her reply.

Standing too quickly, I overturned my chair. It bounced on the floor behind me as I ran to the study, grateful that the sheriff's men hadn't taken my guns when they searched the house. I pulled a twelve-gauge, pump action Browning from the rifle rack and dumped a full box of shells on the desktop. Most of them rolled across the green felt blotter and fell to the floor. I forced myself to stand still long enough to load the shotgun. Then I scooped up another handful of shells, stuffed them into the pockets of my blue jeans and ran out the door.

I ignored the winding path and plunged into the woods like a wild man, crashing through the undergrowth straight toward the studio, completely oblivious to the branches that scratched my face and clawed at my clothes. A few yards short of the clearing I came to my senses and stopped, my lungs screaming for air.

Above me, the sunset's afterglow faded to black through the pines. I stood motionless, barely able to see the outline of the building, straining for a sign of my quarry. A chorus of tree frogs and crickets sang surging counterpoint to the sleepy chirps of titmice and chickadees. A dozen bullfrogs rumbled on the lakeshore to my right, their elastic throats supplying the bass notes for the evening symphony.

These were the sounds of home, usually as comforting to me as a mother's heartbeat to a baby. But I needed to hear the intruder. I longed for complete silence.

As if the creatures had read my mind, the calls around me stopped all together, all at once. Maybe the frogs and insects had sensed a threatening presence nearby. Maybe it was me—and maybe it wasn't. I slowly sank to the ground, listening so hard I heard the pulsing blood in my inner ear.

Minutes passed, and still the woodland creatures maintained their silence. So did my prey. He might be very near, watching the woods, having heard me crashing toward him like an idiot. I might be *his* prey.

I waited. More minutes dragged by as I knelt in the soft pine needles, anxiously searching the darkness for a sign. Sweat rolled into my eyes. Finally the need to know if Mary Jo was safe overcame my caution. I rose and slipped through the trees toward the building as quietly as possible.

Bent at the waist to make myself a smaller target, I stepped from the protective concealment of the tree line into the open clearing and jogged to the rear wall of the studio. I stood with my back to the wall and listened again, holding the shotgun across my chest. A metallic sound came from around the building to my right. I inched my way along the wall until I reached the corner. Crouching low, I carefully peeked around it.

Oblivious to my presence, a man was squatting at the door of the studio doing something to the doorknob. It was too dark to see his face.

I stood back and took a deep breath to steady myself. Then I stepped around the corner and said, "You move and I'll kill you." The shotgun was level with his head.

He froze, facing the doorknob, not daring to turn toward me. I said, "Hold your hands up where I can see them."

Immediately, he raised both arms. Above his head in his right hand was a small metallic object. I said, "Drop that thing and turn away from me."

He opened his hand and the object fell to the ground.

As he turned his back to me he said, "Mister, I can explain. Please don't shoot me."

"Don't move or I will."

I took a step closer to him, holding the shotgun level with my waist. His skinny frame flinched as the muzzle made contact with the small of his back. I took great pleasure in his obvious fear. Finally, here was a flesh-and-bones enemy. A small voice whispered: *Kill him! Kill him!* It was a sweet thought, and the growing force of it terrified me.

"Take exactly two steps forward," I said, "and don't try to run."

He did as I told him, which placed him about two yards in front of me as I knocked on the door. "Mary Jo, it's me. Open up."

The light on the wall above us came on, illuminating the man's back in crisp detail. The door latch clicked and Mary Jo opened the door, stepping aside as she did. I felt weak with relief at seeing her unharmed.

I said, "Baby, are you all right?"

She said, "Yes," and the naked fear in that single word renewed my fury.

I stared at the man's back, longing to shoot him, and said, "We're going to be just fine, baby. Now move to the other side of the studio and stand next to the wall. All the way over there where you'll be away from this guy."

When she reached the far wall, I said to the man, "You turn around real slow and follow me inside."

He turned, and I saw that he was Lester Fredricks, the bartender from the Nowhere Club. His face was swollen on the left side and his left eye was completely shut by the worst black eye I'd ever seen. His thin cotton shirt was soaked with sweat. After a quick glance at my face, he directed his attention to the business end of my shotgun.

"Come on, Lester, follow me one step at a time."

Once we were inside, I told Lester to close the door and to sit on the floor with his back against the wall. He grimaced with pain and let out a little grunt as he awkwardly stooped to the floor. Apparently, the rest of him was as sore as his eye.

I sat on a paint-splattered stool about ten feet in front of him with the shotgun on my lap, pointed at his head.

"What exactly were you up to, Lester?"

"I wanted to talk to you, Mr. Reed."

"You sure went about it in a strange way."

He swallowed and looked down.

"Why were you trying to get into my wife's studio?"

The right side of his face looked embarrassed. "I thought this was your house."

"You thought you were breaking into my house? Well, gee whiz, Lester, that's different."

Lester shifted his good eye from me to Mary Jo and back again.

I watched him in silence, basking in the burning rage I felt. For a week I had been fighting a sense of helplessness, a mixture of grief at Ernest B.'s death and my own impotent exposure to catastrophe. I'd been a sitting duck, completely at the mercy of circumstances beyond my control. Now, finally, with a tangible enemy before me, I felt an overwhelming urge to strike back.

I said, "Lester, you were going to rape my wife, weren't you?" Mary Jo sucked in her breath across the room.

"No sir! Look at me. I'm in no shape for that kind of thing. I couldn't even do it with a willin' woman right now."

"Well, Lester, that's how it looked to me. You were going to rape her, and I was lucky enough to walk in and catch you at it, and I had to shoot you in the face to keep you from killing us both."

Mary Jo tried to interrupt, but I said, "Leave this to me, Mary Jo," without looking away from Lester.

He began to shake. Maybe it was the cold of the concrete slab. More likely it was the shotgun barrel I held level with his face. I felt split in two, half of me taking great pleasure in his pain and fear, the other half feeling removed from my actions, afraid of them, knowing I was doing wrong. It was a distant knowledge, and the strength of it faded fast in the heat of my angry desire for revenge.

"Mr. Reed, you just got to believe me, I wouldn't do a thing like that. I wouldn't."

"Well, that's how it's going to be when I explain it to Sheriff Barker. I had to shoot you in defense of my wife. That is, unless you quit screwing around and tell me exactly what you were doing here tonight."

"I will, I will. Just give me a second to get myself together."

His voice faded away as he stared at the gun. When he didn't keep talking I said, "Lester, I'm getting mad."

"Okay, okay. I wanted to talk to you about the other day."

"You mean when we talked at the bar?"

"Yeah. I got to tell you about that."

There was another long pause as he gathered his thoughts. Finally, he nodded as if a decision had been made and said, "I got to tell you it ain't true, what I told you before."

"What isn't true?"

"That stuff about Ernest B. usin' dope." He glanced away from the shotgun, at my face, then quickly back at the gun. "Ain't true, that's all."

I looked at Mary Jo. She shrugged.

"Lester, why would you lie to me about Ernest B.?"

"You was givin' me twenties to tell you what you wanted to hear. I didn't think there'd be no harm in it."

"It still doesn't explain why you were trying to break in here tonight. I need an answer, Lester, or I'm going to have to save Mary Jo's honor, you know what I mean?"

Still looking at the shotgun, he said, "Yeah. Well, I was over here, goin' to try to talk to you, and I saw this place. Thought it was your place."

"You already said that."

"Well, it seemed like no one was home, so I thought I'd go inside and leave you a note."

I laughed. "You were going to say what? 'Hi folks, just broke in to tell you I was lying to you the other day. Sorry I missed you?'"

His gaze shifted to the floor. "Yeah. Something like that."

Rage boiled within me. There was no longer a division in my mind. I knew what I wanted to do. "Oh, come on, Lester! You think I'm stupid? You were going to rape my wife. You knew she was here alone, and you thought you'd have some fun. I think I'm going to shoot you after all."

"No! It's the truth! I swear it!"

"Well, if that's the best you can do . . ." I lifted the shotgun and aimed at his head. All I could think about was how much I hated him.

Mary Jo screamed, "Garr!"

"Mary Jo, you stay out of this!"

"Ask him about his face."

I lowered the gun a little and said, "Yeah, Lester, what about that shiner? Where'd you get that?"

"Nowhere."

"Nowhere? Lester—"

"At the club. The Nowhere Club."

"Who did it?"

He rolled his good eye, showing the white like a beaten dog. His voice rose an octave, pure terror tightening his vocal chords to a higher pitch. "Ain't gonna talk about that. You can kill me here an' now, be better all around than if I was to talk about that."

Very quietly I said, "Oh, Lester. I think you'd better answer my question. Because I will kill you. Sure as I'm sitting here, I will blow your head clean off your shoulders."

He looked at my eyes and saw the truth there. Something shifted in Lester Fredricks then. Perhaps, faced with a choice of death here and now, or a horror if he talked that I could only guess at, he realized he had no hope at all. The knowledge gave him a strange kind of courage. With his eyes locked on mine, he said, "You ain't got the guts."

Whatever its source, his newfound courage released the demon of insane rage within me. I raised the shotgun again and stood to brace myself. I was going to kill him. I felt led to do it. I would enjoy it. The mere thought of it was filled with sickly sweet promises of pleasure. Lester crossed his hands in front of his face and tightly shut his good eye.

Mary Jo screamed. "Stop, Garr!"

Without taking my eyes away from Lester I said, "Mary Jo, God only knows what this animal had in mind. He—"

She pleaded with me. "He's not an animal! You can't do this, Garr. Look how scared he is. Please, baby, don't do this. Please. For my sake." She began to cry with complete abandon, loudly sobbing and gulping for air.

Her tears penetrated my fury more than her words. I might have spared Lester's life, or I might have murdered him. I'll never know. As I stood over him trying to decide, I heard the sound of something tapping on the window. I turned at the hip, keeping the shotgun aimed at Lester.

Jimmy Wilson, the sheriff's deputy, stood outside the glass with his revolver aimed at me. He shook his head and motioned for me to lower the shotgun, which I did. Lester still had his eyes closed and missed it all.

The deputy disappeared from view for a moment, then stepped through the door into the studio. His revolver was still in his hand, but he held it pointed at the floor. He looked crisp and cool, in spite of the heat outside. He said, "I saw you go tearin' out of your house with a shotgun and decided I ought to come see if you were all right. What's going on here, Mr. Reed?"

"I caught this guy trying to break in here where Mary Jo was. He was just going to tell me what he was up to, then we were going to call you guys."

Jimmy looked at Lester, who was still shaking on the floor. "I see. Well I'm here now, so you'd better set that shotgun down over here next to me, all right?"

I nodded and walked over to lean the gun against the wall, shaking now in the aftermath of my rage. Mary Jo was still sobbing quietly. She wouldn't look at me. The deputy turned to Lester and asked, "What he said true?"

"'Course not. I wasn't goin' to break in here. I just came by for a talk and this crazy man's been threatening to kill me. You ought to lock him up." Lester shook his head and muttered, "Man's crazy. Crazy."

Jimmy looked at me with his eyebrows raised, "Well?"

"Look outside the door on the ground. He dropped something when I caught him trying to get in."

Jimmy thought about it, then said, "Either one of you two moves from where you are, I'll shoot, understand?"

I said, "Okay." Lester just nodded.

The Deputy backed to the door and opened it without taking his eyes from the room. The shotgun was against the wall beside the door. He glanced at me, then grabbed the weapon with his free hand before stepping outside.

In half a minute he was back. "Lester, you drop this?" he asked. He was holding a pencil with something dangling from the end of it that looked like a key chain.

"Never saw it before."

"It's a set of lock picks, Lester. Sure you didn't lose it?"

Lester just shook his head.

Jimmy stared at the lock picks a moment, then seemed to make a decision. "Tell you what, Lester, it's two people's word against one here, so I'm goin' to have to take you in. We'll check this thing for fingerprints, and see what we can see."

Lester seemed pleased to be under arrest. The deputy gave the skinny man a hand up, then made him lean against the wall with his feet spread while he patted him down. Lester's blue jeans were wet with urine. He rolled his single frightened eye at me while Jimmy stood behind him, handcuffing his wrists together. The lawman began to read Lester his rights as he led him toward the door.

"Deputy, do you need me to come along?" I asked.

"Yes, sir, if you could. I'll just walk him on out to the car and wait for you there. You might want to drive around and meet me. I'm parked out front of your house."

"I know where you're parked."

He smiled sheepishly and said, "Yeah, I thought you might."

• • •

MARY JO AND I WALKED ALONG THE PATH toward the house. She looked straight ahead and said, "You scared me back there."

"Wasn't trying to scare you. Wanted to scare him."

"Well it worked—on both of us." She paused, then said, "You were really going to shoot him, weren't you?"

"Just for a second. Yes."

We continued along the path in the darkness, my arm around her shoulders, my other hand holding the shotgun.

The frogs and the crickets were singing again. She looked up at me, her red-rimmed eyes searching my face for something. I looked away. She said, "Garr, you know that little man wasn't there to hurt me."

"How exactly would I know that?"

She flinched, as if she'd been struck. It had been a long time since I'd spoken to her in that way. I removed my arm from around her shoulders and walked on in painful silence, wrestling with a jumbled mess of conflicting emotions. I had saved her life—perhaps—and she didn't seem to care. Of course, it was just as true that she had saved me from—something. Part of me felt relief, even as I struggled with vague self-recrimination. Part of me was angry with her for trying to save Lester's life and rob me of my revenge.

No. That's not true.

I was angry because she had proven herself to be stronger than I, keeping her head while I teetered on the brink of moral oblivion. I was angry not because she had saved me, but because I had needed to be saved, because I couldn't subdue my rage and handle my problems alone.

Mary Jo's soft hand slipped into mine and she spoke quietly, "Garr, honey, I think I know what you've been going through. You're feeling hurt about Ernest B., and you're angry. But you've got to let the Lord handle this, baby. You can't deal with it alone. Look what it's doing to you—almost driving you to shoot that poor man."

Anger rose within me at her expression of sympathy for Lester Fredricks. Clenching my jaw, I kept my feelings to myself as Mary Jo went on talking.

"Maybe I'm not doing my part. I don't know, maybe I'm not being a help to you. I'm sorry for that. But I think you need something I can't give, Garr." She paused, then said, "Have you prayed about this anger you feel?"

I remained silent.

After a few more steps, Mary Jo said, "We could pray together if you want to. Would you like to do that?"

I said, "If you think it will help."

She stopped, pulling at my hand. "If I think it will help? Garr, don't *you* think it will help?"

"I don't know. Maybe."

I saw pain and perhaps a touch of anger in my wife's upturned, moonlit face. "You don't *know*? How can you say that? What's happening to you? What's happening to your faith?"

A longing rose within me to share her simple conviction that God would deal with the trouble in our lives. I was hurting her. I was hurting myself. Years of Sunday sermons had taught me the Christian's path to God: believe you are a sinner, believe Christ was God on earth who died for your sins, believe his Holy Spirit still lives today, abandon your will to his, and his Spirit will enter your life and guide you and—

—And I just could not buy it. I never could. It sounded so simplistic. So glib. Perhaps if my problem was a mere bogeyman hiding beneath the bed, such a childish concept would make some sense. But my dilemma seemed so complicated, so multi-faceted, that I couldn't wrap my mind around it, much less sum up the solution in a simple, single formula.

When Mary Jo spoke again, it was with an edge of impatience. "What's going on, Garr? Something is happening to you. I can see that. Why won't you tell me what it is?"

I opened my mouth to speak, but fear had stolen my voice. After all these years of lies and pretense in church and at home, how could I explain to Mary Jo without losing her?

She saw my hesitation. "Garr, you've got to tell me. Let me help."

I nodded and squeezed her hand. We walked on awkwardly as I searched for the courage to tell her the truth. Maybe she was right. Nobody else knew me as she did. If anyone could help me to sort through these terrible raging temptations, she could. I was drowning in something I didn't understand. But if I exposed the truth of my spiritual battle, would she be able to reach through the pain of the lies to save me?

It was worth the chance.

I took a deep, shuddering breath, filled with fear at the risk, but sure at last that my only hope lay in confessing the truth. My mouth was actually open to speak, when we heard the muffled sound of a man shouting something through the woods. The sound repeated itself, then we heard a shot.

"That came from the road," I said. "Go inside and call the sheriff's office. Now!"

I turned to run toward the deputy's car. Mary Jo screamed, "Garr! Be careful!"

"Just call the sheriff!"

When I reached the road, I saw the silhouette of Deputy Wilson standing motionless beside his cruiser. I approached him slowly, careful to keep the shotgun pointed at the ground. As I neared, I could make out the crumpled shape of Lester Fredricks lying on the asphalt at Jimmy's feet. He was curled in a fetal position, his hands clutching at a deep red stain spreading across his chest.

"He was a crazy man." Jimmy said. "Why would he try to fight me like that?"

"Jimmy, is he alive?"

He looked at me. In the twilight, I thought I saw torment in his eyes. "I had to shoot him, Mr. Reed. He tried for my gun, and he got ahold of it for a second, and we fought, and—oh my dear sweet Jesus!" He turned away from me and fell against the side of his cruiser, sobbing and beating the metal car top with his fists.

I knelt next to Lester and felt his neck for a pulse, knowing it was useless.

CHAPTER 20

MARY JO JOINED JIMMY AND ME, and the three of us waited by the roadside in miserable silence. The distant wail of sirens reached us several minutes before the black-and-white cruisers came roaring up our road, their revolving lights flashing in the night. A strong impulse to run and hide came over me at the sight of so many policemen approaching. I was beginning to think of the law as my enemy.

The patrol cars pulled to the shoulder with brakes squealing and gravel flying. Barker stepped from the lead cruiser and marched to Lester's body without a word to anyone. He stood with his back to us, hands on his hips, boots spread a little, looking down at the corpse with his gray Stetson pushed back on his head. The emergency lights on the patrol cars cast alternating flashes of red and blue on Barker, his deputies, the wall of trees on either side of the road, and on the dead man lying near the ditch.

"Shouldn't we cover him?" asked Mary Jo.

Barker answered her without turning. "Not until we're through checking the area for evidence. Got to document how things happened here, keep the namby-pamby A.C.L.U. off our backs." His voice was strange, as if he was thinking out loud.

Beside me, Jimmy stared into the woods like a zombie, deep in shock, the limp muscles of his face forming a surreal mask in the flashing lights.

"Clyde, someone ought to take care of Jimmy here," I said.

He turned and seemed to notice us for the first time. He looked annoyed at the sight of Jimmy's flaccid expression. With a clipped command, he ordered one of the deputies to take him to the hospital. Other deputies began measuring and photographing the area around Lester's body. I hadn't realized Barker had so many men.

While the camera flashed, the sheriff took me a few yards up the road to ask for my story. I told him almost everything I knew, beginning with Mary Jo's phone call from the studio. I left out my interview technique with Lester.

The sheriff listened closely, nodding his head occasionally and prompting me with short questions. Standing so near to him, I remembered he was a little man. It was surprising. He had grown to larger proportions in my mind. His eyes narrowed and he looked up at me with an expression of condescending distaste as I described Jimmy's breakdown after shooting Lester. Neither of us mentioned our earlier conversation on the front porch.

After I finished, he told me to walk back to the car and tell Mary Jo he'd like to speak to her.

Sitting on the trunk of Jimmy's cruiser, watching Barker and Mary Jo in close conversation, I thought about what had almost happened in the studio. The impulse to kill Lester had erupted from some ancient place at my core, a Neanderthal response to the constant pressure of the last few days. I was under attack, and facing Lester with a shotgun had been my first real chance to fight back. It was tempting to tell myself I had only used the momentum of the situation to get information from him, but I knew better. Watching him squirm on the studio floor had given me pleasure. For the first time since this whole thing had begun, I could reach my enemy and extract a cost for what I was going through. It had been a partial fulfillment of the sickly sweet fantasy I had enjoyed since the morning I found Ernest B.'s corpse.

But now that Lester Fredricks lay on the asphalt with a fist-sized hole where his heart ought to be, the fantasy had mutated into a dull sense of shame.

Although Jimmy was the one chosen by fate to end Lester's life, I could just as easily have pulled the trigger. It was hard to shake the thought that I was to blame somehow. I wanted to kill him—now he was dead. Was it cause and effect?

Mary Jo was speaking forcefully now, waving her hands to stress a point. If only I had her faith, I could close my eyes and ask God for forgiveness, for moral strength. But I didn't have Mary Jo's faith. How could I?

A small voice whispered that I already knew the way. Confession, both to her and to God, was the obvious first step. I longed to take it. I longed for absolution, for delivery from the shame, and an end to the lies. But would Mary Jo forgive me?

Would God?

Jesus Christ himself said that a person who enjoys sinful fantasies is as much at fault as a person who actually commits the sin. I had fantasized a murder, been on the verge of doing it, reveled in the thought of it, and been stopped only by Mary Jo's intervention. Was I not then a murderer in God's eyes?

To pray was out of the question. I was unworthy. I was alone.

• • •

BARKER'S ROADSIDE CHAT WITH MARY JO lasted about five minutes. He spent another few minutes in quiet conversation with one of his men, then he asked me and Mary Jo to follow him into town to make formal statements.

In his office, he interviewed us separately again, as he had on the road in front of our house. The only difference was a stenographer in the corner, recording every word.

He was very polite as I retold my story, saying "please" and "thank you" and calling me "Mr. Reed" for the record. The stenographer's fingers beat a steady clicking rhythm on the keys behind me. My remark that his deputy "just happened to be parked in front of our house" brought a small smile, but no response. My description of Lester's bruised face caused him to frown, but again, he made no comment. It was all very proper.

While Mary Jo was in Barker's office repeating her story, I sat in the waiting area outside. The wasp I'd seen the day Dr. Krueger almost knocked me down the courthouse steps was still beating its head against the yellowed plaster ceiling. I wondered why the sheriff hadn't asked me about Dr. Krueger. His comment when we spoke on my front porch left little room for doubt that he knew I was at the hospital the night Krueger died. And something else Barker said on the porch was picking at my subconscious. Something that didn't fit . . .

I was on the verge of remembering when Mary Jo and the sheriff emerged from his office and Barker sent us away with an admonishment to be careful. It sounded false coming from him.

• • •

I DROPPED MARY JO OFF AT HOME AND WENT for a drive. I could tell she wanted me to stay with her, but I felt a strong need to push harder against the opposition, to hang on to the momentum I had begun by questioning Lester Fredricks at gunpoint. I told myself the deputies out on the road would keep her safe. I told myself she'd understand.

After winding aimlessly along dark country roads for an hour or so, trying to come up with a plan, I pulled onto the gravel parking lot at the Nowhere Club. It was a humid night. A pink neon sign on the low sloping roof crackled as blue arcs of electricity leaped from tube to tube. A modern country and western song seeped out of the roadhouse through the open door, sounding whiney and nasal and silly after what I'd been through. Seems like most of the new music out of Nashville is about some idiot who's cheating on his wife or wishes he was. It gets old. There's far too much of that kind of thing in real life. I prefer the old ones: Tubbs and Cline and Wills and Williams. Their music touched on the low side of everyday experience, but they also painted beautiful pictures with their words. They didn't ignore true love or the beauty of a woman or the joy of being alive.

As I rolled up the truck window and set the brake, I shook my head at the irony. Would I ever rediscover the joy of being alive?

I recognized a few of the men inside. They were day laborers for Reed Construction, spending what was left of last week's paycheck. A couple was kissing passionately in front of the jukebox next to the door. Knife-thin layers of cigarette smoke hovered around the drunks at the bar like spoiled milk drifting through a shark pool.

I pushed between two men who sat at the bar with their backs to each other. They ignored me. Behind the bar, Victor Sickle ignored me too. He was leaning on an ice bin, absorbed in earnest conversation with a buxom redhead several seats away. She wore a low-cut blouse with dozens of tiny sparkling mirrors sewn into the fabric. Even in the dim light, her makeup didn't quite conceal the crow's feet and frown lines on her face, but she made up for it with impressive posture, her back well arched and chest held high.

After a couple of tries, I got Sickle's attention. He walked over to take my order with obvious annoyance. The redhead turned to a man next to her for a light.

Victor Sickle said, "Hey. How ya doin? Man, you shouldn't of run off like that yesterday. Left me sittin' there all alone. Wasn't nice."

"I'm back now."

"Yeah. I can see that." Sickle turned to the right, putting his eyes back on the redhead. "What'll it be?"

"A draw," I said.

As he pulled the beer tap, I looked down the bar. The busty woman was laughing and touching the man next to her on the shoulder with every other word. Sickle brought my mug to me. It looked tiny in his fist.

"Dollar fifty," he said.

I held a five out. When he grabbed it, I hung on to get his attention. It worked. His dark brows knitted together and his empty eyes glared at me. Neon light from a turquoise beer sign gleamed in his oily black hair like the bluish sheen of a crow's feathers.

"Don't be cute, buddy," he said. "Just gimme the money."

I spoke very softly, "Lester Fredricks is dead."

He couldn't hear me over the jukebox, so he leaned over the bar a little. I got a whiff of Brylcreem.

"What'cha say?"

"Lester Fredricks got himself shot tonight. He's dead."

The annoyance in his eyes was immediately replaced by a mask of neutrality. I released the five. Victor Sickle gave me a long look, then he asked, "You shoot him?"

"No."

He nodded and turned to the cash register. His broad shoulders pushed at the seams of his western-cut shirt with every move. He wore a wide leather belt with "Victor" etched on the back.

When he handed me my change, I saw that his huge knuckles were cut and bruised.

I said, "Lester's face was pretty beat up."

"No kidding? Hey. That's too bad, Mr. Reed. But you know, people should watch who they fool with." He turned toward the redhead.

"You own part of this place?"

"No way. This dive is Old Man Martin's. I just tend bar now and then."

"You tend bar at the Easy Money too?"

That got another hard look. The same look I got when the giant pointed me out to him in Deep Ellum the night before. It took him a moment to decide how to play it, then he said, "No way," again and glanced toward the redhead.

"Lester said he had a fight with someone here at this bar."

"He called it a fight, huh?" Immediately, his eyebrows creased again. He hadn't meant to say that. "Look, you want another beer, just ask. Otherwise, I'm real sorry about Lester and all, but I'm too busy to sit around talkin'."

He returned to his position across from the redhead, who ignored him.

• • •

THE PICKUPS ON THE GRAVEL PARKING LOT began to thin out about twelve. By two in the morning there was just one car still parked outside the bar, a dark blue Camaro.

I waited in my truck until three-thirty, struggling to stay awake in the muggy heat. Suddenly, the crackling neon sign went dead. A few minutes later, Sickle came out with the redhead leaning heavily against him. She shuffled along on wobbly high heels like a drunken sailor in drag. Sickle helped her into the Camaro and gave my truck a long stare before he got into the car.

As they pulled out of the parking lot, the Camaro's rear wheels spun, throwing gravel against my windshield. I pulled out behind them onto the road out of town.

Sickle didn't want my company. He drove very fast. We touched ninety once or twice on the straightaways, slowing only at the sharper curves. He led me north, over the Big Muddy bridge and then east on the road that passes my house as it winds along next to Martin Pool.

After driving the length of the lake, he took a turn to the south and we sped onto the dam. The Camaro slowed and stopped about halfway across, next to the roaring spillway overflow. I stopped about a hundred yards behind him. Mist from the pounding flood of the spillway drifted across the road between us, partially obscuring Sickle's car. His taillights were ringed by red halos in the lacy vapor. To my right, the reflections of boathouse lights shimmered along the waterline below. The mirror-smooth lake twinkled under the stars. Tall pines sliced a jagged line of pitch black out of the dark gray sky above the far shore. Beyond the treetops, distant lightning flashed silently in towering thunderheads, warning of another storm approaching.

We idled motionless on the dam for a minute or two, then the Camaro's white reverse lights flashed. The car began backing toward me very fast, weaving a little as it came. I calmly reached to the gun rack behind my seat and took down my shotgun, setting the stock on the floor with the barrel propped against the passenger door. I shifted into reverse. Then I turned, looking out of the rear window with my arm on the top of the seat, and stomped on the accelerator.

Victor Sickle chased me in reverse until we were off the dam and headed down the road through the woods. My pickup truck's gearbox whined like a spinning reel letting out line. I felt elated. I had Sickle hooked. Every few seconds, I looked back to see if the car was still following. He seemed to be losing ground. I slowed a little, playing him in.

The chase ended abruptly. Sickle miscalculated a slight bend in the road. Oversteering, he backed into the bar ditch at about twenty miles an hour and slammed hard into the opposite bank. He was stuck.

I stopped in the middle of the road and considered the situation. Did I really want to go on with this? Things could get nasty, and I'd already almost murdered somebody tonight. But I was finally taking the initiative, and after the frustration of the past several days, it felt good. I had forced Sickle to react, instead of reacting myself. I was fool enough to think I was in control. The temptation to keep the pressure on was too strong to resist.

I put the truck in gear and drove toward the car very slowly.

His lights were still on, but his motor had died, possibly because his tailpipe had been buried in the mud. The car was tilted at a fairly steep angle, bridging the bar ditch with the passenger side leaning down. The driver's side door was three feet off of the ground. The radiator ticked as it cooled. Tall trees lined the ditch, blocking most of the moonlight. I was barely able to see the outline of a head leaning against the steering wheel.

I stepped from the truck with the shotgun in my hands, aimed at the car.

Mud sucked at my boots as I slid down the side of the ditch to the driver's side door. I could see Sickle through the window. His head was propped up by the steering wheel. Blood trickled across his temple. His eyes were closed. The woman was slumped halfway down to the floor on her side, wedged between the seat and the dash. Her legs were spread at odd angles. A streak of moonlight fell across the smeared red lipstick on her face.

It was difficult to open the car door because of the embankment, but I managed. The car's dome light glowed and a little electronic tinging sound began to go off every two seconds. Sickle didn't stir. I pushed him back against the seat and felt his neck—something I was getting rather good at. His pulse was strong and steady. I reached across his lap and felt for the woman's pulse. It was irregular, but I guessed that was from the alcohol in her system.

On the floor between Sickle's small silver-tipped cowboy boots was a revolver. I picked it up with my left hand and flung it into the woods. I squatted to look under the seat. A brown paper bag was rolled up tight and wedged between the metal supports.

Something bumped against my leg. I stood quickly. It was a huge bullfrog. My movement startled him, and he jumped again, landing with a loud splash in some standing water a few feet away.

A breeze stirred the treetops. The air was getting cooler, charged with static electricity. The storm was coming.

Taking care to keep my gun dry, I squatted again and pulled out the paper bag. Inside it was another bag of clear plastic filled with white powder. Thinking of fingerprints, I was careful not to touch the plastic. I rolled the bag back up, and thought about what to do next. The water seeped into my boots.

Between the Camaro's bucket seats was a console storage compartment. I leaned across Sickle again and lifted the lid. Inside were about a dozen cassette tapes. I grabbed a handful of them and flipped them onto the floor of the car. Then I jammed the paper bag into the compartment and left the lid up.

With the car door hanging open behind me, I climbed back up the side of the ditch to my truck. It was only about two miles to my house. The first giant raindrops hit the windshield as I cruised slowly past the patrol car out front and pulled into the driveway. It was pouring as I ran to the front door hopping on one leg. I tugged off my muddy boots on the front porch, then rushed inside to the telephone in the den.

After two rings, a man answered, "Sheriff's Department." His voice was familiar.

"I want to report an accident."

"Who's calling, please?"

A massive crack of thunder shook the window pane. I thought of the call I had made a week ago, reporting the body I'd found on Old Man Martin's stringer. Why hadn't I told them who I was? Maybe I wouldn't be in this mess if I'd told them.

"Who's calling, please?"

I said, "That doesn't matter. You'd better send an ambulance up to the Martin Pool loop road, near the north end of the dam. There's a car in the ditch, and it looks like the people in it are hurt."

There was a moment of muffled conversation, as if the man was holding his hand over the mouthpiece, and then he said, "All right, sir, we're calling the hospital right now. We really need your name for our records, if you wouldn't mind."

"I'm sorry, I don't want to get involved," I said. Same thing I'd told them the other time. "I'd check that car for booze or drugs if I was you, the way they were driving."

I hung up without waiting for a reply. The window pane rattled again with a crack of thunder, right outside. The storm had arrived.

CHAPTER 21

AT NINE THE NEXT MORNING I WAS sitting in the job trailer, trying to function on three hours of sleep while Leon complained about the weather, the engineers, and deadlines.

"We're gonna have to carry the concrete down in buckets and do our digging with shovels, for cryin' out loud. It'll take weeks!"

He looked at me expectantly. When I didn't respond with outrage at the unreasonable demands placed upon him by the county engineers, he said, "Garr, what's wrong? You act like you got a lot on your mind."

I sighed and stared out the fly-specked window at the scarred red earth of the construction site. A diesel backhoe rumbled by, rattling the thin trailer walls.

"You might as well know, Leon. Clyde Barker seems to think I murdered Ernest B. He's had me followed, had my house searched, seized our bank records, and questioned me a couple of times."

Leon looked at me with his mouth open. I went on, telling him about Ernest B.'s drug problem and my theories that they were somehow tied into his murder. Finally I said, "Last night, this guy showed up at Mary Jo's studio, trying to break in. I caught him redhanded. When a deputy tried to haul him off, the guy fought him and the deputy had to use his gun. The guy's dead."

Leon continued to stare at me without speaking.

I said, "Leon, don't tell anyone about this next part, okay?"

"There's more?"

"Well, the dead guy worked at the Nowhere Club. He's the one that told me Ernest B. was using cocaine. He'd already been beat up pretty good when he came to our place, but he wouldn't talk about that. Something he said made me think I might be able to find out why he was breaking into Mary Jo's studio if I asked around the bar. So I went there and sure enough, the bartender, this guy named Sickle, Victor Sickle, had busted up his knuckles pretty good."

"Garr, that's a bad, bad place. You shouldn't ought to go over there alone asking personal questions."

"Yeah. Well, I ended up following this Sickle character when he left for the night. One thing led to another, and he sort of ended up passed out, with his car stuck in a ditch."

Leon grinned. "One thing led to another, huh?"

"That's right. And when I searched the guy's car—"

"You what?"

"Let me finish, Leon. When I searched the car I found a big bag of cocaine or heroin or something, so I called the cops and told them to check it out."

"I'm surprised they didn't bust you."

"I didn't give them my name."

He thought about it in silence for a while, then said, "Garr, you run around chasin' drug pushers and investigatin' murders, you're gonna need someone to watch your back. Next time, you call me."

"You don't want to get mixed up in this stuff, Leon. People are getting killed." I took a deep breath, then told him about Dr. Krueger.

"You think someone killed the doctor?" he asked.

"I don't believe he drank himself to death in the hospital morgue, that's for sure."

Leon leaned back in his chair with a thoughtful look. "I read in the paper yesterday that he had a heart attack from drinkin' too much."

"Interesting timing."

"Yeah, I guess. Hey! That reminds me—there was another article in this mornin's paper."

While Leon rummaged around on the desk for the *Herald,* someone laughed loudly outside the trailer. Then another voice joined the laughter. Leon stood and looked out of the window. "Man, oh man. It sure is gettin' hard to keep those guys from screwin' around all the time. I'll be right back, Garr. Got to go kick a few rear ends."

I followed Leon outside. A group of men were standing together near the parking area. There was a panel truck nearby. "Martinez Kennel and Dog Training" was painted on the truck in sloppy black letters. The men had formed a circle next to the truck, like football players in a huddle. When Leon and I approached, they stood aside.

Crouched at the center of the group was a young Latino man, holding a very active puppy. Leon said, "Gilbert, what in the world are you doin'?"

The man was having a hard time maintaining his grip on the wiggling pup. "I got your dog here, Uncle Leon."

"You what?"

"That's a real bad guard dog you got there, Leon," said one of the nearby men. The others laughed.

Gilbert repeated, "I got that dog you asked for. Ain't he somethin'? Frisky little guy." The little puppy was licking his hands.

"Gilbert, I said I need a guard dog." The workmen laughed again. Leon gave them a dirty look.

The young man said, "I thought you wanted the puppy out here, and the guard dog in town at the office."

"No, I said we need the guard dog out here for our tool shack. We don't store nothin' valuable at the office."

Gilbert looked at the ground and shook his head, "I don't remember it that way, Uncle Leon. I really don't."

"You *know* I wanted you to drop the puppy off in town with Ethyl, and the bad dog out here." The men laughed louder. Raising his voice, Leon said, "Just put the puppy back in the truck and get the guard dog out here where we can see him!"

"Can't do that, Uncle Leon."

"Why not?"

"I already dropped the guard dog off at the office on the way out here."

The workmen howled and began slapping each other on the back.

Leon leaned over and grabbed Gilbert's shirt front with a callused hand. "Gilbert, you better not be sayin' what I think you're sayin'."

"I'm sorry, Uncle Leon. I thought you needed the protection in town."

Leon said, "Gilbert, I want you to think very carefully." The men continued to laugh. Leon turned to them and yelled,

"Shut up!" They immediately fell silent, their faces contorted with the effort of restraining their mirth. Leon turned back to his nephew, pulling a little on his shirt. "Was Ethyl there when you dropped off that dog?"

"Who's Ethyl, Uncle Leon?"

"Mrs. P.! Was she there?"

"No, Uncle Leon, I don't think so. I used the key you gave me and let myself in, and just left the dog there in the front room like you said."

"I *told* you to leave the *puppy* in the front room, you idiot!" Leon went on yelling in Spanish as he pushed his nephew away and ran for the parking area. The workmen burst out laughing again. I ran after Leon yelling, "Hold on, Leon! I'll ride in with you!"

As we pulled onto the road one of the men hollered, "I hope Mrs. P. don't kill that dog!"

"I'm gonna fire whoever said that," grumbled Leon.

As we hurried toward town, I buckled my seatbelt and braced my legs firmly against the floorboard. Leon was a lousy driver at the best of times. Since he was in a hurry, we were all over the highway.

I said, "Watch the road, Leon."

Leon looked over at me and said, "I just thought of something." The truck started to veer toward the bar ditch.

"Watch the road, Leon!"

"Really. This is something you oughta know, Garr."

"All right. What?"

"Remember in the trailer I was gettin' ready to tell you 'bout an article I read in the *Herald* this morning?"

"Yeah?"

"It was about a hit-and-run accident last night."

He looked at me and we headed for the ditch again.

"Leon!"

We were entering Mt. Sinai. An old green station wagon inched out from an intersection in front of us. Leon sped up. My grip tightened on the dashboard. We roared in front of the station wagon with an inch to spare.

"Leon."

"Yeah, boss?"

"They called it a hit-and-run?"

"Yessir."

"Did the paper describe the car that got hit?"

"Said it was a Camaro, I think."

We took a turn too fast and Leon locked the brakes. The truck began a sideways slide, but he recovered in time. As I steadied myself against the door I said, "Was there any mention of drugs being involved?"

"Nope."

"Did they describe the other car?"

"Yessir. Said it was a white pickup truck with a gun rack in the rear window and some writin' on the door."

"Oh, boy."

"Yessir."

We sped on into town in our white pickup truck with the company name on the door.

• • •

ROTTWEILERS HAVE THE REPUTATION OF being one of the meanest, toughest, nastiest, hardest-fighting dog breeds there are.

And then there's Mrs. P.

When Leon and I came around the courthouse plaza, we saw Mrs. P.'s pink Cadillac (bought second-hand from a bankrupt cosmetics saleslady) parked at the curb in front of the office. Leon pulled the truck to a stop beside it. Staring at the office door he said, "Garr, I can't go in there. Would you go on without me? Let me know when it's safe?"

"I thought you said you were going to back me up from now on, Leon."

"Yeah, against dope dealers and murderers. This is different."

"All right. But keep the motor running. We might have to get out of here in a hurry."

I opened the door and stepped out. Leaning back in for a second I said, "I'm serious about keeping it running, Leon."

He grinned and nodded.

I said, "Might need to get that dog to the veterinarian's real fast."

"You think she might hurt it?"

"We'll be lucky if she hasn't killed it with her bare hands."

"Uh, that might put her in a bad mood. You think?"

Staring at him, I said "Leon, you owe me big for this one."

"Anything you say. Just be sure Ethyl's settled down before you call me in."

When I slipped inside the office reception area, the first thing I noticed was a huge, drooling, brown-and-black hellhound. It squatted in Mrs. P.'s chair with its front paws resting on her desk. Its coal-black eyes locked onto mine. From where I stood, its teeth looked to be two feet long. There were at least a hundred of them. Tied around its bulging neck was a candy-striped ribbon and bow.

"Good doggie," I said.

"Grrr," said the dog.

Leaving the door open behind me for a hasty escape if necessary, I took a hesitant step toward the animal.

It said, “Grrr” again, a little louder, and bared its huge teeth.

I froze, deciding I might be more comfortable standing near the open door. I swallowed and said, “Mrs. P.?” My voice broke, so I tried again a little more forcefully. “Mrs. P.?”

The dog barked. Once. Loudly.

Mrs. P. called from somewhere in the back, “Garrison, I’m in here!”

“Are you all right?”

The massive animal barked again, raising its hackles.

Mrs. P. waddled into the front room from the hall with an aluminum pie pan in her chubby hands. In the pie pan was what appeared to be raw hamburger. She said, “Well, Garrison, what do you expect? ’Course I’m not all right. When did you ever know me to be all right?”

She hobbled up to the dog without hesitating and plopped the pie pan on the desk. The huge animal wiggled from head to tail with delight as she slapped it on the rump and said “Dig in, Fifi.”

I stared, fascinated. What had been a killing machine a moment before was now the very image of a domesticated lap dog. Its snout was deep in the pan of food. Its entire rear end wiggled from side to side as it tried to wag a tail that had been chopped off long ago.

I said, “Fifi?”

Mrs. P. looked at me with fire in her eyes. “You got a problem with that, Garrison?” The dog looked up at me and said, “Grrr.” Raw meat dangled from its fangs.

“No. No. No, Mrs. P. You call it—her—whatever, anything you want.”

She nodded her head. Her ample jowls rippled with the aftershock.

Fifi returned to her meal.

"Good," she said. "Now, when I showed up this morning, I was a little surprised to find Fifi here with a note from that fool Leon Martinez sayin' she was a present for me." She stroked the dog's back with her long, shocking pink fingernails. The dog stopped eating just long enough to turn and lick her hand. "I'll admit I was a little aggravated at first. He shouldn't oughta be givin' me stuff without askin' is it all right first." She looked at me to be sure I was paying attention. I nodded enthusiastically. She continued. "But after I thought about it, I decided that it took a real perceptive man to know how well Fifi and I was goin' to hit it off. A deep, soulful man."

I started to speak but she interrupted me, saying, "Shutup, Garrison. Let me finish."

The dog glanced up from the bloody meal and bared its fangs at me. I swallowed and nodded again. She continued, "Anyway, I been thinkin' 'bout it, and I got to tell you this: I'm goin' to be seein' Leon for a while, see how he works out. You might not like that idea much—"

I shook my head quickly and began to tell her it was fine with me if she wanted to see Leon, but she cut me off again.

"I said be quiet! I got somethin' to say and I'm gonna get it said!"

"Yes, ma'am."

"All right." She rubbed the hellhound's ears and said, "I was 'bout finished anyway. Just wanted to say that I'll be seein' Leon for a while, and you better not give me no grief about it."

She stood petting the dog and glaring at me. I waited to be sure she was finished. After a moment she said, "Well? What you got to say?"

I cleared my throat and said, "Mrs. P., if you and Leon want to date each other, that's your—"

"Date!" she yelled. The dog lifted its huge head and lunged toward me with hackles up and fangs bared. Only Mrs. P.'s pudgy hand on its ribbon collar stood between me and a couple of hundred stitches. Mrs. P. didn't seem to notice.

"I didn't say nothin' 'bout no date! I ain't no teenage girl, case you didn't notice. I got some miles on me." She looked down at her ample figure, smoothing her muumuu with her free hand and went on pensively, "'Course they easy, country miles."

"Well, Mrs. P., whatever you want to do, why don't you tell him right now? He's waiting out in the truck."

"Well, why didn't that fool come on in?" she said as she released her hold on the monster and waddled around the desk toward the door.

Fifi returned to her food, pushing the pan across the desk with her nose as she ate. Mrs. P. opened the front door, inhaled deeply (an impressive sight) and yelled, "Leon Martinez! Get in here!"

Outside, Leon opened the truck door and stepped onto the pavement, where he stood uncertainly, looking toward Mrs. P. She yelled, "Come on in here, Leon! I ain't goin' to bite. Least not right away."

Leon's face broke into a small, careful smile as he walked toward the office. I went outside to give the lovebirds some time alone, passing Leon on my way to the truck.

He whispered out of the side of his mouth, "What's goin' on?"

I said, "Leon, it's your heart's desire."

When I got into the pickup truck and looked out through the windshield I saw Leon Martinez, all five foot seven of him, engulfed in the embrace of Ethyl Polanski's huge wiggling arms. He was smiling from ear to ear.

Love is strange.

CHAPTER 22

I DECIDED TO WAIT FOR LEON AT Pedro's cafe, took a table in front next to the window, and ordered a cup of coffee, black. A middle-aged daughter and her elderly mother strolled by, arm in arm, dressed like twin children in bright plaid cotton dresses and straw hats. Across the road, a man bent under the hood of an old pickup truck in the shade of one of the ancient plaza oaks. His truck was at least fifty years old, an Apache 31, with lots of bright chrome, streamlined fenders and bug-eyed headlights. If Bonnie and Clyde had stolen a truck, it might have been that model.

They came to our town, of course. Bonnie and Clyde tore through almost every east Texas and north Louisiana town on their murderous rampage. In Mt. Sinai, they chose to pretend they were benevolent. At a fruit stand just outside the city limits, they passed out ten-dollar bills to everyone present. Two towns farther down the road, they killed a farmer and his nineteen-year-old son. Nobody ever knew why.

And now I had almost killed—would have killed, if not for the turn of events that had left it up to Jimmy Wilson to pull the trigger. The thought left me strangely numb, as if an organ had been removed and the anesthetic had not yet faded. Perhaps it was my heart I had lost.

My thoughts drifted to cosmic things: heaven and hell, the nature of good and evil. How did I fit into the world in my newly adopted role? Had everything changed? I was different. Was the whole world different? I was confused, disoriented, but I knew one thing for sure: I was alone in a private hell, and I wanted out.

I was ready to reach out to God, if I could somehow believe that things really were that simple. I would trade my pride for relief from this emptiness in a second.

But too many doubts remained. If there was a God, would he really be involved with the human race? Would he involve himself with me, a single organism among the trillions here on earth? Because, if there was truly a God, a creator of the universe, then he (or she or it) would have created not just me, a speck on the surface of an insignificant planet in a solar system among millions within the galaxy, but all the millions of other galaxies. If there was a God, what laughable audacity to believe that such power and omnipotence would concern itself with me.

Pedro brought over my coffee.

He said, "Hey, *compadre*, you not lookin' so hot."

"Didn't get much sleep last night."

He sat across from me and began to fiddle with a stainless steel butter knife, twisting it and watching it spin on the table top. "I heard about ol' Lester. That was a shame."

"Yes."

"An' I'm sorry as I can be that it had to happen to you and Mary Jo."

I looked up at him, surprised. Pedro was the first person who seemed to understand that I felt as if I'd lost a piece of myself. I hadn't really understood it either, until his expression of sympathy made it real. I *had* lost something. Something important.

He continued to spin the knife and said, "I lit that candle for you last Sunday, like I said I would. Maybe things'll start lookin' up now."

"I appreciate that, Pedro."

"It's okay."

We sat without speaking for a while, as old friends will. Then I asked, "Do you really believe in God?"

"Whoa! Where'd that come from?"

I said, "I've been doing a lot of thinking lately. You know. With Ernest B. dying and all. So do you? Do you believe in God?"

He looked away, avoiding my eyes. "Yes. Of course I do."

"Why?"

"That's a fool question, Garr. Just get in your truck an' drive around. Look at the trees and the grass. The birds and the whitetail."

"So God made it all?"

"Who else?"

"What about evolution?"

"What about it?"

"Some people think we come from apes."

"You're missin' the point. Don't matter if we come from apes or dogs or my Great Aunt Esperanza. What if we did? They come from somewhere, don't they? Where they come from?"

"I don't know. A black hole or something exploding out in space. Maybe something like that."

"Where'd the hole come from?"

I considered his point for a moment, then said, "Okay, so maybe there's a something that's beyond time, or older than time, or whatever—however you want to put it. Older than black holes, even. But is it God? What I mean by God is something that has logic, something that makes plans. You know, something that's involved in the world."

"Sure. Ain't that what everybody means?"

"But just because something must have been here first—"

"It had to be here always, Garr."

"All right. Always. Just because it's been here always doesn't mean it's got a plan. What if it's a huge, mindless thing that accidentally set the universe in motion, just by being around? What if everything that's happened ever since has been just one accident after another?"

"Impossible."

"Why?"

"There's no such thing as accidents, that's why. See, it's like—well, it's a little bit like spinnin' this knife. Maybe it'll point at me when it stops. Maybe at you. There's no way to tell in advance, right? Pure chance, like roulette, right?"

"Sure."

"Nope. Wrong. Look, you're a bright fella. If you study it some, figure out which way the tabletop slants, how fast the ceiling fan pushes air through here, what the weight of the handle is and the weight of the blade, if you figure out a way to tell just how hard I'm gonna spin it, if you took the time to study all that, wouldn't you know which way it was gonna point? And couldn't you change one of those things to make it point any which way you wanted?"

"I suppose, with some really good tools and a couple of engineers you could predict it pretty well."

"You betcha."

"So you're saying there's no such thing as pure chance."

He snorted. "Of course not. There's reasons for what happens. Reasons you know and reasons you don't. But there's always a reason. And behind every reason is another reason. Never pure chance. The reasons just keep going back until you finally get to the single reason that started it all. Ain't no accidents, ever."

We sat in silence for a minute. I was thinking hard as he spun the knife, over and over. All my life, I'd wondered why people were so sure God exists. People talk about "feelings" and "just knowing." That wasn't good enough for me. I watched Pedro's gnarled fingers as they deftly twisted the knife like a child with a top. Pedro seemed to know there was a God, and his feelings didn't enter into it. He was right: there had to be something at the start of everything. And everything exists according to a set of rules. Maybe there *was* a God; something that cared about the world. If not, who invented the rules?

I said, "You've done a lot of thinking about this."

He raised his cloudy brown eyes to mine for a moment, then looked back down at the spinning knife. After a pause, he said, "It's important."

• • •

I DROVE BACK OUT TO THE CULVERT JOB SITE.

The previous night's thunderstorm had left the air thick with humidity and turned the freshly excavated soil on the job into steaming mush. Red clay clung to everything it touched, caking the tools, equipment, and workmen's boots with a soggy goo that doubled the effort required for every step or turn of a shovel. Still, we had deadlines to meet and no time to wait for the ground to dry.

After sloshing around for an hour or so, answering questions and doing my best to inspire the men to rise above the muddy conditions, I retreated into the job trailer to do a little paperwork. Sitting at the desk, I picked up a pencil, leaned forward until my head rested on a pile of papers, and fell asleep. When I awoke an hour later, I wiped the drool from my cheek and called the office to ask Leon to come take over so I could have a proper *siesta*.

A patrol car was parked in the usual place out front when I arrived at home. I rolled by it slowly enough to see that it was empty.

Mary Jo waited for me just inside the front door. She returned my hug without enthusiasm and quickly backed away.

She said, "I'm glad you're home. We need to talk."

I leaned down to kiss her forehead. "Can you forgive me for last night? I don't know what came over me."

"There's nothing to forgive. But I am a little confused."

"I might have shot him if it hadn't been for you."

"Let's not think about that."

We stood together silently, lost in our thoughts. I said, "I wish I had your strength."

"It doesn't come from me."

"Uh huh."

She stepped back to look up at my eyes. "Garr, you know we only have to ask for what we need."

"Oh, Mary Jo. Could we skip that?"

"Skip it?" She looked away from me for a moment, then, eyes on the floor, she said, "No. We've got to talk about this. Last night you said you weren't sure the Lord would help. It was as if you don't trust him anymore."

"That's not what I said."

"Don't split hairs! It came across that way. I need to know if it's true."

I considered lying. But I was tired of pretending for her. A lifetime of deception was abandoned in the impulse of an instant. Without thought for the enormity of the change that was upon us, I said, "All right. If you really want to talk about it, here it is: I think I do believe in God, Mary Jo. I'm just not sure he would concern himself with my problems."

She stared at me as if I had slapped her face. The color rose in her cheeks. Finally, she said, "Why are you doing this?"

"Doing what?"

"Don't play games! Why are you telling me this? Have I done something? Are you angry with me?"

I sighed. "No. Of course not. This has nothing to do with you. It's just . . . I just . . . I guess I just realized I don't really believe anymore, that's all." It was another lie, to hide the enormity of all the others.

She stood silently for a moment, her lower lip quivering, eyes still on the floor. Then she said, "I don't know what to say to you, Garr."

"Look, I'm sorry. It's just how I feel. I'd pretend to believe in God if it made you feel better. But don't you want me to be honest about this?"

"Yes. Of course."

"Sure you do. Besides, nothing's really changed between us, right? I mean, I'm still here. We're still together. We still love each other."

She looked up and said, "And God still loves you. That hasn't changed, either."

"Loves me? Why would he let these things happen to me if he loves me? Why would he let them kill Ernest B.?"

"You know the answer to that."

"I don't. I really don't."

She touched my arm and said, "Would you give me a lobotomy if that's what it took to keep me with you?"

"Oh, for crying out loud! What do lobotomies have to do with anything?"

"God wants you to be free, Garr. He wants you to come to him because you *want* to be with him, because you love him—not because you have no choice."

"Are you saying that God is doing these things to me because I'm playing hard to get?"

Ignoring my sarcasm, she said, "Of course not. I'm saying we set ourselves up for the pain of this world when we try to live without him. God doesn't inflict evil on us. He allows it to exist as an honest choice, the only alternative to goodness and love. Without it, we'd be like robots. We'd have no freedom."

I said, "Christians get cancer. Christians get murdered. What good is freedom if you suffer and die anyway?"

She leaned against the wall and looked away from me. When she spoke again, it was in a small, scared voice. She said, "I thought you believed in Christ, Garr. All these years, I thought we shared that part of our lives. How could you ... if you really don't ..." She covered her face with her hands.

When she looked up at me again, her lovely green eyes had welled with tears. She said, "I believe that we opened the door to evil in this world when the first person chose to try to live without the Lord. You say you might believe in God. Do you believe that God is love? I do. I believe that's what he *is*, understand? And every positive has a negative. Up, down. In, out. Hot, cold. So if you believe in God, you must believe there's something on the other side—something evil. Satan. The Devil. Negative energy. Call it whatever you like. All right?"

I nodded.

"So the world is divided. A battlefield. Ever since we first chose hate over love, there's been a war going on, and each of us must pick a side. There is no in-between. Choosing good over evil—God over Satan—doesn't get you out of the war, it just gets you on the right side."

"So God can't protect us and we suffer anyway? Is that what you're saying?"

"No! He *does* protect his people, but not by removing them from the battle! As long as there's one person out there who hasn't been given a choice, who doesn't know about Jesus, the war goes on, and we have to stay here and fight. Evil affects us. We get wounded. We get killed. But we don't suffer the ultimate effects of evil. Our spirit is protected—with God's help. We get cancer. We die. But Christians do not despair."

Despair. The exact word for how I felt—standing on the outside watching my life fall apart, so desperate I would murder for relief from the pain of it, but knowing revenge would only make it worse, knowing there was no coming back from that, knowing the longing for revenge was pulling me away from Mary Jo and everything else I cared about.

• • •

WE SPENT THE EARLY AFTERNOON together, silent for the most part, sitting in the heat on the back porch. My confession of unbelief stood like an invisible barricade between us. It was as if I had been unfaithful to her. Perhaps I had. All those years of pretending to share her faith—the most important part of her life. I had told a thousand lies to be with her. But wait—those lies had been for *us*, for the sake of being together. My thoughts boiled with righteous indignation. Didn't she understand that I had sacrificed my own integrity on the altar of our love?

We made small talk, bravely ignoring the new distance between us. We had lunch. We read the paper. Suddenly, Mary Jo put her hand to her mouth, as if she was startled.

I said, "What is it?"

"I don't know how I could have forgotten this—come inside for a minute, will you? There's something you've got to see."

She led me into the kitchen where she opened a cabinet drawer and removed a well-worn man's wallet. She handed it to me.

I opened the wallet and Ernest B.'s face stared at me from the driver's license. There were credit cards, proof of automobile insurance, a brand-new library card—all with his name on them.

Mary Jo said, "So I guess we know what Lester Fredricks was doing last night."

I nodded, looking at Ernest B.'s driver's license photograph. It didn't do him justice. His cheeks looked fat and the whites of his eyes showed under his irises, making him look slightly insane. "Could be whoever beat up Lester wanted to force him to plant Ernest B.'s wallet on our property. Maybe Lester picked the studio instead of the house to avoid running into us."

I continued to flip through the wallet, hoping to find a clue. There were a lot of credit-card receipts, mostly from gas stations and restaurants around Jackson County. I wasn't surprised to see a sales slip from the Easy Money bar in Deep Ellum. I remembered Pedro saying that he'd seen Ernest B. flashing a lot of money around, but the wallet had no cash at all, just lots of American Express receipts. There was one from a scuba-diving supply shop in Dallas. I remembered the unfriendly little postcard message he'd sent from Mexico. Maybe he'd done some scuba diving in Cozumel or Cancun. We used to dive down there together back in the good old days.

"Do you think Lester dropped this wallet on the way to Deputy Wilson's patrol car?" asked Mary Jo.

"Yes. He was planning to frame me, but we caught him before he got the chance. If I'd only searched Lester and found this thing when we had him alone we could have forced him to tell us the whole truth."

As soon as the words were out I knew they were a mistake. She said, "How would you have forced him, Garr? With threats?"

"I have to do something to defend myself!"

"The Lord will defend you!"

"He didn't do much for Ernest B.!"

She sucked in her breath, turned, and left the room. I stood alone for a long time, staring at the wallet, considering the implications of it all. A bright square of sunlight spilled through the window onto the kitchen floor. It had shifted several inches by the time she came back in, her eyes red again. Without looking at me, she spoke in a neutral voice. It was the voice she used with strangers.

She said, "There's something else. A couple of Clyde Barker's men were out walking the ground around the studio most of the morning."

"Good thing you start work earlier than they do, or they'd have found this thing and I'd be sitting in the jail right now."

"Garr, you're missing the point. They were acting like they knew there was something there."

I stared at her, without understanding. Then it hit me. "Jimmy searched Lester before he took him up to the road."

"Exactly."

"And Lester must have had the wallet on him. Why else would he break into the studio? He wouldn't plant it outside and then break in—that doesn't make sense."

"Right."

"So, Jimmy missed the wallet when he searched him, or maybe assumed it was Lester's wallet, and he handcuffed him and took him up to the road. But along the way, Lester managed to drop Ernest B.'s wallet in the grass to avoid being caught with it down at the courthouse."

Mary Jo said, "And if Lester got rid of it before Jimmy shot him, then nobody at the sheriff's department ought to know about it. So how come those deputies were out there searching the woods?" She touched my chest lightly with her fingertips and said, "I smell a rat."

Her earnest expression kindled a familiar warm feeling inside my chest. How could I not love a woman who said things like, "I smell a rat"?

Holding Ernest B.'s wallet in one hand, I pulled her to me with the other. I pressed her close for a minute, rubbing her back as we swayed a little to the rhythm of our heartbeats. The pressure of her body against mine stirred vaguely erotic feelings. I pulled her closer, but the muscles in her back tensed and she placed her hands against my chest. It had been years since she had rejected me. The amorous feeling faded as quickly as it had come, replaced by subtle indignation. All those happy years together—didn't she realize I had lied only to make them possible?

She stepped back.

I sighed. Perhaps it would be best to ignore the situation for now. To give her time. Casually, I said, "I'd guess that whoever gave the wallet to Lester tipped off Barker. Seems like there's a connection with the sheriff's department somehow—like the bad guys have an inside line over there. That could explain why this morning's paper didn't mention anything about the drugs I found in Victor Sickle's car last night."

She squared her shoulders. "What are you talking about?"

I wrapped an arm around her. I tried to pull her back against my chest, to hold her while I described stalking Victor Sickle's Camaro in the ditch, but she pushed away again. When I got to the part about the white powder in the plastic bag, she turned and walked to the other side of the kitchen. She stood rigidly, staring out the window toward the lake until I finished telling my story. I fell silent, watching her with growing uneasiness, absently flipping Ernest B.'s wallet open and closed in my hand. Finally, she crossed her arms and turned to face me.

"Garr, I think you're cracking up."

I laughed.

"No, I mean it. Maybe this is too much for you."

"Why would you say a thing like that?"

"Why would I say that? Why?" She counted the reasons on her fingers, "One, you searched a dead man at the hospital the other night! Two, last night you almost shot a man! Three, you chased a drug dealer down the highway when any normal person would have run the other way! And now you're telling me you're not even a Christian!"

"He chased me!"

"What?"

"Sickle chased me!"

She stared at me for a moment. Then she said, "Oh *that's* a relief!"

"Great. Be sarcastic. That's real helpful."

"Garr, I'm not sure I *can* be helpful. I think you've let yourself go too far for my help."

"What's that supposed to mean?"

"Just what I said. You're changing. You're acting like someone else. You're . . . I don't know . . . you're *scaring* me with all this macho stuff. You're getting mean. You're talking strange. Denying the Lord. You're slipping away from me, becoming someone I don't know."

"Oh, come on, Mary Jo. That's taking things a little too far, don't you think?"

"No! I'm telling you, Garr: You better stop to think about us, and how we're going to be if you keep this up. You'd better think about yourself."

We stood silently for a moment, glaring at each other across the kitchen. But I was much too tired to fight.

I said, "Listen, I'm sorry. I really am. I can't help how I feel about God and everything, but I do promise to be more careful. I will, really. But, Mary Jo, if I don't get out there and try to find out what's going on, who will?"

"If you won't let the Lord handle it, then at least let Clyde Barker do his job, Garr. If you keep running around doing this Sam Spade routine, who knows what's going to happen? It scares me. You could get hurt. I want you to stop."

I tapped my chest with Ernest B.'s wallet and said, "Barker's not going to look any further than right here. He's made that pretty obvious. I've got to try to get to the bottom of this mess without him. I've *got* to, Mary Jo. Please understand that."

She frowned at the floor for a moment, then she looked up and shook her head. I crossed the kitchen and took her into my arms again, nuzzling my face in the fragrant softness of her hair. I said, "Listen, I can't ignore this situation, but I'll stay away from Victor Sickle." I lifted her face toward mine and searched her eyes. "Will that do?"

She sighed and nodded.

I kissed her forehead and said, "Tell you what. When those guys quit searching the meadow, we'll put this thing in a plastic bag and hide it out there. They won't look for it where they've already searched."

"Then what are you going to do, Garr?"

It was all running together: Lester, Sickle, Leon and Mrs. P., and God Almighty. Rubbing my face I said, "I don't know. I can't think straight. Right now I need to get some sleep. I'll figure something out when I wake up."

"Well, let me know what I can expect . . . if it isn't too much trouble."

I stared at her for a moment. Then, deciding to let it pass, I left her standing by the kitchen window. Upstairs in our bedroom, I pulled the drapes closed against the afternoon sun, stripped to my underwear and lay on the sheets. As I stared at the ceiling, bits and pieces of the last week floated through my mind. The giant redheaded doorman at the Nowhere Club, standing next to Victor Sickle, looking at me. The strange smile on Lester Fredricks' face as Jimmy Wilson led him away from the studio in handcuffs. How beautiful Martin Pool had been last night as I waited on the dam for Sickle to take up my challenge. Clyde Barker cleaning his fingernails on our back porch while his men searched my home. The flattened end of Dr. Krueger's nose when I lifted his head from the desktop. Pedro Comacho's spinning knife, proving the existence of God.

I thought about the missing tools from the job shack and how slowly the work was going out there. I was going to lose a lot of money on that project if the weather didn't clear.

Life seems to deliver bad luck in combination punches, like a boxer. A lead with the left followed by a couple of stiff right jabs. Your biggest job gets thrown off schedule, then someone steals your tools. Your best friend turns against you, then turns up dead.

My thoughts began to slip into self-pity. I rolled over and grunted in annoyance. What right did I have to feel sorry for myself? Ernest B. was stone cold dead and his father mad with grief. My problems were nothing compared with that. I thought about Old Man Martin. I hadn't seen him since Ernest B.'s death. Maybe I should drop by the nursing home and see how the old fellow was getting along. Maybe we could help each other. I decided to go when I woke up.

In time, I fell asleep and dreamed that Ernest B. was sinking into a field of mud with a scuba tank on his back. He was running out of air, but I couldn't help him because someone had handcuffed me to Jesus Christ, and neither of us could swim.

CHAPTER 23

A YOUNG NURSE WITH AN EARNEST expression greeted me at the reception desk. She directed me down a hall to the last room on the left. It was four o'clock in the afternoon by the time I got there, but the residents of the Silver Leaf Home were still occupied with discussions of Mr. McKinsey's early morning escape attempt. I heard an old woman say she hadn't had so much fun since Mr. Weeser trapped Nurse Murphey in the men's room and demanded a French kiss. He was a good kisser, too, she said. For a man of eighty-nine.

Two spry old men stood in the hall discussing the morning's excitement. The two had interviewed all concerned: the police, the paperboy, and Mr. McKinsey. Or, more precisely, they'd eavesdropped on all concerned. They were comparing notes, getting their versions of the story straight before dinner. They would enjoy being the center of attention as they laid all rumors to rest with the inside scoop.

I stood nearby and did a little eavesdropping of my own. The story (with my creative embellishments) went something like this:

• • •

EARLY THAT MORNING, NEWSPAPER DELIVERY boy Johnny "J. J." Jones concentrated on his aim as he rode his Huffy Roadster ten-speed bicycle along Tyler Avenue. Lately, several of his customers had complained to the newspaper about being forced to root around in their azaleas for the *Daily Herald.* But at five-thirty in the morning, it was so dark you couldn't see the potholes in the road, much less hit the porches every time. How was a kid supposed to meet his schedule if he had to get off his bike to hand deliver every copy?

J. J. was getting fed up.

As he pedaled slowly down the dark street, watching intently for holes and rocks, he fantasized about growing up to be the mayor, or maybe even president. He'd change things so a person didn't have to work so hard. Shorten up the school day, too. Morning delivery boys everywhere would love him, sending thousands of baseball cards to show their appreciation.

J. J. was nearing the hospital, where the roads got better. His spirits lifted a little. Turning sideways to pull three papers from his bag, he wheeled up the driveway and coasted quickly through the bright lights under the emergency entrance canopy. On the fly, he flipped the papers to the concrete right outside the glass of the automatic doors with practiced precision. "That's what I can do with a little light!" he said to himself.

His next delivery was the worst. The Silver Leaf Home. J. J. had to lean his bike against the white picket fence out front, go through the gate and walk all the way up to the door—just to deliver two copies. A lot of times, even in the dark, the front porch was already full of old geezers sitting in rocking chairs and spitting big goobers over the rail. J. J. usually stopped and spoke to them to be polite. They were old and wrinkly looking, but they seemed to like him. All of the old fellows knew J. J.'s name. In fact, most of them were pretty nice. So J. J. didn't mind talking; it was just that they made him late almost every day, and Mrs. Powell down the street would chew him out if her paper arrived a minute later than six-thirty.

But this morning something was wrong. The old geezers were there as usual, rocking back and forth and hacking and spitting. But no one said a word to him. They just smiled and nodded when he said hello. They seemed preoccupied with something on the other side of the picket fence.

J. J. dropped off the papers and hurried back out to the sidewalk. As soon as he opened the gate, he saw that his bike was gone. His heart sank. He'd slaved for a whole summer throwing papers on foot to save enough money for that bicycle. J. J. looked wildly up and down the street. Sure enough, he saw someone about two blocks away, riding his bike in the glow of a street light.

"Hey, mister! Gimme back my bike!" yelled J. J. as he dropped his newspaper bag to the root-cracked sidewalk and took off after the thief. Strangely enough, he was able to close the distance easily. As he drew near, he could see that although the fugitive bicyclist was pedaling wildly, he was barely moving fast enough to maintain his balance.

J. J.'s pace brought him alongside.

The man on the bicycle was old. He wore striped pajamas, a robe, and slippers. His knees stuck almost straight out to the sides as he tried to pedal a bike designed for a rider half his size. His sparse gray hair stood up on either side of his bald head like tail fins on a '57 Thunderbird.

"Mister, that's my bike!" said J. J.

"Official police business," huffed the old man, still pedaling wildly as he tried to get the bike out of first gear.

"You're not a policeman!" J. J. said indignantly.

The old man made the mistake of looking sideways at J. J. and lost control. The bicycle wobbled, then fell over. The old man hit the street with a quiet grunt.

For a moment, they were frozen in position, the old man lying on the ground with his feet on the pedals and J. J. standing silently, unsure of what to do. The spoked wheels rotated with a steady clicking sound. Then the old fellow said, "Don't just stand there, man—use the radio! Call it in!"

"What?"

Deputy Jake McKinsey (retired) said, "Officer down! Officer needs assistance! Call it in right away, I think I broke something."

• • •

THE OLD MEN LAUGHED AND SHOOK THEIR heads as I walked on down the hall.

E. B. Martin Jr. sat next to his neatly made bed in a rocking chair facing the window. His thick gray hair was combed and parted. His thin lips were set in an angry scowl. For the first time that I could remember, his face was clean shaven. I knocked on the open door.

"Go away," he growled.

I stepped inside the little room. Old Man Martin's body odor was almost overpowering. I wondered why the nurses didn't make him bathe.

"Mr. Martin, how are you feeling?"

He turned his rheumy red eyes toward me. "Well, I'll tell you, I got this nice little room all to myself. Every morning I get lukewarm oatmeal, decaffeinated coffee, an' some orange-colored stuff to drink. Lunch an' dinner I get a canned vegetable, a slice o' white bread an' a little round piece o' meat. I can go to the lounge anytime I like 'tween nine and five and watch soap operas with all the old bags, or I can go sit in a rocking chair on the front porch an' wait for the mailman with the old coots out there. I reckon I'm just fine. How the heck are you?"

He didn't sound so crazy.

"Why don't you go home?"

"'Cause my daughter signed some stupid papers sayin' I'm nuts, an' they won't *let* me go home, you idiot!" he yelled. Then, turning his anger off like tap water, he returned his attention to the window.

"I'm real sorry to hear that, Mr. Martin. Maybe if you called Betsy in California and talked to her, she'd see you're back to normal and agree to let them send you home."

The old man didn't answer, so I tried another approach. "Mr. Martin, can I ask you some questions about Ernest B.? I've heard some talk around town that he was using drugs. I heard that you were pretty mad about it. Is that true?"

"Ernest B.'s a pain in the behind. Always has been."

He continued to stare out the window. I followed his gaze and saw nothing except for a six-foot wooden fence on the other side of a trash-covered asphalt alley.

The old man was clenching his jaw, flexing the muscles over and over. It reminded me of a time when Ernest B. broke his jaw and spent two months eating through a straw. He was about twelve. He said he slipped and fell, but I never believed him. More than once I had seen this old man ball his fist and hit Ernest B. like he was a grown man.

The thought made me feel mean. I said, "You know you might never get out of here, don't you?"

He didn't move a muscle.

I looked around his little gray private room and said, "It's a lot like being in jail, I'll bet." There was still no reaction. I decided to push a little harder. "Mr. Martin, as long as they got you cooped up here, why not tell me the truth? What could it hurt? You might as well be in jail anyway, right?"

Still no response, so I asked him point blank: "Did you kill Ernest B.?"

Without removing his eyes from the window, the old man said, "You're crazy. Ernest B.'s in Mexico. He sent me a real pretty postcard from there, couple of weeks ago."

"Does Ernest B. bring drugs up from Mexico?"

I waited, but he returned to silence. After a few minutes I said, "Well, if you think of something you want to tell me, would you try to give me a call?"

He ignored me. I stood beside his chair for a few minutes, trying to think of a way to get through to him. His attention was solidly fixed on the view through the window. I turned to go. As I was stepping into the hallway, he said, "Daddy's gonna git me outa here."

"Do what?"

He turned to me with a wild look and said, "Daddy said he'd come back and git me."

His eyes gave me an uneasy feeling. "That's real good, Mr. Martin," I said in a soothing voice. "I hope he comes soon."

"Oh, he will. He was gonna take me with him last night, but he said he had some things to take care of first. I figure he'll be back any time now." The old man began to giggle.

Rather than take my eyes off of him, I backed the rest of the way into the hall. When I turned, I almost fell into the lap of an old man in a wheelchair, who sat there as if he'd been waiting for me. His white hair stuck straight out on either side of his liver-spotted bald head. His right leg was extended on a metal support and covered with a clean white plaster cast.

He said, "That old peckerwood is half a bubble off of level, you know. Gets drunk and wanders the halls mumblin' to hisself. Durned if I can figure where he gits his hooch at. Don't worry, though, I heard every word. I'll be glad to compare notes with you, but you got to promise me you won't tell Barker."

"I'm sorry, I don't understand."

He turned the wheelchair and said, "We better not talk here. Come on."

The rubber tires of his wheelchair squeaked on the shiny linoleum as I followed him down the hall and through the reception area. He stopped next to the front door, waiting for me to open it. Out on the porch, the rocking chairs were all taken. The old men who had witnessed Johnny Jones' pursuit of Jake McKinsey were waiting for an instant replay.

At the sight of the man in the wheelchair, they began to clap. Some shouted "Attaboy!" and "Way to go, Jake!"

"Durn fool old coots," mumbled my companion. "Let's go over yonder." He wheeled himself along the porch until we were as far away from them as we could get.

Carefully positioning himself with his back to the old men he said, "Now then. First thing we gotta do is figure out who's bringin' the stuff into town."

"What stuff?" I asked.

"The contraband, of course! What in tarnation was you talkin' to Martin about?"

"Well—I guess I don't understand how you fit in. Maybe it would help if we introduced ourselves."

"Oh. Sorry 'bout that. I'm Deputy Jake McKinsey, Jackson County Sheriff's Department." He held his hand up to me. I shook it. It was like lifting a leaf. "Sorry to stay seated here, got injured chasing a perpetrator this mornin'. You know how it is."

"I'm Garrison Reed, Mr. McKinsey. Glad to meet you."

"Know your daddy real well, Reed. He's a fine man. 'Course he gives us a little trouble over those wetbacks he works his jobs with, but then nobody's perfect."

My father had been dead for years, and he never hired a wetback in his life. But some people consider anyone of Mexican extraction a wetback—illegal alien—even if their grandfather and father were born in Texas. Of course, I'd be a fool to argue such points with a senile old man, so I said, "I appreciate that, Mr. McKinsey. Now what can I do for you?"

Jake McKinsey glanced over his shoulder at the group of old men. They were listening intently. Two held their old-fashioned, two-part, transistor-style hearing aids toward us for better reception.

"Don't mind them," he said. "They couldn't hear us if we was sittin' in their laps using bullhorns. What I wanted to talk about is Ernest B. I heard you askin' his daddy 'bout his dope problem." The old man stared into the distance. "Guess that kinda thing runs in their family. His granddaddy is a moonshiner, you know. Same as dealin' drugs, far as I can see. Just lower prices."

"Do you know anything about Ernest B.'s drug connections?"

"Not much. Sheriff's had me on a leave of absence for a while. Little out of touch. I been mostly concentratin' on findin' ways to improve security around here. Plus I been tryin' to catch Deputy Barker with his pants down." His voice dropped low and he leaned closer to me. "Barker's dirty, you know. I figure Martin's got him on the take."

"Are you talking about Sheriff Barker?"

Jake McKinsey spat on the wooden porch. "*Sheriff* Barker? That'll be the day! That crooked little backstabber'll never make sheriff. Not while I'm alive. Tarnation, boy, don't you know Sheriff O'Ryan?"

I did remember O'Ryan. He had been killed trying to convince a drunken farmer to let his wife out of a water well when I was about six years old. The man had insisted that his wife dig the well a little deeper before he let her up, because the water was still muddy. When O'Ryan had stepped forward to tell the drunk that twenty hours digging at the bottom of a well was a good day's work for any woman, the man had shot him in the forehead. The way I remembered it, Clyde Barker had then shot the drunk and pulled the woman up.

"I guess I'm a little confused, Mr. McKinsey. Are you saying that Ernest B.'s father has been bribing sheriff—ah, Deputy Barker?"

"Not his father, stupid. His grandfather!"

"But his grandfather's been dead for years."

"Horsepucky! Shows what you know." Jake McKinsey turned again to be sure the old men couldn't overhear, then he said, "Who in tarnation do you think I was chasin' last night?"

"E. B. Senior?"

"That's right! I figure he come here to find out how much I told Ernest B. about the coins."

"What coins?"

"The silver dollar treasure, boy! Don't you know nothin'? I thought you been lookin' into this thing!"

"I've been concentrating on Ernest B.'s drug problems. I haven't had time to look into anything else."

"Well, you better find the time. That Ernest B. durn sure did."

"What do you mean?"

"Ernest B. used to come around here all the time, askin' me 'bout his granddaddy's silver dollars. Tryin' to get me to tell him where they was."

I was interested in spite of myself. "Do you know where they are?"

"Sure I do." He leaned back with a satisfied look. His nose was running, but he didn't seem to notice.

"Did you tell Ernest B.?"

"'Course not. Not at first, anyway. If I did, he would've gotten them coins for hisself. He laughed at me when I said it was tainted money."

"So you didn't tell him."

He twisted his pajama shirttail in his hands and said, "When he told me he was goin' to give some of it to the Benevolent Fund, I did."

"You did tell him?"

"Yep."

"When was that?"

The old man stared up at the porch ceiling in deep thought. Liquid from his dripping nose quivered on his upper lip, unnoticed. Finally, he said, "It was Thursday before last."

The night before Ernest B.'s body was found.

I said, "Was he alone when he came to see you that time?"

"Couldn't say."

"How can you be sure it was Thursday before last when you don't even remember if he was alone?"

"Cause I remember havin' to talk to him through the bathroom door."

"Ernest B. was in the bathroom?"

"No, stupid! I was." He sighed as if teaching a backward child and said, "On Thursdays, they always serve spaghetti with meatballs. I always get the runs. When Ernest B. come by, I was sittin' in my bathroom readin' *Field and Stream* like I always do, and we had us a good long talk. He was in my bedroom, I was in my bathroom. We was talkin' through the door. Understand?" When I nodded, he went on, "Ernest B. said he thought about it, and he decided I was right. It was tainted money. But it weren't right to let it just sit there with all the trouble in the world. He was goin' to find it and give it to the Texas Law Officer's Benevolent Fund. So I told him where it is."

"Where is it?"

"In Martin Holler, of course. On his grandpa's land." He wiped his nose with his sleeve.

"That's not exactly news, Mr. McKinsey. Can you be a little more specific?"

He nodded toward the street. "You got a map in your truck?"

"Yes"

"Go get it."

The conversation was getting ridiculous. I was wasting my time talking to a senile old man who thought he was a young sheriff's deputy chasing dead people. Still, what did I have to lose? I went out to the truck and brought back a county map.

Mr. McKinsey unfolded it on his lap, spreading the paper flat with his trembling hands. Then he held up his palm and said, "Gimme a pen."

Leaning forward in his wheelchair with his nose inches from the map, he slowly drew a small circle on the paper with a shaking hand, then filled the circle with an X. The tip of his tongue stuck out of the side of his mouth as he concentrated. For an instant, I glimpsed the young man he'd once been. I could imagine him searching the woods for moonshine during the Depression, when Bonnie and Clyde hid on the back roads of Jackson County. Then he looked up, and the image died when his jaundiced yellow eyes met mine.

"I'd look right about there if I was you. E. B.'s whiskey still ought to be there somewhere. But be careful, he's a mean one. If he catches you around his still you'll never make it out of them woods alive."

I took the map from him and looked at it. He had marked a section of Martin Pool that was very near to the Martin home. I stood quickly and said, "Well, sir, thank you for the help. I've got to get going."

He ignored my outstretched hand, saying, "You ought to look for the still, boy. I know that cracker's up there operating it again. Find the still, find the loot—that's what I told Ernest B."

I thanked him again, stood, and walked back out to the truck. Pulling away from the curb, I glanced at the map lying open on the seat beside me. A real, honest to goodness treasure map with an X marking the spot. Suddenly, I remembered the credit card receipt from the scuba shop that Mary Jo and I had found in Ernest B.'s wallet. I remembered the map that he'd written on, then photocopied at the library; the one with the words "need air" scrawled in the margin. That map and this one were marked in exactly the same place.

I smiled and said, "Shiver me timbers."

Chapter 24

I THOUGHT ABOUT IT QUITE A BIT OVER the next few days: Ernest B. reading about the silver dollars at the library, buying scuba equipment in Dallas, talking to loony old Jake McKinsey at the Silver Leaf Home. It was crazy, the idea of searching for treasure at the bottom of Martin Pool. It was crazy and childish and exactly the sort of thing that Ernest B. might do if he got his mind set on it. Especially if he had to finance a drug habit. By quitting time on Friday night, I'd decided to have a look around the bottom of Martin Pool.

At six o'clock on Saturday morning, I loaded my boat with an ice chest packed with lunch and some cold drinks, a life vest, binoculars, a waterproof flashlight, depth gauge, face mask, fins, scuba tanks (still full of air from who knew how long ago), regulator, and weight belt. Somehow, I'd lost the lid to my coffee thermos, but I packed the thermos anyway.

When I dive, it's always on the buddy system—but Ernest B. had been my buddy. Since I would be diving alone, I decided at the last minute to take along an extra hundred-foot nylon rope to act as a lifeline to the surface. Although it would be safer to bring Mary Jo to watch my safety line, I decided it wasn't worth the argument we'd have.

A couple of years earlier, I had traded my ski boat for a sixteen-foot aluminum johnboat equipped with a steering console and a fifty-horse Johnson outboard with power tilt and trim. The big ski boat's use was limited to the main lake, but with the flat-bottom johnboat's shallow draft, I could navigate the sloughs and channels of the swamp at the top of the lake and on up the bayou for miles.

The boat was suspended a couple of feet above the water in my boathouse. I flipped the switch, and it slowly dropped toward the lake.

Ernest B. and I had begun diving as teenagers, when water skiing and fishing had become old hat. We had quickly learned that the world below the waves of Martin Pool was strange and unpredictable. In the swamp at the top of the lake where the Big Muddy Bayou feeds in, alligators are sometimes seen, and gar up to six feet long are fairly common. There are coots, grebes, cormorants, mallards, wood ducks, a dozen types of water snakes, channel catfish up to seventy pounds, beaver, and nutria.

When seen from a boat or the shore, these creatures are interesting in an abstract way—objects in another world, separate from ours. A submerged encounter with one of them is altogether different. A man under the water has given up his normal existence to join the creatures surrounding him. He is subject to the same shifting currents and, to some extent, the same ruthless laws of nature. Watching an alligator gar cruise in front of your face mask can stir a primeval panic that is completely irrational, given the fact that they never attack anything larger than a perch. The human mind was programmed in the time of the ancients to run from anything that moves with such terrifying precision and is armed with so many sharp teeth.

But it's not all serious below the waters of the lake. A water bird paddling furiously across the surface to escape the tickling assault of your air bubbles is a funny sight to see. Ernest B. and I used to chase them for hundreds of yards, laughing through our mouthpieces.

As I reversed out of the boathouse, I couldn't quite rid myself of the thought that searching for hidden treasure in Martin Pool was a juvenile occupation at best. In a grown-up world, it made no sense.

Of course, with Ernest B., it didn't really matter whether it was sensible. My old friend had always been willing to throw off the thin veneer of adult behavior and pursue a harebrained scheme in the spirit of fun and profit. The year that cars got emergency flashers, he made pretty good money following drivers around the county with his parking lights blinking. The naive unfortunates he "pulled over" often paid "officer" Ernest B. a stiff fine on the spot for "vehicular malfeasance" or some such ridiculous charge.

I had no doubt that Ernest B. Martin had been fully capable of searching for sunken treasure.

But the circles on the maps covered a lot of lakebed. Where exactly would he have looked? Assuming that they'd ever really existed, his grandfather had probably hidden the silver dollars as carefully as his moonshine still. Maybe they were both in the same place. Find the still, find the loot—that's what crazy old Jake McKinsey said.

I turned the boat toward the Martin home place.

Ernest B.'s great-grandfather had built the Martins' house on the east side of a finger-shaped hill that would form a peninsula years later when the waters rose. In the days before Martin Pool, the Big Muddy Bayou flowed beside the hill, just below the home place, and a smaller creek flowed along the west side.

The creek had no name. It sprang bubbling from the hillside, formed by an aquifer that punched through the ground under pressure—a natural fountain. When I was young, my father told me stories of the picnics and swimming parties that he and his childhood friends had enjoyed beside "the fountain" on the Martin place. Years after the spring had been covered by the waters of the lake, he often took me and Ernest B. fishing there, floating over the site of the creek's source. He said that fish were attracted to the cold aquifer water at the bottom of the lake during the hot months of summer.

Because distilling liquor takes a lot of water, I reasoned that E. B. Martin Senior would have put the still near the creek or the bayou. And since whiskey stills stink, it would have been far away from the house. That meant the bayou was too close. The still was probably on the other side of the hill, down near the creek. The place to look was in the deep water of Martin Pool, on the west side of the hill behind the Martin home place, along the old channel that had once been the creek bed.

It was a fool's errand. I knew from experience that fifty years of sediment covered everything below the surface of Martin Pool like the volcanic ash at Pompeii. The murky green water allowed very little light to penetrate to the depths I would be searching. Besides—if the still had just been sitting there, the loggers would have found it when they cleared the trees out of the valley before it was flooded. What were the chances of finding it now that it might be under forty or fifty feet of water? All things considered, only a drug-addled imbecile—or someone trying to retrace his steps—would even try.

The sun was barely over the eastern treetops as I sped along the shore. I passed the Martin place and followed the curve of the hill to the south. A group of ten or twelve mallards rose from the water's surface in front of my boat. With loud angry squawks, they beat their wingtips against the water and paddled frantically across the surface, trying to gain enough momentum to get airborne. Their wakes were swallowed by mine as the ducks parted before me and flew alongside for a while, unwilling escorts on my journey around the peninsula.

When I guessed that I was about in line with the Martin home place on the other side of the hill, I slowed to idle speed. A depth finder was mounted on the steering console in front of me. I turned it on and adjusted the display. Amber and black squares appeared with a beep, outlining the lake bottom in ragged detail. I turned the bow away from shore and began to slowly cruise a zigzag pattern in search of the old creek channel.

About a hundred and fifty feet off shore, I found it.

The amber display showed a V-shaped bottom profile about fifteen yards below. I cut off the motor and plopped a little bell-shaped anchor into the water off the bow. A loud silence filled the morning, broken only by the little scrapes and creaks of my own movements and the hollow sound of gentle waves washing against the metal side of the boat.

I scanned the shoreline with my binoculars.

The hill above the lake still belonged to the Martins, although they made little use of it. The woods were very thick—mature pines mostly, with some post oaks and a lot of scrub brush down low. Wake damage from speeding motorboats had carved away the side of the hill over the years, leaving sandy cliffs six to ten feet tall along the waterline. As the relentless onslaught of the slapping waves had washed away the earth beneath, the trees on the edge of the water had died one by one, collapsing into the lake with their roots precariously balanced on shore. Here and there, the erosion had exposed rusty red limestone outcroppings, the backbone of these east Texas hills. They rose from the lake like giant steps, leading up to a luxuriant cathedral of forest green.

Before Martin Pool was built, an old blacktop road had crossed the valley, several hundred yards to the north. It hadn't been important enough to warrant a bridge, so three brightly painted yellow bollards had been placed where the pavement met the water's edge—a warning to unwary motorists. The road and the bollards were the only signs of human life in sight.

Satisfied that I wasn't being watched, I peeled off my T-shirt and turned to my scuba gear, unused for the past couple of years. A few adjustments to the belt and straps were necessary to allow for the increase in my waist size. I pinched the little roll of fat on my belly and shook my head. Have to work on that. Maybe add a few more sit-ups to my routine. I returned my thoughts to the business at hand. The tank felt familiar once it was on my back. I tied a nylon line to a cleat on the starboard gunwale and hooked my flashlight onto the waistband of my swimming trunks. Holding my face mask in place with one hand and the end of the life line with the other, I sat on the side of the boat, leaned back, and splashed into the water tank first.

Unless there has been a recent extreme change in temperature or a lot of rain, the water in Martin Pool is usually clear to depths of ten or twelve feet. But below that, the muck never quite settles. When I reached the level of constant darkness, I pulled the flashlight from my trunks and switched it on. The fuzzy white glow sliced through the algae soup around me like a miniature spotlight searching the night sky.

I was conscious of an old familiar feeling of melancholy at being so isolated from the world above. It wasn't claustrophobia exactly, since there was no hint of panic. It was more a sense of sad isolation, fortunately easy to repress.

As the depth gauge on my wrist displayed fifty feet, the black lake bottom appeared in the round spot of the flashlight. There was very little plant life so deep. Hydrilla and algae need sunshine to survive. I played the flashlight over the mud below, illuminating a blackish scum that looked like photographs I had seen of a beach recently polluted by an oil slick. Here and there, aluminum cans and beer bottles stuck up through the sludge. There were some old tin cans with twin triangular holes punched in their tops, reminders that our attitude toward Mother Nature has been disgraceful for a long, long time. Hard to imagine throwing garbage into the same beautiful lake where you swim and fish, but lots of people do it every day.

Checking my watch, I saw that it had taken me just under five minutes to reach the bottom. I would need at least ten on the trip back up. That left me about fifteen minutes with a good margin of safety.

In the near total darkness, my search area was gauged by the size of my flashlight beam; about two square feet. With the time limitations of my air supply, that meant I could probably search five or six thousand square feet per dive. A discouraging thought, since at that rate I would finish checking this stretch of the old creek channel in about five years.

I followed the spot of light along the bottom until it illuminated a sharp drop: the bank of the old stream bed. Swimming about six feet above the lake bed, I traced the channel's route north, passing the beam of light along the bottom in a uniform zigzag pattern as I went.

Mud and cans. The comforting click and hiss of the air regulator with every breath. Bubbles. Occasionally, a fish or two, drifting like tethered dirigibles above the black carnage of war. Some old tree stumps, still cracked and frayed where the bulldozers had snapped off the mighty trunks when the valley had been cleared, fifty years before. Once, this had been the floor of an ancient forest, home to black bears and Caddo Indians, cougars and red foxes, timber wolves and river otters—all gone forever. I flew above the ruins like a ghost, haunting the lost world my kind had destroyed, then buried under water in the name of progress.

I was nearing the limits of my air supply when the light from my flashlight seemed to grow dimmer. I shook it to see if the batteries were loose, knowing that I'd recently replaced them. I aimed the light at my hand. The flashlight's beam was still strong. Passing the beam along the bottom again, I discovered the problem: The water around me was growing more murky. As if to take advantage of the additional camouflage, dozens of fish of all kinds now cruised through the water around me.

To my left, I saw a swirling cloud of green and black particles. Something big seemed to be stirring up the bottom. I decided to swim into the hovering debris to get a closer look.

As I entered the cloud, the water around me became bone-chillingly cold. Of course! This was the source of the creek, the "fountain" I'd heard so much about as a child. The cold, clear aquifer was still surging from the ground here, mixing with the tepid water of the lake to create a subsurface whirlpool of bottom muck and mire.

I was in the thick of it, kicking furiously against the current to stay in place. I moved the flashlight beam, trying to pierce the green haze and see the aquifer's opening in the lake bed. It was hopeless—there was too much mud disturbed by the turbulence. But as I played the light around, I realized that something seemed wrong. I switched off the light.

Incredibly, the rushing stream of frigid water below me was glowing, lit from within as if charged with radioactive particles.

I reached toward the glow. The shadows cast by my spread fingers sliced the light into separate beams, like lasers piercing smoke. I wanted to try to swim into the current—to go below the surface of the lake bottom and find the source of the light, but the watch on my outstretched wrist showed less than fifteen minutes of air remaining in my tanks.

To ensure that I would be able to find the place again, I tied the end of my lifeline to a nearby tree stump. As I followed the rope toward the surface, it was hard to be patient and rise slowly; I wanted to hurry back to the house so I could recharge the scuba tanks and return to the lake bottom to investigate the source of the light.

Finally, I broke the surface with a minute or two of air left in the tanks. Raising my face mask to my forehead, I looked around and saw that I had moved about fifty feet away from the boat during the dive. Covering the distance in seconds, I reached the boat and was pulling myself aboard when I heard a familiar voice from far away shout, "Duck, Garr! Duck!"

It was too late.

A bullet tore through my right arm. I collapsed back into the water.

I had never served in the military, never been involved in a hunting accident, never been shot. They say that the pain is usually delayed for a moment, concealed from the senses by the shock of such a massive invasion of the body. Not so in my case. The lake water hit the wound like a searing spike of white-hot steel. Unthinking, I tried to suck in my breath to scream.

I surfaced coughing and spewing water against the side of the boat. It sprayed across the aluminum, mixing with the smear of blood that coated the hull. My eyes focused on the blood on the boat. The small hole in the metal was framed in red. As I watched, that hole was joined by another and then one more before I realized that I was still a target and sank below again, careful this time to replace my mouthpiece.

The initial shock and the pain in my arm were replaced by an overwhelming desire to live. I hovered below the surface, using the last of the air in my tanks, desperately trying to think of a way to escape the sniper.

I decided to swim below the boat and surface on the other side, away from the shore. My right arm was drifting freely, trailing behind me like a leaking wineskin. I was swimming in my own blood. What was the word for death by bleeding? I shook my head—couldn't remember. That was what I was going to do if I didn't get out of the water and get a tourniquet on my arm. Wrap it up. That's a wrap, people. Let's head for the house.

I moved to the bow of the boat and slowly peeked around it. Hide and seek. Peek-a-boo. Can't see me but I see you. A dark Camaro was pulling away from the bright yellow bollards at the dead end road. Always wanted a car like that. Or maybe a Mustang convertible. Nah. Too cold in the winter. Looks like snow. Feels like it too. Too cold.

Slowly, I swam to the stern, where the weight of the outboard motor pushed the sides low in the water. I tried to pull myself aboard with my left arm. It was no use. I kicked off my flippers and set my foot on the motor's stabilizer fin just below the surface. Clawing at the side of the motor with my left hand, I straightened my leg and rose from the water. The searing pain when the air reached my wound was the last thing I remembered before I blacked out.

CHAPTER 25

"GARR? GARR?"

Someone was calling from far away. I didn't really care. Just let me sleep a little while longer, then we can talk.

"Garr? Can you understand me?"

I was so sleepy. Voices mingled. Men and women. Flashes of light. Aching head. What's going on?

"Garr, honey, you're just fine. Can you understand me?"

Mary Jo. She sounds awful. What's the matter? Better go and see.

I opened my eyes to look into hers. They were so beautiful. I'll tell her that. I'll do my best Errol Flynn and say something corny like, *Your eyes are twin pools of pristine blue, glistening beneath the emerald canopy of an endless forest.* She'll like that.

I drifted away again into the black.

Sometime later, I realized that I was awake again, looking at Mary Jo.

"Hey, you," she said.

I said, "Your eyes are ..." and stopped. It came out garbled.

"What?"

My mouth wasn't responding well to the usual commands. I swallowed. It hurt. "You're looking good," I whispered.

The relief on her face was heartbreaking. She smiled and burst into tears at the same time. I said, "Does this mean you still love me?"

She broadened her smile and, wiping her eyes, leaned over me, trying to give me a hug. It was a good one, given the obstacles she had to overcome: tubes in my arm, bandages on my shoulder, a nurse taking my pulse.

When Mary Jo stood back, I asked, "What happened?"

From somewhere else in the room, Clyde Barker said, "We was kinda hopin' you'd tell us, Garr."

I raised my head a bit and saw him standing behind Mary Jo at the side of the bed. I let my head fall back against the pillow. It hurt.

Barker said, "We got an anonymous telephone call sayin' to check your boathouse for a wounded man. When my boys got there, you was stretched out nice and comfortable on the pier next to your boat. Had a real pretty bandage on your shoulder. Professional-like. And the doctor here says he thinks someone gave you mouth to mouth. Still had a little lake water in your lungs when they brought you in."

I looked at Mary Jo. She was stroking my hair. "What day is this?" I asked.

"It's early Sunday morning. You've lost a lot of blood. They had to give you a transfusion. And they operated on your arm for a long time."

My arm. I turned to look. It was slightly elevated on a pillow and wrapped in bulging gauze bandages. "Will it be all right?" I asked.

"They think so. You lost some of your upper muscle, but the doctor said you should get most of your strength back with time." She looked at her hands and said, "You're going to have to do a lot of physical therapy."

After a while, I said, "Clyde, the last thing I remember, I was trying to get in the boat, and then my arm sort of blew up. I guess someone shot me."

"Yep. Size of the holes in your boat, I'd say it was a thirty-ought-six at least. Deer poachers, probably. Crazy fools ought to know better than to fire toward the lake."

"Wasn't poachers, Clyde."

"How do you know?"

"Because one of them tried to warn me."

The sheriff edged his way between me and Mary Jo, tension showing in his face. "What are you sayin', Garr?"

"Well, some of those last couple of minutes are a little fuzzy. But I do remember someone yelling out to me just as I got shot."

"Could be you imagined that. The mind plays strange tricks when you go into shock."

I shook my head—too fast. It hurt again. "No way. I heard someone try to warn me to duck."

He looked at me for quite a while. Then he said, "Did you recognize the voice?"

There was something in his stare that I didn't like. Avoiding his eyes, I said, "No, I couldn't tell who it was."

Mary Jo stroked my hair as I went to sleep.

• • •

I AWOKE TO A DARKENED ROOM, DESPERATE to escape the demons in my dreams. After a moment of frightened disorientation, I remembered my situation and lay still, my mind springing wildly from thought to unrelated thought. There was an urgency to my incoherent mental ramblings. Even though my brain was in the grip of painkillers and shock, I knew I should be focusing on something. Something important.

"You're awake."

The voice seemed to come from everywhere. It was disembodied, unearthly. Maybe I was imagining it.

"You're awake, ain't you?"

For some reason, I chose not to answer. I remained motionless, listening in the pitch black.

"I know you're awake." A minute passed, then, "I'm gonna see you rot in the grave. You're a self-righteous meddler, and I'm gonna fix you." The voice sounded male at first, but it rose steadily higher, becoming frantic and female, "You're dead, Garrison. Garrison *buddy*. Dead, dead, dead . . ."

A soft cloud settled over my face. Soft and cool and smelling of soap. I closed my eyes. I breathed deeply. But the cloud filled my lungs, searching every crevice, blocking the passage of air. I reached out, trying to wave away the softness. My hand touched something warm. I seized it, pulling and pushing and shaking from side to side. Still I couldn't breathe. A new, darker cloud seemed to drift before my tightly closed eyes. With a strength born of desperation, I flailed my arm, trying to wipe away the darkness. My hand made contact with something hard. There was a crash. The sound of metal on metal. The soft white cloud receded and I lay wide-mouthed and gasping, like a fish ashore.

Still, the room was filled with darkness. Or were my eyes closed in a dream? I heard the high-pitched laughter once more. It receded into the darkness, coughing and hacking as it faded away. I lay alone, wondering whether I'd heard it or merely dreamed it. My arm ached. Soon, in spite of the fear, I slept again.

• • •

"TIME FOR A TEMPERATURE CHECK, MR. REED."

I awoke terrified, jerking my head up to look around.

Misunderstanding, the nurse said, "Your wife is just down the hall, speaking with Dr. Chilcott. She'll be here in a moment. Open up now."

I realized I was safe and my heartbeat slowed as she poked a thermometer under my tongue with practiced efficiency and looked at her wristwatch. She checked the flow rate on the I.V. at my bedside and referred to a chart on a clipboard hung from the bed railing. I tried to ask how I was doing—mumbling around the thermometer—but she motioned me to silence. "Keep that mouth shut, Mr. Reed. We need an accurate reading on your temperature, don't we?"

She bustled around the room for another minute or two in silence, then removed the thermometer. She said, "I hear you had some excitement last night."

"What?"

"The night nurse told me you knocked over your I.V. stand. That takes a lot of doing. What on earth were you thinking?"

As I began to answer, Mary Jo entered, looking marvelous. Her thick auburn hair was tied in a loose ponytail at the nape of her neck with a black silk ribbon. A shimmering forest green silk blouse brought out the hazel in her eyes. Her black jeans showcased the firm hips and thighs she worked so hard to maintain. Her beauty comforted me from the instant she stepped into that sterile place. It was born of a calm, soothing spirit. She was one of those women more lovely at forty than at twenty, and she would be lovelier still at fifty and truly incredible at sixty, with even more knowledge behind her emerald eyes, more experience and wisdom. If only things were different between us. I would give anything to undo the pain, to make sure that I would be with her when she turned seventy. By then she would surely be the most beautiful woman in the world.

She smiled. "Garrison Reed, do you have any idea how much trouble you've caused?"

She took my face between her palms and looked into my eyes. She bent and kissed me hard, then straightened and continued to look at me with a worried frown. Could it be? Had she forgiven me so easily?

She said, "I hate to say this with you lying in a hospital bed, but you look awful."

"Getting shot takes a lot out of a fellow."

"No. More than that even." With gentle pressure, she turned my face more toward hers. She said, "What is it?"

I told her about the frightening voice in the night. She told me it was a dream. I asked her to check the window anyway. It was locked. I asked her to talk to the deputy out in the hall to see if he'd let anyone in the night before. She stepped outside for a moment, then came back in, saying, "He didn't think anyone was allowed in, but he's not the night guard. He said we should ask Deputy Wilson tonight."

"Well—you're probably right. Must have been a dream."

But the memory of the suffocating cloud seemed stronger than any dream.

We sat silently for a while, holding hands. I was afraid to speak, afraid to break this new connection we seemed to share. Then, hesitantly, she said, "I brought a Bible. I thought you might like to have me read to you."

I looked away. She was offering a way back, a return to the life we'd had. But could I return to the lies? It would be so easy to say that I'd just been hysterical, overreacting to a moment of doubt. An easy lie that would lead to another lie and soon the world would be made of lies again and we would be just as we'd been.

In a small voice she said, "Well? Would it be all right if I read a chapter or two?"

"I suppose so." A noncommittal response to hold the inevitable at bay for one more moment. But the moment would come. She would probe and hint until I had no choice.

She said, "I don't have to read if it would make you . . . uncomfortable."

"It's not that. It's just . . ." I stopped myself from speaking it aloud. I'd hurt this fine, good woman so much already. How could I add to her pain by telling her how little faith I had in the words of that Bible? I said, "It's okay, Mary Jo. I'm just tired, that's all. I'd like to hear a few verses." Strangely, as the words crossed my lips, I found that this time it wasn't a lie.

She opened the book and began to read:

"*'The Lord is my shepherd, I shall not want.*
He maketh me to lie down in green pastures.
He leadeth me beside the still waters.
He restoreth my soul.
He maketh me to walk in the paths of righteousness
for His name's sake.

Yea, though I walk through the valley of the
shadow of death,
I will fear no evil,
For Thou art with me.'"

It was a most peculiar thing. As my eyelids grew heavy, the words flowed into my spirit. Calming me. Loving me. I actually drew some comfort from the ancient poetry. And as Mary Jo's beloved voice sweetly stilled my anguish, I drifted off to a peaceful sleep.

• • •

THE NEXT DAY AN ORDERLY BROUGHT A potted plant to the room. He put it on the little rolling table near the window and handed me a card in a white envelope addressed to "Mister Reed."

When the orderly left the room, I opened the card. It was one of those flowery things, covered with roses and a line across the top in feminine script that read, "In Sympathy for Your Loss." On the inside, the printed words read, "Words of consolation cannot express the sorrow I feel at the loss of your loved one, but I take comfort from the knowledge that death is but a passage to a better world."

It was obviously a mistake. Why else would anyone send a sympathy card to a patient? But then I got to the message scrawled across the bottom and a chill rose up my spine.

It read, "Been thinking about you—Victor."

CHAPTER 26

DAYLIGHT ASSAULTED MY EYELIDS. I opened them to see a man's black silhouette, a profile sketched by glaring sunshine pouring through the open drapes.

"Wondered if you were set on sleepin' the day away, Garr."

I squinted my eyes to make out his features. It was Clyde Barker. He looked worn and haggard, as if he hadn't been getting much sleep. "You and I haven't had a chance to talk alone since the night Lester Fredricks paid you a call," he said. "I think we ought to clear the air, don't you?"

I coughed and said, "Whatever, Clyde."

He slid a chair next to the bed and sat down, leaning forward with his elbows on his knees, holding his gray Stetson by the brim. Our faces were only a foot apart. His breath reeked of stale coffee. I turned my head away from him and stared up at the ceiling. He said, "I been goin' over your financials, boy. You and Ernest B. had a good thing goin' there. Looks to me like business is off now, though." He clucked his tongue and shook his head. "Seems like he was a real asset to the company. Maybe you shouldn't've been so hasty, runnin' Ernest B. off like you did."

"What are you talking about, Clyde? I didn't run him off. He tried to steal me blind, then he came around the house and darn near killed me, and *you* ran him off. Remember?"

"Oh, sure, I remember your story. But I never did get a chance to hear Ernest B.'s side."

I tried to rise up from the bed. "Ernest B.'s side? If you'd got off your hind end and caught him back when you had the chance, you'd have heard his side, and he'd be alive today." I fell back into the sheets, drained by the intensity of my anger.

Blood rushed to his face. His features twisted into a mask of fury. "You little nobody! Day comes you can tell the likes of *me* how to do my job, I'll—"

His fist rose. For a moment I thought he would hit me. Then, with obvious effort, he slowly straightened his fingers, stood, pushing the chair away with the back of his legs, and strode to the door.

I said, "Why don't you try to find Ernest B.'s killer instead of spending so much time trying to pin it on me?"

With his back to me, and his hand on the door handle, he said, "Garrison, I'm real sorry you got shot, but that don't give you the right to tell me how to handle this thing." His voice began to rise as he went on. "Your daddy was an uppity snob, always orderin' me around like I was his errand boy. As far as I can tell, you're no different. And you still look real likely for this murder. Real likely." He turned and looked at me. "But if you didn't do it, there's things goin' on here you got no idea of. You'd best keep out of it—or so help me I'll put you away whether you killed Ernest B. or not. If I don't get you for this,

I'll nail you for something else. I don't care how I do it, I'll . . ." His voice trailed off. He seemed to realize he was losing control. He stood there a moment longer before leaving without another word.

• • •

IT WAS DARK AGAIN. I LAY IN BED, STARING at a little slit of light streaming in between the curtains. There was an intensely bright street light outside. It cast a sliver of sickly yellow on the bed, slicing across my wounded arm. Special effects lighting, giving my skin a jaundiced look—as if my health wasn't bad enough.

Somebody opened the door. The nurse, come to wake me and give me a pill. Before the door closed softly on its silent oiled hinges, I saw Jimmy Wilson standing out in the hall, dressed in uniform.

I cleared my throat.

"Oh, you're already awake," the nurse said. She clicked on the bedside light. It cast a white circle downward; some of which fell on the bed to join the sliver of yellow from outside. The two patterns of light merged on the sheet like an art abstraction. Mary Jo might appreciate it: "Line and Arc—Composition on a Sickbed."

"Having trouble sleeping?"

I nodded. "Could you ask the deputy to step in here on your way out?"

She pursed her lips and looked at me. "You need rest, Mr. Reed."

I nodded again and turned my face away until she finished and turned off the light. I lay still for a few moments after the door closed, then groped around on the bedside table for a green plastic drinking cup. Gritting my teeth against the pain in my arm, I tossed the cup left-handed. It made a hollow popping sound against the door—not very loud, but Jimmy was alert. The door opened a couple of inches and he peeked inside.

"Come in for a second, please."

Glancing around the hall to see that the nurse wasn't looking, he quickly slipped inside. I gestured toward the table lamp. "Turn that on, will you? I can't reach it."

He stepped to the side of the bed and snapped the light back on. The glow shining on his face exaggerated his features with upcast shadows like a child's flashlight impersonation of Dracula. "Mr. Reed, I'm glad to see you're feeling better."

"Thanks. You're looking better than the last time I saw you, too."

He withdrew his face from the light and said, "I feel pretty bad about breaking up like that. Sorry I wasn't more help to you until the sheriff showed up."

"Jimmy, anyone would've felt the same." He was avoiding my eyes, staring away at the wall, so I went on. "You don't have anything to be ashamed of. I imagine any decent man who had to take a life would feel miserable about it, even if he did it in self-defense."

He nodded. "You ever—kill anybody?"

"No."

He looked at me and said, "It's not—" He paused and looked away again and said, "You can't forget it."

It seemed like an understatement. His baby face was drawn and weary, the freckles across his cheeks fading into dark patches beneath his haunted eyes.

"Jimmy, you couldn't have done anything else. Lester was acting crazy. He probably would have killed you to get away."

The deputy nodded but remained silent, head bowed, eyes on the floor.

"Do you have any idea why he fought you that way?"

He shook his head slowly.

"Did he say anything to you on the walk from Mary Jo's studio to your car?"

Jimmy cleared his throat quietly and said, "Just begged me to let him go is all."

We were silent for a moment, then I said, "It was a good thing for me that you were watching our place and showed up when you did, Jimmy. I was seriously thinking about killing him."

He looked at me strangely. For an instant, I thought I saw something unexpected in his eyes. Was it disappointment? Garr, I thought, you're sick and imagining things.

I said, "I was sure Lester was there to hurt Mary Jo. It made me crazy. I was a second or two away from pulling the trigger when you tapped on the glass." I raised my eyes to meet his. "You probably saved me and Mary Jo from years of suffering because you were there to keep an eye on our place, Jimmy. I'll never be able to thank you enough."

He mumbled something about just doing his job, and we lapsed into an awkward silence. After a minute I said, "Well, anyway, I just wanted to tell you that, and to thank you for being there."

He nodded again and moved toward the door. As he reached for the handle I asked him another question. "Jimmy, am I under arrest?"

"The sheriff didn't put it like that. He just said to stay here and keep an eye on you."

"What if I wanted to leave?"

"I guess you could do that, Mr. Reed."

"Can I have visitors?"

"Sure, Mr. Reed. Anyone you want."

"I thought it was probably okay after last night."

"Last night?"

"Yes. But do me a favor and don't let anyone else in to see me so late, all right?"

He looked at me blankly and said, "What are you talking about?"

"That guy woke me up. He knocked over the I.V. stand."

"What guy?"

"The man you let in here last night."

"I didn't let anyone in."

I looked at him for a moment, then said, "Oh, yeah, it was yesterday afternoon. Sorry. The days and nights run together, you know?"

"Sure," he said. "I'll bet they do. Well, let me know if there's anything else you need."

After he closed the door, I thought for a while. Was it just a dream? But the nurse said they had to come in to pick up the I.V. stand. I remembered the feel of something pressed against my face, something soft and white. A pillow?

Slowly, I raised myself enough to reach the telephone.

Mary Jo answered, half asleep. "Garr! What on earth are you doing up at this hour? You should be resting." Her voice was barely above a whisper, her bedroom voice. I was struck by a mental picture of her, lying nestled in bed, her hair spread across her pillow, telephone cuddled against her ear like a high-tech teddy bear.

I said, "I'll go back to sleep in a little while. Just found myself lying here wide awake and thought I'd call."

"Well . . . I'm going to have to give them a talking to at that hospital. They shouldn't let you sit up all night like this. You need your rest." Her voice sounded distant. Impersonal.

I said, "Aren't you glad to hear from me?"

"Oh yes. You know I am. I just worry about you, that's all."

"I'm all right."

"I hope so." A pause, then, "Your arm's going to be all right too, you know."

I wasn't worried about my arm. As casually as I could, I said, "Is there still a police car on the road out front?"

"Sure. Just like every night. Why?"

"I just wanted to be sure you were safe." It was a lie. I was worried about something altogether different.

We made the kind of aimless small talk you make when neither of you wants to say what's really on your mind. Finally, she said "I love you, Garr" and hung up.

I lay back against the pillow, basking in the warmth of the moment. It was the first time she had mentioned love since the afternoon when I'd told her that I didn't trust her God. Maybe there was hope for us. Then my thoughts returned to the reason I'd called. I found myself wondering why Sheriff Barker had someone watching my house, while I lay in a hospital bed with Jimmy Wilson standing outside the door.

It was a very interesting question.

CHAPTER 27

LEON AND MRS. P. CAME TO VISIT ON Wednesday or Thursday. He stood against the wall tugging on his tie awkwardly. The tie's skinny end hung well below the wide part, and an enormous knot spanned the distance from his chest to his chin like a paisley goiter. He wore it with his denim work shirt and blue jeans. I knew how much he hated wearing ties. It was a touching gesture.

In deference to my tragic state, Mrs. P. had abandoned her floral muumuu, substituting a somber black robe devoid of ornamentation. She wore a huge silver and turquoise necklace draped over her ample bosom to compensate for the uncharacteristic simplicity of the dress. In place of her standard bouffant, she wore a black wig parted in the middle with two curving swoops of synthetic hair passing low on her broad forehead and twin braids that dangled below her round shoulders. The braids were interwoven with brown leather thongs. I suspected the Hiawatha wig and jewelry were an attempt to please Leon by taking a bow in the general direction of his Mayan heritage. To my way of thinking, she stepped over the line with the leather thongs, but Leon didn't seem to mind.

I was glad to see them both. Mary Jo had been spending a lot of time with me, but after five or six days in bed, I was ready for a little diversity.

Mrs. P. waddled over and enveloped me in a matronly hug. Her huge bosom completely covered my face for a moment. It would have been fun if the necklace hadn't been pressing into my nose. When she stepped back, I could see Leon was grinning.

"Love those hugs," he said.

"Yeah, boy. They're something."

Mrs. P. was not amused. She said, "Watch that talk, now. I come here for benevolent purposes, but there's only so far I can stretch this good mood."

"How's Fifi?" I asked.

Mrs. P. said, "She just fine. I got her all set up in your office, since you decided to vacate the premises. She happy as a pig in slop, takin' all your important calls."

"Glad to know the business is in good hands."

"Yep," said Leon. "And all the boys have decided to take a few days off in your honor. Don't it make you proud?"

I rolled my eyes.

After a little more small talk, Leon said, "Garr, I told you to call me before you tried any more of this amateur detective stuff. What's wrong with you, boy? Runnin' around gettin' shot at, and won't let me help?"

"I didn't plan this, you know."

"Yeah, but I known you since you was nothin' but a little guy. You oughta call me when you need a hand. It ain't right."

"Okay, okay. I'm sorry I went and got shot without your help. Next time I'll be sure to bring you along."

"That's good, 'cause you're sure enough in some deep trouble." He turned to Mrs. P. and said, "Show him, Ethyl."

Mrs. P. waddled to the door and leaned against it, her bulk effectively blocking it shut for the moment. She began to hike up her dress hem, then stopped and said, "Ya'll turn your heads."

We looked out the window. After a moment Mrs. P. said, "You can look now."

From beneath her dress she had withdrawn a plastic bag full of white powder. Maybe a half pound. If it was cocaine, it was worth thousands.

"Is that . . . ?"

"You know it," said Leon.

"For cryin' out loud—put it away!"

I averted my eyes again as Mrs. P. replaced the cocaine. She said, "It's a good thing we got Fifi 'round the office, Garrison. She found this stuff in back somewhere. I was talkin' on the phone the other day when she strutted up with it in her mouth, pretty as you please. At first I thought it was sugar."

Leon said, "Ethyl and I been talkin' 'bout this, and we decided you probably didn't put that stuff in the office."

"'Course if you did, we quit," added Mrs. P.

Leon beamed at her like she'd just won the lottery. "That's right, baby."

Mrs. P. said, "We ain't working for no drug kingpin."

"Kingpin?" I said.

She nodded vigorously. The wig slipped a bit lower on her forehead. "That's right. So we had us a decision to make. Is we workin' for a lowdown, drug-dealin', pill-poppin', dope-doin' piece of monkey leavin's—or is we workin' for an ignorant fool been duped into messin' with somethin' he don't know nothin' about?"

"Dope or dupe? Those were the choices?"

"That's right."

"And the decision was . . ."

"Dope," said Mrs. P.

"Dupe," said Leon.

"You're saying there's room for improvement in my approach to this problem."

"Lots and lots of room," said Leon.

"Garrison," said Mrs. P., "as a shamus, you got a pile of potential to improve into. That's a fact."

"Shamus?"

"That's right. Comes to investigatin', you all potential an' nothin' else. 'Course I give you 'bout one more week before whoever's playin' with yo' white behind gets tired of messin' 'round and nails it to the barn door."

"And that's where we come in," said Leon.

"That's right," said Mrs. P. "We goin' to help you figure out who killed Ernest B. and sent that no 'count Lester Fredricks over there to bedevil you and planted this here garbage in yo' office."

"Bedevil?"

"That's right. An' when we find that person, then Leon an' me's gonna kick his chicken white rear-most portions. No offense, Garrison, but I know he's got to be a white boy."

"None taken, Mrs. P. You're probably right."

"You're right I'm right. Was a gentleman of color after you, he wouldn't waste all this time with threats and traps and such silliness. He'd go ahead an' get it done, so he could move on to the finer things in life."

"Like lovin'," said Leon.

Mrs. P.'s hands went to her wide hips, the ancient signal of a woman to be taken seriously. "Now, Leon, I tol' you to watch that talk in public."

"That ain't all I'll watch, Ethyl."

"Oh, you."

I thought about the cocaine. Whoever was setting me up wasn't fooling around. They'd probably murdered Dr. Krueger, sent Lester Fredricks to plant false evidence at my home, and invested thousands in the cocaine they'd planted at my office—not to mention trying to kill me and doing away with Ernest B. So far, I'd managed through dumb luck to discover their attempts to frame me before the damage was done, but sooner or later they'd make it work.

Mrs. P.'s voice broke into my thoughts. "Interesting thing happened, Garrison. A couple of hours after Fifi found that dope, Sheriff Barker showed up. Said he wasn't finished searchin' yo' office. I asked did he have a search warrant, an' he tol' me to mind my business so he could mind his. Say, remember that time Bubba Lean's sister got in trouble? They searched her place out near Henderson an' didn't show no warrant and do you know ol' Bubba—"

"Ethyl!" Leon interrupted. "Why don't you tell us 'bout Bubba Lean's sister some other time?"

She said, "Well, all right, I just thought y'all would think it was interesting. I mean Bubba's just about done servin' that three years hard time, and his sister—"

"Ethyl!"

"What *is* yo' hurry, sugar? Anyway, Barker showed up right after Fifi found the dope, and he spent a long time in yo' office, Garrison. Probably would've stayed a lot longer, except his office called an' tol' him about crazy Old Man Martin wanderin' off from the old folk's home."

"How do you know what they told him?"

"Well, I transferred the call to him in your office, you know. An' sometimes it take me a while to hang up on my end. Anyway, ol' Mister Barker was shore red-faced when he come out. I jus' love it when you white folks get all red in the face. Look silly, like they's a big tomato on yo' shoulders. Give me one more reason to be proud of my complexion."

Leon said, "Oh for cryin' out loud, Ethyl. Will you please stick to the point?"

She drew herself up to her full height, her chest swelling until I thought the fabric of her robe would surely rip at the seams. "You watch that mouth of yours, Mister Mar-teen-nez, or I will see to it that you got no teeth in it at all. Do I make myself clear?"

Leon grinned and said, "Absolutely."

Mrs. P. stared at him sternly without blinking for a moment, then went on. "As I was sayin', when that no 'count cracker Barker walked out of yo' office, I asked him real sweet did he find everything he was lookin' for? He used some extremely foul language, Garrison, insultin' my ethnic heritage. He is not a nice person, that's for sure, and he don't much care for African-American office managers."

Leon waited to be sure she was done, then said, "What do you think about that, Garr?"

"I'm not sure. Either whoever planted the dope in my office called the sheriff, or . . ."

"Or else maybe Barker put it there?"

"The thought crossed my mind. That bag and the amount of powder in it sure looks a lot like the dope I found in Victor Sickle's car the other night."

"The dope that the cops should've found."

"But wouldn't the sheriff just bring the bag with him and then pretend to find it instead of botherin' to break in and plant it beforehand?" asked Mrs. P.

"This is a smart woman," said Leon.

She said, "You keep that in mind, we gonna get along fine."

I slapped the bed with my free hand. "Somebody's tryin' to get me killed or carted off to Huntsville! They plant evidence against me, and Barker's right there every time, looking in the right places. Either he's in on it, or he knows who's doing it."

"Settle down, Garr," said Leon. "You're gonna bust your stitches or somethin'." Turning to Mrs. P. he said, "Maybe we ought to let Garr rest a while, Ethyl."

With his hand on her wiggling elbow, they moved to the door. As they were about to open it, I thought to ask, "Hey, what are you gonna do with that cocaine?"

She said, "Oh, we'll prob'ly drive over an' dump it in the lake."

Leon grinned. Giving Mrs. P. a squeeze, he said, "While we're there, maybe we can get in a little smoochin', huh, baby?"

She punched him in the stomach with a good short jab, so hard I could hear the air rush out of his lungs from my side of the room. "Leon Martinez, I tol' you an' I tol' you. Do not discuss such things in public!"

As they were leaving, I asked, "Whatever happened to Old Man Martin?"

Leon was still trying to regain his breath, so Mrs. P. answered. She said, "You mean with him runnin' off from that nursin' home an' all?"

"Yes."

"I heard they found him sittin' in the middle of the road over in front of his place. Everybody figures he walked clear out there."

I said, "Isn't that something?"

"Shore is. Well, we'll be seein' you, Garrison. Y'all take care." She pulled Leon from the room. He was mumbling something about "love taps."

• • •

FOR THE NEXT FEW HOURS, I LAY IN BED thinking. My wits had been numbed by the painkillers for the past few days, but a lot was starting to come back to me.

I remembered seeing Ernest B.'s file, dog-eared and worn, in the sheriff's office the day Barker tried to tell me there was no drug problem in Jackson County. I thought about the cocaine I'd seen—and left—in Victor Sickle's car. Why hadn't it been mentioned in the newspaper? Interesting that it was packaged exactly like the bag Mrs. P. found later at my office.

The sheriff had assumed that I was the killer from the very first—long before the phony wallet and the cocaine was planted. He argued with Dr. Krueger in his courthouse the day before the doctor was murdered. He sent his men to look around Mary Jo's studio on the same day she found Ernest B.'s wallet there, obviously planted by Lester Fredricks. And Lester was so afraid of going to Barker's jail that he was willing to fight Jimmy Wilson for his gun, even though he was wearing handcuffs.

Although I still wasn't sure exactly what was going on, I was pretty sure Clyde Barker was mixed up in it somehow.

But I had many more questions than answers. What was the significance of the tattoo snapshot I found in Dr. Krueger's pocket? Why had Krueger been unwilling to speak to me at Ernest B.'s funeral, only to ask for a meeting less than an hour later? Why had Ernest B. developed such a strong interest in his family's legendary treasure just before he died? What was the source of the light in the spring under Martin Pool? Who was trying to frame me for Ernest B.'s murder? Who killed Ernest B.? Who tried to kill me? Who pulled me out of Martin Pool and called the cops?

For the first time since I regained consciousness in the hospital room, I began to reconstruct the final events before my blackout in Martin Pool. It wasn't easy. Shock, along with a week of floating in and out of awareness, never completely free of the influence of painkillers, had taken a toll on my short-term memory.

I tried to place the voice that had warned me to duck. It was familiar. But recognition hovered just out of reach, obscured by the trauma of events and the passing of time. I twisted the sheets in frustration. I was sure there was something else I should remember. Something to do with the bollards and the old road . . . yes! I had it. The Camaro. The dark blue Camaro I saw driving away just before I passed out.

The last time I saw that car, it was in a ditch with Victor Sickle at the wheel.

What to do? There wasn't much point in passing the information along to the deputy guarding my door. Trusting the sheriff's department to find the truth was like asking a hound dog to guard the barbecue.

I was on my own.

CHAPTER 28

AFTER ALMOST THREE WEEKS IN THE hospital, I went home with my right arm hanging limply in a blue fabric sling. Other than a sharp pain when I moved too fast, it didn't hurt much.

Mary Jo showed up at my hospital room at eight in the morning and packed the few things I'd accumulated during my stay. I told her to leave Sickle's card and potted plant behind.

Barker followed us all the way from the hospital parking lot. Conspicuous in a marked patrol car, he stayed just a few feet from our rear bumper as we passed between the moss-covered shady banks of the old road home. We slowed to enjoy the view through the ancient overhanging oaks. Barker didn't seem to mind. When we pulled into our driveway, he parked at the usual place by the road out front. I waved at him left-handed before stepping inside the house. He did not return the wave.

It was good to be home with Mary Jo's mothering instincts in overdrive. She set me up on the sofa with a pile of pillows to support my arm and placed a cold glass of Artesia mineral water on the table beside me. A stack of novels by my favorite authors appeared next to the drink. She opened the drapes, spread birdseed on the back porch, and put our binoculars within reach so I could do some bird watching through the French doors if I got tired of reading. Then she settled in beside me, with her arm around my shoulders.

We sat together without talking for a while. She began to cry. She made no sound; the tears simply washed over her smooth, lovely cheeks and hovered at her chin for a moment before dropping.

I said, "What is it, little one?"

"I'm just so glad you're safe at home." She wiped her eyes with her knuckles. "You don't know how close you came to dying, Garr. The doctor said you almost bled to death before whoever found you bandaged your arm. And they say you almost drowned." She sniffled. "You almost died two ways. When Clyde showed up, I didn't know what he was talking about at first. He ran down to the boathouse, and I followed. You were lying there, looking so pale and gray. All I could think about was that you'd been there all the time, suffering, while I was up at the house messing around, being so . . . mad at you. You could have died, and I was right here the whole time." She pulled a tissue from her pocket and blew her nose. "I realized how easy it would be to lose you. And for a while at the hospital, before they told me you were all right, I thought maybe I would. I felt what it would be like. It was devastating."

She turned sideways on the sofa and put her palm against my cheek. "You are the most precious part of my life, Garrison Reed. Without you, I'd be empty. There'd be no reason to make plans. I couldn't paint. May God forgive me, I don't even think I'd be able to pray. I don't know if I could live without you."

I started to speak, but she pressed a finger against my mouth and said, "Wait till I'm finished. I've got something else to say."

She rose from the sofa and stood looking out of the French doors toward the lake, her back to me. Her copper-colored mane of hair hung loose and wild. Glimmers of sunshine sparkled through it, as if she wore an angelic halo. She said, "Garr, I want you to stop looking into Ernest B.'s death. I know someone's been trying to make them think you killed him, and you could go to jail. But it seems like the deeper you get into this business, the harder they push. And now they almost killed you." She turned to face me. Her eyes were red-rimmed, on the verge of hysteria. "I want my husband alive! Even if it means that you have to be in jail."

"Wait a minute—"

"No! You wait a minute! They want you *dead,* Garr." Suddenly, she knelt before me, holding my hand in hers. She went on urgently, desperately. "We've got lots of money. We can hire good lawyers, fight this thing in court. You haven't done anything wrong. You'll get off, I'm sure of it. We could even run away, change our names. I'll do anything. But I will not have you taking these chances, maybe getting shot and killed. It's not fair of you to ask me to accept that. I'm the one who would have to go on living without you." She began to cry again. Her words came out in short bursts between sobs. "And if it's true, what you've been saying—if it's true that you don't know the Lord, I'll have to live on, knowing that you might not be waiting for me when I come to be with God in heaven. You don't know how that makes me feel. If you get killed, it's over for you, but it's just the start of a living hell for me. Can't you understand? I want you to trust God to take care of what's happening to us."

She squeezed my hands and searched my eyes with fear and love. Then, in a whisper I could barely hear, she said, "I need you to trust Jesus."

Tears flowed across her cheeks, quivering on her chin and falling unnoticed. I slid to the floor beside her and held her as best as I could with my one good arm, trying to decide what to say. Finally, I decided not to say anything at all.

• • •

THAT NIGHT, AS MARY JO LAY CURLED IN THE sheets with her back to me, I stared at the ceiling trying to justify what I wanted to do. I knew how she felt. Sometimes, when she was away, the sound of a distant siren in the night filled me with dread—and, if I was feeling particularly melancholy, I allowed those fears to grow into a horrible vision of life without her. Childish perhaps, but it made my joy at her homecomings more intense and provided a slight margin of preparedness for the dismal existence I would suffer if she went first. In the same way that the sting of a vaccination must be endured to avoid disease, my instinct for emotional self-preservation demanded that I try to prepare myself for a life without Mary Jo by thinking about how it might be.

Her voice came to me unbidden. "Knowing you might not be waiting for me when I come to be with God in heaven—you don't know how that makes me feel." For some reason, things shifted as I remembered her words. For the first time in my life, I realized—really understood—that I was going to die one day. The thought terrified me. What then? Was I simply a mass of tissue, destined for nothingness? Maybe I should hope so. Because if Mary Jo was right about her God, I could be destined for something much worse.

Mary Jo rolled onto her back, tugging at the covers. Almost immediately, she began to softly snore. I envied that peacefulness. Her life was full of uncertainty, violence, and lies—her husband running amuck, the very foundation of her marriage based on two decades of deception; yet she slept like a child, free of the demons that tortured me. She was my rock, the center of my life. Was I the same to her? If so, how could she sleep? I had shown myself to be a liar, a thief of affections, a fraudulent partner, deserving of nothing but mistrust. I was, after all, only human. She was wise not to base her confidence on me.

I had never been up to carrying that burden, and neither, I supposed, was she.

The thought did nothing to mitigate my terror. My life was centered on something—someone—much better than myself, and yet she too was only human. What a fool I had been to lean so heavily on such a frail creature.

And yet, as I watched her sleep, I knew her peaceful center was unshaken. If I was not at that center, if her assurance was built on God, what lesson could I learn from the fact that she enjoyed serene dreams while I struggled with doubt and depression? Maybe I should grant her request. Maybe I should trust in God to resolve the situation with Victor Sickle.

"I want you to trust God to take care of what's happening to us."

Was she right? How could I know he could be trusted? For the first time, aware of my mortality in a sure and immediate way, I felt I wanted to lean on God.

And yet . . . I needed to *know* before I could commit so much.

But Mary Jo was asking so much—asking me to turn my back on corruption, drugs, and the murder of my oldest friend. In a way, the destruction of the only place I had ever called home was at stake. How could I live with myself if I didn't try to stop it?

Mary Jo might not understand, but if I gave up now, she would lose me just as surely as she would if I was killed. Every time I passed the Martin place, I'd have to face my failure. Every time I looked at the beautiful lake at our back door, I would be reminded first of the friend who shared my idyllic childhood, then of the way they pulled his swollen body from the water. I would have to bury my emotions alongside Ernest B. to go on living.

She wouldn't want me that way.

I turned my head. The dull red glowing numbers on the alarm clock read two-thirty A.M. As quietly as possible, I lifted the sheets and slipped out of bed. Padding barefoot to the window, I parted the curtains just enough to peek out at the road. No patrol car. In a way, I was disappointed—it would have given me an excuse not to go.

Moving across the dark bedroom, avoiding the furniture by memory, I collected my clothing with my good arm. I dressed in the study and sat in the red oak swivel chair behind my desk to pull on my boots. When I bent over, blood rushed to my arm, throbbing through the wound with every heart-beat, a reminder of what I was up against. The pain receded slightly when I straightened up, but the point was made. I was far from immortal. My enemies would murder me if they got the chance. If I couldn't share Mary Jo's faith in a spiritual ally, at least I should get protection in the material world.

I crossed the room, removed the twelve-gauge shotgun from the rack, and loaded it, pumping a shell into the breach one-handed by shaking it sharply up and down while holding the slide. It was hard to do, and it hurt my arm to move so fast, but it was possible.

So, I had a gun. But the closer I came to leaving the house, the stronger my fear became. My arm still throbbed in time with my pulse. They had missed my head by only two or three inches, out there in the lake. I would have sunk to the bottom, weighed down by the scuba gear. It would have taken days to find me, if they ever did. I thought of Mary Jo. She would have been a widow and not yet known it, waiting for me on the back deck, staring out across Martin Pool. I remembered what she'd said about heaven, and me not being there when she died. It scared me, knowing what I was about to do and suspecting that she might be right.

If there was a heaven, I wanted in.

So, I closed my eyes and tried to pray. I told God what I was going to try to do, and asked for help. I asked him to bring me back home safely. If he wanted me to die tonight, I asked him to take me up to be with him for Mary Jo's sake. I told him what I was going to do was not about me. It was about justice.

And so, after all those lies to Mary Jo, I lied again; this time to Almighty God. But did it matter? Maybe he wasn't even there. Maybe he wasn't listening. I didn't know. That was the problem. Before I could trust in God, I needed to *know*.

CHAPTER 29

STEERING ONE-HANDED, I DROVE the pickup slowly and checked the rearview mirror often for headlights. I thought about Leon's offer to help. It was tempting, but I decided against calling him. I was probably going to end up in jail. Why involve him in something that might ruin his life or get him killed?

As I passed the ditch where Victor Sickle's car had crashed, I saw deep ruts in the rain-soaked soil where his Camaro had been winched out. Water stood puddled in the ditch, black as an oil spill.

Martin Pool lay like an empty hole on my right as I crossed the dam. I might have been driving at the edge of a cliff, beside an infinite, bottomless void. It was a new way of thinking about the lake, but I was used to experiencing Martin Pool in new ways. I had been raised on its banks but never become accustomed to its changing character. It could begin the day with a misty, romantic stillness and end it by violently hurling itself at the waterline, like a caged frantic animal. Some evenings, with fires blazing along the shore and the wind-lifted voices of weekend campers crossing the waves, the lake seemed a crowded, suburban place. But its desolate stillness at dawn could make you feel that you alone had survived the night.

A mile or so along the tarmac road beyond the dam, the headlights of my truck illuminated a battered steel mailbox with "Sickle" painted on the side in dripping red letters—right where old Pedro had told me it would be. I pulled into the ditch a hundred yards beyond the mailbox and stepped from the truck onto the soggy earth, shotgun in hand.

The woods were alive with the calls and screams of the hunters and the hunted. I thought of these deep east Texas woods the way I thought of the lake, in many ways, according to my frame of mind. Soft dappled shade in the springtime lent the forest an aura of calming peacefulness. Tonight, I was conscious of the violent death that waited within its menacing darkness for thousands of animals at the bottom of the food chain. A high wind rushed through the very tops of the pines, whining like speeding tires on pavement. Higher still, the deep gray clouds raced across the sky.

I felt vulnerable and alone.

Stepping into the woods, I set off between the trees, moving carefully on a diagonal away from the road. I was betting that Victor Sickle's house would be several hundred yards from the highway. A man in Sickle's line of work would want privacy. After struggling through the undergrowth for five minutes, moving slowly to avoid making noise, I came to a gravel drive. I walked parallel to it, a few feet away in the trees.

My heartbeat roared in my ears. I found myself taking short, shallow breaths. I would have been afraid even if Sickle hadn't been a drug dealer. People in Texas have a more highly developed sense of the sanctity of their privacy than most. It's an attitude that began years ago, when Texas law allowed for the killing of trespassers whether they threatened you or not. Inside, outside—didn't matter. If you could prove they were on your property without permission, you could kill them. They changed the law in my grandfather's day, but some people don't much care. It's still fairly common to see signs reading "Trespassers Will Be Shot" nailed to trees in the backwoods of east Texas. Only a tourist would fail to take them seriously. I was very quiet.

The Camaro was parked directly in front of a clapboard house. I stopped beside it long enough to touch the hood of the car. It was warm. In that instant, I thought of going back. Sickle was here, in this house. And I knew that, if I continued, he would leave me no choice. I hefted the shotgun with my good arm, considering its implications. With this weapon I had reduced Lester Fredricks from an enemy to a cowering victim of my own blind rage. With this weapon I had almost done a murder. I ran the risk of destroying a part of myself if I was forced to shoot Victor Sickle. Yet if I went back now, I might never recover the life I had already lost.

I slipped the safety off on the shotgun.

The bottom of the walls of the old farmhouse flared out all around, giving it a solidly rooted look. The windows were dark. The recent hard rains had splattered mud up onto the wood siding. A deep porch spanned the front, several steps above the ground, piled high with junk: an old washing machine, a wooden box full of dull black metal parts, a Harley Davidson chassis without wheels or motor, a couple of folding chairs with frayed plastic webbing.

I inched along the side of the house, ducking as I passed the windows. In the back, a mercury-vapor yard light hung high on a creosote pole, dumping its stark white glare on everything. I reached the back corner of the house and crouched beneath a window in the brilliant white light.

Katydids strummed in rhythmic pulses throughout the woods for miles around. I heard a woman's voice.

I double-checked the safety on my shotgun. Then, very slowly, I raised my head above the window sill to peek inside.

The flashy redhead I had first seen talking to Victor Sickle at the Nowhere Club was sitting on a bed four feet away, clearly lit through the window by the pole-mounted light at my back. Her face was turned away from the window. Sickle sat in bed beside her, smoking a cigarette.

The woman's eyes flicked my way. I ducked immediately. After a moment, she spoke loudly enough for me to hear her through the glass. I decided she hadn't seen me. I crouched below the window trying to decide what to do. The bedsprings squeaked.

Why did he have to have a woman in his bed? It complicated things. Then again, maybe it was a blessing. If Sickle was alone in the house, who knows what I might have done?

Then I remembered his little trick at the hotel coffee shop in Dallas, and the fear I'd felt as I ran down the hall toward Mary Jo's room. I remembered how Mary Jo had peeked from beneath the covers when I rushed into the room; her sleepy smile when she said, "Hi, baby. What's the matter?" I remembered the empty eyes Sickle had turned on me as he said, "You're the guy I saw at ol' Ernest B.'s funeral. Hey. Wasn't that a shame?"

The memories added fuel to my longing for revenge.

Slowly, I stood again. The shotgun in my left hand preceded my head above the windowsill by an inch or two. I told myself I only wanted another look—to see what he was doing. My finger on the trigger was just a precaution. I told myself a lot of things—everything I could think of except the truth: The rage was back, and I wanted a piece of Victor Sickle, woman or no woman.

I peeked over the sill. She had leaned over, her head near his, her hands on his bare chest. Suddenly she rolled to the other side of the bed, and Victor Sickle flipped to his belly with a pistol in his outstretched hand, aimed in my direction. He fired. The window shattered. Glass shards exploded past my face, the tiny chips dusting my hair like snowflakes. Involuntarily, I squeezed the trigger too. The shotgun yanked in my hand like a living thing. What remained of the window glass was driven into the room and across the bed. The old plaster ceiling inside was pulverized by the shotgun pellets, dropping a cloud of white powder on Sickle and the woman and obscuring my view of the interior for a moment. The woman screamed. Sickle kept firing, over and over, the slugs whining through the wall all around me.

My nerve broke and I ran like crazy, following the drive until I was about halfway to the road, then cutting directly through the woods to my truck. I was almost there when I heard the deep roar of the Camaro's engine revving up.

Sickle reached the road just as I was speeding past his driveway in the truck. It didn't take long for his headlights to catch up to me as we roared onto the dam.

I drove like a madman, weaving all over the road. Maybe this would work out. If my luck held, he would chase me into town, shooting all the way. There would be a lot of witnesses. The sheriff would have to arrest him. They'd check out his car, and maybe his house, where I was pretty sure they'd find some evidence of his drug deals. With luck, they would even find something that would tie him to Ernest B.'s death. They would overlook my trespassing and the shotgun pellets in the ceiling of his room when they discovered proof that Sickle was involved in murder.

We hit about ninety as we came down off the dam on my side of the lake. The ancient oaks overhanging the road created the illusion of a tunnel, their trunks flashing by much too quickly in my headlights. I was having a little trouble maintaining control of the truck with my left hand alone. As we flew along the section of road in front of the Martin place, Sickle rammed my rear bumper. The steering wheel twisted in my hand. I stood on the brakes. The truck pitched at an angle, tires digging into the tarmac. Sickle hit me again. The front bumper of the truck slammed into the embankment on the left side of the road. I felt the cab tilt. I was about to roll. Sickle cut to the right to avoid driving the hood of his Camaro beneath my truck. As the truck began to flip, it struck the left side of the Camaro. The impact stopped me from rolling and knocked the Camaro sideways into the overgrown brush on the other side of the road.

It was over in a couple of seconds.

I sat at the wheel, steam from the radiator rising through the cracks around my buckled hood. My wounded right arm bled into the sling, soaking the spare shotgun shells. Other than that, I seemed to be all right. Peering through a spider web of cracks in my windshield at the Camaro, I saw that its headlights were still on. One beam shone at an upward angle through the smoke and steam above the road. I thought about that light traveling forever, past the planets, past the stars, never stopping until it shone on some other world where all was well. I struggled with a persistent feeling that none of this was really happening. Maybe I was slipping into shock.

My reverie was disturbed by a small pop and the sight of the yellow muzzle blast of Victor Sickle's gun in the darkness. I shook my head from side to side to clear my mind. Leaning forward to put my face near the cracked windshield, I squinted across the road. Another pop and a flash in the dark over there somewhere. A bullet whistled through the cab. Time to go.

I was lucky the door would open. As I slid from the seat, a hole appeared in the windshield behind me where my head had been. Sickle was getting his range. I squatted behind the truck and pumped a shell into the shotgun one handed. Hot blood flowed from my newly re-opened wound.

I rose to stand beside the hood, laid the gun across it with the butt against my belt buckle, and pulled the trigger. The shotgun roared, slamming back against my stomach. The rear side window of the Camaro exploded. Missed him. I held the gun out from my left side by the slide and shook it sharply up and down, pumping in another shell. Again, using the truck hood for support, I fired. The driver's door was slammed by a hundred pellets in a tight circle. Sickle screamed.

When my ears quit ringing from the shotgun blasts, silence had returned to the woods around us, broken only by the ticking of Victor Sickle's crumpled radiator. I crouched behind the truck and watched the Camaro over the top of the hood until the need to know drove me to reach into the truck cab for a flashlight and slowly approach Sickle's car. Holding the flashlight in my bloody right hand and aiming the shotgun as best I could with my left, I crouched forward as I walked to make myself a smaller target. My boots crunched on the gravel shoulder. Perhaps Sickle would suddenly appear in the window and fire at me point blank. The muscles of my stomach grew tight, anticipating the impact of his bullet.

I reached the door of the car and bent lower to look inside. There was a small glistening circle of blood on the passenger-side bucket seat.

But Sickle was gone.

CHAPTER 30

THE INSTANT I REALIZED THAT SICKLE was not in his car, I clicked off my flashlight and dropped to my knees. He had to be watching from the treeline on the other side of the Camaro, waiting for a clear shot. I slipped the flashlight into the back pocket of my blue jeans and checked my ammunition. There were still a couple of shells in the magazine, and I had six bloody ones tucked into the sling on my arm. Enough to waste a few.

I listened and waited.

The night birds and insects began to sing again. I raised my face toward the sky and sniffed the air. A gentle breeze bore the sweet smell of honeysuckle. Vague wisps of light gray cloud streamed quickly across the strip of moonlit sky above the road. A distant scream floated on the wind, the death cry of a possum perhaps, back broken beneath the claws of an owl. I sniffed again and smelled gasoline and burnt rubber. The wrecked Camaro's radiator continued to tick as it cooled. A soft rustling sound came from the woods a few yards away.

The hunt resumed, and this time I was going to do the hunting.

I stood quickly and fired a round over the car top into the woods. There was a pig-like grunt, and the sound of something big crashing through the underbrush. I hadn't hit him, but Sickle was scared enough to ignore caution and run flat out. I loped around the car, down into the bar ditch and up the other side to the treeline. The woods were very dark, but Sickle made a lot of noise. It was easy to follow him.

I left the flashlight in my pocket and did my best to avoid low-hanging branches and underbrush as I lumbered along in the pale light from the moon. Sickle stopped once, either to listen for me or to try an ambush. I stood motionless beside a tree trunk until his nerve failed him and he began stumbling through the woods again.

Up ahead, the dull yellow glow of an incandescent lightbulb twinkled through the trees. I had expected it. This was Martin land, familiar territory. I slowed to a walk and made my way to the edge of the clearing, just in time to see Sickle slip through the door of the Martins' barn. We had run across more than a hundred acres of deep woods and come to the Martin home place.

I knew the buildings well from many hours spent playing childhood games there with Ernest B. The barn huddled against the hillside behind the house, its rear half buried into the slope. It was one of the oldest structures in the county, built of limestone blocks carved from the hill itself, with a roof of hand-hewn timbers connected with wooden pegs. The mossy cedar-shake roof was steeply pitched to make room for a hay loft in the attic. Behind the barn, the land rose eighty feet or so before dropping on the other side of the hill to meet the water of Martin Pool, near the place where I'd been shot. In the old days, horse-drawn wagons were driven directly into the upper hay loft across a contoured earthen bridge connecting the high ground with the attic floor. Over the years, the lichen and moss that covered the limestone outcroppings grew onto the stone walls and cedar shingles of the barn as well, making it hard to tell where the barn began and the hill left off. The effect was pleasing to the eye, as if the structure was organic, put there by the hand of God along with the land itself.

Sickle was probably inside the old barn with his pistol aimed at the door, hoping I would follow him in. That would be suicide. But I didn't want to spend the night waiting for him to come out, not when I had him running scared. Eventually, the police would find our wrecked vehicles and come looking. It didn't cross my mind to wait for them. I had to keep the pressure on.

It was time to end this thing.

I looped wide around the clearing to my left, staying just inside the treeline. The land rose beneath my feet as I climbed the hill behind the Martin compound. Soon, I stood on the high ground near the second-story wall of the old barn, listening at the hayloft door. I heard nothing, but he was almost surely waiting silently inside, hoping I'd be stupid enough to follow him through the downstairs door. I was willing to bet my life that Victor Sickle didn't know about this upper-level entrance and was devoting his complete attention to the one below.

I pushed the old wooden door open and slipped inside.

The rusted iron hinges screeched as the door swung open and shut. Sickle couldn't miss the noise. I crouched in the darkness near the door and waited for him to make a sound. Above me, pale moonlight shone through the warped and timeworn shingles, casting faint dots of light on the filthy wood-planked floor. It was possible to see some shapes in the speckled moonlight, but no detail. The musty smell of sour hay and horse manure joined with the smell of my own sweat as I held myself motionless, willing Sickle to make a sound. The wait seemed to last forever. My knees ached from the effort of crouching, yet I did not dare to move. After a while, I realized that my legs were going to sleep. I had to do something. I took several deep breaths to steady myself, holding my mouth unnaturally wide to be sure that my breathing made no sound. Finally, I was ready.

Maintaining my grip on the shotgun with my good hand, I reached to my back pocket with the other and took out the flashlight. The movement sent spikes of pain through my arm. I swung the shotgun down in front with the stock braced against my stomach, ready to pan it in any direction. After one last, deep, wide-mouthed breath, I clicked on the flashlight and tossed it across the hayloft with a flip of my wrist, hoping that Sickle would overreact and fire at the light, giving away his position.

Nothing happened.

The flashlight rolled to a stop against an old pile of dry manure, its beam slicing upward through the dusty air, illuminating the ancient, hand-hewn rafters overhead. I froze where I was for four or five minutes, waiting for a sound—afraid to move, afraid to breathe. Finally, it occurred to me that Sickle might have slipped out the front. I decided to risk picking up the flashlight to have a look around.

The hayloft was empty except for a pile of burlap sacks and a stack of old boards. At the edge of the loft platform was a ladder. I would be exposed to the floor below for a few seconds on the way down, but that beat going in through the front door. I backed down the ladder as quickly as possible, sighing with relief when my feet touched the ground. So far so good.

The old barn was divided down the middle by a corridor lined on both sides with low wooden horse stalls. I walked along the corridor, panning the flashlight from side to side, following the beam of light with the muzzle of my gun. Dirt floors, musty bales of hay, cracked leather bridles and other tack hanging on pegs along the walls, the scalloped top rails of old stalls where the horses had chewed the wood—everything I saw reminded me of the childhood games that Ernest B. and I had played in this building so many years ago.

I reached the rear wall where the barn blended seamlessly into the sheer rock face of the hill. We had often made a game of climbing the dry stacked stone, our little fingers gripping the cracks between the blocks as we pulled ourselves up to the dizzying height of ten feet or so—a race to be the first to touch the wooden planks of the hayloft, high above.

Centered on the wall was a rusty metal water trough hanging bottom-side-out on a hook. It was oval, about seven feet long and four feet wide. Something felt wrong. There was no reason for the trough to be hanging on the wall instead of sitting on the ground. I played the light around and saw several boot impressions in the dirt floor nearby and a short groove parallel to the wall, possibly scraped into the soil by the lip of the trough as it was dragged across the floor. But why was it lifted up onto the hook? Why not simply lean it against the stone? The thing was heavy; too heavy to pick up without good reason. I reached forward with the barrel of the shotgun and pushed at the side of the trough. It rocked on the hook like a door on well-oiled hinges. I pushed again with the shotgun barrel, and swung the trough until it hung cocked at an angle. I shone the light behind it.

The stones behind the trough had been removed, and a short timber placed across the top of the resulting opening to support the rocks higher up on the wall. It was a doorway into the hillside. I pushed the old steel trough a little further aside and squeezed through. It rocked back into position behind me, shutting off the outside world.

Shining the flashlight around, I saw I was in a natural cavern—a tunnel, really. The ceiling, about seven feet high, tapered down on both sides. The floor rose to meet the ceiling. There were no walls. A cross-section cut through the passageway would be shaped like a football, coming to points at each end. I sniffed. The air was very still and smelt of soil, fungus, and damp compost. It seemed to lie in motionless horizontal layers, undisturbed for years. I thought about this air going unused by living things, going to waste. It had been hovering here behind the wall when Ernest B. and I had played as children in the barn beyond. This same air still hovered here now that I was middle-aged and no longer playing.

To one side was a dilapidated wooden rack. Potato pallets, I thought, most likely put there by Ernest B.'s great grandfather a hundred years ago. He probably built the barn in front of this natural cave so he could use it for a root cellar.

I said, "Son of a gun," and my voice reverberated against the hard rock walls of the cavern, bouncing from side to side down the tunnel like a drunk in a hallway.

Straight ahead, the passage sloped down into black obscurity beyond the range of the flashlight's beam. I decided to follow it. Walking was difficult; I had to pick my way over an irregular rock floor littered with loose stones. My tentative footsteps scraped and echoed, joining the sound of water dripping in the distance. The ground began to slope steeply down. I leaned on the shotgun, using it as a walking stick to help me descend the slope.

Incredibly, I reached steps carved into the rock. Who had carved them? I thought of prehistoric people, taking shelter here in the dead of an ice-age winter. Maybe Caddo Indians used this cave in the time of Columbus. I remembered the newspaper article Ernest B. had read about a family of Caddos, trapped and mummified beside their campfire in a cave like this. It gave me the creeps.

As I descended the ancient stairway, the sound of dripping water grew louder. The shuffling noises I made bounced against the walls, amplified by the hard rock. The light's beam slashed through the cool air as I lurched along, illuminating the stone floor and ceiling in brief flashes. In some places, water seeped from horizontal fissures in the rock.

I was amazed that a cavern of this size could exist in Jackson County without my knowledge. Growing up around Martin Pool, I had explored every gully, every hill, every inch of shoreline. But I'd never guessed that this wonderful cave was just beyond the wall of the old barn where Ernest B. and I had spent so many playful summer days.

After ten or fifteen minutes of walking and climbing downward, I reached a spot where the passageway widened a little and the shape of the tunnel squared off. There were now irregular walls. I brought the flashlight's beam to rest on a rectangular opening in the wall to the right. It was shaped like a manmade door. Small stones and rock chips were piled haphazardly in front of the opening and beside it. Playing the light around, I could see that the hole in the wall was framed by timbers. Across the top of the opening were several beams, bowed downward by the terrible weight of the hill above.

"Hope it's safe," I mumbled as I picked my way over the pile of stones and stooped under the overloaded timber. The opening led into a short, narrow passage. I followed the smaller tunnel for about ten paces, then found myself in a large room. I caught a glimpse of some sort of equipment standing against the far wall. Two steps into the cavernous space, the stench of human feces and urine assaulted my nostrils. Remembering Victor Sickle, I clicked off the flashlight and silently slipped a few feet along the wall in the blackness to conceal my location.

The air in the underground room was cool, but I began to sweat from fear. This was worse than the barn. There, at least I was familiar with the space around me and a little moonlight shone through the leaky roof to give me something to watch. Here, I was in unknown surroundings and the darkness was total, a blackness beyond anything possible on the surface.

After a minute I heard something: the soft sound of fabric brushing against itself, and a dull clink of metal on stone. It came from within the room, somewhere in front of me. The silence that followed seemed to last for hours. I began to wonder if I had imagined the sound.

Then I heard it again.

I leveled the shotgun waist high and clicked the flashlight on. Quickly sweeping the beam around the room, I saw nothing except the strange equipment against the wall. The stench was almost overpowering, like the inside of a privy in August.

I heard the sound again.

When I spoke, the sound of my voice echoed throughout the room. "Sickle, you can't win against this shotgun. Get out here where I can see you!"

There was a soft moan, then silence. Remembering the blood in the seat of his car, I wondered if he was badly wounded. The sweat of my palm made it difficult to hold the shotgun steady with one hand, but I managed. Slowly, I walked across the cave, shining the light on the objects against the far wall. Cans, pipes, a couple of oil drums, and some bulging burlap sacks were illuminated one by one as the circular beam moved along. A huge metal tank on a wrought-iron stand with four legs. The legs straddled a pile of ashes.

When I realized what it was, I forgot about being afraid of Victor Sickle. I was looking at a genuine part of Texas history. I was looking at E. B. Martin's long-lost still.

I knew how the people who found the *Titanic* must have felt. You grow up hearing about a thing—everyone's heard about it, but no one's ever actually seen it—and you ask yourself: Is it real? This moonshine still had been the subject of tall tales in Jackson County for three generations, the stories building on each other, expanding over time until they assumed a mythical status. People in my generation mostly smiled and exchanged knowing looks when the old folks spoke of E. B. Martin's mysterious still. Who knew if the stories were true? Yet here it was, the one they never found. The federal boys never found it, and they spent years looking. The county boys never found it, at least not in an official capacity. Long after the competition was in prison, or shut down for lack of nerve in the face of the law and the Southern Baptists, long after every other still in Jackson County was just so much rusting junk, E. B. Martin's initials kept popping up on Mason jars full of his home brew. They never caught him. He simply disappeared. To this day, folks still keep those old jars with E.B.M. marked crudely on the lid, empty now (of course), but proudly displayed as proof that Daddy or Granddaddy was a participant in one of the area's finer traditions: getting looped on E. B. Martin's shine.

I moved the light around as I circled the contraption, paying no attention to where I was stepping. On the back side, between the still and the cool rock wall, I kicked something. Another moan rose from the floor at my feet. I sprang back and aimed the flashlight down.

There, curled in a tight ball on the cold stone floor, lay the source of the sounds I had heard and the stench I had smelled.

It was my old friend, Ernest B.

CHAPTER 31

He lay on his side with one end of a steel chain padlocked to his ankle and the other to his grandfather's still. I aimed the light directly at his face, hardly able to believe what I was seeing.

He held a shaking, grimy hand in front of his eyes.

I moved the beam to the wall above him, close enough to make him out in the diffuse reflected glow. With a soft moan, he tried to push himself up to lean against the rock wall. The chain clinked as he dragged it across the floor. He continued to hold his hand over his eyes, making no effort to look at me.

Ernest B. was a big man, about my size. The last time I saw him, he weighed about two hundred and forty pounds. Now, his filthy shirt hung loosely on a bony frame. His thick, prematurely gray hair was tangled and matted, and a short, reddish-brown beard sprouted from his shrunken cheeks. Starvation had transformed his mischievous baby face into a skull with skin.

I leaned the shotgun against the wall and knelt beside him. Touching his shoulder, I said, "It's Garr, Ernest B. I'm here to help you."

For a moment, I thought he hadn't heard or couldn't understand. Then, slowly, he lowered his hand and turned to look at me. Incredibly, he smiled. The teeth between his cracked lips flashed white against his dark red whiskers. He whispered, "Hey, buddy . . ." Then his eyes shifted their focus onto something far away, and he drifted off again.

I shone the light on his legs. The chain was tightly wrapped and padlocked around his ankle, just below the rolled cuff of his faded blue jeans. The other end encircled a copper pipe on the still. I could see bright scratches on the dull brown pipe and bloody scabs around his ankle where Ernest B. had struggled against the chain. I aimed the light at him again. He wore a black T-shirt emblazoned with a white Harley Davidson logo and baggy blue jeans. His belt was wide brown leather, hand-tooled with intricate swirls and secured by a large, silver-plated oval buckle with brass insets. He was proud of that buckle. He'd won it the hard way at the age of twenty, bulldogging at the Mesquite, Texas, Championship Rodeo, riding flat-out until he was alongside a yearling steer, then jumping from his racing horse to wrestle it to the ground in record time. Ernest B. used to be a tough guy.

I patted his shoulder and stood to look around. He had done his best to keep the area around him free of his own waste. It was piled in one spot, as far away as the chain would reach. I shone the light in the opposite direction. What I saw there sickened me.

Two plastic bowls stood side by side on the filthy rock floor, both empty. They were the kind you see in the pet section of the supermarket. Beside them lay a paper bag marked "dog food" and an empty plastic jug. A pair of bolt cutters were propped against the wall a couple of yards away, carefully placed beyond the reach of Ernest B.'s chain. The bolt cutters could snap the chain around his ankle like a knife slicing butter, but he had no hope of reaching them where they were.

Shining the light on Ernest B.'s silent form, I tried to imagine what he had suffered there, chained and fed in the dark like a dog, knowing that the means of escape was inches beyond his grasp. Those inches might as well have been miles.

A cold fury seized me. It was beyond the anger I felt when Lester Fredricks had threatened my wife. It was much deeper than the frustration of being framed for murder. Victor Sickle had led me here to this place, therefore he knew about this depraved torture. I could forgive him for everything else, but an animal capable of this kind of evil deserved no mercy.

I picked up the bolt cutters and cut the chain. Ernest B. didn't seem to notice. How long had it been since his food and water ran out? So long to suffer there, yet it only took a second to cut him free.

Ernest B. was far too weak to stand on his own, but I was able to lift him to his feet and support him with my good arm around his shoulders. The movement seemed to bring him back to the present for a moment. He looked at me with an expression of mild surprise and said, "Where we goin'?" in a hoarse whisper. I was about to answer him when I heard a sound behind me.

I had less than an instant to realize that Victor Sickle was in the room before everything went black.

CHAPTER 32

BEHIND MY HEAD A LITTLE HAMMER tapped on my skull. The throbbing rhythm of the taps matched my heartbeat. It pounded through the drifting black fog of my unconscious mind and made contact with the outside world. I felt pain, therefore I was awake. I opened my eyes. The blackness in my mind matched the blackness all around me—a pool of emptiness. Swirling, nauseating emptiness.

I rolled to my side. The throbbing in my head was nothing compared to the searing misery I felt when my weight pressed onto my wounded arm. I moaned aloud.

Ernest B. said, "You awake?"

I waited for the pain in my arm to subside, then I said, "Yeah. Where are you?"

Ernest B. turned on the flashlight and shone it at me. I shielded my eyes with my good hand and said, "Shine that thing somewhere else."

He aimed the light away.

Layers of dust floated in the flashlight's beam. I said, "What happened?"

There was a long pause, then Ernest B. said, "Cave in. Victor . . . trapped us."

His voice was very soft and hoarse. I think he was having trouble hanging onto consciousness. That made two of us.

I sat up. The little hammer tapped faster. I rolled over onto all fours and vomited on the rock floor, then crawled a few feet closer to Ernest B. He didn't seem to notice. I sat next to him for a while, both of us leaning against the cold stone wall. The nausea began to fade.

I said, "Sickle knocked me out?"

"Uh huh."

"How long has it been?"

He shrugged.

A wave of nausea washed over me. I rode it out, clutching my head in both hands. Then I said, "What did you mean about Victor trapping us?"

He said, "Explosion."

"He blew up the tunnel?"

Ernest B. sat silently for a moment, exhausted by the few words he had spoken. Then he said, "I don't know. Can you go see?"

I took the flashlight from him and stood, using the wall for support. Nausea flowed over me again. I leaned against the stone, waiting for my stomach to settle down. My head felt like it was stuck in a vise and my wounded arm throbbed constantly, reminding me how close I had come to taking the deepest dive of all. I probably had a concussion. What a fool I had been to let Victor Sickle get behind me. My feet were a long way down and hard to control as I stumbled over the rubble and out to the main passageway.

I climbed slowly back up the subterranean stairway toward the barn, pausing every few steps to rest. Dust hung thickly in the air. The hand-carved steps near the top were buried under fallen rocks. I fell once, ripping a hole in my blue jeans, cutting my knee. As I climbed closer to the barn, more and more stones covered the floor until I was reduced to crawling the last few feet on all fours. Finally, I could climb no higher. The opening to the barn was buried by a huge pile of limestone. Somehow, Sickle had completely collapsed the roof of the passageway. I inched over and knelt next to the rocks for a closer look. Some of them were three or four feet across. If I'd had the use of both arms and the proper tools, I could have cleared the opening in several days. But I had only one good arm, no tools, and precious little time. Ernest B. would die soon without food and water.

The downward climb was no easier than coming up had been. When I came to the mouth of the side tunnel that led to the room where Ernest B. waited beside his grandfather's still, I stopped. The sound of dripping water echoed up from farther down the main tunnel. Shining the light ahead, I saw that the floor was smooth and clear of loose rocks. I continued. The tunnel descended gently, and I walked along more easily. The walls squeezed together until the passageway was only three or four feet wide. The dripping sound grew louder. Water seeped from fissures in the stone, slowly oozing down to the floor. As I moved farther along, the seepage increased until the smooth rock under my feet was completely covered with a thin, flowing film of water. The passageway turned to the left, out of sight. I stopped and listened, but heard only the sounds of my own breathing and the ever-present dripping. I stepped around the corner.

All hope of escape faded as I looked at the scene before me. It was another room, much bigger than the one with the still. The floor fanned out and dropped gently down to slip below the edge of a black pool of water. The water spanned from wall to wall, extending forty or fifty feet away to a point where the ceiling also dipped below the surface. There was no way out, but I felt a strange inner peace.

The sloping slab of stone between my boots and the edge of the pool was wet, completely covered by a thin film of water. It oozed from the walls and flowed across the floor, glistening on the red limestone like blood on a beach.

Near the water's edge lay some equipment. The beam of light rested on it for a moment, and I recognized the generator that had been stolen from Reed Construction's tool shed.

I played the flashlight around the room. Drops fell into the pool from the rock ceiling overhead, making circular ripples that expanded and collided. The sound of the drops hitting the pool was echoed and amplified by the hard stone walls. Like a giant kaleidoscope, the constantly changing patterns on the surface of the water reflected the beam from my flashlight up to the dripping ceiling. The dancing lights and hollow water sounds were strangely forbidding, a warning from the underworld to venture no further into this alien place.

I felt drawn to the pool, hypnotized by the sound and the motion. It was tempting to just sit and watch and wait for the end to come, to surrender to the throbbing in my head, to the pain in my arm and my knee. I stared until my vision was unfocused and my thoughts drifted away. The water's surface never stopped moving, like waves on the ocean.

Memories came unbidden—of Ernest B. on the shore of Galveston Island, a tiny figure dancing in the distance on ripples of heat. A string of executed Portuguese man-o'-wars strung along the beach between us, like purple pearls of death. Ernest B., looking up at me, his childish face a dull mask of indifference.

"Will he beat me? You won't let him beat me, will you?"

I thought of Ernest B., stabbing the first man-o'-war over and over. My father, saying "Don't torture it, boys. It's got enough pain just lying there, dying slow."

It occurred to me that perhaps my friend had only been trying to save the animals from a slow, agonizing death. Why had it taken me thirty-five years to consider the possibility that his motives were pure?

I remembered Ernest B.'s voice: "Makes you wonder, don't it?"

I shook my head to clear away the memories and shuffled down to the gasoline-powered generator near the waterline. Several hand tools, an electric winch, a power saw, and some other pieces of construction equipment were piled onto a large wheelbarrow nearby. All of the tools bore the Reed Construction logo. An empty wooden box sat beside the wheelbarrow with "dynamite" painted on its side. Beside it lay a smaller box for blasting caps. At least I knew how Victor Sickle had trapped us here. And I'd solved the mystery of the tool shed burglaries.

The generator was connected to a row of batteries. Attached to the batteries was a bright orange power cord that snaked across the floor and down into the black water.

I stooped to lift the power cord and pulled it up. A small clear plastic bubble rose from the water. It was linked to the cord by a couple of wires. When I pulled again, another bubble appeared. They were low-voltage lights, the kind used by divers for underwater work on oil derricks and salvage operations.

Reed Construction used them to hang overhead in wet areas, such as culvert or bridge jobs.

I remembered the glow I'd seen on the bottom of the lake just before I was shot. It had come from these lights, I was sure of it. Another mystery solved.

Probably, deeper down in this subterranean lake was a current—the underground stream that had sprung from the hillside to form the "fountain" where my father's generation had enjoyed picnics in the old days. It seemed likely that the aquifer had created this cavern, flowing through the rock for a million years, eroding it into tiny particles of sand that were carried along and washed out onto the hillside below.

Ernest B.'s grandfather had probably selected this place for his moonshine operation as much for the ready supply of fresh, clean water as for the privacy.

And then the lake was filled. The water of Martin Pool rose up the hillside to swallow the "fountain" and cover the source of the creek, and likewise forcing itself into the cave and up through the passageway, seeking its own level until it got to this spot. I was sure that the surface of this black pool at my feet was dead level with the top of Martin Pool. The same water flowed in both.

Obviously, Ernest B. had come to the same conclusion. He discovered this cave somehow, and judging from his choice of reading material at the library, decided to search for the famous moonshiner's silver dollars. So he stole some tools and got to work. Small wonder no one had seen him for the last few weeks before his "murder." This was a big job. I remembered the pile of rubble outside the tunnel from the main cave to the small side room where the still was located. It must have taken a long time for Ernest B. to uncover the passageway to the still and to search the cavern down to this pool. Then, his treasure hunt unsuccessful so far, he must have decided that his grandfather had hidden the silver dollars somewhere lower down, in the part of the cavern that was now underwater. So he searched even there, below this strangely forbidding underground pond.

That explained the string of lights in the water and the eerie glow I saw on the bottom of the lake before I was shot. Remembering the receipt in his wallet for a new scuba regulator, hope swelled within me. Perhaps . . . I walked around the equipment for a closer look. Yes! Behind the generator was a complete set of scuba gear—mask, flippers, tanks, and all.

I picked up the scuba mask and knelt at the edge of the pool to fill it with water. Then I hurried back up the tunnel, careful not to spill a drop. Ernest B. sat exactly as I left him, leaning against the cold stone with his legs straight out in front and his hands lying in his lap like a limp rag doll. His right hand loosely cradled a crude wooden cross made from two pieces of charred wood tied together with a strip of black cloth, probably torn from his shirt. I was amazed. Ernest B. had never shown an interest in religion in the forty years I had known him.

At the sound of my footsteps, he looked up and smiled. A dull red bead of blood formed on his cracked lower lip where the smile stretched the skin.

Kneeling beside him, I held the scuba mask up to his mouth. When he realized it contained water, he lurched his head toward the mask, frantically spilling some of it onto his lap.

I said, "Easy, guy. Take it easy, all right? You need to drink this real slow."

Little by little, his sips consumed the water. When it was gone, he leaned his head against the stone and smiled again, licking his lips. The tiny bead of blood was gone.

"Ernest B., I've got an idea," I said. "Let's both go down to the pool and swim out of here. You've got that scuba gear down there. We can use the buddy system, like old times. What do you say?"

He shook his head a little. "Too much current. Couldn't . . . make it."

"Sure we can. We'll go together. We can do it if we work together."

He shook his head again, but didn't speak.

I helped him to stand. The drink of water had its effect; he rose more easily than before. With my good arm around his shoulders and the flashlight in my other hand, we limped past the ancient still, past my shotgun leaning against the wall, past the dog food and the chain, and into the passage down to the pool. Ernest B. clutched the little wooden cross to his chest with both hands.

As we walked along the tunnel, with my arm supporting his shoulders, Ernest B. began to speak. Slowly, haltingly, with long pauses between the words, he told me how he had come to be chained to his grandfather's still. He told me who they had laid to rest in his place up by the Big Muddy Bayou. He told me everything, including why he'd stolen from me, so long ago. He told me a story that began with simple greed. And, like gangrene creeping outward from a tiny scratch, that greed spawned fraud and drugs and drunkenness, blackmail and rage and murder—murder first and last.

The story he told was fantastic. I might not have believed it if it had come from anyone but Ernest B. It touched my home, my friends and family. It was a story of corruption so pervasive that it defiled everything in my comfortable corner of the world, in the life I'd once taken for granted. This was not about a simple murder. It was not about a common drug deal. It was about crimes that spanned generations.

An evil at the root of Jackson County.

And as Ernest B. spoke, both joy and anger rose within me. Joy at the knowledge that my old friend had not betrayed me after all, at least not without good cause. Anger at what had been done to him, and at myself for having misjudged him so completely.

Finally, he reached the end of his story, the part where I appeared "like God with a flashlight." He stopped shuffling along and began to sob—great, heaving sobs that shook his shoulders and forced him to gasp for air. There were no tears. His body had no moisture to spare.

"Garr," he said, "when you were lying there after Victor hit you, all I could think about was how I'd got you killed, maybe. I couldn't stand it, thinking that, on top of everything, I'd got you killed."

We walked a few steps, his weight solid against me. He calmed down a bit. Then he went on speaking slowly, with long pauses between some of the words. "I learned to pray down here, Garr. I was all alone for so long. I thought about you and Mary Jo and the way you believe in God and Jesus."

I felt embarrassed and ashamed, that he would think of me that way.

He said, "I tried talking to God . . . just started talking like he was in the cave with me."

I said, "What did you say?"

"Oh, you know. I apologized for being such a sorry ol' boy all these years . . . and I asked for some help."

"Well, here I am."

He smiled. "Yes. But you know, I didn't feel like he was listening at first. I talked and talked . . . finally I gave up worrying about getting out alive and started asking him not to let me go to hell . . . Lord knows I belong there . . . and I told him I was ready to die or to do whatever he wanted . . . whatever he wanted." He stopped and looked at me. "You ever think about getting nailed to a cross? I been thinking about that a lot . . . what Jesus did for me. I decided I'd rather starve than die like that. At least this way you get numb after a while."

Anger surged within me again. I began to curse the man who chained him to the still, but Ernest B. interrupted me. He said, "Don't talk that way, Garr. I don't hold it against him. I think that was when God started listening . . . when I quit being mad and quit asking for things and started thinking I'd take whatever came . . . whatever he wanted. When I learned to forgive. And when you showed up, I felt so fine knowing you were all right . . . so fine. . ." His shoulders shook a little.

After a moment we started walking again. He said, "I want you to know something. When I was lying there all that time, lying in the dark and dying for a drink and listening to that awful dripping, I kept thinking you might show up. I kept thinking that, if anyone would come, it would be you."

I smiled. "Like I said, here I am."

"Yeah. After all that prayin', here you are, all right. Makes you wonder, don't it?"

I pulled his shoulder a little closer and smiled again. I had my friend back.

And yet, was he the same man I had known all these years? Glancing sideways at his dim profile, I thought about his words. "I learned to pray down here." There was something new about his face, beneath the grime and the whiskers. Something I had never seen before. He was softer, yet stronger. He was hobbling down the tunnel leaning heavily on my shoulder like a ninety-year-old, yet I felt as if he was supporting me. There *was* something new about my friend, something important . . . And then I knew what it was, this new thing I saw in Ernest B.

It was courage.

CHAPTER 33

WHEN WE REACHED THE POOL, Ernest B. pulled away from me to stoop beside the generator. He did something to the equipment and the water came alive with the unearthly yellow-green glow of the low-voltage lights shining below the surface. The colored light on his face gave him an unhealthy pallor as if he was deathly ill. In a way, I suppose he was.

I had to help him back up to his feet. We stood together, looking down at the water.

Ernest B. said, "We'll never make it."

"Don't talk like that."

"Maybe you can get through without me, but I've got no chance, Garr. I could barely get around down there . . . when I was in shape. If I go with you like this . . . I'll only get you killed."

I began pulling off my boots and blue jeans and said, "I looked at the cave-in, Ernest B. The mouth of the tunnel is totally gone. If I did leave you here, and I did manage to swim out, it would take days for anyone to dig through to you." I looked at him and said, "Do you think you could hold out here for even one more day?"

He lifted his chin and said, "Sure."

I smiled. "No. There's no way, buddy. We've got to get you out of here now, while you still have a little strength."

"You could swim back in with some food."

"Could I really? Could I swim back against the current?"

He opened his mouth to speak, then closed it again. In the green glow from the water, I saw him shake his head hopelessly.

I said, "So going out with me now is your only chance."

"It's too dangerous, Garr. You'll have a better chance without dragging me along."

"Ernest B., think about it. How would you feel if you left me here, knowing I was in the shape you're in? Could you do that?"

He looked at me for a moment, then slowly shook his head again.

I said, "So stop that foolish talk."

"But there's not much air in the tank, Garr."

"Then I guess we'll have to hurry."

He smiled a little at that.

I helped him get undressed. His eyes lingered sadly on the little wooden cross as I laid it on the floor. It wasn't easy putting on the scuba tank with one arm. He tried to help. With his strength almost gone, the best he could do was to hold out the straps and guide my bad arm through, sling and all. I considered letting Ernest B. wear the face mask and flippers, but it made more sense for me to use them. I'd have to do the swimming for both of us.

We stood face-to-face at the water's edge with the sickly yellow-green light shining onto us like the plague. Ernest B. closed his eyes and said, "Jesus, please see to it that whatever you want to happen, happens."

I stared at him for a moment, unable to resolve his newfound faith with the Ernest B. I had always known. He returned my stare with a smile. Such confidence. Such strength. Such . . . peace. Where did it come from? Was this really what faith in Jesus meant?

Still staring at him, I said, “Amen.”

I bit down on the mouthpiece and took a breath of canned air. I passed the mouthpiece to Ernest B. My hand shook. He inhaled without comment.

It was crazy, what we were going to do. I thought of Mary Jo. I thought of our home. I thought of finer times with Ernest B. Climbing the water tower. Floating down the bayou on a foam raft. Standing together on that big rock the night my mother died. We turned and walked slowly into the water. I had to support Ernest B. with my good arm.

I cringed as the frigid water reached my thighs. The limestone sloped gently below the surface. We sank only a couple of inches with every step. Every inch sent another frigid shock through my body. I knew what was coming and tried to prepare, but the pain when the icy water hit my wounded arm was so intense I almost passed out. A wave of darkness lapped at the edges of my mind. My knees buckled and I sank under the surface. Ernest B. sank with me.

A current sucked at my legs. It was much stronger than I thought it would be. Frantically, I jammed the air hose into my mouth. After a deep breath, I removed the mouthpiece and shoved it at Ernest B. His hand came up in slow motion to take the hose. We were on our way.

At first, with the string of lights above and the current pushing us along, it went like a carnival ride. The red stone walls flashed by quickly. Silvery air bubbles from the regulator hit the roof and flowed beside us, wiggling and changing shape like giant globs of mercury. With Ernest B. holding onto my shirt, we had a fairly easy time of it, passing the mouthpiece back and forth.

Then we came to the first turn.

I was holding the air hose out to Ernest B. when I slammed backwards into the wall. The current pinned me hard against the rock, and I might be there still except for Ernest B. He managed to maintain his grip on my shirt as he whipped past, his momentum carrying him around the bend and pulling me along. My face mask slipped and filled with water. I dropped the regulator hose when I hit the wall, and couldn't find it. I panicked.

Ernest B.'s hand touched my face. A moment later, I felt the mouthpiece on my lips and desperately bit at it. The air hit my lungs. I calmed. The face mask was useless, so I yanked it off. Without it I could see only vague shapes in the eerie yellow-green light. We were whirling quickly through a series of gentle bends in the tunnel. Ernest B. was ahead of me, with his back to our direction of flow.

I passed the hose to him.

A black shape slipped by on one side. The horrible thought flashed through my mind that it could be an opening to another tunnel, maybe even the way to the surface. Too late, I realized that the cave might have several passageways. We could be rushing toward a dead end in an underground lake. Perhaps our bones would surface at some secluded spring a hundred miles from here.

But the lights were still with us, the tiny glowing balls flashing by overhead like street lights on an underwater freeway. I took comfort from the fact that Ernest B. had been there before and returned alive.

He passed the air hose to me.

I wondered how Ernest B. had managed to string the lights. He must have worn a lifeline that he could use to pull himself up when the time came. There was no way he could swim back against this current.

I passed the hose to him.

With my good arm I blindly trailed my fingers along the rock wall. Nothing but rock. Then my fingers touched something else. A rope. I lost it. Moving my hand around to try to find it again, I felt Ernest B.'s arm. He was holding the rope, trailing it through his fingers as we slipped along. He knew it was there all along. I felt intense relief. Ernest B. *had* been there before. He knew where we were, where we were going. Perhaps it would be all right.

He passed the hose to me.

Our legs intertwined as we drifted through the cave. We held each other tightly, to share the air and to comfort ourselves with a human touch in that alien place. I have never felt closer to another man. We were as we always had been. A life lived together—growing, learning, sharing everything—a lifetime together had created bonds strong enough to withstand the temporary insanity that had seized us. We were two wounded and weak travelers, rushing toward an unknown fate, unable to speak, alone together in an impossible underworld that existed only for us. We might escape—or we might die, our bodies bobbing forever along that underground river. Only Ernest B.'s presence kept me from panic and madness. But where did he get *his* strength?

I gave him the air hose.

At that moment, as our hands touched to pass the hose, we slammed into the wall again. The stream had forked, and we were pressed against the rock dividing the two directions. On Ernest B.'s side, the current raced away into darkness and oblivion. On mine, the lights and ceaseless flow continued around the corner. I held Ernest B.'s shirt, willing myself to pull him toward the lights. The furious current pressed us against the rock without pause, fighting every movement and stretching the loose skin of my face. Ernest B. was caught in a slight depression in the face of the rock wall, both arms flung straight out, pinned to the rock by the unremitting flow, his hands palm out, his fingers trembling in the rushing water, his legs bent at the knee and cocked to the side. Again and again I pulled on his shirt, but Ernest B. was wedged so tightly against the rock that I could not move him. Nothing could move him.

Then, incredibly, with his left hand he slowly managed to place the mouthpiece of the air hose between my teeth.

I pulled at his shirt again and again, desperately trying to yank him away from the wall. He pointed to my watch. He was telling me we were running out of air. Then his hand touched my face and lingered there for a moment.

I will never know if it was a deliberate caress.

He moved his hand to mine, to where I held his shirt. Slowly, methodically, he grasped my fingers and began to pry them away. I shook my head violently and tried to scream "No!" past the mouthpiece and the rushing water. Perhaps he heard me.

With our faces inches apart in the dim watery haze, I saw him smile at the moment that he pushed against my chest, setting me free. In the next instant, I was gripped by the current and torn away from my dear old friend, forever.

CHAPTER 34

THE LAST OF THE LIGHTS WERE ONLY a few yards farther along. I passed the final bobbing glow and sped into the blackness beyond with the certain knowledge that I was about to die. There was no point in struggle. The unceasing flow was too strong for a man with one arm to resist. Better to simply ride the current in a fetal position and prepare myself for death.

But death and birth are two halves of a whole. A pale oblong glow appeared in the distance, dim and dancing in the black water like an oncoming motorcycle headlight on a bumpy road. It was a hole in the floor of Martin Pool. I was through it and bobbing slowly along the bottom of the lake, awash in an afterbirth of swirling mud and algae before I fully realized that I had been thrust from the earth's womb. High above, the surface of the lake shimmered in the early morning light. It was beautiful to see that light.

I rose. I reached for the surface while I was still yards below it, stretching with everything in me to feel the air and to see the sun. Details came into focus through the hazy green. Chased across the calm surface by a gentle breeze, parallel ripples splintered the light into softly shimmering rays trickling down through the sun-warmed water. I kicked and stroked with feeble muscles, willing myself to the top. When my face broke the surface, the aquamarine sky hovered overhead like a proud new mother sheltering her child.

I shook the hair from my eyes, dropped the scuba tank and began the long swim to shore.

As I swam, I wept.

My cries echoed from the hillside.

My tears joined the waters of Martin Pool. I suppose they are there, still.

Chapter 35

As I swam, my mind filled with a confusing jumble of images: the sudden, searing pain in my arm as I reached for my boat the last time I swam in those waters, the moment of amazement and joy when I saw Ernest B. lying in the cave, the second and third bullet holes popping side-by-side in the aluminum hull beside my head, the delayed cracks as echoes of the rifle shots reached me before I sank below the surface, Ernest B.'s hand touching my cheek, then pushing me away, and the voice warning me to duck, just before I was shot. Maybe it was because I was again in the same waters, but I heard the voice again, as clearly as if it were real.

The voice was Clyde Barker's.

When my weary one-handed swim brought me to land, I was near the yellow bollards and the dead-end road where the dark blue Camaro had parked. I sat on the dull red limestone and stared across the still surface of Martin Pool. My arm was bleeding slowly from the reopened rifle wound. I pressed my palm against it. Long after my breathing returned to normal and my tears no longer flowed, I continued to sit beside the water, searching the early morning mist for some sign of Ernest B. Of course, he never came.

This tranquil place of swaying cattails and honeysuckle-scented breezes would be his grave. Here, below the cool green waters where he and I had learned to swim so very long ago, he would lie, forever a part of the lake that bore his family name. It was a wonderful resting place, a good trade for the little metal urn down by the Big Muddy where we'd laid the ashes of another man. Yet he was so terribly young to die, with so much more he should have done.

And he died so that I could live.

He died so I could live. How many times had I heard a preacher use those words about Jesus Christ? How many times had I heard them say that he had died in my place, to pay for my sins?

I didn't understand it. Why would God require such a thing? How could Ernest B. have accepted his fate so calmly? How could he have changed so much? How could he forgive the man who chained him to the still, even as he walked toward his death? Was it faith in Jesus that let him smile as he pushed me toward life and accepted his death?

How could I become such a man?

A warm breeze stirred the water, driving waves along the lake from east to west. Staring across Martin Pool, I thought about Ernest B.'s calm prayer before we began that final swim: *"Jesus, please see to it that whatever you want to happen, happens."*

How could he have been so serene when I felt such fear and isolation? I was *still* afraid, sitting safely on the shore. And the feeling had little to do with fear of death. I'd been plagued by fear since Lester Fredricks was killed, since I had almost murdered him.

I shook my head at that.

No, this was no time to sugarcoat the truth. These emotions went even deeper, even further back. Standing at the brink of committing murder, I had felt them clearly for the first time in years, but my life had *always* been played out against a backdrop of dread and loneliness, against an emptiness that spoiled everything, poisoning the good times, confirming the bad times, like acid rain in a peaceful garden.

I thought it was that way for everyone. All those years in the church pews, enduring stale speeches and dull ceremony beside men and women with problems that far outweighed my own. Cancer victims, widows, orphans. Surely they too felt this aching solitude.

Somehow, Mary Jo rose above it.

I wondered how. She claimed, of course, that Jesus gave her inner peace, but I never believed it was so simple. Perhaps my cynicism was born of pride—a stubborn desire to make it on my own. Perhaps it was anger at the God who let my mother die so young. But today, I had seen Ernest B. die young with a smile on his face.

I had wounded my beloved wife and failed my finest friend by longing for violence and murder. I had sunken so low that my pride was a distant memory. But now, to my surprise, I discovered that the anger I once felt so strongly had faded with the pain of losing Mary Jo and Ernest B. Nothing was left but quiet despair and a guilty conscience.

A wave broke against the rock below me, spraying lake water across my legs. What should I do? I was out of touch with the holy rhythm of life. I was willing to murder. I longed for violent retribution, as if that would end my suffering. But Ernest B.'s and Mary Jo's God would not countenance such a thing. Their God would expect me to forgive, as Ernest B. had forgiven his murderer in the cavern. Ernest B.'s God would expect me to turn the other cheek. He was a loving God, a gentle God, a forgiving God.

A forgiving God.

If God would want me to forgive, why could I not believe that he might forgive me? Pedro's spinning knife came to mind. By his logic, Pedro was right to conclude that the beautiful symmetry of nature was no accident. God must have been involved in its creation. But if he cared enough to create the world, would he care enough to remove the despair that was driving me deep into a hell of murder and revenge?

The despair was still there, deeply ingrained in my psyche, even now that Ernest B. had revealed the truth about the murders and I knew that I would be allowed to return to my life as it had been before. I despaired because I knew that I was an aberration, a flaw in God's creation. If God is perfect, as the animals and plants and every other part of his creation are perfect, I knew that I could not measure up. I was imperfect by choice. Every time I ignored the small voice and chose wrong over right, I enlarged the imperfection.

In me, God had created a clean white piece of paper, a place to write his poetic message of love, but I had stolen the pen and scrawled my pitiful graffiti instead.

Like most people, I was not evil in the extreme. I was no Hitler or Caligula, but over the years I had stumbled drunkenly through the streets of New Orleans and cursed friends in anger. In recent weeks I had longed in my heart of hearts to torture and murder and avenge the death of Ernest B. I hadn't actually killed anyone, but so what? I had chosen the low road often enough. Even now, the evil intent was there, festering behind my civilized facade. The paper was flawed and so was not worthy—why should God write his wonderful poetry in the margins of a selfish wish list? I needed to erase the mess I made of the life he gave me, but I did not know how.

I remembered Mary Jo's words: "We don't suffer the ultimate effects of evil. Our spirit is protected—with God's help. We get cancer. We die. But Christians do not despair."

A miracle happened then.

I believed.

In the end, it was not logic that led me to my faith, it was simply that my need was so great, my desire so deep, that I knew I *must* believe.

On that limestone boulder beside Martin Pool, I closed my eyes and asked God to save me. I didn't want a solution to my problems. I wanted inner peace. I wanted more than anything not to go through the rest of my life alone. I admitted that I couldn't beat the imperfection within me. I had already tried and failed. I begged for help. I pleaded with Jesus for forgiveness. I offered myself to him.

And then . . . and then . . . how can words describe the serenity that settled onto me? It is impossible to convey the slightest sense of it. Calming? Loving? Those are hollow sounds compared to the tender truth that washed my spirit and left me . . . *clean*.

There are some who say that man invented God. That Jesus Christ was simply a good man who died long ago. If that is true, why did revenge suddenly become so unimportant to me? What power washed away the evil in my heart, if not Christ's Holy Spirit? I asked him to take me, I told him I believed, and in that instant I was freed from the sour, rotting curse of vengeance that had clawed at my sanity for so long.

In that instant, my life became simple and clear, like Ernest B.'s last smile. In that instant, finally, I was at peace.

Chapter 36

I LEFT THE FLIPPERS LYING IN A LITTLE pool of water on the limestone and walked away from the lake on the crumbling asphalt road, wearing nothing but my white underwear and wet cotton shirt. It was a long walk home, but it was early and no one passed me. A red-wing blackbird stood on a cedar fencepost alongside the bar ditch, holding a squirming nightcrawler pinned against the wood. Head cocked to the right, it watched me closely with an unblinking obsidian eye until I passed, then pecked at the worm again, dismissing me. Death for some, life for others: nature's way. If it could think, would the worm resent its role? Would the bird, when its turn came? Or did they submit to the holy rhythm of life with innate understanding?

As I had submitted.

A police car stood in the driveway at home. I walked past it, stepping gingerly along the gravel drive in my bare feet. Mourning doves cooed softly. A deputy I didn't know was standing near the door when I went inside. He looked at me as if I had risen from the dead. Close enough.

Mary Jo must have heard the door shut. She rushed from the living room into the entry hall wearing her houserobe and slippers. Her hair was wild from sleep, her eyes red from crying.

"Oh, baby," was all she said when she saw me standing there, pressing my palm against the bloody wound, half-naked and shivering.

"I tried to save him, Mary Jo. I did my best."

"Who you talking about, baby?"

I said, "Ernest B." and walked upstairs to bed, past Mary Jo's searching eyes and the deputy's puzzled frown.

• • •

THEY DIDN'T LET ME SLEEP FOR LONG, OF course. A doctor woke me to look at my arm while Mary Jo hovered in the background. I slept again. Then I awoke to find Mary Jo sitting beside me on the bed, stroking my forehead. She was leaning over me, her lovely auburn hair falling across my pillow, forming a soft enclosure for our faces. When she realized I was awake, she pushed away from me.

She said, "Are you all right?"

"Yes. My arm is sore, but yes."

"Will you tell me what happened?"

I told her almost everything: the chase, the cave, Ernest B., and the river underground. For some reason, I said nothing about my epiphany on the lakeshore. It was still ripening within me, a strange and splendid evolution that my psyche had not yet fully grasped. Perhaps I wanted to hold it close, to bask in the unfolding warmth and comfort of it until I understood. When I was done, she turned away, facing the window. We sat together in silence for several minutes. Outside, the doves were still cooing, loud enough to hear through the glass.

Finally she said, "I thought you weren't going to keep after them, Garr. You said you would stay away from Victor Sickle. You lied to me."

"Mary Jo, try to understand. I said I'd stay away from him, yes, but that was before he shot me."

"Shot you? Are you sure it was this Sickle person who did that?"

"Pretty sure, yes. But, Mary Jo, I—"

"Clyde Barker's downstairs. He says he's got to talk to you now and won't wait."

"All right. I'll go down and see him. But I want you to understand why I did what I did."

"You'll never make me understand. How could there be a good enough reason, a reason that was strong enough for you to risk—everything?"

"There wasn't. I didn't know that then. But I do now. I do. I've changed, Mary Jo."

She nodded and looked away. Why wouldn't she meet my eyes? Just as I was about to speak of my revelation at Martin Pool, someone rapped sharply on the bedroom door.

She said, "That'll be Clyde or one of his deputies. Just tell me one more thing. Is it over now?"

I reached up and cupped her cheek in the palm of my good hand. I said, "Yes, it is. I guess it is at that."

She stood suddenly, leaving my arm extended, my palm touching the empty air where her face had been. She walked away and opened the door to them.

• • •

BARKER SAT IN THE BACK PORCH SWING cleaning his fingernails with his pocketknife as I shuffled past him to the rocking chair.

Without looking up, he said, "Somethin' kinda familiar 'bout this set-up, ain't there, Garr?"

I looked over his shoulder at the woods. A couple of squirrels chased each other in tight spirals around a big hickory trunk, chattering and jerking their bushy tails. They rose out of sight into the deep green canopy overhead.

I said, "It's time for straight talk, Clyde. I know it wasn't Ernest B. we buried."

He looked up from the pocketknife and used it to push his Stetson back on his head, laying eyes on me for the first time since I had stepped outside. There was a distinct line across his forehead between the white skin usually covered by his hat and the tan skin below it.

"Maybe you better explain."

So I told him about the cavern below Martin Pool. I told him about the gunfight with Victor Sickle, about the hole in the back of Old Man Martin's barn, about the still, the chain around Ernest B., the dog food, the bolt cutters—all of it. I told him about the cave-in that Victor Sickle engineered, and the last desperate swim that Ernest B. and I took together. I told him how Ernest B. died.

I didn't tell him who chained and tortured Ernest B. He could draw his own conclusions about that.

Barker lowered his attention to his fingernails. His eyes were hidden behind the brim of the Stetson. He said, "Sickle's dead, Garr. We found y'all's cars wrecked up the road yonder, and your tracks goin' back into the woods. Jimmy and I followed and got to the Martin place just in time to see the blast when he blew up that old barn they got back there. He was standin' over by the house, out in the clear holdin' a pistol. When I called for him to drop his weapon, he fired instead. Jimmy shot him where he stood."

"How's Jimmy taking it?"

"A lot better than he did with Lester Fredricks, I'll tell you that for sure."

I thought about Jimmy in my hospital room, so shaken by his experience with Lester Fredricks, yet able to shoot another man so soon afterwards. I thought about my concern for him, my pity for his guilt and sorrow at having to kill a man. How could I have been so foolish?

I said, "Clyde, why did y'all search the grounds around Mary Jo's studio?"

Barker looked up for a moment, then returned his attention to his pocketknife and said, "We was lookin' for evidence, obviously."

"Yes, but why there? Why right then?"

"Got a phone call, said there'd be something lyin' on the ground out there. Somethin' we'd be interested in."

"Do you remember who took the call?"

He scraped the knife along his left thumbnail. "Jimmy did, I think."

"How about your visit to my office while I was in the hospital? Was there a call then, too?"

"Yes. Matter of fact, yes."

"Who took the call?"

This time when he looked up, his eyes held mine. He said, "I think it was Jimmy."

"And you were looking for what? Cocaine?"

"Yes. How'd you know that if—"

"Mrs. P. found it, Clyde. Just a few hours before you showed up."

His face began to turn a darker shade of red. Before he could speak, I said, "Don't get mad yet. There's more."

"It'd better be good."

"Just tell me this: Who found Victor Sickle when his car was supposedly run off the road?"

"Jimmy."

"And did he tell you about the anonymous phone call he got telling him where to look?"

"No. That's not how we found him. Jimmy was just drivin' by, and . . ."

I saw understanding begin to rise within him.

I said, "Clyde, I'm the one who ran Sickle off the road—sort of. And there was a large bag of cocaine in his Camaro when I left it. I called your office and told the deputy who answered to look for the drugs. I thought at the time his voice sounded familiar. Did Jimmy report finding cocaine in Sickle's car?"

"No."

"There was a big bag of dope in that car when I left it. Exactly like the bag of cocaine Mrs. P. found in my office a few days later."

"Go on."

"Remember when you came to my door all hot and bothered 'cause Mary Jo and I left town for our anniversary?"

"Sure."

"You were very ticked off. You said we shouldn't have gone to Dallas without checking with you. That bothered me, but I couldn't figure out why—until I realized that I hadn't told you where we went. How did you know Mary Jo and I were in Dallas?"

His eyebrows were so tightly knit they formed a single ridge across his forehead. "I'm pretty sure Jimmy told me. Didn't you tell him?"

"Nope. The only people from Jackson County who knew where we spent the weekend were Mrs. P., Leon Martinez—and Victor Sickle, who saw us there. You can ask, but I'll bet neither Leon or Mrs. P. told Jimmy about my travel plans."

"You're sayin' Jimmy's dirty. Dealin' dope with Victor Sickle."

"Clyde, it's worse than that. When Jimmy handcuffed Lester Fredricks that night, Lester was facing the wall and Jimmy was behind him."

Barker nodded and said, "Sure. Standard procedure."

I thought about Lester's hands clutching at the hole in his chest. I looked at Barker and said, "Remember where Lester's hands were when we saw him up on the road?"

It took a moment, then he understood. "He moved the cuffs around front so his story about a struggle would be reasonable."

I nodded.

"Why didn't I see that?"

"Don't be too hard on yourself, Clyde. I saw him cuff Lester from behind with my own eyes and didn't figure this out until Ernest B. told me Jimmy was crooked. Then I started trying to think of ways to prove it to you. Jimmy's good. He's got that all-American grin and aw-shucks attitude. Nobody would see past it without a reason to look."

"But why kill Lester Fredricks?"

"The first time I went to the Nowhere Club looking for information, I paid Lester to tell me about a fight between Ernest B. and his father. I figure Lester knew just enough about Jimmy and Victor's business to realize that they wouldn't want me to hear the truth. Unfortunately, he chose a lie that was just as damaging from Victor and Jimmy's point of view. Later on, they beat him and threatened his life to get him to try to plant that false evidence over at Mary Jo's studio. Of course, I caught him in the act, and when I did a little threatening of my own, Lester screwed up again: He told me that his earlier story about Ernest B. was a lie. I figure Jimmy was listening outside and overheard him. He decided Lester had to go."

Barker snapped his knife shut and slipped it into the front pocket of his chinos. He said, "You know who we buried at the cemetery, don't you?"

"Yes."

"And why I let it happen?"

"I can guess."

His steel gray eyes searched mine. Finally, he said, "What are you goin' to do about it?"

Like gleaners in the cottonfields, a flock of chickadees and titmice fluttered through the woods around us, alighting on the moldering, leaf-strewn ground to peck for grubs; chirping, preening, tapping branches and bark with tiny beaks, moving on, flitting from tree to distant tree. I said, "This morning, I remembered the voice that tried to warn me before I was shot."

His eyes remained locked on mine.

"If you hadn't called out to me, I would have climbed two feet higher up the side of my boat, and Sickle would have put a bullet in my back instead of my arm. And I guess it was you that pulled me out of the lake and patched me up. I figure I owe you one."

He continued to hold my eyes with his for a moment. Then nodded curtly and stood. He said, "I done a lot of things for them Martins over the years. A lot of things. But there's just so far I'll go, and no further." He nodded his head. "Yessir, just so far."

"Clyde, before you leave, tell me something. Why did you come after me so hot and heavy? I mean, what made you think I had anything to do with all this? Was it that trouble I had a couple of months ago with Ernest B.?"

"It was a lot simpler than that. We found the top to your coffee thermos in Old Man Martin's boat when we went to pull that body out of the lake. It had your name on it." Clyde Barker shook his head. "I probably would have left you alone if you'd just told us you was the one who found the body. Couldn't figure out why you'd lie about a thing like that unless you had something to hide."

The porch swing rocked for quite a while after he left.

CHAPTER 37

MARY JO DROVE ME TO THE HOSPITAL that afternoon. My arm was bleeding again. She drove silently, with both hands on the wheel, eyes straight ahead. I rode with my head propped against the passenger-side window, staring at the barren brown cotton rows flashing by.

I had tried to explain to her a couple of times, but she'd answered me with short replies and let the conversation drop. I told her I'd been born again—using the words her church would understand, although they hardly seemed adequate. She stared at me and said, "You've lied to me for so long. How can I be sure of you now?"

I gave up.

Riding into Mt. Sinai, a strange dichotomy of sensations overwhelmed me—sorrow that I had driven Mary Jo to such unhappiness, and joyful certainty of my union with all creation. It was terrible. It was wonderful. It was confusing.

The cotton harvest was over. The roads to town were littered with white puffs all the way to the gin, and the storefront windows were covered with brightly painted announcements of sales and special bargains. Behind the corrugated metal building that housed the cotton gin, the gravel parking lot was packed with flatbed trailers, their tall chicken-wire sides flecked with tiny white survivors of the shakedown into the hoppers. The sidewalks around the courthouse plaza were jammed with customers, large, weathered, raw-boned men in gimme caps and faded denim overalls, following their brightly dressed wives from store to store. This was the season when cash registers trolled for cotton money like anglers for bass in the bayou, a Mt. Sinai August ritual for more than a hundred years.

We drove into the shade-dappled residential section, past the hiss and click of lawn sprinklers, along the magnolia-scented avenue to the hospital. Mary Jo pulled under the canopy at the emergency entrance.

She stared straight out through the windshield as she spoke. "If you don't mind, I think I'll go do some shopping while you're here. I'll come pick you up in an hour or so."

"Mary Jo . . ."

She stopped me with a shake of her head. "Not the time or place, Garr. Just go get your arm looked at, will you?"

"You've got to know I felt I didn't have a choice."

Her face was set in a neutral mask. I knew the look—it meant she wouldn't talk about it no matter what I said. I opened the door and stepped out into the heat. She pulled away from the drive before I reached the hospital doors.

• • •

An intern removed my torn stitches and replaced them. I was ready to go in thirty minutes.

Instead of turning right in the hallway to the lobby, I went left, deeper into the hospital. A short walk along the silent and starkly lit corridor brought me to a dead end with two doors. One led outside to the alley and the other to a landing and some stairs. You could step inside and go straight down to the morgue or up to the rooms above. I stepped outside.

The heat and humidity of the east Texas summer opened the pores of my skin like a faucet, drenching me in sweat before I took ten steps. Along the alley, dented metal garbage cans stood against sun-bleached wooden fences. Deep-throated dogs bellowed through the slats, protecting their captive world from backyard invaders. A hundred feet of cracked asphalt strewn with litter was all that stood between me and Old Man Martin's window at the Silver Leaf Home.

I circled the nursing home and went up the front steps, past the elderly men in their rocking chairs. Inside, a nurse directed me to his room. I told her I knew the way.

He lay in bed, the sheet neatly folded across his shallow chest, both arms lying limply above the covers at his sides. His head was propped up on two crisp white pillows, turned toward the alley window. He must have seen me coming.

I walked around the bed, pulled the easy chair over between him and the view, and sat facing him.

"What the devil do you want?" he said.

I didn't answer at first. I just looked at him, wondering where to start. Finally, I said, "I saw Ernest B. this morning."

He gave a short bark of a laugh.

"Yep. Saw him over at your place. He wasn't looking too good, but he was hanging in there."

The old man stared through me with no expression on his face at all.

I looked into his vacant eyes, searching for a sign of life. Then I said, "Why'd you have to torture him like that? Why not just kill him quick and clean?"

He rolled his head away to face the ceiling. His gray whiskers made a scratching sound against the cotton collar of his pajama top. He said, "He didn't deserve nothin' quick or clean."

It was hard to keep from slapping him. I prayed for self-control. "He deserved better than you gave him. He was your son."

"Wasn't no son of mine after what he done."

I didn't trust myself to speak at first. My fingers dug into the soft vinyl upholstery of the chair arm as I willed myself to be calm. I wanted to drive my fist deep into his upturned face, to beat him for Ernest B., for Lester Fredricks, for Mary Jo and Dr. Krueger and everyone else this evil man had harmed throughout his miserable life.

But the small voice spoke out against those feelings. And this time I listened.

After a while I said, "You figured out it was Ernest B. who swam to your boat and hooked the body on your stringer."

He continued to stare at the ceiling.

"Or did you really lose your mind? Ernest B. said he came here a couple of times afterward. Always on the sly, in the middle of the night. Said you talked to him like he was your daddy. Said crazy Jake McKinsey did the same thing, even chased him down the road on a bicycle. You told me your daddy was coming back to get you, remember? So who was it you thought you were chaining up down by the old still, your son or your father?"

His thin blue lips turned up a bit at the corners. I looked away from him, unwilling to continue to stare at the face of insanity.

"Either way, it doesn't matter. You snuck home a couple of weeks ago, while I was in the hospital. You met your boy down in the cave. And when Ernest B. turned his back, you cold-cocked him, and you chained him to your daddy's still with a little water and a bag of dog food. Then you walked up to the road doing your crazy act and sat down to wait for someone to find you."

The little smile remained on his face, framed by a stubble of gray whiskers.

I leaned forward at the waist, bringing my lips closer to his ear. I wanted to be sure he couldn't ignore me. "Ernest B. told me the whole story this morning. You murdered your father fifty years ago because he refused to sell the land to build Martin Pool. You saw a chance to get rich, but he was holding up your real estate deal. He wanted the valley to stay as it was. He cared more about the land than the money. So you knocked your daddy out and you dumped his body in his still."

Martin turned to look at me again. The emotion in his eyes was hard to define. Anger at being found out? Fear at learning that I knew the truth? Or insanity, pure and simple?

I said, "Must have been quite a shock to see your dear ol' dad floating on that stringer. Looked like he was forty-five and freshly drowned, didn't he?"

The look in his eye changed a little. I thought I saw an unspoken question there. I said, "Haven't you figured out that part yet? It's simple. Your father's body floated in that still for fifty years, soaked in alcohol, pickled like pig's feet in a mason jar.

"Must have given Ernest B. quite a fright when he dug through to that room and found a body floating in that tank looking so much like him. Of course, this whole nightmare was based on that family resemblance. Jimmy probably told you how the other deputies thought it was Ernest B. when they first pulled the swollen thing out of the lake. It was so deformed that even I thought it was him. You decided to let us go on thinking that way. It would give you lots of time to torture Ernest B.

"But you had a problem with the autopsy. You knew Dr. Krueger would find out the truth. So you took a little stroll down the alley here and met with him the day they buried your daddy. You probably offered him a deal. He probably took it—you've got a lot of money. And after he changed the autopsy report, it wasn't hard to talk him into taking a drink to close the bargain, was it? You must have had a few yourself—Jake McKinsey told me you were weaving around the halls that night. Then when Krueger passed out, it was a simple matter of covering his nose and mouth with a wet towel—I found the towel under the gurney. It was a perfect murder: just another alcoholic overdose."

I couldn't stand being so near him. I rose and walked to the window. A skinny dog was scraping around a dull gray garbage can in the awful heat outside. It rose on its hind legs and peeked over the top, scratching to climb in. Just as it was about to succeed, the can fell over and rolled to the center of the alley with an explosive rattle. The skinny dog ran away, tail tucked tightly between its legs, flinging furtive wide-eyed glances back at the garbage can. It was a cowardly dog. It would not eat today.

I turned from the window and said, "You were almost home free, except for one thing. You needed someone to take the fall for the body in the lake. That's when you thought of me. Or maybe it was earlier, when I showed up at your house with the covered dish. Doesn't matter. Either way; I was the perfect fall guy. You knew all about my business problems with Ernest B. For all you knew, he might have told me about your old man, us being such great pals and all. And Jimmy probably told you they found my thermos lid in your boat. So I was both a threat and a likely suspect. You decided to put Jimmy onto me and he got Victor Sickle in on the frame. Between them, they've made my life a nightmare for weeks."

His smile was wider now, probably fueled by the thought of my troubles.

I said, "I couldn't figure out Barker's place in all this. The searches, the constant pressure—at first I thought he was pushing me for personal reasons. But he really thought I was dirty. He was after me like a coon dog following a false scent—all because of you and Jimmy and Sickle, laying the trail for him.

"Of course, even if Clyde had believed I was involved somehow, he knew I didn't kill Ernest B., because he knew the body in the lake was your father. He saw Krueger's autopsy report before it was changed. I think he had a loud argument with Krueger about that report at the courthouse. He was probably trying to get the doctor to leave out certain facts. And Barker kept patrol cars outside my place day and night. Who were they watching? I knew they weren't there to keep an eye on me, because they stayed in place while I was in the hospital. Since our property's next door to yours, I figure Barker was keeping an eye out for Ernest B., parking down the road to avoid being too obvious about it.

"So why did Barker let them bury your father's ashes in Ernest B.'s grave?"

The old man coughed, long and loud. In spite of his heaving chest, his eyes danced with amusement, daring me to go on. I decided to bluff him with my best guess. I said, "Barker's always known you killed your old man. Barker was new on the force back then, maybe twenty years old. Times were tough. Your daddy's moonshine was the best business going and he was famous for never getting caught—hard to do without help. Barker warned him before the raids in return for kickbacks. And when your daddy showed up missing, Barker figured out where he was. He probably went down into that cave and saw what you'd done. You've been paying him off by keeping him in office ever since. Only my father's influence kept you from backing him all the way to the state legislature, maybe even further."

I thought about that poker game so long ago, about my father's reaction to the news that Barker was a cheat.

I said, "One hand washes the other. Barker's never lost an election, and he's never looked too hard at your business deals. I don't think he actually covered for your drug operation. He's too smart to get in that deep. He just ignored the signs, let Jimmy handle the dirty work."

The old man's evil grin slipped away.

I continued, "Oh, yeah, I know about the drugs. Ernest B. told me all about it. May the good Lord forgive me, I even made the mistake of thinking Ernest B. was involved."

He laughed again, a short crackling laugh that quickly became another bout of coughing. I decided to cut to the part he wouldn't enjoy.

"Your dope business rolled along just fine with you handling the finances and Jimmy and Victor doing your leg work. You kept your hands pretty clean around here, hiding the shipments in the woods and selling the stuff out of your nightclub in Dallas. Barker pretended to be tough on drugs in Jackson County, and you got a safe haven to divvy up the dope for weekend runs to the city. Then Sickle and Wilson figured out how much Ernest B. loved you—only God knows why he loved you, but he did—and they figured out that you killed your father. They told Ernest B. they'd see you fry for murder if he didn't pay them off. Of course, Ernest B. didn't know yet that you were dealing drugs. He thought you were just a crusty old man who made a bad mistake a long time ago. So Ernest B. paid them everything he had. He even stole from our business, but they said it wasn't enough. Then he remembered the old stories about your daddy's silver dollar treasure. He decided to search for it to get enough money to pay off Jimmy and Victor once and for all. He never found the coins, of course, but your pals kept up the pressure all the same. Finally, in desperation, he went to you, thinking you would have to help him pay. But you just laughed at him for being stupid enough to pay blackmail money to your employees.

"Ernest B. told me it was your laughter that made him finally face what you are. The pain of it drove him a little nuts. He went to Mexico on a month-long drunk. When he came back here, he decided it might be interesting to stick your father's pickled corpse onto your fish stringer. Then he went back to looking for the treasure as if nothing had happened."

I smiled, thinking of all the trouble my old friend had managed to stir up.

"With your daddy's body lying down at the morgue, Jimmy and Victor were out of the blackmail business, and ol' Clyde lost his leverage on you because he wasn't the only one who knew the truth anymore. He was scared silly that the facts would come out in a way he couldn't control, that you'd be caught and implicate him. So he accepted the frame-up, figuring I was involved in it somehow. Then he and Jimmy took turns watching your place in case the real Ernest B. showed up.

"But when Barker saw me about to be shot in the lake behind your house, he drew the line. Barker never murdered anyone, and he couldn't be a part of it. He called out the warning that saved my life. I owe him for that." I sighed and said, "Unfortunately, Clyde let Jimmy guard my hospital room, and Jimmy let you in the night you tried to smother me with a pillow."

Again, the old man laughed out loud. Again, his laughter rose until it degenerated into coughing. As he held a gnarled fist to his mouth, I went on, my voice rising above the sound of his hacking. "It's all out in the open now. Sickle's dead, and Barker's got an arrest warrant out for Jimmy."

The old man's eyes grew wide above his fist. I said, "That's right. Jimmy's going to jail, and he'll talk for sure. And I think Barker's had enough." I leaned close to the vile creature on the bed and said, "You're finished, old man."

He whispered something between coughs. I couldn't make out the words.

"What?"

He motioned for me to lean closer. I put my ear near his lips. His arms rose from the sheets and he gripped my neck in both hands. I felt his teeth sink into my ear. I tried to pull away, but the strength of his hold on my neck was amazing. I felt the flesh of my ear tear. His teeth clicked shut like a rabid dog's, and he grunted, pulling hard against my neck and quickly biting down on my ear again, taking more of it into his mouth. In my bent-kneed position, I could only reach him from the chest down. I drove my good fist into his sternum. Air hissed from between his teeth. Hot, foul breath curled against my cheek. I did it again. And again. I heard him draw a deep breath. Finally, his teeth released their grip and he coughed violently against the side of my face. I twisted my neck in his hands until I could get my good arm between us, then pushed against his chest with all of my might. His face was less than four inches from mine. My blood glistened on his lips and chin. Incredibly, the old man's strength seemed to be a match for mine. He opened his mouth, baring his bloody teeth. His hands behind my head pulled my face slowly closer.

I stared at his eyes and saw nothing there—absolutely nothing.

As suddenly as it began, it was over. He drew a deep, bubbling breath and coughed with an all-consuming heave of his body. My neck popped from his grip and I staggered back.

His spasm continued. He covered his mouth with one hand and hugged his chest with the other. Bright red blood flew between his fingers and dotted the white sheet. Perhaps it was his, perhaps it was mine. He looked down at it and continued to cough, the sound rumbling up from his frail chest like gravel through a pipe. I saw more blood spreading across the whiskers on his chin. Definitely his blood. He rolled toward me onto his shoulder and reached for the emergency call button, coiled at the end of a wire on the bedside table. I took one step and lifted the button before he could reach it. He fell back against the bed, the coughs racking his body like a man possessed.

I stood with the call button in my hand, watching him suffer. He had begun to curl inward, his shoulders nearing his knees as he fought the horrible thing within his chest. I looked across the room at the dresser mirror. The top of my ear was badly mauled. Blood coated my shirt. Carefully, I laid the button on the floor, out of his reach, and crossed to the little bathroom. I looked in the mirror above the sink. The ear looked terrible. I opened the medicine chest and found some alcohol, cotton, and white tape. I thought about the life the old man had led, his fortune founded on the murder of his father. I tore several strips of tape from the roll and tacked them along the edge of the sink. I thought about Martin Pool, the center of Jackson County, built on murder. I poured alcohol onto some of the cotton balls and gently swabbed my wounded ear. The pain was so intense I had to stop and lean against the wall to avoid falling. Outside the bathroom, the old man still coughed. Gingerly, I lifted the flap of skin that had been my ear and placed a wad of cotton balls against it. I thought about the misery he had caused me. The look in Mary Jo's eyes when she had dropped me off at the hospital. Would we ever be the same? I pressed the tape strips against the cotton balls one by one, then stood looking at the bloody red cotton where my ear had been.

I wanted to watch him die. I wanted that more than almost anything. I went back into the bedroom and stood next to the bed. He was still hacking like a man possessed. Blood now coated his chest as thickly as it coated mine—his blood, coughed up from whatever was eating at his insides.

I stooped down and picked up the emergency call button. I wanted him to see that I could save him, that I had it in my power. I stood there, watching, trying to convince myself that it would be good to watch him die.

But it was no good. I had changed. I had been forgiven.

I pushed the button.

CHAPTER 38

IT IS LATE AUTUMN, AND MOST OF THE leaves have fallen. We can see through the trees all the way down to the water. The summer green of Martin Pool has changed to slate gray, reflecting the cold clear sky above. Here and there the sweetgums still cling to their bright red foliage like a modest bride on her honeymoon night.

Mary Jo and I have begun to heal our wounds, both physical and emotional. Perhaps it was my willingness to forgive Old Man Martin that convinced her I had truly come to know the Lord. I have no doubt that God spoke to her heart on my behalf. As Mary Jo said, he hears us when we pray.

After more than a week of silence, she came to me one evening and embraced me, molding her body to mine from head to toe.

But still, there is a difference, a distance that was not there before. I live in a roller-coaster world of emotions, filled with a peaceful joy born of my newfound faith, yet aching with sorrow at the loss of Mary Jo's trust. Will we ever regain what we lost? Jesus says we must turn the other cheek, forgive those who have trespassed against us. And she has done that, as I have forgiven Old Man Martin. But Jesus said nothing about renewal of trust. Can she learn to trust me again? Perhaps. Only time will tell. Only God knows.

The other day, I got a telephone call at the office from the man who owns the tattoo parlor in Dallas. Seems it was a military tattoo, and the S.A.W. stood for Spanish American War. I thanked him and hung up and crossed the street to the leaf-covered plaza. Standing in front of the bronze statue there, I read the list of veterans at the bottom. It's a short list, with my grandfather's name and Ernest B. Martin Sr.'s, and five or six others. I should have remembered.

Barker has retired and moved to Arkansas. I never told anyone what I know about him. It was all just guesswork. I have no proof—and besides, the man saved my life. Maybe it's wrong, but I cannot bring myself to cause him harm. I forgive him, too.

The Nowhere Club and the Easy Money are both closed now, shut down for good after Old Man Martin was arrested. He has been diagnosed with throat cancer and spends his days in conversations with lawyers and doctors. When he talks, it's with a little buzzer that he holds against his neck. They will start his trial this winter, if he survives the chemotherapy and is judged to be sane.

It still bothers me that Jimmy Wilson got away. No one has seen him since he walked out of the courthouse the day I swam up from the bottom of Martin Pool. I think he may be in Mexico, lying low with the drug dealers he knows down there.

They decided to leave Ernest B.'s grandfather's ashes in the crypt. A stonecarver simply added "Sr." to the marker. Jake McKinsey was the only one left alive who'd actually known the moonshiner, except for Old Man Martin, so no service was held. Mary Jo and I leave flowers there sometimes.

There was another memorial service for Ernest B. out on Martin Pool. It was strange seeing bass boats and ski boats all tied together over the spot where the "fountain" pours up into the bottom of the lake, tied together while we spoke again of losing him. That time, I did not cry. I will not cry for Ernest B. anymore.

And although I want more than anything to forget the madness that almost destroyed me, I know now that can never happen. Three days ago, I read in the paper about a man who caught a thirty-pound catfish near the Martin place. There was nothing unusual about that—they catch one or two that size every year. But when the man got home and cleaned the fish, he found a 1933 Walking Liberty silver dollar in its belly.

As I set the paper aside, I could have sworn I heard Ernest B. Martin laugh and say, "Makes you wonder, don't it?"

We want to hear from you. Please send your comments about this book to us in care of the address below. Thank you.

ZondervanPublishingHouse
Grand Rapids, Michigan 49530
http://www.zondervan.com